Also by Margaret Porter:

A Change of Location

The Myrtle Wand

The Limits of Limelight

Beautiful Invention: A Novel of Hedy Lamarr

A Pledge of Better Times

Praise for *Sequins and Starlight*

"Porter writes in a clear and appealing manner that makes the complicated world of dance accessible and attractive. ... The complex relationships are engaging throughout, always keeping the reader hooked. A page-turning romance for those who adore the worlds of theater and dance."

—*Kirkus Reviews*

"Porter's juxtapositions of personalities and worlds are nothing short of exquisite . . . A compelling story . . . Immersive descriptions, strong characterization, and challenges."

—*Midwest Book Review*

"Another standing ovation for Margaret Porter! Anglophiles, theatre kids, and balletomanes everywhere will devour her delicious and delightful Sequins and Starlight."

—*Leslie Carroll, author of Temporary Insanity*

"Made me fall headlong into the luscious story set in England, with ballet, burlesque, and theater, as well as love bruised by family expectations. Romance readers will adore Sequins and Starlight."

—*Literary Redhead*

Praise for *A Change of Location*

"Porter has perfectly captured the romance trope of finding unexpected love while traveling to new places. The author also deftly portrays the machinations of a twentysomething career woman who's somewhat closed off to romantic intrigue. Porter skillfully immerses readers in the fictional Milver Vale and vividly evokes British village life, from pubs to fun characters to countryside exploits . . . A charming sojourn to the English countryside for readers who enjoy smart love stories."

—*Kirkus Reviews*

"Hannah's ability to navigate and analyze unfamiliar surroundings and people becomes a driving force in a novel that explores her international sojourns, matters of the heart, and the people and places that motivate her to step away from her former successful patterns and into different relationships and milieus . . . A revealing novel of new possibilities and life that covers unemployment, romance, heartbreak, other cultures, and new lives . . . The perfect ticket for a warm account of movie-making and personal magic."

—*Midwest Book Review*

"A triumph! A Change of Location hits its marks perfectly on both sides of the pond. I had so much fun with Porter's quirky, thoroughly lovable characters that I couldn't put the novel down."

—*Leslie Caroll, author of Royal Affairs.*

"Perfect for romantics who adore stately homes, all things England . . . and delicious budding romance . . . Highly recommended!"

—*The Literary Redhead*

Sequins & Starlight

Sequins & Starlight

A Novel

MARGARET PORTER

GALLICA PRESS

"Great artists are people who find the way to be themselves in their art."

– Margot Fonteyn

Act 1

*"Do you want to take your clothes off in front of people?
Well, if you're young and beautiful, maybe you do."*

—Cyndi Lauper

Chapter 1

Ellie sashayed into the wings, timing her movements to the clash of symbols and the bass drum's insistent thud. The club host beamed at her before he glided onto the stage to close the show.

"Aren't we fortunate," she heard him say, "that Stella Nue chose Archway Cabaret club for the final performances of her farewell tour?" His enthusiastic words drew vigorous applause. A few exuberant cheers indicated the presence of Americans or Aussies, less inhibited than Londoners.

She adjusted a rhinestone star ornament, loosened by the velocity of her pirouettes. Hairspray residue stuck to her fingers.

Camille hurried over. "How did you feel out there?" She handed over Ellie's green velvet robe.

"All right, I think. I was concentrating on the music and the changes to our choreography. It's been years since I was on a stage that small." She pulled the fabric over her glittery star-shaped pasties and covered the half-moon at her crotch.

Her aunt's cat-eye glasses frames matched her magenta

column dress, a bright note of color in the backstage gloom. "I went out front to check the volume. Exactly what we requested. Let's hope the techs can maintain consistency for the rest of the month."

Earlier in the day, as soon as they stepped off the train from Paris, Ellie's countdown had begun. Twenty-four times to repeat her routines. Two performances per night, three nights a week, for four weeks.

And then, she thought, I'll say a final farewell to this bizarre, beautiful world of burlesque.

Stella Nue's persona would live on after retirement. The stage name was attached to lucrative branded products—her signature fragrance, a popular lingerie line, and other items offered for sale on her website. Her latest commercial endorsements included a television advertising campaign for a luxury automobile and a print promotion for a high-end botanical-infused vodka, contracts that would continue for two more years.

When Ellie and her aunt reached the headliner's private dressing room, they could hear muffled chatter from next door. At the start of her career she'd belonged to that gossipy girl gang, never imagining that she'd become a worldwide sensation as Stella Nue, the Naked Star. They were joined by the scantily clad girl responsible for gathering up the garments the performers incrementally discarded during their routines. She placed her burden on a chair in the corner.

"Thanks, Lisa." With a smile, Ellie asked, "Or do I call you Lola?"

"I answer quicker to Lisa." She was lean and long-waisted with contrasting curves. "I didn't officially become Lola LaFlamme till I came to the Archway." One hand indicated the red and orange flames embroidered on the front of her silver lamé halter top and forming side pockets in the matching short skirt.

"I'll check on your men," Camille told Ellie.

She reached inside her robe to ease off her pasties. "I started out as a stage kitten," she confided.

"Where?"

"In the States. New Jersey."

"My first gig was in Blackpool," Lisa said. "Stripping. The manager, a racist bumhole, called me Hot Cocoa. I told him I'd take less pay if I could be Lola LaFlamme instead. But it meant a longer slog to save up for my move to London." She knelt down to open Ellie's stage case. "D'you got any professional tips? 'Cause I'm working up my solo act."

"Do I ever. Let's meet for lunch or coffee. I'll have morning ballet class, but I'm free after that."

"That'd be brilliant." Lisa rocked back on her heels. "I work the afternoon shift at a burger bar near my flatshare in North Acton. Midday is good for me."

"Soon as I'm settled, we'll make a date."

She relished any opportunity to share hard-won knowledge and several years of experience with an eager neophyte. At its worst, burlesque could be a bitchy business, but never enough to destroy the prevailing camaraderie.

"Oh—I forgot." Lisa pulled a piece of paper from her flame appliqué pocket. "We're not allowed to pass notes or gifts to performers, it's against the rules. I'm supposed to give this to that lady. Your manager."

"She's not here." Ellie took it. "And I'll never tell. Is it from a man?"

"An awfully polite one. 'Would you be so kind?' 'Thanks very much, indeed.' He wanted me to tell you 'break a leg.' I should've let him know that round here we say 'pop a pastie.'"

"For ballet dancers, it's *'merde'*"

"That's French for 'shit.' I wasn't taught that word in language class, but I know it."

"The classier version is *'toi, toi, toi.'* In Australia, *'chookas.'*"

"You were a ballerina?"

"Once upon a time." She didn't refer to herself as one, but people outside the profession used the term indiscriminately.

"You wore a tutu and went up on your toes like they do?"

"I'll dance on pointe in the second show."

"Wow." Lisa draped Ellie's crystal-studded corset over the clothes rail. "Best be going, before I get told off for being a pest."

"You're not," Ellie assured her. "But when my guys barge in, which they soon will, there won't be room for all of us."

"Just ask if there's anything else I can do. I memorized your props list and wrote down where to place everything like you want."

"Thanks. When you give up kittening for burlesque stardom, it'll be a loss to this club."

Lisa grinned. "No *merde*."

Although Ellie relished her solitude, she was denied silence by the noise on the other side of the wall. An occasional shriek or excited squeal rose above the chorus of voices that she knew so well from years in prestigious ballet companies, and when she and the cast of her Stella Nue show toured major cities throughout her homeland and other countries. Returning to her dressing room, spartan or lavish, she'd face the mirror and ask herself how many performances until she figured out how else to use her meticulously trained body. And she would ponder where next to direct her ambition.

She crossed to the chaise longue crammed against one purple wall and sank onto its unyielding cushion. With relief, she closed her eyes, conscious of their dryness—from the spotlight's glare and heat, plus insufficient sleep on the Eurostar from Paris. She couldn't remember whether she'd replaced the bottle of lubricating drops in her show kit before leaving her suite at the Ritz Hotel.

Approaching footsteps halted at her door.

"Decent?"

"Bare-ly."

Zack Adams, lively and effusive, had the ability to cheer her on her lowest days and brighten her darkest moods. He had also danced at City International Ballet in New York, until an injury limited his ability to perform his *tour en l'air* and *grand jeté*—feats not required of a male support dancer in a burlesque act.

Eyeing the lavender liquid in his martini glass, she asked, "How's your Aviation?"

"Sublime."

George Karras, his spouse, was drinking white wine. An excellent listener and a source of carefully considered aesthetic guidance, he choreographed their routines. When she started in burlesque, he'd designed her costumes, sourced the materials, and constructed the garments. Another reject from their ballet company, for failure to maintain the mandated weight standard, he was supremely elegant in his black tailcoat and tuxedo trousers.

The trio's shared experience of constant evaluation of their physiques and humiliating criticism resulted in close comradeship.

Leaning against the doorframe, George said, "Don't worry, I won't let him order another. We can't have him dropping you during a lift."

"Hasn't happened yet," Zack shot back.

"Camille's giving the stage crew instructions about the set for tomorrow's first act. Aren't we doing *Treasure Chest?* Did you check out your new doubloon pasties?"

"Not yet. How's your rental apartment?"

"Great," Zack replied. "Despite being so far from the best shopping."

"George will take you anywhere you want to go. The Tube map is imprinted in his brain." She unscrewed the top of a water bottle to break the seal.

"Camille says your club contract stipulates that a limousine will pick you up at the Ritz and take you back after the show."

"Her idea, not mine. It can't be much more than a five-minute walk along a well-lit stretch of Piccadilly."

"Take advantage of all the perks," George advised. "You're about to lose them."

"Don't talk crazy," Zack retorted. "She's a multi-millionaire. She can ride in style whenever she wants. For as long as she likes."

Her aunt joined them. Peering into the mirror, she smoothed her smoky silver hair, arranged in an artfully layered bob. "Don't let the management overhear. I fight hard for contract riders." She turned to Zack and poked his shoulder. "Save the yakking for after the show. Let her have some peace and quiet." When the two men departed, she asked, "Did somebody bring you tonight's menu?"

"I seem to be sitting on it." Ellie shifted her bottom and retrieved the leatherette folder. "I'll have the plain flatbread with hummus. Caviar makes me thirsty," she said regretfully. "I can't drink much water before going on again."

Harry had always ordered caviar for her whenever he took her to his favorite New York oyster bar. They'd gone each Friday afternoon, after their last class of the day and before their respective evening rehearsals. When she left Juilliard to join the ballet company, they maintained the tradition.

"Something sweet?"

"Chocolate-dipped strawberries."

Ellie waited until Camille was gone to pry open the note Lisa had delivered. The staple's sharp tip pierced her thumb, and she pressed it against the paper to blot the drop of blood, leaving a red mark.

Dear Ellie, I look forward to seeing you again and wish to present a proposal that will benefit us both. Please ring or text at your earliest convenience. G.

No name, only the initial, followed by a telephone number with a UK prefix.

"Nice try," she murmured.

Her fans and followers often sent handwritten messages. Through intensive online research, the most passionately devoted had discovered that Stella Nue's birth name was Estelle and knew that during her dancing years she'd been billed as Ellie Lowery. Seeking to create a personal connection, they inevitably provided contact information—phone number, email address, social media handle. The creepiest obsessives maintained their anonymity while urging her to respond to their overtures.

She crumpled the paper and dropped it into the wastebasket. It landed on top of discarded tissues, strips of paper backing from her pastie tape, and a single uncooperative false eyelash.

Chapter 2

"I didn't expect a strip joint to draw a crowd like this," Dan Wheeler admitted. The group at the adjacent table wore formal attire, as though they had arrived from the sort of dressy event that occurred nightly in the ballrooms of the luxury hotels lining Park Lane and Piccadilly. Other people were dressed respectably, as they would when dining in Mayfair's more upscale establishments.

"It's a cabaret," Lou retorted. She turned to her partner, adding, "He didn't want to join us. Maybe he's worried people will think we're a throuple."

"That possibility never crossed my mind."

"Chill," Lou said. "Enjoy. We're celebrating your birthday. Better late than never."

Kelly smiled at him. "And your new status as Director of Operations."

"Different title. Same duties."

Lou made a derisive sound. "As a company finance officer, I happen to know your compensation increased. Next time we go out, you're paying for drinks."

Kelly shook her head. "Stop teasing your boss."

"He's used to it. When he wrote my brilliant annual review, he referenced my appealing sense of humor."

With mock sternness, Dan said, "Ms. Ridley, if you don't mind your manners, there will be an addendum. Forcing me to attend a peep show could be regarded as a violation of the moral turpitude clause in your employment contract with Latimer London Estates, Limited."

"You won't," Lou said. "I've always wanted to see Stella Nue in person."

"Not jealous," Kelly murmured. "Not much. I mean, not at all."

Lou sipped her cocktail. "My primary reason for coming here is to watch Dan blush when the ladies disrobe."

His companions, paired by a lesbian dating app, were a testament to the occasional value of the similar algorithm that had let him down so many times. He marveled that his brash Director of Finance had found a soul mate in the serene artisanal baker who shared her Shepherd's Bush flat.

Lou stirred the contents of her glass. The pink plastic swizzle stick had the shape of a naked woman in profile. "I never asked what birthday present you got from your dad."

"A voucher for Angler's Attic, the rod and tackle shop not far from Thornbury and Tayer Court. His unsubtle and unnecessary reminder that I'm due for a visit. Brian drew a picture for me. A fish, according to the note his rehab specialist enclosed."

"Did your mum send anything?"

"No."

Not a card or a letter or a present. No telephone call.

He was relieved to see a disembodied hand parting the crimson swags of the curtain. The compere, wearing formal attire, stepped out.

"On behalf of the Archway Cabaret stars and staff, I warmly welcome you to the second show," he said, beaming.

"Please be attentive to our protocol. Photography, videography, and audio recordings are forbidden while an act is in progress. Table-hopping during a performance is not allowed. Kindly refrain from rude gestures or shouting inappropriate comments. At the conclusion of each act, feel free to express your appreciation, enthusiastically but respectfully. The curtain call is your opportunity to take pictures—without flash. Take as many selfies as you like outside. Pose under the arch. Stand at the entrance. We want our sign to be visible."

His listeners laughed at this aside.

"Most important of all, enjoy the program! Club regular Holly Hollywood is our opener. Also featured tonight, the ever-popular Audrey in Amethyst. And Luscious Liz, recently returned from her tour of the shires. Following a brief interval, headliner Stella Nue will grace the stage."

The friendly, informative oration drew heavy applause. As it waned, two showgirls sporting feathery headdresses swept in from either side of the protruding half-moon stage. Turning their backs on the audience, they cocked their knees and wiggled their bottoms to the drumbeats produced by the sound system. Each one took hold of a curtain, placed a hand on a hip, and marched in opposite directions, pulling the heavy fabric as they went.

Platinum blonde Holly Hollywood, sheathed in a strapless, hot pink satin gown and wearing opera gloves of the same material, perched on the top step of a gleaming white staircase. Her rhinestone jewelry—earrings, necklace, and bracelets—sparkled beneath the stage lights. Dan, who favored vintage films, recognized her attire as a facsimile of Marilyn Monroe's iconic costume from *Gentlemen Prefer Blondes,* and wasn't surprised when the sound system erupted with the familiar strains of "Diamonds Are a Girl's Best Friend." Unlike the movie star, Holly didn't sing or lip-sync—or keep her dress on. She shimmied and swayed, removing the tearaway skirt before taking off the bodice, corset, bra, and knickers. As the tune faded, she strutted off, wearing sequined circles over her nipples and a diamond-shaped thong, recipient of applause, cheers, and wolf whistles.

A girl in a revealing halter top and shorts darted onto the stage, smiling and winking, as she gathered up the scattered clothing.

"We didn't get the full Monty," Dan murmured. "Will we?"

Lou shook her head. "Unlikely, in the Borough of Westminster. I reckon there are restrictions."

Prince's "Purple Rain" set the mood for Audrey in Amethyst, a statuesque Black woman sporting a shag haircut like the late singer's. She peeled off a succession of violet-hued draperies.

Luscious Liz, who wore a sequined jumpsuit, stripped to a frenetic disco number.

"Enjoying yourselves?" Dan asked his table companions during the interval.

"Definitely," Lou replied. "You?"

Curling his hand around his tumbler of whisky, he replied, "Of course." Given his work colleague's habit of friendly mockery, he withheld overt admiration of the ladies who had pranced upon the stage. Not that he fancied any of them.

This place, in addition to being unfamiliar, was far livelier than his usual evening haunts. At the end of a normal working day, he abandoned his Latimer Row office and climbed the stairs to his top floor flat. After a solitary supper, he reviewed financial and property news online or in print, streamed an old movie, or watched sports pundits analyze recent football matches and speculate on the outcomes of future ones. Before a fishing weekend, he researched possible waterways and suitable accommodations. A regular supply of complimentary tickets was one of many benefits derived from his employer's prominence as a lord of the realm and owner of a compact but immensely valuable section of Mayfair. Dan used them, if the play or concert appealed to him. Once or twice a week he dined at his gentlemen's club, exclusively masculine and populated by members of his dad's generation and a lesser contingent of his own contemporaries. Hearing them overshare about wives and mistresses and children and dogs, none of which he possessed, he was convinced he needed to shake up his staid routine.

Tonight was a start. Although he didn't envision becoming an Archway regular.

The host's reappearance enticed the audience from the bar and lobby back to their tables.

"The entire Archway Cabaret family are honored by the return of a lovely and talented lady who needs no introduction. She enjoyed her earliest international success here, and ever since has drawn capacity crowds wherever in the world she performs. My friends, we proudly present Stella Nue in *Everything's Coming off Roses.*"

The curtain pullers carried out their task less demonstratively than before, accompanied by lilting chords from a harp. The set consisted of three pieces of furniture. Sheer curtains enclosed a circular bed covered in pink satin. A bench and narrow table were positioned to one side of the stage. Various toiletry items were arranged on the gleaming white surface: hairbrush, hand mirror, oversized powder puff, old-fashioned scent bottle with squeeze bulb, and a bouquet of pink roses.

Riotous applause, clapping, and whistles drowned out Stella Nue's entrance music. She was a petite young woman whose reddish hair flowed to her waist. Her face was heart-shaped, with large eyes set beneath smoky brows. Bright red lipstick accentuated her mouth. She was more delicately built and less voluptuous than the performers who had preceded her.

Slowly she made her way to the table, her diaphanous pale pink robe fluttering with her movements, synchronized to a classical piece that Dan vaguely recognized and eventually identified. She held up the mirror and pressed the powder puff to her brow and cheeks, chin and neck. With a suggestive sideways smile, she reached inside her garment to swipe the tops of her breasts. Picking up the flowers, she held them close to her face and inhaled.

Dan didn't notice the satin pointe shoes until she rose onto her toes and began to dance. Her version of the Rose Adagio from Tchaikovsky's *Sleeping Beauty* score was scaled down to fit the limitations of the performance space. He was acquainted with the ballet, firmly embedded in the repertoires of London's major and minor dance companies.

A series of arabesques moved Stella Nue and her flowers upstage to the bed. She parted the draperies and placed her roses on the pillow. Lying beside them, she closed her thickly lashed eyes.

A handsome dark-haired man vaulted out from the wings, the black tails of his coat floating behind him and whipping about during a brief solo that roused the slumbering lady. Leaving her bed, she joined in a romantic *pas de deux* punctuated by several daring lifts. Facing the audience, she pulled the thin fabric from each shoulder, letting it fall to rest on her hips. She plucked the sash and opened the robe to reveal a transparent nightgown. Slipping off the outer garment, she offered it her partner, who executed multiple turns and carried it into the wings.

Bending forward, she unfastened ribbons at the back of the gown and took it off. Her remaining layer was a pink satin corset and lacy underpants. Waving the filmy fabric like a banner, she returned to the bed, granting her audience an enticing glimpse of her shapely back and bottom. A pink sequin rose was positioned over each rounded cheek.

Reclining against satin sheets, she ran her hands up and

down her torso. She kicked and scissored her bare legs. As if summoned by her frantic, sexualized motions, a second man, a near-twin of the first, appeared. He seized her hand and pulled her towards him. As the music swelled and cymbals crashed, they performed a dramatic dance duet before he waltzed away.

Smiling at the audience, she sat on the bed. Gradually, enticingly, she unlaced her corset and let it fall open to expose the rose-shaped sequin pasties attached to her breasts.

The stage lights went out. When they came on again, Stella—in her peignoir—curtsied in every direction and extended her arms to the male dancers. Each of them clasped a hand and kissed it.

After they led her away, Lou murmured, "She's a gorgeous ginger. I wonder whether the carpet matches the curtains."

"Don't be crude," Kelly objected.

"She's got a natural redhead's skin tone but dark eyebrows. Probably penciled in."

The entire cast came onto the stage to bump and grind and shimmy and blow kisses. The host, after announcing that Stella Nue would be the featured act for the remainder of the month, wished everyone goodnight.

Dan followed his companions into the lobby. A queue stretched from the merchandise display to the opposite wall. Stella Nue fans could purchase perfume or lingerie or autographed boudoir photos.

"I'm peckish," Lou announced. "Let's go somewhere suitably festive, but not far from Green Park tube station."

"I know the perfect place," Dan announced.

Chapter 3

Moonglow penetrated the clouds muddling the sky, but the stars were outshone by the streetlamps and the brightly lit buildings that lined the busy thoroughfare. The Pink Full Moon, they called it back in New Hampshire, where Ellie had learned the traditional names and associated lore for each month. An April shower had darkened the pavement and created shallow puddles churned by cars, taxis, and buses.

The breeze felt deliciously cool against her bare face. Before leaving the club, she'd washed away thick makeup and plucked off her false eyelashes and arranged her hair in a casual semblance of a ballet bun. Pearl studs replaced the pink rhinestone earrings she'd worn on stage. She hoped her navy trouser suit was sufficient camouflage, because she'd forgotten to put on her non-prescription eyeglasses before handing off her stage case to Camille. They must be buried in the jumble of items she carried to and from the theatre: cosmetics, pastie tape, sewing supplies, tiny plastic pouches of colored sequins and crystals for costume repairs, hair products and accessories, pill case, and more.

She reached into her pocket for her vibrating cellphone and moved beneath a hotel awning to prevent pedestrians from colliding with her. "Hi, Mom. Shouldn't you be in the studio?"

"Not yet. Renée is leading the little ones through their barre exercises. How was your opening?"

"Stella's last stand is a total love fest. I've come full circle, to the site of my debut overseas gig."

"Your dad and I ordered flowers. I hope they reached you before showtime."

"They're gorgeous and the perfect shade of pink. I used them in my final Rose Adagio—never to be repeated."

The flow of traffic had slowed to a crawl, and horns blared.

"What's going on? Where are you?"

"On Piccadilly. Walking to the Ritz."

"You're supposed to have a limo."

Like members of her entourage, her relatives were obsessed with the perks conveyed by her star status. "I let Camille and the guys take it. Don't worry, I'm incognito. I'll call tomorrow and tell you everything. Give Daddo a kiss for me."

There was no need to join the steady stream of pedestrians moving along the hotel's iconic covered walkway. The entrance was located on the Arlington Street side, where fluttering blue flags bracketed the blue awning.

Before she set foot on the carpeted steps, the top-hatted doorman beamed at her, saying, "Lovely flowers you've got there, m'lady." Saving her the trouble of navigating the central revolving door, he pulled open the one near where he stood.

"Good evening, Mrs. Colman," the night clerk greeted her when she paused at the reception desk. "How may we assist?"

"I planned to walk from here to Seven Dials tomorrow,

until I saw showery intervals in the forecast. Would it take long to go by taxi?"

"That depends on the time of day."

"It's a lunch meeting."

"I should think you'd have a ten-minute journey, approximately, barring delays for roadworks. Shall we arrange a cab for a particular time?"

"Not yet. I'm waiting for my friend to confirm."

"You can ring in the morning and let us know. Anything else we can do for you?"

She placed her roses on the curved desktop. "I could use a vase."

"Certainly, Madam. One of our staff will locate one and deliver the flowers to your suite."

After thanking him, she said, "My aunt is meeting me in the bar. Is it still open?"

"Until half past eleven. Plenty of time to enjoy yourselves."

As she stepped around the circular table in the center of the rotunda, she admired the enormous and very fragrant arrangement of mixed, long-stemmed flowers. The chosen location for the traditional post-performance assessment was supremely Art Deco in style, with glossy gold-accented wood walls and smoky Lalique glass *bas relief* panels. She scanned the room, seeking a vacant two-top, a term she'd learned waitressing at her dad's restaurant. Couples had claimed them all. The larger table with four chairs was too near the door for her liking but preferable to perching on a barstool.

A server in a pristine white jacket and black trousers presented the drinks menu, but she already knew what she wanted. Her cocktail, an icy combination of gin, ginger syrup, ginger ale, and crushed mint, arrived in a tall glass. Although she rarely drank spirits, first nights were sufficient cause—especially her final first night. She savored the mix of flavors as she waited for the alcohol to decrease the level of post-show adrenalin.

"Hello, Stella."

She glanced up. A man was leering down at her.

"I saw your show. Genius. Absolute genius." He pulled out the chair opposite hers and sat, smiling in the suggestive, close-lipped way she knew so well. "What luck to find you here."

"I'm waiting for someone," she stated crisply, hoping he'd take the hint. Was this the mysterious author of the note she'd discarded? The best way to avoid these unwelcome encounters was to hide out in her hotel room, a drastic measure that prevented her from living a semblance of a normal life during a tour.

"Last time you came to London, you put on quite an extravaganza at the O2. Supporting acts, lots of showgirls, a full orchestra. The place was packed. Why aren't you booked in over there?"

Feeling a hand press on her shoulder, she stiffened.

"My sincere apologies for turning up so late," intoned a male voice, distinctly British.

Double ambush.

The fellow seated across from her got up. "I was telling Stella how much I enjoyed her performance tonight." He made a speedy exit.

Meeting the intruder's gaze, she said calmly, "I could've handled him myself."

"That's what I told my work colleague. But she and her partner insisted that I come over and rescue you."

His reply eased Ellie's wrath, as did his confidence in her ability to ward off a nuisance. "Thanks. To all of you."

"Since we arrived, they've been glued to their mobiles, trawling the internet for information about you. Fangirling. Ignoring me. We were also at the Archway Cabaret. Second seating."

Why would any right-minded female ignore him? He was gorgeous. His hair was very dark brown, but the low light prevented her from determining the precise color of his eyes. Blue, maybe, with a grayish tinge.

She waved her hand towards the three vacant chairs. "Join me. You can scare off predators until my official chaperone arrives." After he accepted the invitation, she told him. "Tell your friends that only my website and social media accounts, managed by trusted individuals, are accurate sources. Most of what they'll find online either contains the slightest fragment of truth, or none at all. I'm sure they've stumbled on fake photos with my head stuck on a different woman's nude body."

"That must be frustrating."

"My most faithful and passionately supportive followers are vigilant about reporting deepfakes and refuting the misleading gossip. Many of them are young women who uphold me as a model of femininity and feminism—which aren't mutually exclusive. They read or listen to every interview. They buy the merchandise. They stand in line to get my autograph. I love them for it."

"Lou and Kelly neglected to inform me that the famous Stella Nue is also a ballerina. I daresay you've had extensive training."

"From the time I could stand up." Over the years, she'd edited down the history of her ballet years to the essential facts. "My mother and one of her sisters danced professionally in Montreal and later established their own studio in New Hampshire. I was their pupil, before being accepted into the dance program at Juilliard. I had to drop out when I aced my audition for City International Ballet. After a very brief stint as an apprentice, I joined the corps. I was still a teenager when they promoted me to soloist." Despite being undesirably curvy. Skipping past the excruciating body-shaming saga, she concluded, "Eventually, I left."

She wouldn't, she couldn't, mention Harry.

"For a career in burlesque?"

Ellie shook her head. "Not then. Somebody I trusted had fled to Ballet Bruxelles. When one of their soloists left on her maternity break, he recommended me to the artistic director, who had been a *répétiteur* at CIB. Eventually she offered me a season contract, and I had the chance to take on major roles. Rafe became a huge star, invited to perform as a guest artist with European companies, in full length ballets or at galas. Whenever he could, he took me with him."

"You performed with Rafe Lawrence?"

"My former partner. Dance partner," she clarified, in case he jumped to a wrong conclusion. "We've known each other nearly a decade, and for five of those years I was his work wife. Lawrence and Lowery, dancing our way across Europe. In those days I was billed as Ellie Lowery, my real name. One of them." Within the ballet company, she'd often been referred to as Rafe's Waif.

"I'm Daniel Wheeler. Dan."

The waiter stopped at their table and asked if they wanted anything else from the bar.

"Whisky for me, please. What will you have, Ellie?"

"Another Ginger Rogers." She didn't care that it would subdue her habitual reluctance to engage with a stranger. Handsome Dan appeared to be genuinely interested in her backstory, and she was curious about him.

"What prompted you to give up what sounds like quite a successful ballet career for burlesque?"

She was grateful for the waiter's timely return. The presentation and placement of their drinks gave her a chance to frame her response to the familiar question. "I like change. And challenges." She smiled. "After I pulled George and Zack into my act, I went back on pointe, just in a different way. We've had a lot of fun."

"So why pack it in now?" he asked.

"We're ready. Even more so after our grueling year-long farewell tour. Europe. Australia. New Zealand. Japan. Thirty North American cities. We've just completed our final set of full cast shows, in Paris. For sentimental reasons, I tacked on the Archway gig." She stabbed the ice cube remnants with her straw. "I'm not abandoning show business. I've enrolled in the stage acting program at the Muriel Baker School of Dramatic Arts, near Regent's Park."

"Buck up," he muttered. "Fangirls approaching."

"We have to leave now," the tall, spiky-haired female announced. "Our train doesn't have a twenty-four-hour service on Thursdays." To Ellie, she said, "I'm Lou. This is Kelly."

"We loved the show," the shorter woman told her. "Especially your act."

"I'm so glad." After the women were out of earshot, Ellie asked, "Whose idea was it to go to the Archway, yours or theirs?"

"Lou's. On my birthday I was in Liverpool giving a conference presentation, and ever since she's been going on about how I missed having a party. I didn't care. But when we both received a promotion, she insisted we had to celebrate everything."

"What sort of work do you do?"

"Property management. At the executive level." Staring into his whisky glass, he added, "My father is a devoted supporter of the arts. Classical music is his primary interest, but his generosity extends to dance companies as well."

"British Ballet Theatre?" she asked. When he affirmed it, she told him, "Tomorrow I'm meeting Rafe, their artistic director, for lunch. Before I get insanely busy with publicity stuff. And apartment hunting."

For several seconds he regarded her without speaking. "My role at Latimer London Estates requires knowledge of the rental market. What are your requirements?"

"Safety, security, privacy. I won't consider anything on the ground floor or basement level. Otherwise, I just want the basics. Fully-equipped kitchen, living room, two bedrooms, bathroom with shower and tub. Clean. Reasonably attractive décor. Plenty of windows to let in the light. Price isn't a consideration."

"Obviously not. This is an expensive, world-class hotel. Do you seek a long-term or a short let?"

"However you define immediately until the end of June."

"Any specific location?"

"This area would be ideal, because I know it best. Or Marylebone. I'd like access to green space."

"I'll have someone on staff research current listings. By end of business tomorrow, I can provide some recommendations."

"That would be fantastic."

"I'm happy to review them with you, if you care to stop at our office in Latimer Row. Unlike Lou, I've got an incredibly short commute. Two flights of stairs."

A fleeting grin revealed that two of his bottom teeth were slightly misaligned, the one physical imperfection she'd detected. Hers were more obvious: black Irish eyebrows that contrasted with her russet hair and the permanent crook in her little finger, broken in a childhood softball game. Too much bust for ballet.

"You work from home?"

"Almost. I live above the shop. My employer owns all the buildings on both sides of the street. I pay him a peppercorn rent for the privilege of occupying the upper story flat." He removed his cellphone from his inside jacket pocket, and after swiping, he presented it to her. "Add your details to my contacts."

She passed her device to him. "You can do the same." As she pressed digits, she said, "Mine's a New Hampshire number. I'm including my email, if you need to attach images or a document."

She was shoving her phone into her jacket pocket when a flash of color attracted her attention. If the bar's occupants were asked which of them was the celebrity, Ellie had no doubt that the woman in the magenta dress and matching eyeglasses would be the choice. She introduced Dan to her aunt, explaining about his offer to assist their property search.

"One less London checklist item for me," Camille said. "The Ritz is an expense we're willing to bear temporarily, not indefinitely. Ellie prefers to meet journalists in a private hotel suite instead of a restaurant or pub, where she'll draw attention."

"Aunt Camille is my tour manager."

"Not for long." The older woman told the hovering waiter, "Cosmopolitan, please."

"Another for you, sir?"

"I've reached my limit. Just the bill."

"We'll pay," Ellie said. "You're about to do us an enormous favor."

"Even if I delegate the task?" He placed both palms on the surface of the table. "Flats located in desirable areas are in high demand and get snapped up quickly. Will either of you be available for viewings at short notice?"

"Not before the weekend," Camille told him. "Ellie's schedule is packed. Fashion shoot. Media availabilities—television breakfast show, newspaper interviews. Where she goes, I go."

"I'll keep that in mind. Enjoy the rest of your evening."

Watching him depart, Ellie was impressed by the grace of his stride. Not exactly balletic, but he didn't display the awkwardness that some long-limbed men possessed. He could be a male model—runway and print—with that combination of smooth gait and striking features. Or a movie star. His voice was also good, crisp yet sonorous, and he spoke with the classiest sort of English accent.

"Since when do you let a strange man cozy up to you in a bar?"

To avoid her aunt's penetrating gaze, she drew circles on the table's surface with her straw. "He's a hero. When one of those assertive Stella fans was pestering me, Dan came over and displaced him."

"I'm sure he had an ulterior motive."

"Possibly."

"Probably." After a pause, Camille added, "You don't seem to mind."

"Maybe not," she admitted.

"High time you emerged from your shell. I suspect your Mr. Wheeler would be happy to coax you out of it."

For Ellie, the prospect was equally comforting and terrifying. "Time will tell." Her tone was cheerless when she added, "Better a businessman than an actor. Never again."

"You're tempting fate. Never is a dangerous word."

She didn't respond to the warning. "I'm supposed to decide on the routines for our second week of shows. Thoughts?"

Camille sampled her cocktail before replying. "At this late hour, I'm past the point of giving advice or making decisions. This drink isn't helping. Let's discuss it in the morning over coffee. Our minds will be clearer when the caffeine kicks in."

Chapter 4

Ellie tapped her credit card against the taxicab's contactless pay device. Bidding her driver a cheery farewell, she darted through the drizzle to the café entrance. When she joined her lunch companion, seated in the least populated section, he rose and kissed each of her cheeks.

"Here's a sight to brighten a dreary day," he declared. "The beautiful burlesque star formerly known as Rafe's Waif."

She reached up to smooth his windblown brown curls, noticing the strands of gray that had appeared since their prior reunion. "Wonderful to see you. Last year when I was here, you were far away in—where?"

"Bali." He pulled out a chair for her. "Don't ever travel halfway across the globe to save a relationship. I got myself a magnificent beach tan. Like the lady, it vanished."

"Her loss." She removed her glasses. Unfolding her napkin, she used it to wipe raindrops from the lenses.

After they ordered food, he asked, "How is the Beast of Ballet Bruxelles?"

"Unchanged. The day after I arrived, I treated her to dinner at a brasserie near the Jardin Botanique. I ordered a seafood salad with framboise vinaigrette dressing, and she still complained that I was eating too much. I didn't need to ask if I could attend morning class. She ordered me to."

"On YouTube, there's a video clip of us in *Sleeping Beauty,* and every time I check I find that the viewer count has gone way, way up. We left City International ages ago, and during that time our Act Three *pas de deux* has become legendary. I wonder if Mireille knows how popular it is?"

Ellie grinned back at him. "I'll never forget those coaching sessions. 'Foreplay, foreplay. Zay are *not* flirting. Puss in Boots is wanting sex. White Cat makes him crazy for it.'"

"'Zay leave zee stage to fuck. Zay come back happy and purring in zee *Polacca.'* It's a miracle we got through those scenes without laughing."

"She also wanted to know if I'd be interested in returning as a demi-soloist, although she would require a remedial period of intense preparation. I almost face-planted in my salad."

"And you declined?"

"No *en arrière* moves for me. It wasn't a realistic option. On my night off, I went to a performance and found out which *coryphées* had been promoted, and saw how well the veterans were holding up."

"Did you see anyone in Brussels worth stealing from her?"

"Do your own scouting," she shot back. "I'm no ballet spy."

"You're welcome to join class at BBT. Have you met Anya Semerova?"

"Never. I've seen her on film. Everybody has."

"I'll introduce you, properly and deferentially. She resembles a fragile fairy but can be just as intimidating as Mireille. Our quintessentially English dancers are adapting—somewhat—to her preference for the Vaganova technique. I'm curious to see what she thinks of you, with your mixed-up training. The Cecchetti qualities you got from your mother. And at Juilliard and CIB, you were immersed in the Balanchine style so many American teachers perpetuate."

"I'm uniquely me, I suppose. I looked at the schedule for the last weeks of your season. Tell me about the new work you've choreographed. Is it abstract?"

"Yes." With obvious regret, he said, "I'm restrained about incorporating contemporary pieces. 'Not too much of that modern muck,' one of our board members tells me. *The Day Dream* is inspired by Samuel Taylor Coleridge's poem of that name, set to Scarlatti's Sonata in F minor. Our dramaturg and I are finalizing *Virtuosi*, which we'll debut at the Autumn Gala. A short narrative ballet about Frederic Chopin's affair with Georges Sand, and the relationship between Franz Liszt and Countess Marie d'Agoult. Four dancers. Music by the two composers. Very classical in style. I'll present it on a double bill. With *Les Sylphides*."

The ballet she loved best, as he knew. "A perfect combination."

"We're starting *Onegin* rehearsals." His voice dropped when he said, "Stirs up so many memories. Monte Carlo. And our last night performing it in Brussels."

"Don't go there," she warned.

"Your retirement was voluntary." He wagged his shaggy head. "Advancing age and an injury-prone body forced me out."

"Since coming back to England, you've done great things. One of the world's premier ballet companies made you artistic director. As choreographer, you'll have lasting influence. Like Ratmansky and Wheeldon and Peck and Forsythe."

"Flatterer."

"It's the absolute truth. Don't pretend you're unaware."

"Enough about me. I'm interested in your latest endeavor.

I don't see why you need a training program when you've got professional acting credits already."

"I lucked into the roles of Stella Kowalski in *Streetcar Named Desire* and Beatrice in *Much Ado about Nothing*. There's a lot more to learn than a couple of shows in a summer stock company could teach me. That's why I chose a London drama academy with a broad curriculum."

"When do you begin?"

"Next month. It's an eight-week course. Improvisation, voice and diction, and movement. There are sections on character development and scene study. Performing for the camera, audition technique, and safeguarding issues. We'll also rehearse a one-act play and present it to staff and students and invited guests."

"Is there a graduation ceremony, like Harry had at Juilliard? Will you receive a diploma?"

She felt the smile leave her face, and her breath stilled. "A certificate. To add to the accumulated ballet competition awards at my parents' house." She hadn't finished high school or earned a college degree.

He laid his cutlery across his plate. "I suppose you'll return to New York."

Shaking her head, she replied, "I've set my sights on Boston and environs, where there are several well-established theatre companies. I'd be near my sister. And not far from our parents. And just a couple of hours away from the lake cottage."

"Stay here, love. With all the other American actors who have invaded the West End theatres."

"They're movie stars," she said dismissively. "Or have a string of Broadway credits."

He plucked a credit card from his wallet. "Afraid I really must dash. Full cast stage rehearsal for *Day Dream*. Piano only. Come along and watch."

"Wish I could, but I'm booked for a photo shoot. Professional hairdresser and makeup artist. Fashion stylist. The works."

"Then I'll look for you at morning class. Ten o'clock, every day but Sunday."

"I'd better visit Freed."

"You've given up your cheater shoes?"

"No. That's an outdated term. Mindens are ubiquitous, have been for years. I'll be shopping for tights and practice skirts. And a leo. Or three."

"I look forward seeing you extravagantly kitted out tomorrow."

"I wish. I'll be on a television studio set, answering questions about stripping and being a sex object. I'll deflect by describing my version of burlesque as an extension of my dance career. Anyway, this is apartment search week. Somebody's working on it for me, and I'll have to check out whatever he finds."

Outside the café, they walked away in opposite directions. The showers had subsided, so Ellie didn't put up her raincoat hood. After weaving through the shiny black Seven Dials bollards, dotted with raindrops, she paused to check the map she'd downloaded to her phone. Turn on Monmouth Street, follow it to the corner of St. Martin's Lane and Cecil Court.

Her partnership with Rafe Lawrence had started in Manhattan and ended in Brussels.

In addition to dancing White Cat to his Puss in Boots in New York, they'd been paired for the Peasant Pas de Deux in *Giselle*—her well-developed bosom wasn't such a liability when portraying a village girl. After his promotion to principal, their onstage encounters were fleeting. When he performed Prince Siegfried in *Swan Lake,* she was either cast in the first act *pas de trois* or in the third act as the Polish princess. At Ballet Bruxelles, far less hierarchical, they often performed together, and she had joined him at galas elsewhere in Europe. Seated in a railway compartment, rattling across international borders, or huddled in airport lounges, they had shared artistic angst and personal anxieties, disappointments, and dreams. Until early onset osteoarthritis and a dodgy spinal disc pushed the celebrated *danseur* into the premature retirement that forced consideration of administrative positions.

Ellie's stroll through the city revived her strong affinity for London. Its vibrancy and international flavor had long appealed to her, and as she passed pedestrians conversing in various languages, she wondered whether they were residents or tourists. In New York, living within the bubble imposed by her strict CIB work schedule, she'd had little available time for exploring or expanding her limited geographical range. With Harry guiding her from place to place, she'd never had to learn the intricacies of the street layout or the subway system. For Sunday lunch they ate dim sum in Soho or went to the oyster bar or a Blarney Burger. When his parents left Long Island to spend time at their city apartment, she and Harry dined with them at restaurants far fancier than the ones they frequented.

Her brief but productive shopping spree at Freed of London provided her with footless tights, wrap skirts in several lengths and pastel colors, and a pale blue knit warm-up top with long sleeves. The sales assistant was placing the purchases in a carrier bag when Ellie's cellphone buzzed for an incoming text from Dan Wheeler, property bro.

Good news—perfect flat found. Need to discuss. When can we meet?

Busy 2day & 2moro, she responded. *Sunday best 4 me. You?*

Yes.

Coffee my suite 9 am?

Good. Need to see govt issue id. Will explain.

Ok.

His mention of flat, singular, startled her. She was expecting a collection of internet links for available properties that met her specifications.

She halted near the door and texted back. *Can u send web listing?*

Sorry, no. Doesn't exist.

Baffled, she exited the shop. She was close to Leicester Square underground station where she could board a Piccadilly line train for Green Park station. There was just enough time to race to the Ritz, drop off her Freed bag, and order a taxi to deliver her to the photographer's studio. The stylist, she hoped, had accommodated her request for classic casual attire and elegant couture gowns rather than revealing lingerie or a showgirl costume. And she counted on the professional makeup artist to save her the hassle of fixing her face for tonight's show at the Archway.

Chapter 5

Although Dan frequented the Rivoli Bar and had attended functions in the William Kent Room, he'd never visited a Ritz Hotel guest. The opulence of Ellie's deluxe suite was breathtaking. Its windows overlooked Green Park and framed an expanse of treetops.

"I'm not convinced it's worth the fortune we're paying for the privilege," she acknowledged, offering him the cup of coffee her aunt had poured.

In her oversized gray top and black leggings, with her auburn hair tied back in a loose ponytail, she was a stark—and attractive—contrast with her elegant surroundings. Her curving brows appeared to be naturally dark, and so were her lashes. She had greenish eyes.

Sitting across from him, she said, "Tell us about this mysterious flat you've discovered."

"It belongs to my employer, Martin Latimer. That's what he prefers to be called, but in fact he's the Marquess of Milverston. His ancestors owned Latimer House. Like most private aristocratic mansions, it was sold and demolished between the wars and replaced by a multi-level building. He's the landlord. And he inherited a huge, five-bedroomed flat on the top floor. Modern kitchen. Two sitting rooms, formal and informal. A terrace balcony with view."

"I said we're not overly concerned about cost, but it must be astronomical. You've described the floor space of a whole house. In Mayfair."

"Martin is willing to forgo market price. He'll be satisfied with a thousand pounds."

"A week?" Camille asked.

Before he could reply, Ellie said, "Done."

"Per calendar month."

Her rosy lips parted in disbelief. "Is that what you called a peppercorn rent?"

"Correct. Martin and his wife and toddler son live on his Somerset estate, and they don't come to London as often as they used to. Hannah might need to stay overnight in order to attend meetings, but she says your presence wouldn't be problematic for her. If you don't mind hers."

Ellie shook her head. "Not at all."

"Your requested safety features include a separate residents' entrance, on-duty day and night porters in the lobby, security cameras, smoke alarms, and fire suppression system. Your prospective neighbors are quite respectable. Some are undeniably posh. Round the corner you have the Latimer Row shops and restaurants. And the numerous amenities that Piccadilly offers, which you know about. You'd be situated about halfway between the Green Park and Oxford Circus underground stations. If you wish to proceed, I'll conduct a basic background check. May I please see your passports? And driving licenses, if you've got them."

Camille went to the adjoining room.

Ellie stepped around a portable ballet barre to reach the designer handbag on the window seat. She extracted three passports and placed them on the table. Two had blue covers: one embossed with the American eagle, and another was stamped with a coat of arms. The third was burgundy, adorned with the Irish harp.

"I thought only spies required multiple identities," he commented.

"I was born in the United States. Through my mother, I qualified for Canadian citizenship. And Irish, because Grandpa Lowery emigrated from County Clare to Boston." She handed over a pair of laminated cards.

Camille returned and placed her trio of passports beside the silver coffee service. "When traveling internationally, we have multiple options for entry. The Canada papers are especially useful for other Commonwealth countries."

He returned his attention to a certificate of birth card for Estelle Aurelie Lowery. "Like me, you have a March birthday." Noting a discrepancy, he held up the driving license. "Here, and on your passports, you're listed as Estelle Colman."

"My husband's surname. Professionally, I've always used Lowery."

His cursory data gathering hadn't provided information about a spouse. Were they divorced? She didn't wear a wedding band.

Noting the direction of his gaze, she murmured, "He's deceased."

"I'm so sorry." After a pause, Dan commented, "He must've been quite young."

"Twenty-three. An automobile collision. The other driver, who was intoxicated, survived with minor injuries."

His personal experience of sudden, shocking loss made him sensitive to hers. Out of consideration for her feelings, he shifted his gaze to Camille Martel. "Are you the aunt who was also a ballerina?"

"Not me. Never. I've got very flat feet," Camille said. "When Charlotte and Renée established their dance school, I was their office manager, handling enrollments and accounts receivable, doing publicity, and ordering supplies. I work for Ellie, when she's touring. I also have a small local business of my own."

"Camille's Closet is a clothing consignment store," Ellie told him.

"I'm primarily responsible for developing a Stella Nue line of reproduction vintage clothing," Camille added. "We're sourcing fabrics domestically, and the garments will be constructed in a renovated factory building in New Hampshire. We're ready to establish official Stella boutiques in select cities, starting with Boston. And eventually New York and Beverly Hills. Perhaps Chicago and Atlanta."

When he returned their passports, Ellie asked, "Are we approved?"

"All that remains is for you to inspect the premises to see whether they suit. If so, we'll need to determine the mode and timing of payments, whether weekly or monthly. If you choose direct deposit, my office can provide a routing number to your bankers in the States."

"Add the dollars-to-pounds conversion fee to my rent. I insist."

"I'll inform the billing department. Would you like to see the place this morning?"

"The sooner the better."

Dan's assertion that Latimer House was an easy stroll from the Ritz was confirmed. Its pale stone façade contrasted with the older, heavier Victorian architecture that prevailed on the adjacent street. At ground level, separate entrances served office employees and the occupants of the flats on the upper floors, which had decorative bow windows.

Dan introduced Ellie to the doorman as Ms. Lowery, adding, "Her grandfather is an Irishman."

"Born in County Clare, between Limerick and Ennis," Ellie clarified. "He emigrated to Boston in the United States."

"I'm from Galway," Lorcan declared with pride.

"These ladies are interested in becoming Martin's tenants," Dan explained before leading them to an elevator.

Ellie's expectations for the Latimer apartment were high, and nothing about it disappointed her. In the spacious drawing room, damask-draped windows on two sides let in plenty of light. It was furnished with an eclectic mix of antiques and modern pieces. The colors of the Persian rug beneath her feet remained bright despite its apparent age. Heavy gold frames surrounded large landscape paintings and the mirror over a fireplace. Family photographs representing several generations filled the wide space between the pair of porcelain vases on the mantel. The dining room contained a mahogany table with eight chairs, a crystal chandelier above, and a sideboard.

Studying the kitchen cabinetry and sleek, ultra-modern appliances, Camille commented, "Very nice."

The room Dan referred to as the study was a cozy retreat with sofa and armchairs arranged in front of a widescreen television. A corner desk supported a computer. Framed travel and concert posters decorated the walls.

"The extra bedrooms are along this corridor," he said, showing them the way. "How does this one suit you?" he asked Ellie.

She admired the graceful sleigh bed, part of a matching set that included a dressing table and a tallboy. The ensuite bathroom was luxuriously appointed.

Camille expressed her approval of the room across the hall.

"I'm unaccustomed to showing residential property," Dan admitted. "Typically, it's office or commercial space.

But I've been here often, and I'll do my best to answer any questions."

"How soon can we take possession?" Ellie asked.

"You may rock up here at any convenient time."

She turned to Camille. "We're booked at the Ritz for a full week, right?"

Her aunt nodded. "I'll inquire about the cancellation policy."

"Shall I inform Martin that you're taking the flat?" Dan asked.

"Please do. Though I can't believe he's willing to let complete strangers live here."

"Stella Nue is not just anyone," he replied in his calm fashion. "My cursory vetting process confirmed the existence of your mother's dance academy. And your father founded the Blarney Burger restaurants."

"Daddo's local burger joint was so popular that he built it into a regional chain. The conglomerate that bought him out established franchises all over the country. Instead of retiring on the proceeds of the sale, he opened another Irish pub—my brother Liam is co-owner and manager. They can't legally use the Blarney Burger name, so their signature menu item is the Shamrock Burger."

"The bun is different," Camille said. "Patrick and Liam use toasted slices of Irish batch loaf."

"Sounds tasty." Dan tossed his key fob and caught it. "Our contracts department will draft a letting agreement for your review, and we can make adjustments. It's not an absolute requirement, but if you're interested in a short-term insurance policy, I can provide details."

"I am, if it ensures peace of mind for your boss. And you. Nobody will come here except George and Zack. I'm not planning any raucous parties or raves during my residency."

"If you do, I want an invitation."

"As soon as we're settled," Camille told him, "you'll be our first dinner guest."

"I accept," he said promptly. "Am I being cheeky if I request your best approximation of a Shamrock Burger?"

On Thursday afternoon, Ellie returned to the Archway Cabaret for a pickup rehearsal with Zack and George before embarking on their second group of shows. In recent days, her act had often faded from her thoughts, and she needed to redirect her focus.

After moving from the Ritz to the penthouse flat, she and Camille spent their days, rain or shine, exploring the shops of Latimer Row and its environs, stocking up on food and wine. Even before receiving the elegant floral arrangement from Martin Latimer, designed and delivered by the florist housed in one of his many historic buildings, they already felt at home.

She was using the plastic tweezer to pull a false eyelash from its compartment when George barged into her dressing room. "How's the best boss in showbiz?"

"Almost ready." After applying the eyelash glue, she asked, "Where's your other half?"

"My nuttier half, you mean. He's taking pains with his hair, and I was tired of being asked to comment. I'll know he's satisfied when he posts his selfie." Crossing to the clothes rail, he examined her costumes. "I dread doing what he calls your pirate peel. Our puffy shirts are a hazard. Every time we wear them, I'm afraid a flouncy cuff or neck ruffle will snag on your spangles or catch in your belt buckle." George shuddered.

"I bet you've got enough time to convert them to tearaways. I have sewing supplies in my bag. The audience would love seeing your pecs. You won't need those shirts after tonight."

"Don't make me. Please." He placed his palms together beseechingly. "We'd be out of sync with the music. Say, when will we see that fancy penthouse apartment Camille told us about?"

"Soon. If Zack promises to be civilized. I can't have him snooping through his lordship's desk drawers or her lady-ship's wardrobe."

Their comedic *Treasure Chest* routine, one of George's early choreographic efforts, was always a crowd-pleaser, and its final presentation was no exception. Returning to her dressing room, Ellie pried off her doubloon pasties and replaced them with a pair shaped like scallop shells to match the aquatic theme of her forthcoming act. In *Ondine Undone,* she personified a water nymph, emerging from the sea to dance with mortal men.

She reached into her bag's external compartment and dug out pointe shoes dyed to match her diaphanous teal-col-ored costume. After acquiring them from a Berlin shop rec-ommended by a friend at the Staatsballett, she'd worn them there and in Brussels and in Paris. Recalling their enduring stiffness, she decided more breaking in was required. She placed a foot on each toe box, pressing down as hard as she could. When the stage kitten delivered the transparent frilled shirt, black beaded corset, and red velvet tearaway trousers that made up her pirate queen costume, Ellie was smashing a shoe against the concrete floor.

"What did it do to piss you off?" Lisa asked.

"Standard practice." Ellie bent the sole back and forth to test its pliability before squirting hand sanitizer inside the toe boxes. "The alcohol content loosens the glue. Normally I'd rub it on the outside but can't risk diluting the color." She would miss the suede platform and shock absorbing interior of her Gaynor Mindens.

Thank goodness for silicone toe shields, she thought on her way to the stage. And the softening properties of antibiotic gel.

Twirling about, weaving between Zack and George, she wasn't entirely pleased with the precision of her footwork. Her Ondine costume, layers of pastel chiffon secured by satin ribbons, was the most comfortable to dance in. It was also the simplest to remove, which she did until she wore nothing but the shell-shaped pasties and scallop modesty patch.

After the curtain call, she retreated to her dressing room. Shoving the teal pointe shoes into her show bag, she was thankful she'd never wear them again.

The usual clamor and chatter from the adjacent dressing room had died down. On a weeknight, cast members with day jobs didn't linger, neither did those who had children. The showgirls who could sleep in tomorrow would head to the nearest pub, as a group or with a date. They had invited Ellie to join them, but she wanted to rest up for morning class at British Ballet Theatre.

Camille popped her head around the door frame. "If you want to leave by the front door, the lobby has been cleared. Except for some English guy claiming he was Harry's room-mate at Juilliard."

Ellie put down her hairbrush. "Tell him I'll be there in a few minutes."

Chapter 6

Her short journey to the deserted lobby allowed no preparation time for an unexpected encounter with an individual from her distant past. Sandy-haired and lean, he was more impeccably dressed than he'd been during their student days. He hadn't worn glasses then, and she couldn't decide whether they made him look nerdy or professorial. He'd grown a moustache and a scruffy beard, like a male dancer returning to work from a lengthy hiatus. She preferred clean-shaven men, but his whiskers suited him.

"Hello, Gil."

"Ellie." As he kissed her cheek, his stubble rasped her skin.

"Thanks for coming. I hope you enjoyed the show."

She recalled none of his history after he left Juilliard and had no idea when he'd returned to London. Had he attended Harry's funeral?

Memories of that day were fragmented, either piercingly clear or hazy.

A spray of white lilies and fern fronds had been spread

over casket lid. Unable to look for more than a moment, she'd fixed her gaze on the enormous floral arrangements packed in between the communion rail and the altar of the Colmans' church. The minister who baptized an infant Harry had spoken in a refined, British-flavored accent. She learned things about her husband that he'd never told her. A female cousin described amusing incidents from summers in the Hamptons, drawing faint laughter from the congregation. His high school drama teacher was overcome with emotion, wiping his eyes with a handkerchief as he regretted the loss of an exceptional and promising talent.

"I dropped off a note on your first night but couldn't stay. Father was waiting for me at the Garrick Club."

She didn't admit that anonymous messages annoyed her, or that she'd thrown his away. "How is he?"

"He's rehearsing the revival of Rattigan's *A Bequest to the Nation* at the Sovereign Theatre. He plays Admiral Lord Nelson, our famous naval hero."

She'd met Sir Francis Cooke when he crossed the Pond to witness Gil's performance as Freddy Eynsford-Hill in Shaw's *Pygmalion*. Harry had played Professor Higgins. Brilliantly.

"When you're not so knackered, I'd like to discuss your foray into stage acting."

"You know about that?"

"Last year, at the start of your farewell tour, you mentioned it in an interview. Here's my card."

Reading the small print, she said in surprise, "You're a playwright."

"My true calling, as I belatedly discovered. My failure to inherit Sir Francis Cooke's talents persuaded me to follow a different professional path. With better hours but worse pay."

"I'll phone you," she told him, and meant it.

"Soon," he insisted, leaning in for another kiss. It landed at the outer edge of her mouth.

Her aunt appeared, necessitating introductions. Gil accompanied them to the limousine and opened the passenger door for them, pre-empting their driver.

As the car proceeded through Mayfair traffic to the calmer environs of Latimer House, Camille asked, "How well did you know him?"

"We saw each other constantly. He and Harry shared a dorm room. More than once, he barged in when we were—when we weren't studying. Poor Gil, he was so embarrassed. We did try to find him a girlfriend, so he wouldn't feel like a third wheel, but never succeeded. He liked hanging out with us."

"Did he and Harry compete for parts?"

"We were all competitive, dancers and drama students, within our respective disciplines. Hard work, high hopes. I sort of related to Gil, and empathized with him. Both of us felt the pressure of living up to parental expectations. He wanted to fit in but didn't. Not at the school, not in New York. It was nice seeing him again. I hope he'll find success with the play he's written."

Overnight, her subconscious carried her to the Lakes Region summer stock theatre where she and Harry had played lovers and spouses. He was feeding her lines, with an audience present. Terrified of making a mistake, she parroted the words. She was wearing the wrong costume. None of their props was in the correct location, and the stage furniture was poorly arranged. Like every dream about a performance, this one morphed into a full-blown nightmare, and she forced herself into wakefulness to escape it.

In the aftermath of his death, Harry had often appeared in her dreams. Lately, she'd seldom seen him.

Shaken and sad, she got up from the sleigh bed. After a quick shower she poured a cup of coffee and put together a simple breakfast of yogurt and diced figs. Camille helped her assemble a selection of nibbles that would energize her through a strenuous morning.

Ellie placed her empty bowl and orange juice glass in the dishwasher. "How will you spend the day?"

"My accountant and I have a video call to review my tax return before the filing date. No matter where we are in the world, Uncle Sam demands his due."

Ellie picked up her bag, checked her reflection in the gilt-framed mirror in the vestibule, and exited the flat, ready to strive and stretch and soar and sweat. At Piccadilly Circus station she boarded the Bakerloo train for Regent's Park. At her stop, she followed the signs for the Way Out and squeezed into the crowded lift.

The historic Crescent Theatre, located on the south side of Regent's Park, housed British Ballet Theatre. At the time of Ellie's prior visit, early in Rafe's tenure, he'd given her a tour, showing off results of the costly renovation that revived its faded grandeur. The stage, he'd boasted, had the best sprung floor in the entire dance universe, as though that fact might tempt her to audition for his company.

She headed for the multi-level modern annex, containing administrative offices, rehearsal spaces, orchestra room, on-site wardrobe storage, music library, scenery construction shop, physio suite, and more. At reception she received directions to the space reserved for morning class. She stepped into an elevator large enough to accommodate fully half the *corps de ballet*. After its doors closed, she switched off her phone and tucked it into her bag.

From the studio doorway, she scoped out the spacious square room. Two barres, upper and lower, were permanently affixed to three of the mirrored walls, and rows of moveable ones stood in the center. Her nostrils were assailed by the aroma she'd encountered from childhood to adulthood, everywhere in the world: stale perspiration. Unfamiliar with the principals' and soloists' preferred locations, she faced the usual problem of finding a place to work.

Spotting an apparent vacancy, she removed her thin warm-up jacket and draped it over the bottom rail. Thousands of damp palms had smoothed and darkened the top one. She pulled her loose shirt over her head and stripped off the drawstring garments, revealing a figure that differed from the typically androgynous ballet girl. The top portion of her black leotard—best for hiding inevitable sweat patches—was designed for the well-endowed dancer, with broad straps and extra spandex layers for bust support. A curving bosom and the slight flare of her hips made her lean torso appear disproportionately slim, and she accentuated her small waist by tying on a filmy black chiffon skirt. Black tights, cropped at the calf, exposed the lower portion of her legs before she pulled on her leg warmers. To ensure optimal traction, she'd scuffed the split leather soles of her soft canvas slippers with a serrated kitchen knife.

After a quick check to make sure her bun was well-secured, she balled up the discarded garments and jammed them into her bag. She shoved it against the wall, leaving plenty of open area for footwork.

The long mirror reflected dozens of contorted bodies. As in every professional class, Ellie was surrounded by attractive faces and spare, muscled physiques. Although the majority of dancers were white, the company was ethnically mixed. She detected foreign accents and languages. Two men were speaking French. One blonde, whose English carried a Russian or Polish inflection, chattered with a brunette who must be German or Austrian. Joining the communal warm-up, she completed a series of hip and hamstring stretches and splits. She sat on the floor and used her stretch bands to pull on each big toe, then the smaller ones, an exercise that reinforced balance. Bending over, she touched her nose to her knees, feeling the morning pinch in her back muscles. She rolled her head to loosen her neck. Holding her right calf, she lifted her leg high and pulled it inwards until it was parallel with her torso. She performed the same movement on the left side.

She exchanged a nod and a half-smile with the girl closest to her, who had earbuds in. Making friends wasn't a priority, but she didn't want to offend anyone. The young male dancer on her other side stared so intently at his reflection that she didn't bother to engage.

Rafe breezed into the room. Spotting her, he came over to offer a casual greeting before he approached Semerova. From the way he bobbed his leonine head in her direction, Ellie deduced that she was the subject of their dialogue.

Don't stay, she silently pleaded and exhaled her relief when his panther-like stride carried him from the studio.

The ballet mistress ended her consultation with the pianist and clapped her hands. "We begin now."

Ellie eased into the predictable pattern of basic exercises she and everyone else in the room had learned long ago. *Pliés. Ports de bras. Tendu* to front, side, and back—slow tempo, then fast. *Rondes de jambes á terre, petits battements, battements frappés, grands battements.* Semerova's narrow hands and bony fingers marked the movements, and gradually she added complexity to her combinations.

Ellie held her spine straight while maintaining a looseness in her shoulders. A glimpse at her reflection showed that her breasts jutted out over her flat, toned midriff. Her butt, a mass of muscle, curved outward more than those of other girls.

Semerova circulated through the room, often trilling "la la la" in time with the piano. Pausing at the blonde girl next to Ellie, she gave a correction. "Too stiff arms, Gemma. Loose and light. Ah, better."

She regarded Ellie, her expression blank. "Friend of Rafe. Danced for Mirielle. Knows Sven also."

Responding, Ellie suspected, would be a breach of etiquette. If she nodded affirmation, she'd miss a beat—or more. Her eyes didn't move from the girl in front, whose pale blue leo was already marked with damp blotches.

During the brief break that preceded center work, the men moved the portable barres against the wall. The dancers shed outer clothing. The girls sat down to remove their slippers and tie on their pointe shoes.

After a quick swig from her water bottle, Ellie unzipped her bag's outer compartment. Empty. As panic escalated, she rummaged deeper into the jumble of t-shirts, leggings, lambswool, and toe guards. At the bottom she found the turquoise shoes she'd worn in *Ondine Undone*. Her lowly status as stranger was about to plummet to unimagined depths. She would forever be infamous as Bosomy Chick Who Wore Colored Pointe Shoes.

At least, she consoled herself, they're fully broken in.

Head high, conscious of the disdainful glances directed at her feet, she followed the blonde who had worked beside her at the barre.

"Bold choice."

"Unintentional. Morning mix-up." She plucked at her leotard, fused to her lower spine by perspiration. "I'm Ellie."

"Gemma Banks. Are you a late-season hire?"

"No. Rafe invited me to attend class. We've known each other forever. He partnered me in New York. Brussels. Elsewhere."

"Gosh, you've had quite a career. Principal?"

"First soloist. The kind who gets to dance the big roles." Shaking her head, Ellie admitted, "I never stayed anywhere long enough to officially move up the ladder."

Gemma's shoes were appropriately pink, supple yet supportive, with neat white stitching around the toe boxes.

Semerova gave instructions for center work—arabesque, promenade, *pas de basque*, repeat. Ellie, in the second group, was relieved that she had a chance to study the combination before performing it. She just managed to keep up the pace during a series of jumps and arabesques performed to the strains of the Act Three polonaise from *Sleeping Beauty*. During a sequence of diagonal pirouettes, she wobbled on the first one and messed up her timing.

"New girl in silly shoes, do again with next group. Back row."

She redeemed herself with the *glissades* and *échappés*, without expecting—or receiving—acknowledgment. The session wrapped up with a series of *grands jetés*, the exuberant leaps she most enjoyed and executed satisfactorily. It was heaven, dancing on a shock-absorbing floor again after the Archway's unrelenting wood.

When class ended, nobody lingered. Everyone had some place to go—a rehearsal, the canteen, the physio room. Ellie, unsure of her status with regard to the women's changing room, gathered up her things.

Anya Semerova beckoned, her gesture reminiscent of the commanding Myrthe, Queen of the Wilis, in *Giselle*.

"Your name."

"Ellie Lowery."

"Why you are here, Eeley? If for keeping fit, better to join barre class in gym to exercise."

"No artistry. No challenge."

"I see. And for this I am to have you as a distraction every morning?"

"I'll stay in the back row. You don't have to coach me or give corrections. I'm not auditioning."

"Never again come with those bad color shoes. Is clear?"

On a grateful sigh, she replied, "Very."

"I improve you, but to no purpose. You are how old?"

"I just turned twenty-nine."

"In the prime. Is sad." Anya's gaze shifted to the door, where Rafe was watching. "Great waste," she added, in a carrying tone, directed at him.

Ellie ignored the faint flutter of an ambition she'd buried

years ago. She reminded herself that she sought the pure pleasure of movement, and the cathartic rigor and discipline that ballet demanded.

"What a fab bag," Gemma told her as they were packing up. "I've never seen that type."

"Designed for tennis players," she explained. "My brother gave it to me years ago. Lots of space, and plenty of separate compartments for shoes and water bottle and more."

Rafe greeted her with a grin. "You survived, I see. Makes me wonder if Anya's doing her job."

"I'm on the verge of collapse," she confessed.

"Care to observe a rehearsal? I'm coaching Leah Sternberg and Drew Mason in *Onegin*. The final *pas de deux*. We'd welcome your input. You danced Tatiana superbly. Reckon you could again."

"I doubt that. But we'll always have Monte Carlo," she murmured.

He'd drawn to the surface memories of portraying the heroine in one of the most dramatic and emotional ballets in the repertoire. Tatiana's story arc accurately reflected her own journey from dreamy, besotted girl to mature woman capable of relinquishing a deeply ingrained love. Ellie knew every note of the score. Sometimes, to help herself fall asleep, she played back the music in her mind.

Her yearning to hear it again convinced her to stay. "At the moment, I'm desperate for coffee. Tell me where to find you."

"Studio A, our largest, at the far end of this corridor. It matches the dimensions of the Crescent Theatre stage. We start in a quarter of an hour."

Chapter 7

Revived by fresh air and a caffeine buzz, Ellie emerged from the lift on the studio level, and made her way to a space larger than the one used for company class. Natural light streaming from a strip of window was reflected by a mirror opposite. The usual wall-mounted and portable barres were present. A small desk and straight-backed chair were placed at one side of the room. Drew Mason, in a loose, long-sleeved t-shirt and tights, sat stretching on the floor. Leah Sternberg's frothy tulle calf-length practice tutu floated up and down as she performed a series of *relevés* on pointe.

The accompanist, a middle-aged bearded fellow sporting a ponytail, was seated at a gleaming black Steinway. He greeted Ellie with a broad smile. "I'm Barry." Lowering his voice, he added, "The one person in the building, apparently, who recognizes Stella Nue."

"Ellie," she said firmly. "Lowery."

"I know. Rafe told me. You caused rather a stir in the ranks this morning. Without anybody realizing there was greater cause for amazement than your unconventional choice of footwear."

She dropped her bag onto a chair. "Can I purchase your silence with complimentary tickets to one of my shows?"

"They'd be no use, I'm afraid. I spend my evenings pounding out popular tunes in a hotel piano bar. Never fear, your secret's safe with me. But don't expect it to remain one for very long."

While waiting for Rafe, the dancers asked Ellie about her experience with Ballet Bruxelles and wondered what Mireille Charpentier was like.

"A swan forged from steel," Ellie told them. "Unchanged from her time at City International, where she first coached me."

Rafe came into the room. "Grand, everybody's here." When he placed a chair for Ellie, he asked his ballerina, "How's that ankle?"

"Ready for anything."

"Excellent. We'll begin from Drew's entrance." He handed her a piece of paper. "After ignoring your pleas to remain, your husband Prince Gremin has departed. You pick up Onegin's letter to read it again. You hear him outside the room, though you don't see him yet. Drew, you're upstage behind the scrim, crossing from one side to the other, searching for her. Not that fast. Do it again. Much better." Turning to Leah, he said, "Before he enters, sit at the desk—defensive, preparing yourself to defy and deny him."

Ellie watched them carry out Rafe's directions.

"When he moves downstage, you do the same, without looking at him. Keep still as his arms encircle you and slide down your body. Drew, when you collapse at her feet, reach up—slowly—and take her hand. Hold tight, so she can't escape. Barry, let's have his entrance music, please."

Even if a single piano didn't do justice to the emotive score, for Ellie it was hardly less powerful than the orchestral version. It dragged her backwards through the years and a time when the steps and positions and had been imprinted on her mind and her body. She recalled all the physical manifestations of Tatiana's agonized yearning for the man whose rejection had wounded her as an impressionable young girl. The frantic, flailing of the arms, each lift and toss, the gravity-defying *jetés*, reluctant yet passionate embraces.

She'd trained for a profession that depended on an acute memory and the ability to retain what she learned. In class, combinations had to be absorbed quickly and performed immediately. Through constant repetition, choreography and timing movement to music became second nature.

It doesn't matter that I remember so much, she told herself. I won't perform this role again.

She could also recall the fierce blast of applause whenever she remained alone on the stage, facing the audience, depleted and bereft. Numbed by exhaustion and grief, tears trickling down her face, struggling for breath, she'd gripped Rafe's hand for the duration of a protracted curtain call.

His sing-song voice pulled her back to the studio.

"Dum, da, dum dee da. Leah, relax all your muscles as he carries you. You're limp with longing and lust." Rafe's shoulders sagged. "You're almost, almost succumbing to him. You're a married woman now, not the innocent girl you were when you first fell in love with Onegin. You know exactly what he wants. And you want it just as much. Drew, show us exuberance and elation whenever she turns towards you. It's proof, you believe, that you've won her."

Ellie saw the sprung floor dip slightly when Drew landed with force after his *tour en l'air.*

"John Cranko's choreography is sheer brilliance," Rafe said, "deserving of accuracy and precision. We'll take it again. Same place, Barry."

After letting them go through the section once more, he glanced over at Ellie. "Any comments?"

"Leah, you were perfect when Drew tossed and caught you, but your feet wobbled slightly on the landing. To keep your balance, angle your body in a sequence." She rose to demonstrate. "Head. Torso. Hips. And on the arabesques, use the extension of your arms and stretch your neck for maximum uplift. Like this. Exactly," she approved after Leah copied her. "And when I tore up Onegin's letter, I ripped it in time with the bass drum's downbeats. When you shove the scraps into his hand, some of them will fall to the floor, and he'll drop the rest. Don't be nervous about slipping on them, because after that you won't be on pointe."

Leah nodded.

Rafe, solicitous of his dancers' psyches, advised them to release all the angst of the climactic *pas de deux* on leaving the studio. "Don't neglect self-care. You're both on tonight."

Before Leah left, she told Ellie, "I would've liked to see your Tatiana. Rafe says you were superb."

"At City International," she replied, "I was cast as her sister Olga. During that closing scene I always stood in the wings, watching. Wondering if I'd ever dance it myself."

"So did I."

"If you search online," Rafe said, "you'll find a video of us."

That's not all they'll find, Ellie thought. Barry was correct, it wouldn't be long before she was outed as Stella Nue.

"She never put a foot wrong," Rafe went on. "I did, but I hope nobody else notices where."

Before raising her water bottle to her lips, Leah said, "I hope you'll come to tomorrow's rehearsal. The bedroom scene. Tatiana's dream."

"Our happy *pas de deux,* we called it." Ellie's eyes found Rafe. "I'm convinced carrying me back and forth and up and down the stage forced you into retirement."

"That's my incentive to head for the gym and partner the

weight machine," Drew announced, holding a towel to his perspiring neck.

"I better grab some nosh before my Swanilda costume fitting. Not much," Leah added, tapping her partner's shoulder. "For your sake, I promise not to put on a single gram of weight."

As soon as the pair departed, Rafe put his hand on his back and told Ellie, "Watching him lift and throw her about and catch her and drag her around brought on sympathy pains in my maimed spine. How was it for you?"

"I anticipated everything she did, from the biggest jump to the minutest gesture."

"You tempt me to put your name on a cast list."

He was joking, but she couldn't muster a laugh. "Hell, no."

"Burlesque's loss could be ballet's gain."

"You sound like my mother."

"We should heed our mums. They always know best." He peered down at her and asked, "You didn't mind coaching Leah?"

"You know I can't resist a challenge. I wasn't sure I could see *Onegin* again. Now I want a ticket."

"You've got it. And another one for *Coppelia*, which closes out our season. A cheery contrast to Russian despair and remorse." He took his phone from his pocket. "If I don't hurry, I'll be late for our monthly managers' and administrators' lunch. Stop at the front desk to pick up a membership form for Friends of British Ballet Theatre. If you won't let me put you in a ballet, you can make amends with a sizeable donation."

"All right. But I want to be listed as Anonymous in the annual report. Can't have your dancers complaining that I bought my way into company class."

"You'll be back tomorrow?"

"Definitely. To prove to everyone that I possess proper shoes."

Leaving the annex with the membership brochure, she was determined to find her way to the tube stop without opening a map on her phone. Noticing a weary but cheerful family group laden with souvenirs from the London Zoo, she followed in their wake, correctly guessing that they were also bound for Regent's Park station.

Dan, monitoring a Latimer London Estates investment committee meeting, heard his mobile ping. The chairman, assuming the company head was the source, encouraged him to read and respond as necessary. But the message came from Ellie Lowery, not Martin Latimer, and it was a dinner invitation. He'd refrained from contacting her, despite his increasing desire to do so. Her lengthy silence indicated that she required no further advice or assistance.

On the appointed evening, he put on a coat and tie before strolling over to Latimer House with a bottle of prosecco and a bouquet from the Latimer Row flower shop. Before Ellie answered his knock on the door, he heard a disconcerting burst of masculine laughter. He wasn't her only guest. Masking his disappointment, he beamed at her.

Shiny gold flecks dotted her pale blue sheath, and a thick braid of hair was coiled atop her head.

"How thoughtful," she said, accepting the bottle and the flowers. "I need your help luring Camille and George out of Zack's way before he has a meltdown."

Dan caught a whiff of jasmine as he followed her. To prevent further crowding, he halted in the kitchen doorway.

"Almost ready," the man standing at the cooker reported. To Dan, he added, "Beef crown rib roast. Hope you're not vegetarian. Or vegan."

"I should've asked about that," Ellie said on a contrite note. "Are you?"

"Not since a brief spell when I was an undergraduate."

"Zack, our chef, created the menu."

"I'm George, his husband," said the other man. "Your server this evening."

Camille held up her glass of red wine. "And I'm the sommelier. What'll you have, Dan?"

"Same as you, please."

"Prosecco for me," Ellie declared. "It's a superior one—with a cork. George, will you do the honors? I'll put these flowers in water."

Seeing Ellie's lookalike dance partners, he detected dissimilarities that hadn't been apparent when they were onstage. Although both men were tall and dark-haired, Zack had bright blue eyes, and George's were brown.

Zack lifted his glass. "To Dan, who provided our Ellie with this spectacular apartment. George and I are emerald with envy."

"I'll melt if I stay here," Ellie declared. "Dan, take this, please." She handed over her prosecco and picked up the vase of flowers. "We should all leave Zack in peace."

"No, no. You can't steal my sous chefs," he insisted. "George can carry the hors d'oeuvres tray to the parlor, but I want him to come back. Camille, you're dicing mushrooms."

When they were out of earshot, George murmured, "I'm getting a preview of my future existence. Did Ellie tell you about our bed and breakfast?"

"Not yet," she said, setting the vase on a low table separating the sofa from the armchairs. "Return to your mate and do his bidding."

"Yes, madam." After a butler's bow, he retreated.

"They raided the Fortnum's food hall and the butcher shop in Latimer Row. Help yourself to smoked salmon. Truffle cheese and biscuits. Chutney." She handed him one of the small plates stacked beside silver cutlery and napkins.

He eyed the book atop the pile on a side table. *"Understanding the English.* Is it helping?"

"I haven't started. I'll let you know when I finish. I was curious about whatever common attributes define Englishness. And how they've been preserved in an era of individualism and among a diverse and multicultural population."

"For a start, there's cricket. Real ale. A monarch as head of state. Grumbling about the weather—too wet, too warm, too anything. What was your friend saying about a B&B?"

After a single sip, she said, "The guys are about to become innkeepers in a lakeside town claiming to be the oldest summer resort in America. Two years ago, they purchased The Maples, a five-bedroom, five bath historical house on three acres. It has wide pine floors and fireplaces. Huge kitchen. And many more original features. There's a nineteenth century barn, big enough for weddings and private events. Apple orchard, blueberry patch. It's set back from Wolfeboro's Main Street but within walking distance of restaurants and shops, the lake and the boat docks."

"They won't have time to miss performing."

"True. The house was renovated to some extent, but its kitchen and the overall décor were dated. Between our tours, they zhuzhed it up and moved their collection of antique furniture from a storage unit. On Fourth of July weekend, the first guests arrive. They're booked through the summer and filling up for foliage season, when the leaf-peepers show up. The mountains and ski resorts are close, so they'll have wintertime customers as well. Best of all, from my perspective, their place is less than fifteen minutes from my summer cottage and on the same side of the lake. We're almost neighbors."

"You own a lake property?"

"Co-own with Cousin Phil, who teaches at the boarding school in Wolfeboro. Grandpa Lowery—the Irishman—left it to all his grandchildren. I bought out my brother and sister. Liam has permission to use it anytime he wants, whether or not I'm there, but he's too tied to the pub to get away much. Marie is a medical researcher, living in a nifty upmarket Boston condominium with her partner. They also have a quaint little holiday home on Martha's Vineyard and didn't want or need a third house. A vintage one at that, requiring lots of annual maintenance."

"I've been doing things all wrong," Dan said. "I'm older than you. Gainfully employed and amply compensated. But I'm still renting. From my boss."

"I've seen the street where you live. Most people would say you lucked out, big time."

"When you're not touring, or on your lake, where do you live?"

Her face lifted, revealing a smirk. "With my parents, in our Birchmont house—my home since I was two days old. After Daddo sold his company, they expanded it. I occupy the guest suite, with my own separate entrance and a tiny covered patio. It's easier and far less costly than purchasing my own place."

"Even though you could afford to have any number of houses, if you wanted to."

She poked a thin salmon slice with the tines of her fork. "I found better uses for the assets I inherited from my husband and the money Stella Nue brings in. She turned out to be a massive earner. Touring and product licensing are extremely lucrative. My aunt and I and our financial advisers are constantly strategizing in order to keep the income stream flowing."

Camille, overhearing this comment, said, "After my Montreal trip, I'm responsible for putting our plans into action. And because I won't be traveling around the world any longer, I can adopt a cat."

"Zack and George want a dog." Smiling over at Dan,

Ellie said, "Guess who wants a laid-back Golden Retriever. And who's insisting on a fluffy, fashionable designer breed."

"Lab for George. The fancy one for Zack."

"The other way around. What news from the kitchen?" she asked her aunt.

"Decisions about plating and presentation are underway. Did you invite Dan to the Saturday show?"

"Not yet." Smiling, she asked, "Are you interested in attending our grand finale? I'm happy to offer my comps to you and Lou and Kelly."

"I'll ask them and let you know."

"And I hope you'll stay afterwards, for Stella's retirement party."

"You always refer to her in the third person," he commented.

"Because she's a separate entity. A role I've been playing."

"It's that easy to compartmentalize?"

"I've done it all my life. I wasn't *just* a ballet kid. I rode a pony and played softball and dove off the dock into the lake and paddled around the bay in my granddad's canoe. I waited tables at The Shamrock and flipped burgers whenever Daddo was short-staffed." Her greenish eyes landed on him speculatively. "I'll bet you have different ways of being and doing, depending on where you are and who you're with."

He nodded. "Executive Dan, at Latimer London Estates. Countryside Dan, who goes fishing at the weekends." Brother Dan, Brian's visitor at Harding Hall, his care home. Son Dan, companion to his father, who was permanently and irrevocably estranged from the woman who abandoned them both.

George stepped into the room. Bowing, he uttered a formal announcement that the meal was served.

The salad was an artful creation, the beef was expertly roasted, the potatoes had been perfectly crisped, and the broccoli amandine was a triumph. Hardly any of Mayfair's finest dining establishments, Dan declared, could have improved upon what Zack had produced, a compliment that momentarily deprived him of speech.

"I wanted to bake something splendid. But after a heavy meal, it's obscene to present a multi-layered cake. Which, I assure you, I could've done."

"I can attest to that," George said. "My dance career would've lasted longer if I hadn't packed on the pounds from his cooking."

"Boo hoo." Zack sawed the air with his hand, playing an invisible violin. "You're exaggerating. Sven Eilert offered you a place in his company. You chose to work with Ellie instead of him."

"No regrets. After hopping from continent to continent with her for the past three years, I can settle on the shore of Lake Winnipesaukee and cater to people who haven't yet tired of living out of suitcases. Am I serving the dessert, or you?"

"Both of us." Zack pointed at Ellie. "Stay where you are. We'll clear the table."

"That inn of theirs," her aunt murmured, "will suck up a lot of their energy. They're going to be busier than they realize. You, too," she told Ellie. "Ballet class six mornings out of seven. Weekday afternoons at drama school. You're the all work, no play type, Estelle Aurelie Lowery Colman."

"Am not," Ellie contradicted. Ignoring her instructions to stay seated and confirming her relative's accusation, she gathered up floral-patterned bowls and saucers from the sideboard and arranged them at each place.

George returned, bearing a silver tray of macarons.

Zack followed, a silver bowl cradled between his gloved hands. "Passion fruit sorbet. My own creation."

"You're a marvel," Dan declared.

"When investigating the contents of the kitchen cabinets,

I found an ice cream maker. As soon as I saw the passion fruits at Fortnum and Mason, I knew exactly what to do. Peel and puree, make a simple syrup, blend and chill. Into the machine. Vroom, vroom. Voila!"

After the final course, they returned to the drawing room. George and Zack passed around miniature glasses of port.

Accepting hers, Ellie said, "Dan is a fly fisherman. An angler. If you want advice about attracting fishing enthusiasts to your inn, you should consult him."

George's brown eyes regarded him with curiosity. "We don't know a thing about it."

Zack added, "Our place is beside a lake and near lots of rivers and streams. There's a sports shop in Wolfeboro that sells fishing licenses and all the equipment. We hope to provide lodging for their out-of-town clientele."

"You'll need to link up with experienced local fishing guides," Dan said. "They'll know what species are running in a given season and the best spots for casting."

"It would be great to have another add-on to our excursion packages."

"What's included?" Dan asked.

"Boat trips around the lake. Driving tours through the White Mountains, in summer and during foliage season. Agricultural fairs. Farm visits for animal petting and hayrides and wandering in corn mazes."

"Outlet shopping," Camille added. "On rainy days."

"If you ever come to New England," George told Dan, "you're staying with us."

He should've answered, truthfully, that such a visit was unlikely. Instead, he heard himself say, "I definitely will."

Chapter 8

By the time ballet master Marcus Baldwin dismissed class, the slight twinge at the base of Ellie's spine had morphed into full-blown ache, and her thighs and calves vibrated from exertion. Discomfort while in motion was bearable. Standing on the tube station's concrete platform was worse. She pawed at the interior of her carryall, desperate for ibuprofen. It wasn't yet midday, but she was surrounded by people wearing Friday expressions, welcoming the weekend's proximity. She longed to soothe her muscles with a soak and sweat in the bathtub but barely had time for a hasty shower.

She found Camille in the drawing room of the flat, stuffing tissue paper between the layers of shimmering, glittering Stella Nue costumes before sheathing them in plastic.

"You'd better tell me which of these I'm shipping to New Hampshire," she said. "And how many you'll keep here to donate to the fashion museum."

"Can we discuss it later? I need to clean up."

Camille surveyed the disarray. "I hope Gil Cooke isn't coming here."

"We're meeting at the Sovereign Theatre, just off Shaftesbury Avenue."

"One more question. Do I pack this?" Camille held up a white bustier embellished with faux pearls. "You could wear it under your black velvet jacket, with the black silk trousers."

Shaking her head, Ellie said, "Your vision of my London residency is at odds with mine. I'm not anticipating many dress-up occasions. But leave it here, just in case."

Before entering the shower, she examined her bare feet. Reddened areas of chafing on two toe knuckles looked like blisters starting—tomorrow she'd stick a piece of gel or moleskin over them. A broken and jagged toenail needed attention.

During too few blissful minutes under the water, she shampooed and rinsed her hair. When she finished with the blow dryer, she decided that she'd visit her London salon after her closing performance and have several inches hacked off.

Sir Francis Cooke's image, clad in the martyred admiral's uniform, adorned twin vertical banners hanging on either side of the Sovereign Theatre. Unobtrusive in size and structure, the building was dwarfed by the larger venues nearby, which boasted the most popular brand-name productions. Pushing the brass door handle, she approached the box office and told its occupant she was meeting Gilbert Cooke.

"Ms. Lowery? This is for you." He handed her a lanyard with a badge marked VISITOR. "Step on through, he's waiting in the auditorium."

Ellie paused beneath the overhanging balcony and placed her hand on the curved wooden back of an aisle seat. "Hello." Her voice rang out in the cavernous space.

Gil, seated in the dress circle, hopped up. "Spot on time. What do you think of this old place?"

"Very grand. Impressively historic. Worthy of Sir Francis Cooke and Lord Nelson. He's getting raves—as expected."

"This revival forces a reconsideration of the play, hardly a success when first presented. We hope the good reviews and positive press will help it compete against all the long-running musical extravaganzas and ensure an extended run. When would you like to see it? You can have a ticket to any evening performance or matinee."

"I'll let you know."

She wondered if Dan Wheeler might enjoy a history play about England's naval hero and his scandalous mistress Lady Hamilton. Her obligation to him was immense, and she hadn't yet figured out how else to repay him for placing her in Latimer House. He'd apparently enjoyed the dinner party. He and his office colleague and her partner were included on her guest list for Saturday night's finale and champagne reception. She wondered whether *A Bequest to the Nation*, starring an actor knighted by the late queen for services to the theatre, recipient of multiple Academy Awards and BAFTAs, would appeal to him more than *Onegin*. He might regard a ballet performance as more of a penance than a privilege.

"The stage is Father's true home. He accepts film work for the money, and because it ensures a full theatre when he's appearing in a play."

"You've got a staff badge," she noted. "You're an employee?"

"Front of house assistant. Thirty hours a week, on contract. Would you like to sit in the royal box?"

A narrow stairway took them to the Royal Circle. He led her through a discreet door into the private lounge, carpeted in dark blue, containing damask covered chairs and sofas. A velvet and gold-fringed curtain separated the space from the royal box.

Gil moved a gilded chair close to the balustrade. "Try it."

Her view of the stage and its safety curtain was partly obstructed, but she could see the rows of chairs below and a portion of the upper tiers. "I can now say I've sat where a royal person does." Had she and Gil ever spent time together when Harry wasn't present? She didn't think so.

"Before long, you'll take your place on the boards," he said, sitting next to her. "You were right to turn down the cinema roles you've been offered."

"How did you know about those?" She'd never spoken about them to an interviewer.

"Father receives film industry newsletters and shares them with me. But why study at Muriel Baker's academy? She's too infirm to teach, although I daresay they roll her out occasionally to pontificate to the students."

"I wanted an all-ages adult program. Most places I investigated cater to children and teens."

"You're no neophyte. You had major roles at a summer theatre."

She drew a quick breath. "*Much Ado*. I was Beatrice to Harry's Benedick. And Stanley Kowalski's wife in *Streetcar*."

Stella for star.

"What, I wonder, would he say about your career of undressing for voyeuristic audiences?"

Disregarding his question, she said, "Tell me about your play."

"*Fractures in the Heart* is a two-hander, a drama in two acts, about a twenty-something couple from different backgrounds. He's British, she's a Yank. Their marriage is failing. They rushed into it without knowing one another well. They have trust issues. And diverging aspirations." His gaze veered away from her and towards the safety curtain. "My current draft is entered in a competition sponsored by a new play festival and will have a public reading. I paid an additional fee to receive critiques from the judges and feedback from the actors."

"I hope it does well. I'd love to read it."

"You will. After I make any suggested alterations."

"What's your father's opinion of it?"

"He's rather cross about there being no meaty role for him."

"Next time," she said brightly.

"That's what I told him."

"It's a huge achievement. He must be proud."

Gil made a face. "He respects the hard work I've put in, on this script and all that came before. But that can't negate his regret that I was a dismal failure as an actor."

"What happens after the festival?"

"My agent and my father will recommend my revised script to the Sovereign Theatre Group managers. At the moment the producer is scrambling to recast next season's first play, because the Hollywood actress who would've starred suddenly turned up pregnant and withdrew. Financing was contingent on her participation." He cocked his head. "When there's a table read for the management here, I want you as Lyla. The wife."

"Sure, if the timing works." A reading, she knew, was an ephemeral event early in the process, a baby step on the winding path towards production. "I promise I'll be here on your opening night."

"Indeed, you will. On that stage."

His response startled her. "It's too soon to audition. For anything."

"You might not have to."

Even if he did manage to insert his play into the Sovereign's upcoming season, he wouldn't be responsible for casting.

"You danced dramatic parts in ballets. You played leads opposite Harry." Gil lowered his head, breaking eye contact. "Your very public life as Stella Nue is an act, isn't it? On Sunday morning, when you wake up, you'll be one person. Ellie Lowery."

"And Colman," she murmured. Her gaze shifted to her left hand, where the gold wedding band used to be.

After lunch on Friday, Camille set out across Green Park for Buckingham Palace and the current exhibition at the King's Gallery. Within minutes of her departure, Ellie's masseuse arrived with her collection of ointments and oils, and set up her portable table in the study.

"You'll think I say this to all my clients," the woman commented midway through the session, "but you're the best to work on. Well-defined muscles. No flinching. Not squeamish about nudity, either."

Ellie laughed.

"Hold still. What's so funny?"

"I'm famous—or infamous—for removing my clothes, with hundreds of people watching." Closing her eyes, she tried not to wince as Ingrid's industrious fingers manipulated the ball of each foot and every toe. She was startled to hear the click of the door lock. "We're in here," she called, surprised that Camille had returned so soon.

"Hello," an unfamiliar female voice responded.

Ellie sat up, holding the towel against her chest.

The woman who returned her gaze had dark, curling hair and a warm smile. "I'm Hannah."

"Ellie."

"Dan didn't warn you I was coming?"

"He said you might."

"I promise I won't get in your way. Carry on. We can get acquainted later."

"Who's that?" her masseuse whispered.

"My landlady. She and her husband own this place."

"Fine gaff they've got. Lucky you."

When Ingrid finished, Ellie climbed down from the table and put on her robe. She tapped her credit card against the payment pad, making sure to add a generous tip.

"Ta. You can hydrate yourself but wait at least an hour before showering or having a bath."

"I know."

"If I didn't remind you, I wouldn't be doing my job. See you on Tuesday."

Ellie accompanied Ingrid to the elevator and pressed the button for her.

She went to the kitchen to remove her water bottle chilling in the fridge.

Hannah joined her and announced, "I'm popping over to the greengrocers. Can I bring you anything?"

"We're already well-stocked. Camille—my aunt—is a regular at the Latimer Row shops. Help yourself to whatever you see that you like."

Watching slender, petite Hannah study the shelves of refrigerator and cupboards, Ellie noted that they were of equal height. "Were you a dancer?"

The curly head turned in her direction. "Not me. Why?"

"Your body structure is ideal for ballet." After a pause, she said, "Sorry, that was way too personal."

"I'm flattered you think so. If you don't mind, I'll tuck into this yogurt. Maybe toss in strawberries and a little granola. I'm famished and won't see food again for hours. Business dinners start with several rounds of drinks, and it could be eight o'clock before somebody suggests ordering. Will you join me in a bite?"

Ellie waved her bottle. "This is all I need. I'll graze before heading to the Archway Cabaret for tonight's show."

"I have to know more." Hannah spooned lemon curd yogurt into a bowl. "Let's go to the terrace. You're fine as you are, nobody will see us. If they could, they'd never guess that's your dressing gown. It's gorgeous."

Tightening the belt at her waist, Ellie said, "I bought it on Rodeo Drive, during awards season. We weren't introduced, but I saw you at the Academy Awards after-party I attended."

Hannah looked up. "Nobody told me Stella Nue was there." Slicing a berry, she added, "Acorn Films wasn't in contention. We were in schmoozing mode, talking up our next release, a between-the-wars semi-tragedy set in Vienna. It deserves as many nominations—and statuettes—as *Forsaken Fortune* won. But it'll be up against all the apocalyptic and dystopian special effects productions with box office clout. We might have a shot at the costuming award. Not to mention Critics Choice. And the BAFTAs."

"*Forsaken Fortune* was a lovely movie. The kind that stays with you. I saw it at the independent cinema in Concord."

"Massachusetts?"

"New Hampshire."

"I'm a Mainer, from Falmouth. So is Dad—his family have lived there forever. My mother's English and Welsh. Dan told Martin you're a New Englander, too, but I wasn't privy to any details. During pre-production, there's a limit to the amount of information I can take in."

Following her to the terrace, Ellie belatedly recalled her aristocratic status. Based on their conversation thus far, Hannah hadn't fully assimilated into that rarified realm of privilege.

Hannah was lifting a spoonful of her concoction to her mouth when Big Ben's chime, located somewhere on her person, rang out faintly. "Better take this." She pulled her cellphone from her pocket and held it to her ear. "I didn't expect to hear from you yet. Everything okay?" Listening, she scrunched her face. "Put him on. Hello, Richie-roo. Mummy misses you." She went quiet again. "When Ariel chased it, did she catch it? Oh. I see. Well, that *is* exciting. Please hand Daddy's mobile back to him." She rose and moved to the terrace railing. "Martin, did our son witness the murder of the 'wittle wabbit?'"

"Yikes," Ellie murmured.

"That's a relief. Help him understand he cannot keep it as a pet. That's illegal. Tell him it must go to the wildlife sanctuary in Little Milver. You can both take it there. The staff will foster it until it's mature enough for release. Do whatever you can to make this a learning experience. I'll talk to you tonight. It might be late."

She returned to the table and laid her phone on the glass surface.

"Is the rabbit okay?"

"Fortunately, yes. Richard is in no way deprived of animal companionship. We have two dogs, plus the estate manager's, as well as any number of barn cats. And our horses."

"Sounds like you chose the right time for a London meeting."

"Meetings," Hannah corrected. "Tonight's social gathering is a warm-up for tomorrow's main event. I don't mind getting away from Stanwell House occasionally. I adore our staff—they're family. But I do sometimes yearn to make myself a grilled cheese sandwich like Grammy Jane taught me, without feeling like I'm intruding into the cook's territory."

"I know what you mean. Whenever I'm on an overseas tour, I get a mad craving for a Blarney Burger." Hearing herself, she clarified, "Shamrock Burger."

"I love me a Blarney Burger."

"My dad invented it."

"He's a genius. What's a Shamrock Burger?"

"Essentially the same, with tweaks. For legal reasons, Daddo had to rename and alter his masterpiece after selling his regional restaurants to a much bigger company. He and my brother own a pub in Birchmont. My hometown."

"I was one of his best customers," Hannah told her. "In Portland. In Boston. Just talking about the Blarney makes me want one in the worst way."

With a conspiratorial grin, Ellie announced, "I know how to make it. A Shamrock, I mean."

"You're rapidly becoming my new best friend. Satisfy my craving, and I'll put you in one of my movies. Pinkie swear." Hannah held up her hand.

"Thanks, but no thanks. Yours isn't my only offer."

"I bet."

"I turned down plenty of blink-and-you'll-miss me roles. Strippers, obviously. Call girls. A slutty casino worker in a heist movie who ends up dead. The smart-ass chick on the production line who sleeps with the factory owner and gets shipped out of town so his wife won't find out."

"Yuck."

"I won't name the famous producing team that approached me about an animated series about a burlesque star based on Stella Nue. My image would be used, but somebody else would do the voice. Nobody knows what I sound like, they said, so authenticity didn't matter. Their version of my alter ego would've had a breathy, Marilyn Monroe quality."

"Of course. Was it greenlighted?"

"A rival production company swooped in and swallowed up their studio, so the project was shelved. Thank goodness. Tomorrow, Stella Nue hangs up her G-string forever. On Monday, Ellie Lowery starts drama classes at the Muriel Baker School of Dramatic Arts."

After absorbing this revelation, Hannah announced. "I'm prepared to barter whatever I can for that burger. I've got loads of contacts—agents, producers, directors. Here and in the States. On the West Coast. And I don't mean Cornwall."

"I might have an acting gig lined up, sort of. A playwright acquaintance invited me to take the lead female role at a table read of his debut work. He's Sir Francis Cooke's son. I've known Gil since we were teenagers at the Juilliard School in New York."

"I've never met him, but I know his dad. Sir Francis won the Oscar for Best Supporting Actor in *Forsaken Fortune* and received an Emmy nomination for the sequel, *Tender Treasure.*"

"I met him. A lifetime ago." When Harry and Gil were in *Pygmalion.* If she hadn't been preoccupied with planning an elopement, memories of the celebrated English stage and film actor might be clearer. "I'm not allowed to shower till a half-hour after Ingrid leaves. It might take that long to organize my stage case. It's a mess."

"I'm free tomorrow night," Hannah said. "How do I get a ticket to your last show?"

"Let me take care of it. I reserved a table for Dan Wheeler, and Lou from his office and her wife. You can sit with them."

Chapter 9

On Saturday, patrons packed the Archway Cabaret. Tables were rearranged to make room for extra chairs at the back and both sides of the room. Dan and his three companions squeezed their way to the prime spot Ellie had provided. They requested a round of drinks and an *amuse-bouche* tray that would be served during the interval between the two shows.

Hannah, who had ordered a mocktail, commented, "This is a high-class operation." Turning to Lou, she added, "Forget I'm your employer's spouse. I'm not here to spoil anybody's fun."

"Martin's the opposite of the stiff I worked for before joining Latimer London Estates," Lou responded.

"He sent flowers and wine for my birthday," Kelly volunteered. "And booked a table for us at the restaurant in White City that everyone's raving about. He told Lou we should order whatever we wanted and put the bill on his personal account. Best dinner of my life."

"What did you have?" Hannah wondered.

During the recitation of menu items, which Dan had

already heard, he studied the crowd, picking out faces from television or filmdom. When the women's conversation shifted from fine dining to the star of the evening, he listened closely.

"When Martin said Stella Nue would be our lodger," Hannah said, "I expected to find a diva, behaving like she owned the place. Quite the contrary."

Curiosity got the better of him. "Does she ever talk about her husband?"

Hannah regarded him in surprise. "She has one?"

"Had. She was twenty when he died. He was three years older."

"That's awful. What happened?"

"Motorcar accident. I located his *New York Times* obituary online."

"Well, well," said Lou. "Private investigations. We know what that means."

Ignoring her comment, he recited, "Henry Lionel Matthew Colman. The Fourth. Three residences were listed—two in the state of New York and one in Barbados. Like Ellie, he trained at Juilliard. He won a lot of acting awards and was tipped for professional success."

"Our Dan is smitten," said Lou, manipulating her straw into a trapezoidal shape. "No one better to console a grieving widow than a man in need of consolation himself."

Three pairs of sympathetic eyes were directed towards him. "Thanks for the thought, but I'm all right." True, the tragedy that ruptured and divided his family was a point of connection with Ellie, yet he hoped they had more in common than the death of a loved one.

With a glance at Dan, Hannah asked, "Are you as excited as I am about our Shamrock Burger?"

"What's that?" Kelly wondered.

He subsided into silence while Hannah presented the history of the Lowery family's famous culinary products.

Lou wasn't mistaken about his interest in Ellie. Her attractiveness was one reason, of course. And he was intrigued by the bold and risky choices she routinely made, stepping out of an established career and gliding into another. She was reinventing herself once more, jettisoning her famous Stella Nue persona to enter a demanding profession in which similar success was not necessarily assured.

After the opening acts ended, the compere returned to the stage to remind the audience of the prohibition against photos, video, and audio. "Now, in her next to last appearance on this or any stage, the magnificent Stella Nue!"

A lengthy bout of applause drowned out the entrance music flowing from the sound system, an orchestral version of "You Stepped out of a Dream." Dan instantly associated it with the iconic Busby Berkeley sequence in the MGM musical *Ziegfeld Girl,* featuring glamor girl Hedy Lamarr and starlet Lana Turner.

The parting curtain revealed Ellie on the pink satin bed, slumbering. In her dream, she conjured up partners—George and Zack—to dance with her. Throughout their romantic waltz, she plucked away the diaphanous pale layers of a costume similar to Lamarr's. Everything came off, even her white satin slippers, until all that remained was a pair of glittery star-shaped pasties and sparkly G-string. Her pale skin glowed like the moon in the half-light, and her movements were sublime. And though she was the essence of desirable femininity, her twist on the original scenario offered a sly upending of gender roles.

"Oh, my," Hannah breathed, when the routine concluded. "That was lovely. I didn't realize her performance included so much dancing. I assumed all burlesque acts were flashy, with lots of hip wiggling and shimmying and mugging and teasing. Brassy trumpets and trombones, cymbals crashing, and bass drums thump-thumping. Ellie is suggestively sexy, but so, so subtle. And very romantic."

"A blatant depiction of female empowerment," Lou contributed. "She was totally in charge of those men."

The server delivered their tray. Conversation flagged as they loaded their small plates with bite-sized delicacies. Ushers guided newcomers to their tables, and other staff members took drink orders. During the second show, the ladies performed with verve, and the girl responsible for removing the discarded clothing and props repeatedly dashed in and out from the wings.

The spotlight's flare against the closed curtain quieted the buzz. Two men appeared, the tuxedoed host and a gentleman in a three-piece suit, who held the microphone.

"On behalf of our Archway Cabaret family, we express deep gratitude to this month's headline act, for choosing our humble venue to close out her spectacular career." He passed the mic to the compere.

"For the final time, it's my privilege to introduce the beautiful, the talented, and the forever to be remembered *artiste* Stella Nue. Please tuck your phones away, and enjoy her in the debut—and one time only—appearance in *Swan of the Lake*."

The painted backdrop displayed a moon hovering above a tree-lined lake. Ellie entered, poised on the tips of her pointe shoes. She timed her steps to a harp's cascading notes, the start of the most famous *pas de deux* in the entire ballet canon. Her calf-length costume of snowy tulle was decorated with tufts of trembling feathers. In each hand she carried an oversized white feather fan, moving them up and down in graceful wing-like motions. No Prince Siegfried appeared to partner this Odette, who danced alone to the pensive strains of a single violin. As the music faded, she cast aside her props, slipped off her headdress of spangles and white down, and let her long hair fall.

The tune and tempo shifted, multiple strings soared, light and bright—the Siegfried-Odette reconciliation *pas de deux* in Act Four. Ellie pulled her sash to release the top layer of tulle. Then another. She slipped off the feathery bracelets on her wrists. Pausing, she unhooked the front of her white satin bodice, and with a flourish, pulled it away.

"No corset," Lou murmured.

Hannah whispered back, "It's a bustier."

Dan was less interested in wardrobe terminology than the symbolism and underlying significance of her finale. Watching her dart across the stage, clad in the scanty top and fluffy knickers, he tried to make a connection between her milestone moment and the ballet's theme. Ellie danced in code, and he wanted to crack this one.

After she removed her bustier, her pale round breasts and pink-tipped nipples were visible through a thin and transparent layer of shimmering silk. The crowd gasp in unified amazement.

Turning away, she let the insubstantial covering slip to expose well-defined shoulder blades and a narrow torso. When she turned, beaming and bare-chested, she was rewarded by resounding cheers and thunderous applause. With shocking abruptness, the stage went dark. The curtains closed.

"What a way to go out," Lou said. "That's practically the full Monty, which she's never done. I'm gobsmacked."

Kelly nodded. "So is everybody else."

The house lights came up. Ellie, wrapped in a green velvet dressing gown, emerged from behind the curtain to curtsy and blow kisses. Zack and George entered from opposite sides, kissing her cheek before presenting a white rose bouquet. She cradled her flowers in the crook of one arm and fluttered her free hand before she was escorted into the wings.

Checking the time on her phone, Kelly said regretfully, "We can't stay for the after-party, or we'll miss our train."

"Don't they run late on Saturday night?" Hannah asked.

"It's a dodgy service," Lou responded. "We learned the hard way."

Dan intervened. "I hereby authorize your homeward journey by taxi or rideshare and use of the company card for payment. I'll cover the charges as a personal expense. I want Stella Nue's most fanatical fans to be able to congratulate her."

Ellie's colleagues filled her dressing room, their excited chatter bouncing off the purple walls as they examined the garments and accoutrements she was giving away. Before her first show, she'd privately handed over several items to stage kitten Lisa-Lola, with assurances of a future coffee date at a mutually convenient time.

"You aren't keeping this?" asked Holly Hollywood, holding up a red velvet corset with half its satin bows untied. "Wish I could fit into it."

"I reckon I can." Luscious Liz pried it away.

"If you stuff the top," Holly shot back, and everyone laughed.

"Cow," Liz retorted, though her tone was affectionate.

Using both hands, the other girl pushed up her prominent bust.

"Ooh, this bralette," someone else cried, holding it up by one strap. "Covered with crystals."

"They're the really expensive ones, aren't they? Always the best for Stella."

The girl with the bralette approached Ellie. "Will you autograph the inside, please? Here, along the seam."

Ellie dug into her bag for a permanent marker and scrawled her Stella signature on the white satin lining.

Camille had already removed the swan costume. Ellie stood still while her ambitious young friend pulled up the zipper of her aqua blue party dress.

"You're gorgeous," said Lisa, peering past Ellie so she could see the mirrored reflection. "Fit and flare suits your figure. But so does anything. What'll happen to all your merch?"

"I hope most of what I signed this afternoon sold during intermission or after the show. Whatever's left gets packed up and shipped back to an office in the States, to fulfill website orders."

"Run along to your party. I'll keep an eye on this lot and make sure your things are evenly distributed."

"You're a peach." Ellie's lips brushed Lisa's cheek.

Stepping into the club, she was greeted with clapping and cheers. On being handed a glass of champagne, she supposed this was how a prima ballerina felt on entering her retirement. With the essential difference that she felt relief rather than regret.

The Archway's manager and front of house staff showered her with compliments and best wishes. She thanked the technical team for maintaining a consistently seamless production. Zack and George sat at a corner table, sipping colorful cocktails. Camille, swathed in silver lamé, spoke to Hannah Ballard and Dan and his co-workers. Ellie joined them.

"You were magnificent." Hannah hugged her.

"We loved it," the exuberant Lou told her.

"Let's have some food," suggested Kelly, taking her partner's arm. "I spy caviar."

"Lumpfish roe," Dan said. "More affordable."

"And from an environmental standpoint," Ellie acknowledged, "preferable to beluga or sturgeon."

"I need a refill." Hannah held up her glass of clear liquid before following the others.

Standing so near Dan, Ellie was glad of the designer stilettos that added several inches to her height. "I hope you enjoyed the show."

"Further evidence of your partiality for Tchaikovsky compositions."

"When creating a routine, the guys and I often choose

music from ballets we used to dance. It suits my style—either fantastical or a gentle and humorous tease. I've avoided fetish tropes—schoolgirl, cheerleader, French maid. It took a lot of convincing before I agreed to be a lady pirate. And I never sexualized or demeaned real professions, like nurse or cop or secretary. Or ballerina." She lifted and lowered an arm, as she'd done during her performance. "So, I'm *Swan of the Lake.*"

"That one was a puzzler."

"Because I stripped down at the end? George and Zack dared me. I had to."

"I was intrigued by the symbolism in your Swan Queen. Self-imposed death in order to achieve liberation? Destroying your Stella Nue persona to achieve freedom?"

"You're very perceptive. Or I'm too transparent." She stared into her champagne glass. "I can relate to Odette. Not just because she loses her man. One dance critic referred to her as a divided soul. She has two identities—maiden at night, swan by day. Whereas I've got several. You'll encounter most of them, if you hang around me long enough."

"I should like that."

Ellie felt a surge of delight as he gazed back at her. She sensed that he'd responded to an overture she hadn't intended to make but in retrospect didn't regret.

"Tomorrow, I'll present myself to you in an entirely new identity. Shamrock Burger cook." A sense of duty overcame her desire to linger. Without hiding her reluctance, she told him, "I should be mingling." She needed to move away from him before the event photographer captured them together.

"Without Stella making demands on your time," he said, "you can experience some of London's nightlife beyond this cabaret. It would be my pleasure to serve as your guide."

He wants to ask me out, she realized.

She hoped he would. Very soon.

Act 2

"Have a belief in yourself that is bigger than anyone's disbelief."

—August Wilson

Chapter 10

On Sunday morning, Ellie stood on damp pavement and handed her aunt's luggage to the uniformed driver, who was loading each piece into a minivan.

Camille, eyes on her phone, said, "I texted George to let him know I'm on my way. I hope there's enough room in the vehicle for the extra suitcase Zack bought for all his purchases. I'm sure he'll moan about our early departure."

"Remind him that he'll have several hours to enjoy the luxuries of the first-class passengers' lounge. Wish I'd had a chance to tell them goodbye."

"You'll see them this summer when you're at the lake. Don't forget to contact the man in the fashion museum's Theatre and Performance Department."

"Tomorrow," she promised.

"I couldn't provide professional quality photographs of your swan costume, just the ones I took on my phone when you had your fitting, and a few before you went onstage last night. I've got the design sketches at home—I'll scan and send them to him. His conservators will clean and preserve the garment. Oh, he also asked about the pannier gown you wore in *L'Ancienne Regime* during your tour before this one. Tell him to contact *Vogue* about reproducing the pictures from their fashion spread. If he wants that one for his collection, I'll remove it and your wig and accessories from storage and ship them over here."

"Stop being a manager. You're supposed to take a break from business."

"That'll be easier when I'm in Montreal."

"Give my love to Grand-mère and Tante Sylvie."

"I will. *Au revoir, chérie.*"

After a hug and exchange of kisses, Camille stepped up into the van, and the driver slid the door panel into place. Ellie watched until the vehicle turned the corner and vanished from view. From this moment, her relationship with her aunt and her dance partners had shifted. They would reunite two months from now, in New Hampshire, under different circumstances and with altered perspectives.

Back in the flat, she passed the den where Hannah sat at the desk, phone clutched to her ear, scribbling notes. She set down her pen and pinched her fingers together leaving an inch of space, indicating that her call would end soon.

The suitcases filled with Ellie's stage costumes and assorted paraphernalia had vanished, headed for the cargo hold of a Boston-bound jetliner. Opening the tall wardrobe that held her civilian clothes, she pondered what to wear during the week ahead. A directive received from the Muriel Baker School of Dramatic Arts recommended comfortable, non-restrictive garments and soft, flat-soled shoes for classes. She pulled out several lightweight linen tops and experimentally paired them with casual cropped trousers. Her footwear collection was limited to ballet shoes, two pairs of stiletto heels, and the GaitGuard sneakers she wore when trotting around the city.

Hearing Hannah's knuckles tapping the doorframe, she looked around.

"After that conversation, I need a run to clear my head. And burn off some calories before eating a Shamrock Burger. When I get back, I'll whip up Eton mess for dessert."

"Sounds good. I'm going to Selfridges this afternoon to look for shoes. And I've got a hair appointment."

"Do you have the ingredients for tonight's feast?"

"Of course."

Wincott & Sons in Latimer Row had supplied the requisite Irish cheddar. She'd purchased batch loaf at the bakery and Irish butter from a supermarket. At the greengrocer's, she picked up spuds and tomatoes and mushrooms and leafy salad greens. Without a deep fryer, she couldn't produce French fries—chips, in Brit-speak. She'd substitute oven-crisped potatoes seasoned with garlic and sea salt, a specialty of Zack's.

Beneath a gray-clouded sky, she walked towards Oxford Street. The Berkeley Square nightingale was silent, unwilling to compete with the combined roar of cars, taxis, motorbikes, and commercial vehicles. Davies Street was a mixture of historic and modern architecture and high-end boutiques. Claridge's Hotel loomed at the intersection with Brook Street. Focused on its intricate brickwork façade, she didn't immediately notice that she was in danger of colliding with two men approaching the bar entrance.

The younger one was an American movie star she'd met in Hollywood, at the same Oscar party where she'd spotted Hannah Ballard. He'd concluded their brief dialogue by suggesting that she accompany him to his room at the Beverly Hills Hotel for a nightcap—and no doubt more. The man with him must be his agent, or a producer. Neither of them recognized her. The actor didn't respond to her smile, unwilling to be accosted by a glasses-wearing female with wind-blown hair, whose lips shone with pale pink gloss instead of Stella Nue's vibrant signature crimson. Amused, she knew he would've been offended if she hadn't recognized him. If she pursued him into the bar and declared her identity, he would assume she was belatedly accepting his invitation to get physical.

Selfridges, a combination of the United Nations and the Tower of Babel, teemed with shoppers clutching bright yellow carrier bags. Ellie maneuvered through an endless stream of humanity to the directory at the escalator. Wandering the shoe galleries on an upper level, she saw nothing in the designer boutiques that met her specific but simple requirements—comfortable, flexible flats with soft soles. She was telling herself she'd have better luck at a discount store when her eyes lighted on pale pebbled leather loafers with a rubber sole and an attractively pointed toe. They were on sale. She hailed a shop assistant and stated her European size.

"We should have it in stock," he replied. "Small sizes don't sell out as quick as medium."

He returned with a cardboard box. "Your lucky day." Removing the lid, he brushed aside the tissue and pulled out the stretchers. She pulled off her GaitGuards, glad that her sports socks concealed feet that had spent nearly two decades in pointe shoes.

"How's the fit?" he asked.

"Perfect. Where have these been all my life? Cushiony, with good arch support. Although I wish they were dark, so scuffs and dirt wouldn't show."

"The black ones aren't ever marked down, they're too popular."

"Doesn't matter. I want them."

She left with two pairs, pleased to have spent less than a hundred pounds.

The hair salon receptionist guided her to a cubicle, saying, "It's been an age since you visited us. Jeremy's ready for you."

The stylist greeted her as though she was his long-lost

friend rather than a client he saw once a year. "Delighted to see you again, angel. But oh, dear. That color!"

"I know," she said, settling into his chair. "A month ago, it was worse."

Pulling at a strand, he shook his head. "At least it's temporary and will fade. So, shampoo, cut and blow-dry?"

"Yes, please."

"How much are we taking off?"

"Lots. But please leave enough for—for an updo."

She'd almost said ballet bun.

Ellie paused at the mirror in the foyer. Her hair swept down past her shoulder blades and the ends were even. Before leaving Selfridges, she'd taken advantage of a cancellation at a beauty kiosk and let a makeup artist work on her.

"You're stunning," Hannah told her. "Dan's going to be knocked out."

"I didn't spiff myself up for him."

"If you say so."

"I do." She hoped her emphatic reply was convincing. Hannah's smirk raised doubts.

"Can I be your sous chef?"

"And steal my dad's secrets? Thanks, but no thanks."

She changed into a casual top and cropped trousers with a drawstring, no different than she'd wear to The Shamrock. She didn't want Dan assuming, as Hannah did, that she was trying to entice him. It might scare him off. Her readiness to enter a relationship—with the right person—was new and untested. Though possibly not for much longer.

When Rafe was between marriages, she'd sometimes imagined sleeping with him. She hadn't, from reluctance to take advantage of his vulnerability, and her dread of being swayed by grief into a bad decision. From countless rehearsals and performances, their bodies were well-attuned and intimately acquainted. He was a considerate and sensitive dance partner, which she guessed would carry over from studio and stage to bed. But their platonic friendship was so essential to her wellbeing that she wouldn't jeopardize it. Mutual understanding of this reality was the basis of a longstanding joke about the torrid affair that would never happen.

Her desire for a meaningful relationship didn't stem from loneliness, or because she felt incomplete without a significant other. Until she found one, she would to some extent feel defined by past events. There hadn't been space for romance during the busy globetrotting years. She certainly wasn't interested in hooking up with an algorithmically selected stranger from a matchmaking app. Or any *danseur* or staff member at British Ballet Theatre. Mutual attraction was a requisite. The perfect person would want to be with Ellie Lowery Colman, not Stella Nue.

Distinguished, droll, devastatingly handsome Dan Wheeler matched all her criteria.

When she let him into the flat, she kissed his cheek before accepting the wine bottle he'd brought. The fleeting contact of her mouth and his smoothly shaved skin caused a lightheaded sensation. When he reciprocated, the ankles that adequately supported her entire weight when she balanced on pointe felt decidedly wobbly. After supplying him with a drink, she led him to the drawing room. She remained, chatting with him and Hannah for a few minutes before returning to the kitchen to prepare the main component.

In her effort to recreate a pub atmosphere, she served dinner on the terrace. Rejecting the silver cutlery and crystal glassware as inappropriate, she'd arranged the table on the terrace with simple white stoneware and plain cloth table mats.

The meal received positive reviews.

"That was hands-down the world's best hamburger," Hannah gushed.

"I've no point of comparison," Dan said. "But it's a rave from me as well."

Gratified by their appreciation, she defied all efforts to extract the recipe. "Daddo made everyone in the family sign a non-disclosure agreement." She reached for the serving tongs and added more crispy potatoes to her plate.

"Look at you," Hannah said, "going for seconds. Don't dancers live on nuts and berries?"

"Food is our fuel," Ellie said. "Protein, carbs—we need plenty. I don't have rehearsals or performances, so I'm not burning maximum calories. And nobody's lifting and carrying me. But in class, during the *grand allegro,* I'm supposed to soar high off the ground." She passed the platter to Dan.

"I'm saving room for Lady Milverston's excellent Eton mess."

"I keep forgetting she's a ladyship," Ellie admitted.

"So do I," Hannah said.

"Shall I refill your wineglass?" Dan held out the bottle of malbec he'd provided.

She tapped her glass. "Alcohol free for me."

"How is it?" Ellie wondered.

"Better than I expected." Hannah fidgeted with her napkin. "As Rosalind from *Forsaken Fortune* would say, I'm with child. Around six weeks is my best guess. Every time I droop and turn green making breakfast, Martin presses me to see the doctor. When I get home, I will. His mother knows, but we aren't saying anything to Richard till I start to show. Neither of you can breathe a word about it."

Ellie counted on her fingers. "A Christmas baby."

Hannah nodded. "Close. Unless it's late. From a work perspective, the timing is ideal. Film production slows down during the holidays. Caring for a newborn during awards season, which seems to arrive ever earlier and last longer each year, will be a complication. My perfect excuse to stay home and give it a miss. Liz Gregorio can represent Acorn. She enjoys all the hoopla. Me, not so much."

Ellie didn't let them help her clear the table. When she rejoined them, they were monitoring the sunset and commenting on its brilliance.

Dan held his glass in Ellie's direction. "To your first day of theatre school."

"And another week of ballet class," Hannah added. "That's a tough schedule."

Ellie said, "Not so bad. I've been way busier."

"How do you mean?" Dan asked her.

"Daddo didn't want us turning into spoiled rich kids after he sold Blarney Burger. When he opened The Shamrock, he put us to work. Liam bussed tables till he was old enough to serve at the bar. Marie, our nerd, used her analytic skills as junior bookkeeper. I waitressed. And cooked, if I had to. In addition to school and my dance lessons."

Hannah chimed in, saying, "I helped out in my dad's vet practice. I was a production assistant on Mum's horticulture shows for public television."

With a glance at Dan, Ellie said, "I doubt you can match our woeful tales of lowly servitude."

"On the contrary. I spent my youth weeding and deadheading and raking, and received a pittance for it. My dad is a passionate gardener with an extensive collection of roses and other plants." Smiling, he added, "Would the two of you care to join me for dinner tomorrow at the bistro in Latimer Row?"

"I won't be here," Hannah said. "I leave for Stanwell in the afternoon."

Regretfully, Ellie told him, "My foundation's Board of Directors scheduled their quarterly meeting to accommodate the time difference. They're in New York."

Dan set down his empty wineglass. "What's your mission?"

"Scholarships. For young dancers who need assistance paying for classes or summer intensives. And we started a program that supports people training to work with special needs dance students—all genders, all ages, all ethnicities. Neurodiverse or autistic, Aspergers or Down Syndrome. They all benefit from physical therapy and exercise. Pupils can apply for financial support grants to cover tuition and fees, if needed."

Her companions exchanged glances.

"Have you told her about your brother?" Hannah asked Dan.

"No."

"You should."

Chapter 11

"**B**rian's the youngest," Dan began. "I'm the middle one. Oliver was older than me."

A change in Ellie's expression told him she'd noted his use of past tense.

"Immediately after we graduated, my mates and I traveled to France. It was meant to be a brief trip. My parents had planned a celebration like the one Oll had when he took his university degree. Grandparents. Cousins. Friends of the family." All these years later, and after everything that happened, he recalled everyone who had been invited. "It never took place. Because of the accident."

Hearing his staccato sentences, he reached for his glass and drank, hoping to ease the constriction in his throat.

"Oll and Brian were paddling a canoe on the River Severn, not many miles from our home. The wind came up, as it often does. They took on a lot of water and capsized. A nearby motor craft sped over. The men on board rescued Brian, after he'd been submerged for several minutes. They couldn't find Oll. Although he was a strong swimmer, it was spring tide, when the current is at its most powerful. Before nightfall, searchers recovered his body."

"I'm so sorry," Ellie whispered.

"As a result of oxygen deprivation, Brian suffers from frontal lobe hypoxia, a form of brain damage. From the day he was discharged from hospital, he's lived at a residential care home near Thornbury. Close to Tayer Court, our family home."

He spared her the gruesome aftermath. Oll's funeral. Dad's stoicism in the face of tragedy, seeking solace in roses and classical music. His mother's inability to cope, her abbreviated journey through grief counseling, leading to her abrupt desertion and eventual remarriage. His own resolve to stick by his father and to be as present as possible for Brian.

"Does your brother remember what happened to him?" Ellie asked.

"He's severely impaired." Mustering a semblance of smile, he admitted, "Probably not a good candidate for therapeutic dance classes." He stared over the terrace railing at a panorama of buildings and rooftops, gilded by the sun's slanting rays. "My apologies for dampening spirits on this most pleasant occasion. Let's talk about that new baby."

Picking up the cue, Ellie asked Hannah, "What is the age difference between this son or daughter and your little boy?"

"About three and a half years. Richard was born in March."

Ellie glanced at Dan. "Like us."

"If you don't have plans this weekend, you ought to come down to Somerset and experience our annual Milver Vale Flower Fete—the subject of my lengthy phone conversation. You wouldn't be our only celebrity, because hordes of them live in or near Bruton. Plus all the poshos scattered about the countryside. You and Dan will stay with us at Stanwell House."

"This," said Dan, "is where she informs you that it's got twenty bedrooms."

"What's it like?" Ellie asked. "The fete, not the house. I saw it on the screen, and my tv."

"Not much different from any New England agricultural fair. There's a gymkhana and a costumed pet parade with prizes. A rubber duck race on the river. Marquees for food and drink. Games and competitions. You don't have to make up your mind now. If you're able to join us, let me know, and I'll send you train info." Hannah turned to Dan. "Or you two could drive down. Together."

"Indeed." He'd been undecided about going but was perfectly willing to chauffeur Ellie. While she was at Stanwell, he could run up to Harding Hall to visit Brian and stop at Tayer Court to see Dad.

"Our vicar is doing her part," Hannah added, "saying special prayers to keep the rain at bay."

Dan hoped Ellie would accept the invitation. For him, driving her to Stanwell House—a two-hour journey, each way—was a most appealing prospect.

"I hope it wasn't a mistake, encouraging Dan to tell you about Brian," Hannah commented over an early breakfast.

"He didn't seem to mind," Ellie pointed out. "And it helps, knowing a little about his past."

"Where and how you did you meet him? You've never said."

"At the Ritz, where I stayed during my first week in London. After my opening performance I went to the Rivoli Bar to wait for Camille. Dan and Lou and Kelly were seated at another table, although I didn't know they'd seen my show. A man who had also been in the audience came on to me. Happens all the time. I'm used to it. Dan rescued me, pretending he was my date. We chatted. I mentioned I'd soon be apartment hunting, and he said he has connections in real estate. He offered to show this place to me and my aunt. We loved it on sight."

"I'm glad. I've enjoyed having you for a flat mate."

"You're easier to live with than my lazy, messy roomie at Juilliard. Harry accused me of marrying him just to get away from her."

"Did you two have a big wedding?"

"We eloped to New Jersey. After his parents calmed down, they insisted on a fancy afternoon reception at their East Hampton house. Nearly all the guests were their friends, or people Harry knew from various schools. My family flew down from New Hampshire. I was Cupid in *Don Quixote* that night, so Mom and Daddo went back with us to the city so they could see me dance."

"What was he like, your Harry?"

"Handsome and talented and super smart and very rich. I was the envy of everyone at Juilliard, girls and boys. Why's he with her, they all wondered, when he could have anybody? The meanest ones said it to my face."

"That was jealousy talking. You're a total babe."

Staring down at the remaining strawberries in her bowl, Ellie said, "Tell me what else I should know about Dan."

"He used to be in the legal department at Martin's firm, negotiating and writing up contracts. Because he wanted a change and more responsibility, he requested a transfer to management. He gets headhunted so often that he was pushed up the ladder to a directorship. He can be a calming influence on Martin, who tends to get overly excited when exploring business opportunities. Dan and his dad, Sir Terence, are incredibly close."

"His father has a title?"

"He's a baronet. Who married an earl's daughter. After the accident, they divorced. According to Martin, Lady

Lucinda Wheeler ran off with her therapist's brother to the wilds of Scotland."

"Grief changes people," Ellie acknowledged. "In unexpected ways."

"It does. But if, God forbid, my child was brain injured and institutionalized, I wouldn't desert him. Lady Lucinda Whatever-her-name-is-now didn't stop being a mother to two surviving sons. Dan doesn't talk about her. Neither does Terry." Hannah gathered up her plate and cutlery. "I'd better prepare for my marathon meeting. Will you be here when I come back for my luggage?"

"I'm in drama class till four-thirty."

"Here's a piece of parting advice that I hope you don't mind. If you're interested in a man, it's important to share significant events from your past sooner than later. Something I learned the hard way with Martin. If the full truth comes out at the wrong time, it's seriously damaging."

"I know that."

"Dan carries burdens lightly and silently. I wouldn't call him a loner, but he hasn't many friends and divides his time between work and family—what's left of it. He and Terry take fishing trips. They're members of the same gentlemen's club. Which, my husband says, consists of chaps who dine and drink together while they share investment tips and rehash their schooldays. He needs someone to add excitement to his well-ordered, predictable existence."

"And you believe I'm that person."

"I've said enough. You've got ballet class, and I'm already behind schedule. Come to Stanwell for our fete, if you can. If you can't, keep in touch."

Ellie followed her halfway down the hall. "I'm leaving London at the end of June, you know."

Turning, Hannah said, "Even so, you have the freedom, the flexibility, and the financial resources to live anywhere you want to."

That didn't mean she was willing to stay in a city without any employment and a small number of friends, gambling on the chance of making a love connection.

When she exited Latimer House, her bag was stuffed with necessities that would carry her through the day. Her loose tunic and cropped trousers matched the recommended attire for drama class. She boarded her underground train, and while the wheels beneath her zoomed along tracks, she considered Hannah's advice to reveal her complete history to Dan. Laying out the details of her marriage, she concluded, could serve no positive purpose at this early and uncertain stage of their relationship. When the door of her carriage opened with a pneumatic gasp, she flowed with the crowd towards the Way Out sign.

She'd been provided with an unassigned locker in a dim corner of the women's communal changing room. She stripped off her street clothes and changed into her leotard and tights. Anya was leading class, which banished thoughts of Dan and everything else. The slow, soothing cadences rising from Barry's piano eased Ellie into a state of concentration. During *grande allegro*, completing each revolving *tour* and soaring across the floor in the final *jeté*, she felt invincible.

"Is better, Eeley Lorry," Anya intoned from the front of the room. "Straight back, soft arms, quick feet."

Despite a firm faith in her talent, she possessed the chronic perfectionism common to everyone present. She was gratified by Anya's rare praise, yet dreaded stirring hard feelings among the other dancers. Or worse, an antipathy that would poison her pleasure in being here.

"You did a good class," commented Gemma, while they sat on the cool floor untying the ribbons of their pointe shoes. "One of these days you'll get recruited."

"No way." Ellie raised her bottle for a mouthful of coconut water and flexed her feet and calves. "Transformation time." Standing up, she slung her bag over her shoulder and padded from the room on taped feet, pulling out hairpins on her way to the dressing room.

She claimed an available sink and turned on the taps. When the basin was sufficiently full of tepid water, she plunged her head in. Squeezing a blob of shampoo from a travel-sized bottle, she washed away the sweat. She removed tights and leotard to clean the rest of her body. After drying off with a fresh towel and applying deodorant, she slipped on her underwear and covered it with the thigh-length tunic and drawstring trousers. She was plugging in her portable hairdryer with British plug when dancers not scheduled for rehearsal drifted in.

Clean and refreshed, she crossed busy Marylebone Road and mapped her way to a café in Regent's Park. There she found several dancers who obviously favored the offerings here over those of the company canteen. They waved her to their table. Accepting their invitation with a nod, she joined the queue for coffee. While waiting her turn, she scrolled through a daunting flow of texts and decided none required an immediate response. She made note of the fact that Gil Cooke had returned from the play festival he attended over the weekend, and wanted to meet up as soon as possible.

The BBT group, a mix of soloists and corps members, asked probing questions to determine her professional experience. They laughingly referred to her initial pointe shoe mishap. She listened as they aired opinions of casting decisions, shared their workout routines, and exchanged familiar complaints about juggling work demands and personal schedules. Nobody said anything negative about Rafe or anyone on his staff, either because they were reasonably satisfied with management, or because they thought she was his spy. Before long they began to scatter, departing for a rehearsal or a coaching session, or an appointment in the company gym or physio suite. Ballet dancers, like athletes, spent hours on body conditioning and cross-training for the strength and stamina that was as necessary as technique. Exercise regimens were developed to lengthen muscles rather than bulk them up.

With more time to kill, Ellie explored the portion of the park. She found Queen Mary's Garden, a sizeable area of arbors and borders where the roses were heavily budded and many were already blooming. She looked forward to seeing the flowers when all of them opened to reveal their full glory.

Ellie located Weymouth Street more easily than she'd expected to. She meandered slowly along the side street towards the modernist building that housed the Muriel Baker School of Dramatic Arts.

The nervous flutter within her ribcage carried her back to the day she started at City International Ballet. Harry skipped his morning class at Juilliard to go with her. All these years later, she could remember him walking beside her, swinging her well-worn duffel by its shoulder strap.

Today, carrying a different bag, she arrived by herself.

But oh, he was there, inside her head. Saying all the things he would if he were physically present.

Not now, Harry.

Impatient to begin the next phase of her professional life, she pushed the door open and stepped up to the reception desk. The staff person on duty directed her to an upstairs room, smaller than a dance studio and lacking barres and mirrored walls.

"I'm Maxi," a middle-aged Black woman told her. "Your instructor."

"Ellie Lowery."

Maxi checked her list for the name and made a mark beside it. "Seven to go. Half female, half male. Various ages and ethnicities. One American—you—and a Canadian. According to your application, you've worked professionally."

"In ballet. And a short summer stock season. Two plays." She doubted her career as an internationally renowned burlesque artist was pertinent.

When the full group was assembled, they received name badges and were invited to give self-introductions.

"Pay attention," Maxi told them. "This is a memory exercise."

The students described prior stage experience—plays at school or with amateur dramatics societies in their borough or city or town or village. Ellie drastically edited her performance history—stressing dance, briefly mentioning summer theatre without naming her lead roles, and again eliminating burlesque. Maxi listened carefully and made notes. When everyone had spoken, she stressed that each person's individuality and uniqueness would be valued throughout their training. Class participants were expected to be supportive of each other rather than competitive. She reviewed the information provided in their enrollment packets and took questions.

"Do you teach all our classes?" asked Simrat, who had self-identified as Punjabi.

"A different instructor is in charge of the acting for the camera segment. We bring in talent agents and stage directors to discuss audition technique and professional issues. Yes, Ellie?"

"Who directs the play?"

"That's decided later, after the group reaches consensus on the material. You'll be given scripts to consider. A member of staff will be assigned to lead your rehearsals. I'll attend as I'm able to mark your progress. Right. Let's begin, shall we? Time to stretch those muscles. And vocal cords."

After a ninety-minute class using flexors and tendons her

companions probably never heard of, Ellie joined them in raising both arms towards the ceiling, extending her neck, rotating her shoulders, bending to touch her toes, and more. Unlike her morning activity at the barre, this warm-up included facial exercises. And lots of vocalizing. She joined her cohorts in sounding out vowels while pushing the breath out through her diaphragm. They leaned over and grunted. Through pursed lips, they made popping noises. They repeated tongue-twisters. Everyone laughed, infectiously and uproariously, the most effective ice breaker of all.

Maxi put them through a simple improvisation exercise. When they finished, she dismissed them for a ten-minute break. They returned to find she'd arranged the chairs in a circle for a group discussion. After inviting each person to name a favorite actor, actress, play, and film, she collected the name badges.

Passing out blank sheets and pencils, she said, "I'd like you to write down the name of each colleague, starting with yourself and moving in a clockwise direction. When you hand in your paper, you may go. I'll see you tomorrow."

Ellie studied the group and without hesitation wrote in the names in alphabetical order: *Ellie, Rose, Archie, Val, Declan, Graeme, Simrat, Tony.* She rose and hoisted her bag to her shoulder.

Simrat, following her down the stairs, said, "Feel like I've known those people for weeks instead of hours. But goodness me, I'm exhausted. I'll need a liter of strong coffee to stay awake at work."

"What's your job?"

"Call center manager for a firm in Leytonstone. I was working daytime hours, but when I said I wanted to start drama studies they switched me to the evening shift. My boss says if I'm cast in a play, he'll put me back to morning or afternoons, or move me to half time. I've worked there forever, and they don't want to lose me." The younger girl flicked back the black braid trailing down her shoulder. "I need to eat something before clocking in."

"See you tomorrow."

They passed through the door and went in different directions. Ellie set out for Welbeck Street, where several hotels were located and she could probably hail a taxicab. The tube might be quicker, but not by much, and she'd have to cram herself into a stifling carriage with a multitude of passengers.

"Ellie!"

Thinking a male classmate was calling her, she spun around.

It was Gil Cooke.

Chapter 12

Gil reached her, disheveled and short of breath. "How's old Muriel Baker?"

"She wasn't there, Ellie replied. "I did get your message," she told him. "I meant to respond but haven't had a chance."

"It's teatime. Let's find a place where we can sit and chat."

She wanted to hop in a cab and return as speedily as possible to Latimer House. Hannah might not have departed for Somerset, and she wanted to share the day's events with someone. Not Gil. "To use your terminology, I'm knackered. I doubt I'd hold up my end of a conversation. Another time?"

He frowned. "Don't you want to know how my play fared at the festival?"

"Tell me."

"I won! *Fractures in the Heart* received the top prize."

"I'm happy for you."

"Be happy for both of us. You're my Lyla."

"For a reading, you said."

"Winning a major competition increases the chances of getting the play into production. My agent set up a meeting with the management at the Sovereign Theatre. If they aren't interested, she'll put me contact with other producers. I've started thinking about who should read Randall."

"Everything's happening so fast," she commented. "I haven't seen your script."

"Not until I've made the minor alterations suggested by the judging panel. You'll have the improved draft by the end of the month."

"Great." Her store of enthusiastic responses was depleted. Of course she was glad for him, but his determination to cast her as this unknown character Lyla was perplexing. A role in a two-person contemporary play—in London's West End—demanded skills she didn't yet possess. Her single acting lesson had resembled playtime, not formal instruction. Audiences at the Lakes Region summer theatre had been easily pleased.

"You need an agent, too. Father and I can help. If you're affiliated with a performers' union in the States, that could complicate matters."

"When City International hired me, I became a member of the American Guild of Variety Artists. Harry belonged to Actors Equity, and he made sure I joined as soon as I qualified."

"I imagine you'd be accepted into our actors' union if you submit proof of past professional employment."

"Okay." She wasn't sure how to end this discussion without either hurting his feelings or offending him. At Juilliard, she and Harry often conspired about how they could ditch Gil, and success invariably resulted in mingled relief and guilt. "If you find out how I can apply, I will. And I promise to reply quicker than I could this afternoon."

She walked away with purpose and turned at the corner without checking the street name, confident that eventually she'd locate Welbeck. Before she did, she spotted an available taxi. Frantically waving, she signaled for the driver to wait and trotted over the zebra crossing. The man lowered the window, and after giving her destination, she climbed inside.

Leaning against the seat, she removed her phone from her trouser pocket and texted Hannah.

Have u left L House? Need advice. Any recs for London talent agents?

The reply came instantly. *On my train, already past Reading. Plenty of recs. Can u wait till after Flower Fete?*

Yes, Ellie typed.

As the shock of being tracked down by Gil wore off, she couldn't decide whether to be flattered or disturbed by his persistence. Even though his play had fared well at the festival, she wasn't sure about committing to it. Gil had no idea who would be cast as the husband. And Harry often told her that chemistry was essential for stage couples.

In *Much Ado About Nothing* she'd matched wits with him as a sparky Beatrice, debating and insulting and teasing his roguish Benedick. If he hadn't pushed her, even harder than their director, she'd couldn't have risen to the challenge of Shakespeare's complex language and phrasing. Their characters' relationship in *A Streetcar Named Desire* was fraught in a different way, devoid of comic aspects. What a downer, she'd commented, when they studied lines together on the dock at the lake cottage.

Opening her photos icon, she swiped through images accumulated over the years, until she found Harry waist deep in the water, his light brown hair haloed by sunshine, a panorama of mountains behind him. He'd shot the one of her picking blueberries from the tall bush that grew on the shore. A blurry video captured a pair of loons in the bay and their plaintive cries. Scrolling past a succession of sunsets, each uniquely and dazzlingly colored, she landed on an image her cousin had taken at the funeral.

She stood with her parents and siblings, wearing a sleeve-less black dress borrowed from her sister Marie because she expected the Colmans' church to be stuffy in waning days of summer. But the air conditioning system was powerful. When Liam and Daddo escorted her down the aisle to take her place beside her in-laws, goosepimples sprouted on her chest and along her arms from shoulder to wrist. The limousine that transported her to the cemetery had been just as cold.

Holding back tears while constantly shivering. That was the clearest, most lasting memory of that endless day.

As a ballet dancer, Ellie had endured grueling and physically demanding hours of company class and afternoon rehears-als, frequently followed by an evening performance. During her years performing burlesque, she'd smiled and shimmied for her audience all night and after the show signed auto-graphs and posed for photos. She'd tumbled into bed at a late hour, sleeping through half the morning. She'd spent the rest of the day working on the act with Zack and George, or practicing it with their supporting cast.

By the end of the week, she had settled into her new and different routine. To fill the two-hour gap between dismissal from ballet class and her afternoon at the drama academy, she sampled the healthiest fare at nearby eateries. Weather permitting, she explored more of Regent's Park on foot or took the bus to the London Zoo.

On Friday afternoon she arrived at drama school later than usual, the result of a lengthy catch-up conversation with Rafe. She dropped her dance bag on the floor and took the vacant chair between Simrat and Declan. Aware that one member of the group was missing, she was surprised when Maxi laid out the day's curriculum.

Val held up her hand. "Shouldn't we wait for Archie?"

"He dropped the class. When that happens in the first week, we admit a wait-listed person, but we didn't have any. Let's begin with our warm-ups. Lots to accomplish this afternoon, as we don't meet again until Tuesday."

They spent the next hour on diction exercises, exploring vocal tones and textures and projection. As usual, Maxi required them to do improvisation, and wrapped up the session with a scene study.

Later, Ellie and Simrat made their customary visit to the Asian restaurant in New Cavendish Street. Over spicy calamari and avocado spring rolls, they shared impressions of their activities and their classmates.

"It's a shame about Archie leaving us," Ellie said. "He's talented at improv. And funny."

"He told me he wasn't sure he could afford the course fee, and then his work hours got reduced. Stepping out before the end of week one means he gets most of his money back. With a small amount deducted for the days he attended."

"Doesn't the school offer financial support? Scholarships?"

"Before classes started, anyone could apply for a bursary. By now all those monies will have been allocated."

"I see." Ellie squeezed the remaining morsel of squid with her chopsticks and carried it to her mouth.

Overriding Simrat's protests, she took care of the bill. After they parted, she returned to the academy, hoping she could have a private conversation with Maxi.

"You want to pay Archie's tuition," the instructor repeated.

"Yes. And I don't want him finding out," Ellie insisted.

"Orla in the business office will give him whatever plausible explanation I invent. Unspent funds in the scholarship account, or something like that."

"Are there other students who need financial support? I'm willing to help them, too."

Maxi half-shuttered her dark eyes. "I won't pretend I'm not aware of why you can afford this. An internet search for dancer Ellie Lowery brought forth an avalanche of Stella Nue links. Your classmates can do that as well, you know. And here's me, teaching you stage movement."

"Totally different from burlesque. Or ballet."

"Let's consult the school's accounting guru and re-enroll Archie. Don't be surprised if Orla asks if you're interested in funding fresh paint and the shower room tiling job in the top floor flat. We could raise the rent if we do some upgrades."

Ellie grabbed her bag. "Human needs are my jam, not capital improvements. That said, if she can show estimates for the necessary work, I might reconsider."

After emerging from the creation of fiscal year-end reports, and returning from his holiday weekend in Somerset and Gloucestershire, Dan contacted Ellie. She'd remained in the city to read and walk and explore. During a brief coffee shop meet-up, he learned about the drama class and her voluntary patronage of the academy. Her enthusiasm for giving away money, whether as an individual or through her foundation, was admirable but unexpected. He'd supposed Americans were consumed by a passion for making it and holding onto it.

His workday seldom ended after leaving the office, but as evening progressed, he closed his file folders, powered off his laptop, and relaxed with a film. Recent choices had sharply veered into ballet territory. Vivien Leigh was transcendent as the tragic Myra in *Waterloo Road,* a ballerina turned streetwalker after the presumed death of her suitor in the First World War. He'd rewatched *The Red Shoes,* despite being put off by the creepiness of the obsessed impresario. He hadn't previously seen *The Turning Point,* and wondered how accurately it reflected the peculiar universe Ellie had occupied for much of her life. The profession's detrimental effect on personal relationships was exposed, but several fine performances and entertaining dance sequences compensated for a hackneyed and predictable plot.

It's not too soon, he decided, to make plans for the second May Bank Holiday.

Phoning Ellie, he proposed an early dinner at a South Bank restaurant, followed by an offering at the film noir retrospective at the British Film Institute.

"On the Saturday night, they're screening *Lady of Burlesque*," he told her. "Barbara Stanwyck. RKO, 1947. Based on a novel by Gypsy Rose Lee titled *The G-String Murders*. Do you know it?"

"No. I'm intrigued."

"I'll book a table at the brasserie I've been wanting to try, not far from the cinema. Let's hope the incessant rain will let up by then."

On Thursday, when he tuned in the late news broadcast on television, he saw alarming reports of flooding that had devastated southern portions of Somerset. Grabbing his mobile, he texted Martin Latimer, who rang back straightaway.

"We're in a disaster zone," his employer said. "The River Milver overflowed its banks, causing all manner of property damage in adjacent villages. Debris blocks the drains, where they exist. Fields are sodden and roads impassable. I'm trying to locate pumping equipment and more types of supplies than I ever knew existed. In addition to supporting the efforts of our parish councils to provide emergency shelter for residents whose homes are inundated. They desperately need citizens' advice."

"I reckon you could use an assist. I'm available."

"Trains are running, as far as I know. I can send Hannah or someone from staff to collect you at Newbridge station."

"I'll get my car out of storage and drive myself."

"Brilliant. The private lane to Stanwell is choked with mud—you'll have to enter through the front gate. How soon can you leave?"

"Lou and I are close to finalizing the reports we're required to submit at the end of the month. I could wrap up my portion in the morning, if I start early. You'll see me before teatime."

"I'll let Hannah know. Thanks, mate."

This emergency trip forced Dan to break his date with Ellie. Wasting no time, he placed the call.

"How awful," she responded, when he shared Martin's news. "Could I help out, do you think?"

"You don't mind spending your holiday weekend in a flood zone?"

"Martin and Hannah let me rent this place, and I pay practically nothing for the privilege. I want to do whatever I can for them."

"All right, then. I'd like to get away around midday, to avoid the westbound outflow of holiday traffic. You'd have to miss your afternoon class."

"I'll ask Maxi about making it up."

"Where should we meet?"

"You tell me. I'll be at BBT for morning class, which finishes at eleven-fifteen. I'll take a taxi to the flat and wait for you there."

A three-day visit to distraught friends in stressful circumstances might not be the best choice for their official initial date. But, he consoled himself, it ensured a different sort of quality time with Ellie than a restaurant dinner and a movie.

Chapter 13

"If I hadn't seen news footage of flooded streets and submerged cars," Ellie said, "I'd never guess parts of the countryside are waterlogged. It's a gorgeous day for a drive."

"The Milver Vale didn't suffer as badly as nearby areas," Dan replied, "despite the river breaching its banks." Decreasing speed, he eased his Jaguar into a different lane. "This car spends more time in lock-up than on these streets. An expense I'm willing to bear. No faffing about with train schedules if I want to visit Gloucestershire to see my father and Brian, or decide to drive somewhere for a fishing weekend. And it's convenient when Martin summons me to Stanwell." His foot pressed the brake pedal as he joined the line of vehicles waiting for the traffic signal to change.

While he stared straight ahead, she angled her gaze just enough to study his profile. Dark-rimmed sunglasses enhanced his movie-star looks. His fingers tapped the black leather steering wheel, indicating impatience.

"After Hannah left London," she said, "I watched *For-*

saken Fortune again and streamed all the episodes of *Tender Treasure*. I'm excited about staying in the house where they were filmed. But I wish we weren't going there because of an emergency."

"Martin will insist on giving you the complete tour, from cellar to attics. He's steeped in the history and lore of the place. Because it isn't open to public view, he relishes any chance to share his vast knowledge." He tilted his head in her direction, saying, "You're in charge of the radio."

Taking this comment as evidence that he was disinclined to converse when behind the wheel, she fiddled with the presets until she landed on a classical station.

Speaking over the strains of a violin concerto, he said, "I suppose orchestral music puts you in a dancing mood."

Ellie smiled. "It depends on the piece. Rafe can listen to anything and make a ballet. Although I collaborated with George on my burlesque routines, he devised most of the choreography. With input from Zack."

"How are the innkeepers?

"The first batch of guests arrives in just over a month. They swear they'll be ready. Zack sent me photos of the house, inside and out."

"It's your project as well," he pointed out. "You financed it."

"Not entirely. And I don't care if they fully repay what I loaned them. Without George and Zack, Stella Nue wouldn't have been the worldwide sensation she so quickly became."

"Your philanthropic spirit is unusual for a person your age."

"I benefited from other people's generosity as a young dance student. Before Daddo sold his company, I relied on scholarships for summer dance intensives. I couldn't disappoint organizations or individuals that supported me by not pursuing a career. Good preparation for a profession that's nothing but pressure. All the time."

"Were you ever tempted to do something else?"

"I was too determined to prove myself. I felt driven to work hard enough to overcome my physical defect."

"I don't understand."

"In every respect but one, I matched the standard for ballet. Ideal height—short, with long legs. Small bones, stable weight. But when I hit puberty, I developed more flesh on top than a dancer is supposed to have. And it's impossible to deflate a full bust by dieting. Because I was talented, City International very grudgingly put me on the roster of soloists, and occasionally cast me in principal roles. But the artistic director and his minions never stopped treating me as inferior."

"That must have rough."

"I was pretty fed up by the time Harry encouraged me to audition with him at the summer theatre. He wanted me to switch to acting. Halfway through the season, on a horrible day, I woke up a wife and went to bed a widow." She drew a sustaining breath. "Rafe assured me Ballet Bruxelles would be a safe space, that I'd be happy dancing there. And I was. Until I wasn't."

"Did you experience the catfights and rivalries portrayed in ballet movies?"

"They're real, though rarely as toxic as you've seen on the screen. Close friendships, even if somewhat competitive, are more typical than feuds. I've known Melinda since we roomed together one summer in New York, and she's still at CIB." She laughed. "When I interviewed burlesque queens for my student thesis, an examination of the New York scene in the middle of the twentieth century, I heard crazy stories. Itching powder in pasties. Sabotaging stage props. Antics that stemmed from a combination of insecurity and outright jealousy. A lesson in the seamy side of show business."

"Yet it didn't deter you."

"The season after Rafe retired, I left Ballet Bruxelles and

went home to Birchmont. I had no idea what to do next. One of my interview subjects had kept in touch with me. Her nephew managed a club in Hoboken, New Jersey, and was looking for a stage kitten. That sounded like fun, and in neo-burlesque my figure wouldn't hold me back. After a few months, I put together my own act for the revue. George and Zack helped with choreography and costuming. It was a lark. Then I got completely sucked in."

She lapsed into silence, aware of his concentration while navigating his way out of central London to the motorway, and used her phone's map app to trace their route. Beyond Basingstoke, he left the busy M3 for the A303. The landscape opened up, revealing vistas of green meadows and low, rounded hills where sheep grazed. White daisies bordered the roadside and fields were carpeted with bright yellow flowers.

When she asked if it was a crop, he answered, "Later in the year, the seeds from those plants will be harvested and pressed to make an oil used in cookery or for industrial purposes. There's a rapeseed processing plant in the Milver Vale, one of several area businesses that Martin helped develop."

"What's he like?"

"The opposite of whatever you envision a stuffy English aristocrat to be. For a start, he refrains from using the title. He thinks of himself as an ordinary bloke. Who just happens to own a street in Mayfair and a chunk of Somerset and a global investment company. He's hardworking. Self-deprecating. Intensely attached to his region, although he wasn't raised there. Devoted to Hannah and their son, and utterly enchanted by them. As he will be by the baby, when it arrives."

"You're describing a friend more than a boss. Or a landlord."

"Because he doesn't treat me like an employee or a tenant." Eyeing his satnav display, he told her. "We can stop at Barton Stacey services. There's a petrol station where we can buy a sandwich and a drink."

Leaving the highway, he parked close to a cluster of buildings that formed what Ellie identified as a rest area, with coffee shop, restaurant, and chain motel. Inside the gas station, she chose a fruit smoothie and examined a tempting array of chocolates and unfamiliar candies. Deciding a road trip was no excuse for a lack of discipline, she selected a packet of almonds and joined Dan, who purchased a sandwich and packet of crisps.

He rummaged around in the car boot, shoving aside fishing gear, and removed a folded piece of canvas.

Spreading it over a damp patch of grass, he acknowledged, "Hardly a picturesque—or quiet—spot for our picnic."

When they resumed their journey, Ellie continued studying fields and farmsteads. She spied a grouping of tall stone pillars that towered over people scattered around them. "Stonehenge! You didn't tell me it was next to this highway."

"Have you never been there?"

She craned her neck as they sped past, keeping the landmark in view as long as possible. "This is my first trip beyond London. Unless you count Heathrow airport."

"I do not," he said drily. "High time you broadened your horizons, and experienced the real England." His hand left the steering wheel for an expansive gesture. "The West Country is the best part."

"In your biased opinion," she teased.

"Right. You can take the lad out of Gloucestershire . . ." He trailed off, letting her to complete the phrase for herself.

They had moved onto a narrow road bordered on both sides by white-blooming hedges that he identified as hawthorn. Portions of the grasslands were soggy in places, limiting the available grazing area for sheep and their lambs and dairy cows.

Slowing down to enter a village, he announced, "Here's

Little Milver. The deconsecrated church and its parish hall form the Rural Heritage Center, fortunately sitting on higher ground. The prince presided at the opening ceremony, and ever since it has received accolades and awards." He slowed down so men carrying shovels could cross from one side of the road to the other.

Farther on, at the bridge over the river, a barrier blocked the road. A man in a high visibility vest walked up to the car, and Dan lowered his window.

"Sorry, sir, nobody's allowed to pass—safety issue. We're waiting on inspectors to find out whether there's structural damage down below. The branches and leaves have been cleared away, and two chaps are bringing over a gurt big seine to catch the bits and bobs floating downriver. We've seen kiddie toys. Plastic flower pots. A garden gnome. Where're you bound?"

"Stanwell House."

"You can't get there by Home Farm Lane. Best backtrack to Newbridge and take the main road. That's what all residents in Milver St. Mary and Milverston village must do, till we get the all-clear for the bridge. Shouldn't be long. It's stood strong for centuries, t'isn't the only flood it survived."

"Where's the worst damage?"

"Round about the church, I'd say. If you know the millpond, you'd not believe how it's swelled. And nor can the waterfowl."

"You're sure the main road is clear?" Dan asked.

"Water did overflow the place where it dips, but Newbridge emergency services sent word it's receded enough for vehicles to pass through."

Dan backed up the Jaguar to a spot where he could reverse and passed through the village again to access the recommended route. "When we reach the market town," he said, "you'll recognize places along the High Street from *Forsaken Fortune* and *Tender Treasure*. Minus horse carts and carriages and extras in eighteenth century clothing." The wheels crunched pebbles and grit deposited by rising waters.

As they crossed over the swollen river, Ellie observed that the bridge did not look new, despite the town's name.

"Used to be. Three centuries ago."

The parking lot of an enormous home improvement store was crammed with cars and the customers carrying their purchases—buckets and mops and shovels and others items necessary for clean-up. Near the entry to a roundabout stood a chain motel and a petrol station. Dan took the third exit, signed for Milverston Magna and Milver St. Mary. Ellie was entranced by the verdant pastures and yellow flowered fields, scattered houses with colorful gardens and profusely blooming lilacs. Treetops rose above an extended boundary wall.

"We're here." Dan turned at a paved drive marked with two stone pillars and stopped in front of the metal gate, which promptly opened. "Someone's monitoring the security camera." The car moved forward and the gate closed. "This is the Home Park."

They were surrounded by a sea of tall grass and wildflowers bent by the breeze. Ellie leaned nearer her open window to inhale fresh and scented air. Each curve of the drive revealed a cluster of towering hardwoods. She wanted him to slow down so she could absorb the landscape, but the male of the species hated being told how to drive. Another bend revealed the broad building of pale golden stone, and the reality exceeded its on-screen magnificence. In the sunshine, the windows' diamond-shaped panes glistened like gemstones.

"I can't imagine what it must be like, living here," she said.

"You're about to find out."

Hannah came down the shallow front steps, followed by

a dark-haired man. "Nico will take care of the luggage. Dan, give him your key so he can move the Jag to the stable yard."

Ellie followed her to an entrance hall with wood paneling and a minstrel gallery at one end, opposite a tall window of clear glass and colorful heraldic shields. Paintings of uniformed horsemen lined the walls, separated by antique swords and shields arranged in intricate patterns.

"Our historic Great Hall," Hannah explained. "Martin loves showing people around, but you'll have to wait till he gets back. Richard is still down for his nap. Ron, our house manager, is exercising the dogs. All of which accounts for the present—very temporary—peace and quiet. Would you care for tea, or something else?"

"Tea for me," Dan responded.

"The same." Ellie gazed at the broad fireplace, wondering how often it was used, until she felt Dan's hand on her shoulder blade.

"This way. Keep close, or you'll get lost."

Chapter 14

Ellie trailed Dan through a series of grand rooms and along a corridor that led them to a bright and spacious modern kitchen. Sunshine streamed in from windows on two sides, glancing off the white-painted cupboards and island and the shining marble countertops. Only in commercial kitchens had she seen this many appliances—a pair of high-end ovens set into the wall, a broad green enamel range with multiple burners, a massive refrigerator, microwave, and something that appeared to be a wine cooler. The wooden dining table was of sufficient size for a banquet, with ample room for ten chairs.

Hannah had already set out three mugs and was spooning loose-leaf tea into a brown ceramic pot. She reached for the electric kettle and poured. "Anything to eat? To tide you over till dinner."

"Not for me," Ellie told her.

"We stopped for a bite on the way," Dan added.

"Martin will be ravenous when he gets back. He drove off after breakfast, and I doubt he got any lunch." Along with mugs of steaming brew, Hannah provided a small pitcher of milk and a bowl of grainy, caramel-colored sugar. "Muscovado, I think. Or demerara. Oh—that's Martin now, I hear his Defender coming up the drive." She took a fourth mug from a cabinet and poured tea into it. Crossing to the glass door, she opened it and called, "Take off those wellies before you step inside. Gosia mopped the floor." Laughing, she added, "Don't give them to me. Leave them outside."

Ellie recognized the tall, shaggy-haired man from family photographs scattered about the Latimer House flat.

He grinned down at her. "Welcome to Stanwell, Ellie. You're brave to venture into a disaster zone."

"I'm here to help."

"Tremendously kind of you." He sat at the table.

Hannah set down his tea. "Too busy to message or ring me since dashing off this morning?"

"Afraid so. I visited the bank in Newbridge to open the relief fund account. The charitable division of Latimer Global made a substantial donation."

"So will Acorn Films UK," she said, "soon as you give me the routing number. Where else have you been?"

"Little Milver. The school cafeteria provides meals to villagers whose kitchens aren't functional, and they're feeding the cleanup crews. I left before the bridge inspectors completed their examination. I had to backtrack to Newbridge and took the long way round to Milverston Magna to reach Milver St. Mary. The church's lych-gate is surrounded by something resembling a lake. The millpond looks like a reservoir. I've got photos." He handed his phone to Hannah.

"Dreadful," she said, swiping, then handed it to Ellie. "I rang the catering firm responsible for craft services during our film and television shoots. Where do you want them to set up?"

"Inside the tithe barn. They can unload their lorries in the car park."

"Did you stop at Holly Cottage? How is Isobel?"

She referred to Martin's mother, whose artistic talent was evident in the watercolors and oils hanging in the Latimer House flat.

"Surrounded by other members of the Women's Institute, all making sandwiches and organizing a clothes collection. I offered one of our estate vans and a driver to deliver food and everything else to the undercroft of All Saints church, for distribution."

"I don't suppose you got lunch."

"Packet of crisps at The Peacock. Poppy met me there and we toured tenant farms—the ones we could reach. And checked the watercourses. Every stream is a river."

Hannah went to him and pressed her curly head against his. "You don't have to solve all the problems. Let the helpers help. Top up?"

"Yes, please."

She lifted the teapot and poured the liquid into his mug. She passed him the milk pitcher.

Focusing gray eyes on Ellie, he said, "If you aren't already, you'll soon wish you were back at Latimer House, high and dry."

She smiled over at him. "Take your wife's advice and give others a chance to step up. Over the past couple of decades, my home state of New Hampshire has experienced several one-hundred-year floods. My ballet class participated in a fundraising telethon, answering phones and taking credit card payments. Mom brought in principal dancers from Boston to join us for a charity performance. All the proceeds went to flood relief."

Martin said, "In time, we'll have to think up entertaining ways of raising a load of dosh. For now, our priority is restoring essential services and providing necessary supplies." Eyeing his wife, he asked, "Where's Richard?"

"Asleep on the library sofa. If I don't wake him soon,

he'll be groggy and grumpy the rest of the afternoon. And make a mighty fuss at bedtime."

"Take him outside for a ramble. Especially if he's been indoors all day."

Ellie said, "I'd like to stretch my legs."

"You'll want wellies," Hannah told her. "I've got an extra pair you can wear. I'm guessing we're close to the same size." She slipped off a shoe. "Try this."

Ellie removed a canvas flat and eased her foot into Hannah's clog. "Perfect."

"I'll fetch the boots and the boy."

When she reappeared, she brought with her a toddler whose brown hair lay flatter on the side he'd slept on. His blue t-shirt and shorts were rumpled, and his socks—printed with dolphins—sagged around his ankles. He tugged his hand out of his mother's and launched himself across the room.

"Hello, Richard," Dan greeted him.

"Why are you here?"

"I wanted to see you."

"Who's that?"

"Ellie. She came with me. From London."

"Oh." He stepped behind Martin's chair. An instant later he peeked around and beamed at Ellie. "I'm a *nurl.*"

"Technically, he's a commoner, not an earl," his father explained. "At his birthday party, his great-grandmother Alicia told him about his courtesy title. She's a dowager duchess and obsessed with rank."

"And," Richard announced, "I'm a dragon."

"That he is," Hannah acknowledged, threading her fingers through her son's curls. "We christened him Richard Dragon Rufus Latimer. Come along, fire-breather, let's get your wellies on."

"Can we go to the river?"

"If Daddy says it's safe."

Martin met her gaze. "Obstructions upstream have been cleared away, and the water is rushing with enough force to weaken the bank. Best to keep well away from it."

"We'll be careful," Hannah promised him. "You're not coming?"

"I should dig through the fridge and larder. Unless you or Jan already decided what we're having for dinner."

"I'm afraid not," she confessed. To the guests, she added, "The advantage of marrying Martin—he's a willing and creative cook. He worked at a restaurant in Venice."

"Just one advantage?" he teased.

"Do I have time to change into jeans?" Ellie asked.

Hannah moaned. "I'm a complete dud as hostess. No plan for feeding our company, and I haven't shown you to your bedroom. Any objections to floral chintz?"

"None."

Dan said, "Do you mean the room you stayed in before you and Martin married?"

"Yes. The North Bedchamber."

"I'll take her."

Ellie grabbed her handbag and went with him. She paused halfway up the staircase landing to study the portion of landscape framed by an oval window. A man and two dogs, one shaggy and light brown, the other black with white markings, were crossing the lawn.

"Ron, the house manager, with Martin's lurcher Ariel. Jewel is Hannah's. Just a matter of time till Richard has his own dog." When she joined him in the upper landing, he told her, "I know a least four ways of reaching the guest quarters. This is the quickest and simplest." He proceeded along a broad and lengthy corridor of closed doors, until coming to one that was half-open. "Your flowery bower."

His description was accurate. The fourposter had a chintz coverlet and canopy, the curtains were made from matching fabric, and it covered the window seat where Ellie's duffel had been placed. Pale purple wisteria fronds encroached on the windowpanes.

"I love it."

His presence and their proximity to that bed made her wonder if his imagination was moving in the same direction as hers. To reorient her thoughts, she asked, "Is your room as nice as this? Where is it?" As a blush heated her cheeks, she regretted the second question. He might assign an unintended significance to it.

"They always put me in the Paneled Bedchamber, halfway down the passage. A more masculine vibe."

"With everything else going on, Martin shouldn't be making dinner. Is there a decent restaurant in the area, close to Stanwell, or in that town where we detoured?"

Dan shook his head. "He loves cooking, and it's something to think about besides crisis management. Text me when you're ready to go downstairs. I'll guide you."

Standing at the edge of the River Milver, still perilously close to flood stage, Ellie watched the water swirling round willow trunks and littered with sticks and broken cattails. The flattened and muddied grass beneath her feet was evidence of how far the overflow had extended.

"Martin moored his narrowboat over there," Hannah told her, pointing. "When he inherited this estate from his uncle, he had *Emotional Rescue* transported from Little Venice in London. Hard to believe at the moment, but the river is too shallow for a vessel that size, so he sold her." She knelt to speak to Richard, who tugged her shirt hem. "What is it, love?"

"A boat for me." Widening his eyes, he added, "Please."

"Next summer," she said calmly, "when you're four years old, we'll fly across the sea to Maine. Great-grampa will take you on his lobster boat."

"A lobster has claws." Ellie held up both hands and mimed the opening and closing of a crustacean's pincers.

"Lobster," he repeated, his tiny thumbs and fingers copying her movements. He leaned down to touch one of his socks. "Fishes."

"Those are dolphins," Hannah told him.

"Fishes!" he insisted.

His mother released a sigh of surrender. "Why don't you show Ellie where you found the baby rabbit?"

He whirled around. "Over there!" he shouted, and raced off.

Hannah rested a hand on her abdomen. "I'm hatching a girl egg. They told me at my week ten blood draw. It's been at least a century, Martin says, since the head of the Latimer family produced a daughter."

"Even more cause for rejoicing."

When they joined Richard, he pointed out the place under a clump of faded daffodils and related a marginally intelligible tale of the bunny's discovery by Ariel the dog.

"Let's look for the deer herd," Hannah suggested. "The keeper couldn't locate them where they usually graze. He thinks the storm drove them into the Home Park, to shelter under the oaks and chestnuts."

Ellie had never felt as earthbound as she did sloshing through puddles and stomping through damp grass in borrowed rubber boots. When her cell phone ringtone drowned out the bird calls and buzzing insects, she pulled the device from her jeans pocket. Reluctantly, she accepted the call.

"Hi, Gil."

"How about meeting for drinks after your drama class? If you've not yet been to the Wolseley, it's worth going. And only a few streets from your flat."

"I'm in Somerset."

"Whatever for?"

She could hear Hannah and Richard singing a ditty as

they moved ahead of her, hand in hand. From the frequent pauses, she guessed that its tune and words were improvised.

"Ellie?"

"I'm staying with friends in the Milver Vale."

"All weekend?"

"That's the plan. Back to London on Monday."

"We should discuss *Fractures in the Heart*. Soon. What days next week are you free?"

"None. Ballet class every morning. Maxi's drama classes all afternoon."

"I'm scheduled to work at the Sovereign for every evening performance. Sunday?"

It was more than a week away. "I'm not sure," she hedged. "I'd better hang up." With a laugh, she added, "I might be in danger of attack by a wild deer. Bye for now." She hurried to catch up with her companions.

Richard faced her and held up his arms. "Carry."

"You can walk," his mother told him. "Better yet, you should run."

"That was Gil Cooke," said Ellie, pocketing her phone. "He wrote the play I told you about."

"Is it any good?"

"I haven't read it. But he won the top award at a play festival. Two characters, a man and a woman. He asked me to read the wife when he presents it to theatre producers. That's why I asked for an agent recommendation."

"Cait Murray. Not too young, not too old. She represents Lucas Daltrey for stage and film work, and a number of equally prominent actors and actresses. I'll contact her, talk you up."

"I'd appreciate that."

Richard bounded towards them. "No deers," he said mournfully. "All gone to bed."

"I expect so." Hannah bent over to tug up his sagging shorts. "We can take Ellie to meet the horses."

The barn's inhabitants greeted the visitors with whinnies and head bobbing. Hannah lifted her son so he could pat Étoile, his father's horse, before returning to the house.

"My workplace," she told Ellie, indicating one of several structures that formed the stable court. "A vacant staff flat before I claimed it. Acorn Films UK leases space at Hartcliffe Studios near Bristol, not quite an hour by car. My assistants are based there. At least twice a year I fly to Boston, for strategy sessions with Liz Gregorio. And to spend time with my family in Maine. I'll be going this summer, before my tummy gets so large I can't travel comfortably."

A sage green vehicle came up the drive and parked beside Dan's Jaguar. A leggy blonde climbed out, followed by a black Labrador.

"Millie!" Richard hurried over to greet the dog.

"Our estate manager, Poppy Dean." Hannah went to meet the young woman, saying, "This is Ellie Lowery, our Latimer House tenant. She came with Dan. How's everything at The Peacock?"

"Jack sent me away. He's got a dozen people making meals and serving tables." For Ellie's benefit, she added, "My husband owns the pub in Milverston Magna. The better of the two, by far. My mobile hasn't stopped ringing all day. Time to hole up in my office to return the calls I've missed. Is Mart around? He's supposed to contact firms that do water damage remediation."

"You'll find him in the kitchen."

"Jan won't be here to cook for you tomorrow. Her daughter's house is a mess, and she's got the whole family at hers."

"We'll manage. If she needs anything, Kateryna can pick it up at the supermarket in Newbridge tomorrow, when she shops for Isobel. And us." As Hannah stepped past the mud-spattered Land Rover, she said, "I'll get the bank papers Martin mentioned, with the routing number for the flood relief account." She opened the passenger door and retrieved a folder.

"I want to contribute," Ellie told her.

She removed the borrowed boots and set them outside the double glass doors beside Martin's. Richard plopped on the ground and struggled to tug his off. When he stood, Hannah brushed dirt off his backside. They found Martin and Dan still seated at the kitchen table. The dogs were there, and the man who had exercised them. Introducing himself as Ron, he grinned and declared that he was the real master of Stanwell.

"Not far from the truth," Martin affirmed. "But don't believe his boast that he's a finer chef than me." He bounded up from his chair. "Ready to see the house, Ellie?"

"Now?"

"I'm tagging along," Dan announced, "to keep Martin honest."

"You think I don't know the difference between colorful family legend and recorded history?"

After granting Ellie time to admire the ground floor dining room's gleaming mahogany table and sparkling crystal chandeliers, Martin moved into areas associated with visiting royalty.

"Do you and Hannah use these grand rooms?" she wondered.

"Occasionally. Before visitors arrive, Gosia the housemaid removes protective cloths from the antique furniture and dusts the surfaces."

Dan muttered, "None of that sprucing up happens on my account."

Martin concluded his tour in the Long Gallery. "We bring Richard here on stormy days and make him run up and down until he's worn out. Several times this week we had to lure him out of the fireplace. He was hell-bent on climbing up the chimney flue all the way to the rooftop."

"Takes after his dad," Dan said. "I'll wager Martin did exactly the same as a boy."

Ellie looked at Martin. "You have a disrespectful employee."

"I make allowances."

"I'll behave," Dan said. "I certainly don't want to get sacked. Not after the monumental difficulty I had landing the job."

"Difficulty?" Ellie repeated. "Hannah described you as quite the catch. Professionally," she hastily added.

"For two years after qualifying as a solicitor, I worked at a Bristol firm. When I found out Latimer London Properties were recruiting, I immediately applied for a position. I was one of two finalists. They hired the other chap."

"Not my decision," Martin declared. "I had no part in that process. The only reason you missed out, I discovered, was because he was based in London and they didn't want to cover relocation expenses." Turning to Ellie, he said, "Four months later, that fellow gave notice and went out to Dubai to work there. I contacted Dan. Vetted him myself."

"About ten minutes into that conversation," Dan added, "we realized my dad and my grandfather had both been acquainted with his uncle."

Martin's gaze shifted from one to the other. "Fate is generous in bringing people together at the perfect time. Don't you agree?"

Chapter 15

Martin's question, and its intended implications, revolved in Ellie's mind during her morning calf stretches. When she wondered how Dan had received it, she lost her count and had to start over. Holding the back of the dressing table chair, cocked her left leg and rose onto her right at the moment someone tapped on the bedroom door.

It was Hannah, wanting to know what she fancied for breakfast.

"Not much, after the delicious dinner your husband served last night."

"You're welcome to use our exercise room. It's fully equipped. Machines and everything. I'll show you later. Kateryna's coming over, and I'd better put together her shopping list. Come with me to the kitchen. We both need breakfast."

Ellie indicated her tank top and leggings. "I'll change."

"Don't bother."

Conscious of the stretchy fabric accentuating her breasts, she grabbed a loose cotton shirt from her duffel and put it on. She slipped her bare feet into her leather flats and followed Hannah.

They found Kateryna and Richard surrounded by toys in the bright kitchen corner that was set up as a play area. Last night, prompted by Martin, Dan had spoken of his successful effort to arrange the Latimers' sponsorship of the young Ukrainian refugee. Although her primary job was organizing events at the venues in the three adjacent villages, she ran errands and assisted the couple as a child minder.

"When I finish buying things," she said, rising from the floor, "Poppy will have me make sandwiches at the pub. All holiday weekend activities I was planning and promoting at museums are stopped for the flood."

Hannah said, "The relief workers will be glad of any and all assistance. I'll be at The Peacock, too, helping with lunchtime service."

Ellie looked away from her bowl of yogurt and berries. "I'm going with you."

Hannah and Kateryna studied the contents of refrigerator and freezer and surveyed pantry shelves to determine what items should go on the shopping list.

When Kateryna returned from her trip to Newbridge, she dropped off Hannah's requests and departed for Isobel Latimer's cottage to do the same. Ellie encountered her again when she and Hannah arrived at the pub across from the village green, to prepare meals for displaced villagers and hungry road repair crews.

Spreading soft butter over pieces of whole wheat bread and passing them to Hannah, she commented on the cohesion of the community.

"A crisis does bring out the best in people," responded Hannah, adding slices of cheddar to the sandwich. "But don't assume it's all sweetness and light around here. Martin deals with conflicts between residents whose interests and opinions differ. Some of them take pleasure from stirring up pointless controversies."

"Bellyachers. In Birchmont, they come to the annual town meeting for the express purpose of making mountains out of molehills."

They remained until a fresh crew of Poppy's recruits arrived for the afternoon shift. Back at Stanwell House, Ellie accepted a toasted and buttered crumpet to go with her tea. The two men returned, attractively disheveled, bearing a parcel of fresh fish filets, shrimp, and scallops.

"Purchased at a discount from a market desperate to sell its wares at a time of reduced demand," Martin explained.

He submitted to Ellie's request that he let her assist with preparation for his stew. While he diced pollock and she shelled and deveined the prawns, they traded tales of kitchen labor in diverse settings—his canal side restaurant in Venice and her dad's pub. Hannah, enlisted as salad-maker, let Richard shred the lettuce.

Dan, typing notes into his laptop, looked up to say, "When Martin and I stopped at the bank to discuss relief fund disbursements, we learned about a large donation received just before closing time yesterday. From an account registered to Estelle Lowery Colman."

Pulling off a shrimp tail, Ellie said, "My small way of assisting recovery efforts in the Vale."

Martin shook his head. "I wouldn't describe a five-figure sum—in which the first number is two and the second is five—as small."

"Oh, Ellie," Hannah murmured. "That's so generous."

Dan added, "With no quid pro quo. Because she contributed to a foreign entity, she can't claim a charitable deduction on her tax."

"I could've arranged the donation from the Lowery-Colman Foundation, but there would have been a delay for admin approvals and documentation. It's also a holiday weekend in the States. Direct deposit from my personal account was the speediest method."

They dined on the terrace, in view of the garden areas behind the house. An ancient wisteria twined up the back wall, and the branches of blooms reached all the way up to Ellie's bedroom window. When everyone finished eating, they carried empty dishware to the kitchen. Hannah handed over the dessert plates and followed with a rectangular shaped object on a platter.

Ellie studied the checkerboard pattern of pink and yellow, wrapped in a substance resembling pale putty. "What's that?"

"Battenberg cake. Sponge encased in a layer of marzipan."

"Where did it come from?" Martin wondered.

"Jan's kitchen. To keep her grandkids occupied, she gave them a baking class. While they faffed about with shortbread biscuits, she created this masterpiece and Kateryna delivered it to us." She began cutting.

Richard, who had been served his meal before the adults had theirs, climbed up on his chair and pointed at the cake. "Big piece."

His mother gave him a thin one.

Ellie's resolve to do a strenuous morning workout intensified when she accepted her portion. "The loveliest cake I've ever seen. How is it made?" Her first delectable bite convinced her that it was well worth any amount of trouble.

Martin severed a piece with his fork. "The batter for the sponge is mixed and divided for coloring. After baking, the assembly process is somewhat fiddly. Each section is held together with apricot jam."

"I never had anything like this," Ellie declared. "Not in Paris, the capital of decadent desserts. Or Tokyo."

"What fun, eating your way around the world," said Hannah, on an envious note. "Knowing you'd work off the calories on stage."

Ellie shrugged. "My diet as a burlesque artist didn't permit any more indulgence than when I was a ballet dancer."

"What did you do between tours?"

"Prepared for the next one. I made promotional appearances and did interviews. I was booked for advertising shoots, print and film. I had meetings with designers at the companies that produce my merch. When not otherwise occupied, I coached my Mom's students at Birchmont Dance Academy—all ages, from beginner to advanced and pre-professional." After a moment of uncertainty, she chose to make a humiliating confession to her extensively educated audience. "I left school before I turned seventeen. Whenever my schedule permitted, I would enroll in community college classes. History. Sociology. Marketing. But I never managed to complete a course."

"Ellie is a constant reader," Dan volunteered.

"At the moment, I'm working my way through Stanislavski's writings. The latest translations."

Martin rattled off names of single malt whisky distilleries and asked Dan's preference. He returned with a bottle and two cut crystal glasses. Ellie accepted Hannah's offer of a non-alcoholic elderflower cordial spritzer. Richard, whose lips were speckled with cake crumbs, sat down on a stone step to toss a tennis ball for the dogs. Black and white Jewel was a skilled retriever. Ariel the lurcher disliked giving up the ball, and the child chased after her to reclaim it.

"I've decided to drive up to Tayer Court after breakfast," Dan announced. "After I visit Dad, I'll pop over to Harding Hall to see Brian. I'll be back for dinner."

"Why not take Ellie with you?" Hannah asked. "Terry's roses will be marvelous. Ours certainly are."

Dan smiled at Ellie. "Would you like to go?"

She didn't want to admit how much. "I might be needed here."

Martin said, "You've both been a huge help, but I doubt

there's anything left for you to do. In the morning we've got a community worship service at All Saints. Afterwards there'll be an informational assembly in the parish hall for residents of all three villages. The councils and the staff from emergency services will give updates on repairs and so on. Besides, if you overnight in Thornbury, you can drive on to London early enough Monday to beat all the holidaymakers rushing back at the end of the day." With patently false sternness, he added, "I want the employees of all Latimer divisions to be at their desks promptly on Tuesday morning."

Richard, drawn to the table by the adults' laughter, wanted to know the cause.

"Daddy's being silly. Bath time for you, Richie-roo." Hannah stood up and took him by the hand. "When you've got your jim-jams on, we'll read a story in bed."

"About the hedgehog."

"Please," she prompted.

"Please!" he shouted.

"All right."

Looking up at his father, he said, "Be the fox. *Please.*"

Martin stood. With a smile at Dan and Ellie, he said, "Sorry to desert you, but I'm duty bound to perform. Help yourself to the libations."

After the couple took their child inside, Ellie asked Dan if his family home was as palatial as Stanwell House.

He choked back a laugh. "Oh, no. But it's even older, a combination of eras and styles. Original medieval features overlaid with Georgian embellishment in places. My great-grandparents were enraptured by William Morris, so the Arts and Crafts esthetic was imposed nearly everywhere." He draped his arm over the back of her chair. "I can't predict how well Dad would cope with an overnight guest at short notice, so I'll arrange a room for you at the castle hotel. I can make a dinner reservation at its main restaurant. Do you mind if he joins us?"

"That would be great." When she tipped back her head to scan the heavens, it landed on his upper arm. She felt his palm stroke her hair, released from the loose ponytail she'd worn all day. The sensation was intensely pleasurable. Her voice was noticeably uneven when she said, "Star light, star bright. The wishing star."

His caressing hand blocked out all wants and needs except her urgent desire for him to press his mouth to hers.

And because she refrained from speaking her wish, it came true.

After breakfast, Dan, phone in hand, excused himself to phone his dad and make hotel and restaurant reservations. Martin remained at the table, jotting down notes for his address to the community. Hannah prepped Richard for a day at his grandmother's and tried to dissuade him from taking along a supply of dog biscuits.

"Ernie has plenty of treats at Holly Cottage."

"Exactly the same," Kateryna assured him.

"Jewel and Ariel want him to have theirs."

"Just one," said Hannah, relenting. After she zipped a miniature backpack bulging with stuffed animals and plastic toys, she kissed the top of his head and handed him over to Kateryna. Standing at the window, watching them cross the stable yard to the car, she said, "I spend more time and effort getting him ready to leave the house than I do on myself."

"Not always," Martin protested.

"I guarantee I'll be dressed and ready for church before you are."

Left to her own devices, Ellie made her way upstairs to the exercise room Hannah had shown her yesterday. This was the right place to work off nervous excitement at the prospect of meeting Dan's parent. She stepped around a weight machine and the stationary bicycle to remove a rolled-up yoga mat in the corner. After a completing her favorite stretches, she picked up the remote-control device and pointed it at the widescreen television attached to a wall. She found the YouTube icon. She searched for "World Ballet Day" and selected BBT's portion of the twenty-four-hour livestreamed event featuring ballet companies across the globe. She scrolled past the introductions and stopped when she located Rafe's morning class. Positioning herself beside the treadmill, she used its handrail for a barre and eased into a *plié*.

The familiar combinations should have come easily. But her thoughts strayed to her kissing session with Dan beneath a night sky dotted with glittering stars. Smiling at the memory, she bent from the waist in *port de bras devant*.

His background and life experience were nothing like hers, she reflected. She and Harry hadn't had anything in common either, apart from dedication to their respective art and a shared passion for performing. He'd been born into the wealth and status his family had enjoyed for generations. Whereas she and her industrious parents, descended from laborers, were fully aware of the extent to which timing and luck had contributed to their achievements.

From her initial encounter with Dan Wheeler, she'd been conscious of his attractiveness and an appealing hint of humor. He hadn't concealed a reciprocal interest in her, which had effectively erased her instinctive wariness. Since then, she'd discovered his mesmerizing blue-gray eyes and a family tragedy. Her fame had hampered past relationships, all of them casual and fleeting. Dan wasn't bothered by it.

I want to know everything about him, she realized. *His past. His hopes and dreams, concerns and fears. But he'll expect me to share aspects of myself and my history, and that could damage rather than strengthen our connection.*

Rafe's voice drew her out of her reverie. "*Fondu* to front. *Tombé*. *Piqué*—on demi-pointe. Hold two counts. Repeat to the side. *Rond de jambe en l'air* once, repeat twice, and three times."

He started on the *grands battements,* and Ellie swung her leg high in unison with the figures at the parallel rows of Studio A barres. Front, side, back. The cameraman focused on the pianist—Barry, so friendly towards her when she attended *Onegin* rehearsals.

She looked forward to seeing Leah and Drew and the other members of the first cast perform it. Should she invite Dan to go with her?

"Energetic start to your day." Hannah came into the room.

"Force of habit. If I don't move and stretch, I'll regret it on Tuesday morning. Especially if Marcus Baldwin leads class. He's merciless."

"Do your muscles and joints hurt afterwards?"

"Ibuprofen and deep tissue massage take care of any aches. Severe pain is different—and dangerous. If ignored, it can result in major injury. I don't know any dancers who are actual masochists—a myth that adds drama to films and tv shows. We can cope with the twinges. For something worse, we get an assessment from the physical therapist. Or the medical staff."

"Pointe shoes must be really uncomfortable."

"Not if they're correctly fitted. We have ways to cushion the toes and heels to prevent blisters, which are absolute hell. I used to be constantly on pointe, practically all day and night—class and rehearsals and performance. After all that my feet were screaming for an ice bath. Nowadays I can leave the studio after two hours, counting warm up and cool down."

"Sorry I interrupted, but I wanted to say goodbye before we have to leave for All Saints."

"I'm done. No way can I do *petit allegro* in here—I need open space for *jetés.*" She reached for the remote and switched off the television. Spotting a box of tissues on a shelf, she pulled one out and dabbed at her brow and upper lip. "It's been interesting, getting a glimpse of your life here. Although I don't know how you manage to be a wife and mother and a movie producer."

"With excellent spousal and staff support. And through sheer stubbornness." Hannah's hand flicked back her curls. "I'm fortunate that before Richard arrived on the scene, Acorn Films UK was well-established. After wrapping the fourth iteration of my mother's gardening series for Serve-Flix, I began scaling back. I commit to just one major project per year. Most of Liz Gregorio's Thomas Hardy biopic will be filmed on location in Dorset, an easy drive from here. We'll shoot some interiors at a Hartcliffe Studios sound-stage, less than an hour away. If the traffic isn't bad."

Ellie stifled a yawn.

Hannah's brows shot up. "Our Dan kept you up late, did he?"

"Not the way you're thinking. Lots to mull over in the night. Meeting his dad feels like a major step. Towards what, I have no idea. And I wish I'd brought something nicer to wear besides one of those boring travel dresses that rolls up and unrolls without a wrinkle."

"What color?"

"Black."

"Of course. Come along, Cinderella. Let me be your fairy godmother."

Ellie went with her down the corridor to a room of tall, wooden wardrobes and an entire wall of open shelving. "Wow."

"Jacobean mansions don't have clothes closets. This dressing room was my idea." Hannah yanked open a ward-robe door, revealing a row of garments on hangers. She tweaked sleeves, mumbling to herself. Taking out a paisley-patterned chiffon blouse, she held it up for inspection. "If you wear this as a jacket, it will add pizazz to your little black dress." Moving to a shoe rack, she said, "I've got a spiffy pair of slingbacks that should fit. While you try them on, I'll find a sensational piece of statement jewelry."

"You really do have magical powers," Ellie said.

Chapter 16

The bridge that spanned the River Milver's receding waters had passed inspection, so Dan was able to cross from Milver St. Mary to Little Milver and connect with the road he preferred. Despite the likelihood of holiday traffic in Bruton, popularized and glamorized by an influx of celebrities and politicians, he stuck to the familiar A359, heading towards Frome.

Did Ellie have morning-after regrets about what happened last night on the terrace? He definitely didn't. As a classical piece flowed from the speakers, he recalled running his fingers through her auburn hair, and the feel of her soft lips moving against his. He'd discovered the texture of her skin and the contours of the figure concealed by a long-sleeved navy and white striped shirt and a pair of dark blue trousers.

She pressed the control on the touchscreen and increased the volume. "Chopin's mazurka in D major. I know it from dancing in *Les Sylphides*. So did Nijinsky and Pavlova and Karsavina, when they were with Diaghilev's Ballets Russes."

Her hands darted in various directions, and she angled her head from side to side. When the music faded, she lowered the sound and continued, "City International revived it when I was a member of the corps. It was my debut as soloist, when we repeated it for a gala performance. In Brussels, I was paired with Rafe Lawrence for the opening *pas de trois,* and the *pas de deux* in the waltz section before the finale. By far the best partner I ever had."

Until this moment, her affectionate tone when referring to the former male star hadn't troubled him. Overnight, Dan had developed a startling degree of possessiveness. He reminded himself that at Ellie had disavowed any off-stage partnership with the director of British Ballet. But she was seeing him six days a week. It wasn't unheard of for a lengthy professional alliance to ripen into something more.

"There's no plot," she continued, "or characterization. One male poet and twenty-three sylphs in long, Romantic-era tutus. Flowers in our hair, tiny fairy wings attached to our backs. Many picturesque tableaux—static poses—by the soloists and the corps. It's about half an hour long. The choreography is simple, with focus on the movements of the head and arms and hands and feet. Not a favorite among show-offs who want to impress with their technique."

"Sounds familiar. I must've seen it."

"You're probably thinking of *La Sylphide,* a story ballet. Men in tartans and kilts and a witchy woman who casts spells. A wedding procession at the end."

"That's the one. I saw it with my dad and his lady friend."

"He has one? How long have they been together?"

"Four years. They met at the Chelsea Flower Show. Pamela Ames is head of public relations for a building society that sponsored one of the important display gardens. He sees her whenever he's in London. They attend plays and concerts. And ballets."

"He's got a title, so he must manage acres and acres of countryside property. Like Martin."

After a shake of his head, Dan explained, "Nominally he's partner in a firm of solicitors based in Bristol, primarily serving as a legal consultant on certain types of cases. As for land, my Wheeler ancestors spent generations acquiring large tracts of it. The house I grew up in was on the estate, and Dad and I moved from there to Tayer Court while my grandparents were still living. After he inherited, he reduced his holdings, selling off the majority of the tenant farms and houses. Part of the proceeds went into an income-generating trust that pays for my brother's care. Dad's preferred occupation, rose breeding and cultivation, isn't at all profitable. Hannah's mother, the garden guru Wendy Edney, filmed an episode of her television series at Tayer Court. You'll find it on ServeFlix."

"What did you tell him about me?"

"That you're a former professional dancer embarking on a career as an actress. I didn't mention that you're also an excellent kisser."

She responded with a soft laugh. "Takes one to know one."

"The darkness and the starlight emboldened me. And your head resting against my arm. I assure you what happened after that was . . . meaningful."

"For me as well." Her hand moved across the center console to settle on his forearm. "I want that dinner date. And Barbara Stanwyck in *Lady of Burlesque.*"

"I'll check whether it's available on one of the streaming platforms. What was Martin saying to you when I was telling Richard goodbye?"

"He apologized for not having time to show me around the factory where the organic rapeseed oil was produced." Hannah had sent them off with three bubble-wrapped bottles, stowed in the Jaguar's boot.

"We did accomplish a great deal over a short period. I compiled all my research into a document he'll hand out to the property owners and tenants at the community meeting. They're desperate for guidance about making insurance claims for repairs to residences or businesses."

"Additional hardship for people in dire straits."

"It requires meticulous record-keeping. They'll have to provide photographs of flood damage to loss adjusters, in addition to various types of documentation—purchase receipts, copies of bills of sale, product warrantees. In some cases, temporary accommodation is required, before and during restoration, with reimbursement of costs, if that's included in the policy terms."

"When a crisis shatters normality," she said reflectively, "the complexities are overwhelming. Before and after my husband's funeral, I wanted to be left alone. But I had to meet with a lawyer and trust officers. The minister of his parents' church. My grief counselor. In retrospect, I sympathize with them, having to deal with a twenty-year-old zombie. I was disoriented. Detached—from myself and everybody else. Awake most of the night. Sleepwalking through the days and weeks and months."

"I remember." The accident on the river had occurred nearly a decade and a half ago, and if he let himself remember, it felt like it happened yesterday. "I experienced all of that."

Folding a granola bar wrapper in half, she asked, "Does Brian spend time with your father at Tayer Court?"

"He becomes agitated if his routine is disrupted. When he had his appendix out, the brief stay in a Bristol hospital was hard for him. But his case manager isn't entirely opposed."

"I hope it works out."

"I'm taking you to the house to meet Dad and have a look round. Before I drive to Harding Hall, I'll deliver you to the hotel. I did request a superior room, but they couldn't guarantee it would be available at such short notice."

"I've never spent the night in a real castle. Wherever they put me, I'll be satisfied."

At Alveston he left the main road, thereby avoiding the larger town of Thornbury. Proceeding northwards, he entered territory where his Dimery ancestors had raised crops and livestock as tenants of his Wheeler forbears. He saw nothing like the devastation that plagued the Milver Vale, although the recent deluge had pushed mud onto the tarmac here and there and raised the height of a brook dividing one field from another. He proceeded along a tunnel of hedgerows thick with white hawthorn blossom.

Sunlight bathed Tayer Court's stone façade and front lawn. A circular bed contained roses and purple lilac blooms, offering a hint of the glorious displays elsewhere on the property.

He switched off the engine. Realizing he hadn't yet informed Ellie about an important individual, he told her, "Sandra, our housekeeper, who also cooks for Dad, is probably still here. She and her husband live in a bungalow down the lane. Don't be surprised when she calls me Daniel—nobody else does. Dad will be with his roses, taking advantage of the fine weather."

He left the driver's seat and went to the boot to remove his wheeled suitcase. Ellie picked up one of the bottles of oil.

Smiling down at her, he said, "It's been ages since I brought somebody here."

"A girl, you mean?"

He nodded. "And never an American one."

"I promise I'll be good."

He released the handle of his case. His palm cupped her chin, and he leaned in for a kiss. As she swayed towards him, circling his waist with her slender ballerina arms, he whispered, "When we're alone, you can be as naughty as you like."

Hearing the crunch of gravel, they both turned.

"You missed lunch," his father said.

As Ellie stepped away, Dan responded, "When I rang, I didn't know exactly when we'd leave Stanwell. And I tried to avoid the major roadways and heavy holiday traffic. That slowed our progress."

"Good afternoon, Miss Lowery."

"I'm Ellie." With her free hand she pushed up her sunglasses, revealing her eyes.

Dan was disappointed that Dad didn't invite her to call him Terry.

She held out the gift. "Milver Vale cold-pressed rapeseed oil. Lady Milverston asked us to bring it to you."

"How is Hannah?" He directed this question at Dan.

"In joyful expectation of delivering a daughter at year's end."

"Splendid." He led them to the front door and opened it, allowing Ellie to enter first.

Dan added, "And frustrated by Martin's futile attempts to stop her from working so hard."

Sandra stood in the hall, beaming. When she tried to take his case, he clung to it.

"Meet my patient friend Ellie, who never complained about traveling every back road from South Somerset to South Gloucestershire."

"No reason to," said Ellie, brightly. "Such lovely scenery."

"Fine day for a drive," the older woman agreed. "Smooth going, I reckon, in that swish motor of his. Leave your case, Daniel, and come to the kitchen. You must be famished."

Bashing his Panama hat against his thigh, Dad said, "I'm off to the glasshouse."

"I lured Ellie here with promises of a garden tour."

"Oh. Well, yes. Certainly."

"Food first," Sandra insisted. "Then the roses."

"You know where to find me," said his father, halfway out the door.

Bees darted from campanulas to columbines and buzzed deep within the tubular flowers of the spiky foxgloves. Dan's mother had taught him the names in the distant days when she'd snipped blossoms with her secateurs and placed them in the trug he carried for her.

Ellie, silent and attentive, listened to descriptions of centuries-old roses, budded but not blooming. Dan perceived that his parent was talking at her, not to her, in a voice that was a shade less than warm. They followed a stone wall of uncertain age, partly obscured by flowering rose canes underplanted with perennials. Broad steps led to the sunken garden, where two men weeded borders crammed with Dad's creations, all of them blooming. In the center was the round pond with a fountain that had proved irresistibly tempting to Dan and his younger brother on hot summer days.

"The varieties I produce," Dad said, "are grown off-site until mature enough for sale." He pointed at a trio of leafy shrubs, flowering profusely. "TC37, my latest and most promising cultivar."

Leaning over, Ellie pressed her nose against the pink petals and inhaled. "Amazing fragrance. Like strong perfume."

"My grower and I expect it to perform well in rose trials. He currently has five hundred grafted plants ready for introduction. After that lot sells out, he'll maintain a reserve list for next year's stock. He means to offer over a thousand in subsequent seasons. If you care to see how new roses are made, come with me."

In the glasshouse, grow lights were positioned above long tables. Ellie paused to study the identifying labels of specimens that were segregated by container size.

"All my hybrids come from seed produced by rose hips. Fewer than half the ones I plant will germinate. Seedlings remain in their pots until the root structure is established enough for transporting to the rose fields where they mature."

An adjacent glass-sided shed held several evergreen bonsai trees undergoing rehabilitation. Herbs and annual flowers and vegetables had been transferred to the borders or the kitchen garden, their next stop. Dad showed off rows of ripening strawberry beds and the fruit cage. Gesturing towards the orchard, he expressed hopes for a decent crop of cherries, peaches, apricots, apples, and pears. With pride he pointed out the two giant yew trees, hundreds of years old, shading a ruin that formerly served as a place of worship for the manorial household.

Hoarse chittering drew Dan's gaze to a magnolia. He counted three dark-feathered birds clinging to the branches, carrying on a conversation. "That sounds like Jack."

"I saw him this morning. The biggest in the flock, and the boldest. He leads the others when they're foraging in the lawn to feed their young. There's a group of nestlings in a crevice in the old chapel wall, clamoring for food." His father moved towards the tree, calling, "Jackie, Jackie, Jackie. Come down, Jackie." A bird soared down to the ground and waddled over. "That's him."

"A crow?" Ellie asked.

"Jackdaw," Dan answered, "smallest member of the corvid family. In times past, people would take a baby bird from the nest before it fledged, to keep as a pet—a practice that's now illegal. The species is notable for its ability to mimic the human voice. My brother Brian and I taught one to talk back to us, or so we believed. This Jack will eat from your hand."

"I wish we had food. What does he like?"

"Anything he's offered. Keep him in sight while I'll get a few morsels from the kitchen."

Best to leave her alone with Dad, he decided. Perhaps

if I'm out of the way, he'll loosen up enough to show the typical Sir Terence charm.

Sandra, muttering in exasperation, was installing a fresh bin liner.

He crossed to the worktop and opened the biscuit tin. "Ellie wants to feed Jack." He removed a digestive.

"I'm about to go home, but I needed to speak to you when Terry wasn't around to hear. You'll be seeing Brian?"

"After I take Ellie to the castle." Noting the worry in her face, dread surfaced. "Is something wrong with him?"

"It's to do with Lady Lucinda."

When he unclenched his teeth, he asked, "What about her?"

"She contacted Harding Hall's chief administrator. Nerys, Brian's physical therapist, mentioned it when I was over there a few days ago. I'm no blood relation, so she couldn't say much. If you want to know more, you might ask Dr. Daventry. Or Brian's case manager."

"I wonder why Dad didn't tell me."

Sandra shook her graying head. "You know how he is about her. But I couldn't let you go over there and find out the way I did. She might get in touch with you."

"She wouldn't know how," he retorted.

"You're a top executive at an important London firm. The office phone number is on the website. Email addresses, too."

With better understanding of his father's moodiness, he returned to the magnolia tree where Ellie waited for him.

"Sorry I took so long. Is Dad chasing after Jack?"

"He went back to the big greenhouse. I'm keeping my eyes on your bird." She pointed to a dark shape on a lower branch.

"Hold out your hand." He broke the digestive into pieces and placed several in her open palm. "Lean down and show it to him. Call his name."

"Look, Jackie. Here's a cookie. A biscuit."

"Keep your hand cupped. That's right." He tossed crumbs on the ground.

The jackdaw swooped over and greedily nibbled them. He cocked his glossy head, inspecting the tidbit Ellie held. Hopping up, he landed on her hand long enough to seize it. Setting it on the grass, he pecked away.

Dan held up his phone. "Might I take photos? To show Brian."

"Sure." When she held out another remnant, the bird approached.

He captured numerous images of Ellie and the bird together, and individually, and shot video. When every speck of biscuit was consumed, he said, "Sandra had to leave, but I'm capable of brewing a cup of tea. If you're so inclined."

She gave him a long look. "I think we'd better go."

"Let me show you the house. It won't take long." He wanted to see her there. He hoped she would like it. "This tour will be considerably less detailed than Martin's."

While she admired the beamed ceilings of the primary sitting room and the dining room, and the Carrara marble mantels, questions tumbled about in his mind. Why, after over a decade of blatant disinterest and complete silence, had his mother contacted Dr. Daventry? Was she contemplating a visit? She had no right or authority to interfere in arrangements for Brian's care. Dad was his legal guardian.

Chapter 17

Harding Hall, located between Thornbury and Bristol, occupied a renovated Edwardian mansion. A modern extension contained the dormitory and a clinic. Family interaction was encouraged—the staff strongly advocated for it. Residents neglected by relatives suffered frequent bouts of depression, unlike those receiving regular visits and cards and emails. Dan and his father and Sandra visited separately, and frequently. They were permitted to attend physical therapy sessions or medical examinations and could observe group activities. Brian's chief carer let them know if he was having a difficult day.

When Dan presented his identification, required by protocol, the woman at the reception desk messaged the attendant to discover Brian's location. Handing over a visitor badge, she said, "He had his tea outdoors this afternoon. Norman is taking him to the day room."

He made his way along the corridor to the rear of the house and the former ballroom, where a wall of windows overlooked a broad terrace. Watching his sibling shuffle alongside Norman, Dan recalled the agonizing vigil in the hospital ward, when tubes and wires had connected the inert body to monitors and machines and bags of fluid. Brian had survived, and basic motor skills were partially restored, but loss of his mental acuity was hard to accept. Progress in rehabilitation didn't equate with recovery. The chatty, cheeky kid who had climbed trees and trained jackdaws and alternately plagued or emulated his two older siblings had vanished. In his place was a young man with a vacant expression and partial deafness, who communicated through unintelligible sounds.

"Brian, here's Dan." Norman, a Bristolian of Caribbean descent, was the son of Windrush immigrants from Dominica, both of them longtime health service employees. "Let's sit and tell him our news."

Brian mumbled.

During these one-sided conversations, Dan always focused on his brother's face while Norman made statements and answered questions. With amplified cheerfulness, he said, "Good news, I hope."

"Brian will participate in our annual Games Day. He and Nerys have practiced ring toss. Next, they'll work on catching and throwing a ball."

"Dad and I will be here to cheer you on." He tapped the photo icon on his mobile and selected a close-up bird photo. "Here's Jack. I saw him this afternoon."

Brian squinted at the image.

Swiping to a different picture, he said, "This is my friend. She fed him digestives, just like you used to. He sat on her hand. Isn't she pretty? Her name is Ellie."

Brian lurched back in his chair and gripped Norman's wrist. When he babbled, Dan desperately wanted to believe he recognized the bird in the photo.

"Best get him to his room," said Norman, his statement tinged with apology. "He's tired. Lots of stimuli today."

"Right. I'll be back soon." He reached over to grip Brian's bony shoulder. "Good fellow."

"If you're able to come back tomorrow, we're screening a film for our residents. Bank holiday treat, and families are invited. Sir Terry said he'll join us."

"Wish I could, but I'll be on my way back to London."

"Quite the challenge, choosing something interesting without scary scenes. You wouldn't think it, but we have to carefully vet the animated ones as well."

"Consider a screwball comedy from cinema's golden age. Fun and lively. Visually appealing, although they're mostly black and white. And you could check out the technicolor musicals from the Fifties or Sixties."

"Thanks for the tip. If our crowd enjoy themselves, we'll do it again when Summer Bank Holiday comes round in August." With a wink, Norman added, "You could bring along that fine-looking lass whose picture's in your mobile."

"I just might," he replied.

The wardrobe in Dan's bedroom contained items more appropriate for rural activities, but he did locate a white dress shirt, dark coat, and a pair of quality trousers. When he went downstairs, he discovered his parent wearing a casual cashmere jumper and corduroys.

"It's a country hotel," his parent said defensively, "not the Savoy. The jacket and necktie are surplus to requirements."

"Not for a castle. Besides, this is my sort-of first official date with Ellie. You're our chaperone."

The instant he pressed the Jaguar's start button, it woke with a purr. He reversed and eased into the roadway.

"When you rang this morning and said your travel companion is a former dancer, my interest was piqued enough to investigate. I discovered that Ellie Lowery rose rather quickly through the ranks of a major New York company and performed with Ballet Bruxelles. All well and good. But for reasons beyond my comprehension, she chose to become Stella Nue. A stripper."

"Burlesque artist."

"I understand French. *Nue* means naked."

"A misnomer," Dan replied. "She didn't take everything off." Only once, just on top, in her final performance at the Archway.

"Very little was left to the imagination in images that popped up on my computer screen. You're surely aware that the strict discipline performers apply to their art doesn't often carry over into personal relationships. They lead erratic lives."

"You're very much mistaken if you believe Ellie is incapable of commitment. She was married."

"Was?" The implication was clear.

Dan unclenched his teeth. "She's not divorced. Her husband was killed when a drunk driver struck his car."

In an altered tone, his father said, "How very sad."

"Yes." Dan, knowing hardly anything about Harry Colman, wondered whether Ellie would ever choose to reveal more.

"Unless they are extraordinarily gifted, ballet dancers don't receive much in the way of salary. Removing her clothes in public venues and private clubs apparently provided her with a substantial income."

"She didn't switch professions to make money. Her father made a fortune in the restaurant business. She inherited her husband's trust funds and other assets. Her worldwide tours always sold out, and she earns a great deal from product licensing."

"Where did you meet her?"

"At the Ritz's Rivoli Bar. Six, seven weeks ago. Lou and

Kelly and I went there after seeing her show at the Archway Cabaret in Mayfair. When the curtain closed on her final performance, she ceased to be Stella Nue. She takes classes at a drama academy. You should ask her about it."

During the journey from Tayer Court to the castle, Dan's anticipation of a pleasurable evening dissipated. The marginally gracious welcome his father had extended towards Ellie had annoyed him. The prejudice he'd just expressed was infuriating.

He made a left turn at Castle Street. As he proceeded towards the hotel, he passed the stone church. It was distinctive for the finials and intricate tracery adorning its square and extraordinarily tall steeple, which appeared to scrape the dimming sky. Numerous family members, known and unknown, lay in the churchyard over the boundary wall. Oliver's headstone was there, sited close to the more recent ones marking the resting places of their Wheeler grandparents. Distant ancestors were interred inside the church, under the floor. The more prominent or wealthier ones had been commemorated by brass or stone-carved memorials.

The Tudor-era castle was indelibly associated with Henry VIII, who had ordered its noble owner's execution, and later stayed here with Queen Anne Boleyn during their royal progress through the West Country. The building was topped with ornate brick chimneys and its towers, stout or narrow, were adorned with crenellations.

Drinks first, he decided, as he and his father strolled through the courtyard to the entrance. That'll loosen him up.

Ellie was chatting with the young woman at the reception desk. A silk scarf held back her auburn hair, exposing the small hoop earrings that she frequently wore, and a rectangular onyx pendant hung from the gold chain around her neck. The flowing paisley blouse over her simple black dress was left unbuttoned. Dan appreciated her understated glamor and hoped his father did as well.

During his younger years, he'd occasionally experienced an infatuation. He could tell the difference between that and the overwhelming, all-consuming emotion Ellie stirred in him. It began as a superficial response to her outward attributes—beauty, desirability. But it had progressed from growing awareness of her intelligence and perceptiveness and tenacity. He appreciated her sense of humor. And, as he'd discovered beneath the stars, she was an exceptional kisser.

She greeted his father before asking him, "How was your visit with your brother?"

"Brief. Is your room satisfactory?"

"Positively regal. A tower suite, named for a Queen of England. It was vacated by a couple who had their wedding here yesterday. The ceiling paint is twenty-four carat gold. The furniture has blue velvet upholstery. Stone walls. Two fireplaces. The bathroom overlooks a big church."

"Our family has attended services at St. Mary's for several centuries," his father told her.

"The bed is the largest fourposter in any British hotel. It has a canopy and curtains."

This information conjured an intriguing scenario that Dan struggled to suppress. "We've half an hour before the time of our booking. Shall we order a round of drinks?"

He held Ellie's hand on their way to the vast lounge stuffed with reproduction period furniture covered in tapestry or tartan. Wood paneling ran halfway up the walls, and intricate white plasterwork extended to the ceiling. Beyond the fireplace was a secluded seating area, overlooked by a painting of Henry the VIII with a favorite wife, surrounded by his children and retinue. A waiter speedily arrived to take their orders. To fill the silence, Dan embarked on an uninspired summary of the castle's history. His store of facts ran out by the time they received their libations.

Seeking a way to erase his parent's biases, he said, "Ellie takes daily class at British Ballet Theatre."

Dad looked up from contemplation of his gin and tonic. "How did you arrange that?"

She replied, "Rafe Lawrence, their artistic director, was the *danseur* who partnered me most often, in New York and Brussels and elsewhere in Europe. Dan says you're a ballet patron."

"My mother's influence. In her youth, she trained at a school in Bristol, inspired by ballerina Alicia Markova. When I was a lad, we regularly took the train to London to attend performances."

"You saw Markova dance?"

For the first time, Dad produced a genuine smile. "I'm not quite that old. But I did sometimes encounter her after she retired. Mother served with Dame Alicia on a ballet academy board, and occasionally I escorted her to graduation performances and galas."

"My mom danced professionally before becoming a teacher. There wouldn't have been a Margot Fonteyn, she told me, without Alicia Markova. Before my performances, she always quoted Markova's comment about her relationship with the audience. 'I don't reach out to them. I draw them in to me.' At the time, I felt her attitude was insensitive. Ungrateful."

"How do you mean?"

"She didn't seem to value the people—like your mother—who adored her. But after I was promoted to soloist and could better connect with the audience, I recognized the truth of her words. Ballet lovers want to be enthralled and awed. Drawn in, as she said. Not merely by talent, but by charisma. People attend burlesque shows for the same reason."

Her eloquence had charmed Dan, until she jarred him with a statement certain to revive his father's disdain. He quickly suggested that they move to the dining room. Tudor roses were woven into the octagon blood-red carpet, and images of Henry the VIII and lesser personages gazed down from the walls. He followed Dad's example and ordered the three-course offering. After intense study of the á la carte selections, Ellie requested crab ravioli. After hearing a description of the *gariguette,* a molded dessert of strawberries in various forms, she decided to try it.

Resuming their discussion of dance, Dad asked her, "By what method were you trained? I've heard that during the Cold War, the Russian style lost its popularity in your country."

"My mother and aunt are from Montreal, and the Cecchetti method is dominant in Canada. Because Birchmont Academy's most proficient pupils typically move on to a Royal Academy affiliate in Boston, they are prepared for that curriculum and exam process. At Ballet Bruxelles, I encountered a mix. Some of my colleagues had studied at St. Petersburg's Vaganova Academy. Or in London. Mireille Charpentier began at the Paris Opéra. But as a *répétiteur* and coach at City International, she absorbed an American flavor."

Ellie turned her head towards Dan. "Poor you, sitting through all this ballet chatter."

"He's accustomed," his dad acknowledged.

Encouraged by their apparent bonding over his dad's favorite subject, Dan relaxed enough to enjoy his wine and his meal. It was presented with flair, artistically arranged on bespoke dishes rimmed in green and gold and stamped with coronets. Ellie insisted on sharing her strawberry dessert.

After they left the resturant, she accompanied them as far as the inner courtyard. Pendant lamps illuminated the doorways, the fountain's cascading waters glowed, and bollards topped with bright bulbs were positioned along the intersecting pathways.

Dan offered his fob to his father and hooked his arm through Ellie's. "I'll be a moment. Don't leave without me."

But if you did, he thought, I wouldn't mind.

Since hearing Ellie's description of her giant fourposter

bed, he'd imagined spending the night there with her. Pulling her close, he said, "I can drive Dad home and come back. If you like."

"I would. He wouldn't." Her hand dipped into the pocket of her dress. "Here," she said, handing over an old-fashioned metal key. "I'll get another from reception. Message me in the morning when you're ready to leave Tayer Court. You can find me by following signs for the queen's tower suite. It's at the top of a spiral staircase."

His finger traced her jawline. "You're inviting me to breakfast?"

"No room service before noon. I had something else in mind."

"Oh." He kissed her. "It's all right if I return rather early?"

She sighed against his chest. "Extremely all right."

Chapter 18

Ellie's cellphone ringtone, the *Swan Lake* theme, dragged her towards consciousness. "Good morning," she greeted Dan drowsily.

"I woke you."

"I don't mind. Where are you?"

"Tayer Court. I had to make sure you didn't change your mind. Do you still want me to climb the spiral stairs?"

She eased her legs over the edge of the bed. "Yes."

"I've had breakfast but I need to pack up and say goodbye to Dad. He's already outside, somewhere in the gardens."

Ellie hurried to the bathroom and stripped off her silk top and shorts. She tentatively twisted the shower faucets and checked the temperature before stepping inside. If only, she thought, hot water could melt her concerns about Sir Terence Wheeler. She detected in him the same detachment she'd noticed in early encounters with Henry and Lana Colman, her in-laws.

She yanked a warm towel off the heated bar to dry herself and wrapped another around her head. Moving cautiously across the smooth tiles, she removed the complimentary bathrobe from its hook beside the wardrobe and put it on. Additional garments would be superfluous.

Except for the portions of her anatomy covered by sequined pasties and a G-string, she'd exposed her entire body to Dan at the Archway Cabaret. But he'd been seated at a distance, and the spotlight had washed out any and all flaws. She directed a self-conscious glance at her bare feet, studying the rough calluses that had sprouted on pressure points and the prominent veins pushing through the taut skin.

It occurred to her that Dan might be just as anxious about undressing and showing her all that was beneath his clothing.

He knows I've spent my working life with male dancers. Men who have ideally proportioned physiques, lean and muscled and buffed and toned. Gym rats, all of them, constantly working out in order to maintain the strength and stamina required by their profession.

Don't you dare compare me to them, Harry used to say, before heading to the pricey health club where he worked out twice a week.

To appease his actor's vanity, she always replied, *I never compare them to you.*

She located a hairdryer on a shelf inside the wooden wardrobe and turned on the highest setting before aiming it at her head. Trawling through her cosmetic bag, she took out her compact and applied a dusting of face powder to cover her post-shower flush.

I was way more chill, she remembered, *before Harry and I had sex the first time.*

To quiet the rumbling of her stomach, she ate a portion of the pear she'd brought from Tayer Court yesterday and a whole energy bar. Surging adrenaline wasn't stimulating enough, so for reinforcement she brewed a quick espresso in the machine. Then she brushed her teeth. Twice. And popped a breath mint into her mouth.

What made me think I'm ready for this, she wondered.

Thinking. That's the problem.

Don't think.

Calf stretches required no concentration, only the ability to move and to count. Holding onto the desk chair, she rose on the ball of her foot and lowered her heel into the pale, patterned carpet. When she completed thirty stretches on each leg, she performed *pliés,* aware of her uncovered crotch and the absence of leotard or tights.

When she heard a heavy tread on stone steps, she felt her heartbeat accelerate. Before Dan could knock, she opened the door.

"It's a long journey to reach the lady at the top of the tower. And what appears to be the world's largest bed. You've no idea how much I wanted to stay with you last night. I hope you understand why I didn't."

"Your father. He doesn't approve of me." She sank onto the blue velvet bench at the end of the bed, and her hands fluttered as she searched for words. "He's a Sir. You graduated from a famous Oxford university and work at an important company in London. Your boss is a lord. I'm an American from a working-class family. No high school or college diploma, just some ballet school certificates and competition prizes. I've spent my life in show business. From his perspective, I'm a package filled with complications."

"Whatever they are, none of them matter to me."

Not yet, she thought. "He probably hopes I'm a passing fancy."

"If so, we'll convince him that you aren't. Here's proof." He placed a piece of paper on the desktop. "The code for the lock of my flat's outer door." Setting a key on top of it, he said, "This opens the inner door. Thanks to Martin, I've got yours, though I'd never let myself in without permission. If you don't feel ready for this step, you can say so."

Moved by his action, and his concern for her feelings, she said, "I worried I might be rushing you."

He knelt in front of her, slipping his hands inside the robe. "Have you ever received, altogether unexpectedly, something you wanted but hadn't begun looking for?"

"Yes. This." She released a hum of pleasure as his fingers moved across her back. When she rose, he caressed her bottom, her thighs. Her legs, strengthened by years of ballet training, felt insubstantial. A surge of desire rendered her powerless, but not for long. Her hands, she discovered, responded to her will. They moved swiftly along the front of his shirt, unfastening each button. Pressing her face against his bare chest, her cheek grazed soft hairs.

Taking a sealed condom from his trouser pocked, he placed it in her hand.

They shed the rest of their clothes and pulled back the duvet. He eased her onto the smooth sheets. Before their bare bodies merged, her lips met his. Together they created a tempo that built up to a crescendo, and drew from her a cry of rapture and release.

The highly efficient Hannah wasted no time connecting Ellie with a recommended talent agent, which led to an interview in a Soho office. Deciding they were compatible and equally frank about stating their expectations, she and Cait Murray met a second time at a French brasserie near the Piccadilly Circus underground station.

"I won't let you participate in a table read until you've signed a contract." For emphasis, Cait parked her coffee cup in its saucer with a clatter of porcelain. "You're a professional. The Sovereign Theatre Group must compensate you appropriately. Regardless of how many years you've known the playwright, you don't owe him any favors."

"I haven't even seen his script," Ellie told her.

"I know someone who has." Cait swept the curtain of inky black hair behind one ear. "Another client of mine, a major star, was approached about the husband role. For reasons I don't understand, he's keen to do this play. Because I'm negotiating his deal, I can ensure that you receive equal pay. And billing." After a glance at her phone, she said, "My assistant. We've received the release letter I requested from your New York managers, designating me as your representative for stage work over here. Your aunt provided electronic copies of pay slips from the Archway Cabaret for the dates you performed—those earnings fulfill the requirements for union membership. We can submit that application on your behalf and will be in touch when it's ready for a signature."

Ellie commented, "I've never known my business affairs to be taken care of with such dizzying speed."

"I respond quickly," Cait replied, "when an internationally famous burlesque star hands me a casting offer for the debut play by Sir Francis Cooke's son." She stared through the lenses of her black-rimmed glasses. "Am I responsible for your ballet contracts?"

"There won't be any. Attending company class is the extent of my involvement with BBT. A lifelong habit, not a career plan."

"You must have been quite good, though, to dance in New York and Brussels and Berlin and Monte Carlo."

"Lack of talent was never a problem," she acknowledged.

"What, then?"

She hesitated. "My chest. I refused to take drastic measures—reduction surgery—to conform. European companies don't have such strict physical requirements. It's sort of funny that in ballet, I had too much bust. As a burlesque performer, I sometimes wished for more."

"Don't we all. I believe we've covered everything, for the time being. Oh—one more thing. Do not invite me to your little drama academy play."

Ellie laughed. "No way. It would unnerve me. And my classmates."

The following evening when Dan joined her for supper, she recounted portions of this conversation, leaving out references to her bodily proportions. She did give him an opportunity to demonstrate his appreciation of them.

After he was gone, she texted her mother an invitation to an overdue video chat.

"How long do we have?" she asked when the oval face framed by wavy, silver-streaked brown hair popped onto her screen.

"Almost none. Your Daddo is making a quick supper because I have to be back at the studio in half an hour. We're rehearsing spring recital and reached the point when Renée predicts it will never come together. In private, that is. Only to me. Not when the students and dance moms can hear. We have a couple of dance dads, too. And more boys than usual."

"I wonder why."

Mom's shoulders rose and sank in her Québécois shrug. "Who knows? According to some of our teachers, lockdown practice videos by male ballet dancers generated curiosity or interest. If they stay, we'll need a good partnering instructor. I did ask George and Zack, but they declined—too busy with their inn."

"How many of the senior pupils are doing summer intensives?"

"All the ones who applied. Some received scholarships for places in Boston or New York. That's the extent of my news." After a pause, her mother said, "Isn't it time you told me about the man who helped you get your apartment? Camille says he looks like a movie star. Which one?"

"Basically, any who matches your preferred version of tall, dark, and handsome."

"Are you serious about him?"

"Getting there," she answered. "We spent the holiday weekend in the country, with friends. And I met his father."

"I wondered if you and Rafe might . . . "

"Never. Anyway, we're not spending quality time together. He's too busy proving himself to be the best artistic director in the ballet universe."

"When you do see him, ask if any of his *répétiteurs* can come to Birchmont next summer. Renée and I want to launch an intensive here. Less costly for participants than what major dance companies offer, but an equally high level of instruction."

"If you want Semerova, I doubt you can get her."

"We don't need Anya. We're looking for the right man to train and inspire our boys, and who won't terrify our girls. It's no problem finding a ballerina, especially if she's on the cusp of retirement, or recently unemployed. We can draw on our contacts in Montreal or Boston. Before I go, tell me about your drama school."

"My group is deciding which one-act to perform for the showcase. I had lunch with my new agent today. She'll negotiate for me if I agree to do Gil Cooke's play. Tomorrow, I'm taking Dan to the first night of *Onegin*. I told you about coaching Leah Sternberg."

"It's you who should be Tatiana Larina, *ma chérie*. Dancing *is* acting, And reacting. Why not put off becoming an actress? Mireille wanted you to rejoin her company. I know Rafe would hire you."

Ellie expected to hear this refrain at some point in every conversation. Her mom and her aunt had refined her natural talent and developed her technique, preparing her for a career in which standards for performance and appearance were rigorously applied. The combination of their training and her determination to succeed ensured a speedy and relatively smooth transition from student to apprentice to *coryphée* to soloist. And though they had accepted her decision to exchange pointe shoes for pasties, they hadn't surrendered hope that her departure from the ballet stage was temporary.

"There's not a company on the planet that would have me, after my years slumming in burlesque. Give Daddo my love. And Renée. Camille, too, if you see her. I'll get in touch with my sibs and arrange a family get-together for later this summer. At the lake."

When she and Dan entered the grandiose Crescent Theatre lobby the following night, she recalled her childhood visits to the ballet and the thrill of anticipation. As soon as she settled into a green velvet chair in the dress circle, her thoughts flew to the dancers. Those who appeared in the first act would have left their dressing rooms to warm up on the stage or at backstage barres in the wings. Men adjusted dance belts. Women flexed their feet, checking that pointe shoe ribbons weren't loose or constricting. Everyone awaited the welcoming applause as the conductor took his place, and the overture's opening notes.

Ellie looked forward to witnessing a fresh production of a favorite ballet but couldn't subdue her envy of Leah Sternberg. Tatiana was a cherished and meaningful role.

Dan calmly paged through the printed program he'd purchased. When he offered it to her, she said, "I'll read it later. When I'm able to concentrate." She kept her fingers curled around her handbag strap so he wouldn't see how they trembled.

The charming and lively beginning of the ballet offered no hint of the conflicts and drama that would ensue. Olga and Lensky expressed their love in a lyrical *pas de deux*.

Tatiana, introduced to the dashing and aloof Eugene Onegin, was instantly smitten. In her bedroom dream sequence, she imagined him as amorous and passionate. Drew supported Leah's exuberant arabesques, lifted her high, sweeping her across the stage. In the party scene, she effectively rendered Tatiana's response to Onegin's rejection, and the desperate attempt to avert a fatal duel.

Dancing *is* acting. The truth of Mom's reminder had never been more obvious or profound.

As the stage went dark, Dan leaned close and whispered, "You used to do all that?"

Recalling the beautiful ballroom *pas de deux,* and the passionate finale's physically demanding choreography, she answered, "And so much more."

Ellie sipped a glass of Cava and watched Dan dice artichoke hearts. He'd invited her to his flat for a Spanish dinner, and paella was the main course.

"When I moved in," he told her, "I decided the décor didn't exactly match my taste. I picked up the antique partners' desk when working in Bristol. I changed the armchairs and sofa. Dad gave me the Persian rug. Isobel Latimer, Martin's mother, painted the watercolors of Tayer Court and Latimer Row. It's safe to wander about. My cleaner was here today."

Ellie, curious about his reading tastes, studied the spines of the volumes that filled the floor-to-ceiling bookcase.

"Take whatever you want," he said.

She bypassed the novels, most of them by British authors she didn't know. Examining a book on film history, she asked, "What are we seeing tonight?"

"I found a site where we can stream *Lady of Burlesque.* My expectations of the plot aren't high, but Barbara Stanwyck is well worth watching."

She followed a short corridor, past a powder room, and peered into each of two bedrooms. The one above the streetscape had a wooden floor and just enough space for the easy chair, treadmill, and single bed. It retained the sash windows of other façades along Latimer Row. Dan's room, across the hall, was larger. Fully carpeted, it held a double bed with padded headboard, a chest, and tall wardrobe. The windows were south-facing, with Roman shades. A large building blocked a view that was probably similar to what she could see from her penthouse balcony. The one-way avenue below was lined with art galleries and offices, indicating optimal quiet during the night hours. She assumed she'd find out later.

After dinner they snuggled on the sofa to laugh and kiss during the scenes without Barbara Stanwyck. When her character, the tough and salty Dixie, ordered a champagne cocktail in a bar scene, Dan paused the video. Using her phone, Ellie found a recipe and read it out while he pulled bottles from his liquor cabinet and took a mini-bottle of bubbly from the fridge.

Pointing at the box of demerara sugar cubes, she said, "I thought only restaurants had them."

"For Dad, who stops by for tea when he's in town, though he stays at the club. Next time, you'll join us there for dinner."

"To be perfectly honest, I'd rather not be subjected to another interrogation about why I abandoned ballet for what he clearly regards as a sleazy profession."

"He can't help equating burlesque with the Soho dives where drunks manhandled the showgirls, though I doubt he visited any of them. I explained the artistic aspect. And mentioned your interviews with veteran performers that you did for your school research paper."

"What did he say?"

"That you should've written about Dame Alicia Markova instead."

She doubted Sir Terence had intended that as a joke.

They carried their champagne flutes to the sofa. Before restarting the film, Dan looked at her and said, "I'd love to keep you here till morning, but I know you've got class. Any chance of a sleepover at the weekend?"

"Saturday night. I could be all yours on Sunday as well."

"Yes, please." He pulled her against his torso. "We've exchanged keys. Might as well stash toothbrushes in our respective flats."

"Gosh, you move fast, Daniel Wheeler." She didn't mind at all.

In the afternoon, Maxi pointed out to her assembled students that they'd reached the deadline to choose their one act-play for the showcase.

"I'll be in the teachers' lounge. When you've reached consensus, send someone to get me."

Breaking the silence, Simrat suggested, "Show of hands?"

"Not before discussion," Graeme insisted.

"I don't have anything else to add." Val twisted a strand of blonde hair.

Archie straddled an armless chair. "Option one, the church where a wedding and funeral are booked on the same morning. It's farcical and fun, but there's no substance to the characters."

"Right," Tony agreed. "And even though Molière's play is translated to modern language, its setting is historic. Nobody's heard of all those dead French actors and actresses being ridiculed. Maybe not Molière either."

"What if we reimagined it?" Archie suggested. "Turn it into a royal command performance for the current monarch. We can impersonate celebrities. We could do actors and television presenters and cookery show chefs."

"And a football player," Declan added. "Identifiable by the team jersey."

Simrat smiled. "That's a genius plan."

"We could throw in references to all the places where famous people hang out," said Rose, excitedly. "The Savoy Hotel. Number Eight Hertford Street."

"The upper-class departures lounge at Heathrow." Ellie had spent many an hour there. "I think we just arrived at consensus."

Simrat turned to her. "I see you as Caroline Bryden. Similar hair. And coloring."

"Her accent is so posh. I'm not sure I'd be able to recreate it."

"It only takes a little extra work with our voice coach. If Graeme practices his smolder, he'll be a perfect Lucas Daltrey. You'll both carry your Oscar statues. Declan, who's your favorite footballer? Tony, what famous Canadian will you be?"

"One of our comedians, I suppose. Nobody in this country would recognize an ice hockey player."

Archie stuck his nose in the air. "I'm Francis Cooke. *Sir* Francis, to you."

Everyone laughed.

"I'll find Maxi," Val offered. "We're going to blow her mind."

Despite her misgivings about accurately portraying an actress in possession of an Academy Award, Ellie was in a buoyant mood during her tube journey to Piccadilly Circus. On her way to Latimer Row, she stopped in the chemist's shop to purchase a toothbrush. After discreetly concealing it in a gift bag, she went directly to Dan's office building and asked the receptionist to deliver it to Mr. Wheeler.

Chapter 19

Relying on her raincoat hood for protection, Ellie scuttled towards the Sovereign Theatre. To avoid a tide of pedestrians and umbrellas in Shaftesbury Avenue, she diverted to a side street hoping she wouldn't get confused and be late for her meeting. She came to a sudden stop when she noticed a gleaming green sign above a fast-food restaurant.

She was still beaming when she entered the lobby, where Gil Cooke waited for her.

"Are you hungry?" she asked him.

Startled by her greeting, he said, "Starting to be."

"Come with me."

"I'll fetch my brolly."

"You won't need it. The rain has almost stopped. And we aren't going far. Are you vegetarian?"

"Not currently."

As she retraced her steps, he offered a monologue on the rudeness of audience members who were incapable of switching off their mobiles during performances. When the eatery was in sight, she pointed at the sign.

"Blarney Burger has arrived in Britain."

"What's so thrilling about one more beefburger joint?"

"My father created it."

"Right. That's why Harry liked going there. Do you get free food?"

"I wish. When Daddo sold his company, he didn't include that clause in the transfer document. Londoners probably assume it's an Irish chain, not American."

She wished Dan were with her instead of Gil, because he'd understand—and probably share—her delight. Pushing the door open, she gazed raptly at the illuminated menu board behind the counter. "Wow, major product expansion. For the sake of authenticity, I recommend the regular Blarney, but suit yourself. My treat."

"Oh, very well," he said grudgingly. "Are you having chips?"

"You can. What to drink?"

He studied the menu board. "Limeade."

"Two Blarneys, please. One order of Shannon Spuds. Two Galway Gulps."

Gil followed her to a green chair with shamrock-shaped back and placed their tray on the table's green laminate surface. She detected no significant differences between this franchise and the one closest to the Manhattan apartment where she and Harry had lived.

After sampling her burger, she opined, "A reasonable facsimile of the original product." She reached for one of his chips to try it. "These potatoes were deep fried in a different sort of oil than they use at home. And they're saltier." She picked up her cup.

"How long has Cait Murray represented you?"

Speaking around the paper straw between her lips, she said, "Since last week."

He wagged his sandy head. "I told you I'd help you get an agent."

"I saved you the trouble," she said blithely. "More accurately, Hannah did."

"Hannah?"

"Ballard. The film and television producer. I stayed with her and her husband for part of the bank holiday weekend."

"The director of *Fractures in the Heart*, Joan Wadsworth, plans to cast Lucas Daltrey as Randall. Cait Murray represents him."

Her eyebrows shot up. "She gets points for discretion. When she mentioned a client of hers was under consideration, she wouldn't say who."

"Father gave him an early version of the script. They worked together on *Forsaken Fortune* and *Tender Treasure*. They became even better acquainted when appearing at film festivals and awards ceremonies."

To redirect him from the settled issue of her agent, she asked, "When do I get your script?"

"In approximately a fortnight. The final version is being printed and bound." He shoved aside his empty burger wrapper. "On Saturday evening, the British Film Institute is showing *Who's Afraid of Virginia Woolf*. Useful preparation for *Fractures*. I'll get two tickets."

That night belonged to Dan. "I'm not free," she said, striving for an apologetic tone. "But I'll be sure to see it."

"You haven't told me when your drama class will perform one-acts. I want to be there."

Inviting him to the showcase was impossible. His notoriously pompous parent was being mercilessly mimicked by Archie. And she couldn't expose him to Graeme's hilariously overblown version of the sexy, smoldering actor destined to be Ellie's co-star—whose actress wife she portrayed.

"It's not a large auditorium, and three classes will be presenting plays," she replied before taking another bite of her burger.

The most gratifying proof of acceptance at BBT was being assigned a locker in the women's changing room. She used it to store street clothes, an extra water bottle, and her least presentable leg warmers. Arriving early on Thursday morning, due to speedy connections on the underground system, she added a pair of pointe shoes that weren't quite dead. After changing into leotard and tights, she made her way to the studio.

The bearded and ponytailed pianist was seated at the shining black baby grand. "Rafe says you danced with him."

"Whenever a better partner wasn't available."

Barry returned her grin. "Same sense of humor. No wonder you two get on so well."

"We have a long, shared history of tears and laughs. And venting."

"Favorite role?"

"Tatiana was the most demanding, technically and dramatically. The best kind of challenge. And I usually had Rafe as my Onegin. Swanilda in *Coppelia* is fun, she's such a genuine girl, and wonderfully feisty. As I recently told someone, flying through the air to Chopin's D major mazurka, in *Les Sylphides,* was the pinnacle of happiness. That's not to say I didn't enjoy my *Swan Lake* parts—the Act One *pas de trois* and the Polish princess. I was Drosselmeyer's mechanical doll at the Christmas party in *The Nutcracker,* and the shepherdess in the Land of the Sweets. In *Sleeping Beauty,* I've been a fairy at Aurora's christening and White Cat at her wedding."

"Bold and bouncy characters."

"That's right," she said airily. "I've always been a showgirl, even before my career in burlesque."

Company members ambled into the studio on turned-out

penguin feet. Anya arrived, sporting her usual black tunic and loose, wide-legged trousers. People removed earbuds and placed phones, foot rollers, stretch bands, and massage balls in dance bags.

At Rafe's entrance, everyone at the barre perked up. He greeted Anya and clapped Barry's shoulder before turning a chair backwards and sitting down.

Gemma, hastily inserting her feet into her split-sole slippers, muttered, "What's he doing here?"

"No idea," Ellie replied as she tied a sheer blue chiffon wrap skirt over her tights. "He either finished his paperwork or ran out of millionaires to solicit for donations." She unfurled her striped leg warmers and sheathed each of her lower limbs to the thigh. Readjusting a hairpin, she asked, "What are you rehearsing today?"

"*Coppelia.* One more time in Studio A before moving onto the theatre stage."

"We begin now," Anya called. "Please be ready."

Ellie faced the mirror, placing her fingers on the wooden rail, and pulled in a long, deep breath to center herself. They began with head rolls and *port de bras,* feet in first position followed by second position, and the addition of *tendu à la arrière.* Ellie's hands, in unison with those of her fellow dancers, darted back and forth and sideways as Anya sketched instructions for a combination involving *petits battements.*

Barry began with a slowed down version of the Chopin piece she'd referenced earlier. Fighting her impulse to smile at him, she copied the other dancers' intent and focused expressions. Before beginning center work, people reached for their water bottles and discarded outer layers of clothing. Ellie took up her usual position in the back row of the second group and watched Rafe watching everyone else. During *petit allegro,* one of his heels tapped the studio floor, keeping time. He must long to join the dancers leaping diagonally across the springy floor. She wished he could show them his buoyant *pas de chat* and astonishing *entrechat huit.*

When the last group finished *grand allegro* and the music stopped, Rafe clapped—for the dancers first, then for Anya and Barry. "Thank you, everyone. Excellent energy. I hope it carries you through your busy day and evening. Marcus wants his *Coppelia* villagers in Studio A half an hour from now. Don't be late."

Ellie hadn't reached the door when he beckoned. She recognized his mimed gesture as the same one he'd used as Prince Siegfried in *Swan Lake.*

"Let's talk."

"When?"

"Right now. If convenient."

"I've got an hour to kill." She needn't reveal her appointment at a Harley Street women's clinic for a consultation about birth control.

She went with him, keeping her gaze fixed between his shoulder blades so she wouldn't see how the rest of the group reacted to her being singled out by the boss. Instead of taking her to the elevator, he led her to a narrow hallway and a room with empty bookcases and many cardboard boxes.

She wrinkled her nose. "Smells like the painters just left."

"Welcome to our future library and reading room. The cartons contain our collection of memoirs written by dancers, or ghostwritten for them, and biographies. Bound music scores. A ballet notation archive, mostly Benesh with Labanotation mixed in. My entire staff is busy planning the summer tour and making decisions about the upcoming season. I can't spare anybody to sort the contents and organize them by subject. You're a booklover. Here's a task I hope you're willing to take on."

"Does every item have to be catalogued?"

"No. I envision a simple sign-out system. After the materials are shelved, we'll bring in a sofa and some chairs and tables and reading lamps."

"It can be an extra stop on your public tours." She set down her dance bag.

"I'm not asking you to start now. Wait till the paint fumes dissipate."

"I can't resist digging into a box or two. I might find something interesting to take home."

"Help yourself." Pausing in the doorway, he turned to say, "Let me know if you turn up anything of value. Sergeyev's handwritten notes on the Petipa ballets. Or a long-lost libretto."

She lifted the unsealed flaps of an unlabeled box. It contained several long-forgotten but familiar titles. Like most young dancers, she'd devoured ballerina biographies for inspiration, undeterred by tales of struggle and setbacks. Over time her interest had extended to the history and development of the art. She picked up a volume to study the color photograph of an elegant, middle-aged woman. Opening it, she studied the curling handwritten signature, underlined, beneath the author's name on the title page. After she examined images of a dark-haired juvenile dancer in various costumes, and countless representations of an acclaimed and iconic Giselle, she closed the book and picked up her bag.

The elevator carried her to the administrative office on an upper floor.

Rafe stood at his assistant's desk, reviewing documents being passed to him. "Giving up so soon?"

"I did discover a treasure in your trove." She held up *Markova Remembers*. "Autographed. May I have it, please? I promise to get a replacement copy in a secondhand shop or online, though it won't be autographed like this one. I'd like to give it to Sir Terence Wheeler."

"You know him?"

"We met in Gloucestershire." She'd had no opportunity to inform him about her romance with Dan. "His son arranged my rental apartment in Mayfair."

"Wheeler is on our donor list, and we have hopes of persuading him to join our board. Kindly inform him that Dame Alicia's memoir comes to him with compliments from me and BBT."

"I will."

With his trademark wink, Rafe added, "This seems like an optimal moment for another proposition. Alison, hold my calls."

Ellie followed him into his office. While he pawed through a file cabinet, she looked at the wall posters advertising the company's past performances, before and since he became its artistic director.

"Here it is." He pulled out a single sheet of paper. "The elements of our standard employment contract. At the end of this season, one of our female soloists leaves us for Staatsballett in Berlin. Another, whose husband accepted a job in Edinburgh, will transfer to Scottish National. I've got two openings. I'm hoping you'll agree to fill one."

Chapter 20

She stared at the document on his desk, clause after clause of type that had organized her past life. "Anya would object."

"It was her suggestion. 'Let Eeley Lorry join company.' You have a musicality that can't be taught, she says. I concur."

"She won't want me when she finds out I was Stella Nue."

"She's known all along. I told her after your first morning in class. She doesn't care."

"Your board of directors might."

"The hiring of artistic personnel is outside their purview. They only participate when we interview candidates for the executive staff."

"I spent barely a year in the corps," she reminded him. "My ensemble work is limited to small groupings. *Dances at a Gathering,* or the foreign princesses' *pas de six* in *Swan Lake.*"

"I told you, love, I need soloists. Mireille sometimes cast

you in principal roles, and I'm willing to do the same when I can. You've seen the next season's schedule. *Sylvia.* Our Autumn Gala, to be performed at—wait for it—the Royal Albert Hall. The premiere of my *Virtuosi,* staged partly in the round. Paired with *Les Sylphides.*" He paused to let this sink in, his face impassive as he watched for her reaction.

Rafe, her longtime supporter and occasional savior, had morphed into her torturer. Turning down *Sylphides* was excruciating.

"Wouldn't you like to dance for royalty?"

"I did." She forced a smile. "According to rumor, a certain princely duke came incognito to one of my London burlesque gigs. The tabloids never found out."

"I can guess who it was." Placing his forefinger on the contract, he went on, "Naturally we'll have weeks and weeks of *Nutcracker,* with multiple casts and understudies. *Cinderella.* At least two commissioned works, one of which goes to Prague next summer. A European tour—probably *Giselle.* Oh, when I have a spare hour or two, I study the original notation for *Le Papillion.* I want to create a restored version—before it occurs to Ratmansky to give it a go." He folded his hands and rested them on the desk. "I've known hundreds of dancers, but none like you. You're my unicorn. A rare combination of varied experience and untapped potential."

"I've been on hiatus way too long," she pointed out. "Professionals don't come back after they go away."

"They most certainly do. We grant time off to our people if they want to dance in West End musicals."

"Months, maybe. Not years."

"If you're working this hard to dig up excuses, you must be tempted," he said, with disconcerting accuracy. "Here's an incentive. Join my merry band and the doomed affair we've put off will never, ever take place. Relationships between management and talent are prohibited." His tone was no longer jocular when he continued, "Human emotion and physical attraction aren't easily controlled, of course. That's why we encourage transparency and communication. Last year a situation arose that necessitated placing one individual in a comparable position elsewhere. Whatever our dancers get up to amongst themselves is their private business. Unless it has a toxic effect on them or their colleagues."

She'd observed the many ways he'd upended the harsh systems of control and repression and uneven power dynamics that had driven them from City International. Creating a healthy ballet company was no easy feat, and he'd achieved it.

He picked up the document. "Agreements must be finalized in the next fortnight. I need your answer soon."

"Your faith in me means more than I can express, and I'm deeply grateful. But I can't dance for you. It's impossible."

"You pride yourself on embracing challenges. I'm presenting you with a major one. Think it over. Talk to Anya. Marcus. Me."

"I'm going to sign a different contract, very soon. My theatrical agent has completed negotiations with the Sovereign Theatre Group. At the start of your next season, I'll be performing a major role in a new play."

His eyes narrowed, deepening the creases at the corners. "What is it?"

"*Fractures in the Heart.* Written by Gilbert Cooke, son of Sir Francis. He describes it as the present-day version of *Who's Afraid of Virginia Woolf.* Two characters, Lyla and Randall, a young married couple. Me and Lucas Daltrey."

"An Academy Award winner. That's huge." He placed his elbows on the desk and pressed his palms together. "I'm gutted. And sincerely chuffed for you. If we'd had this conversation sooner, and you were available, would you have accepted my offer?"

She owed him the truth. "Maybe. I can't say. I really do hate letting you down. Especially since you don't have a company school to draft from."

"We'll manage. A couple of girls in the corps are primed for promotion. The apprentice dancers can audition for those places." He pulled a folder towards him and opened it. "We've updated the job prospectus for our development team members. Please consider joining us in that capacity. As a dancer who is also a donor, you understand and can articulate our mission and our needs. Declining government subsidies for the arts forces us to vigorously cultivate additional corporate sponsors and celebrity patrons. In addition to titans of industry, we've got a popular royal duchess and a handful of high-profile retired dancers."

"I'm willing. Provided I can serve as a volunteer, without compensation. As my schedule allows."

"Agreed." He added, "It better not be necessary to point out that my motive for bringing you into the BBT fold isn't wholly mercenary. We're forever partners, Ellie."

"I adore you, Rafe. Always have. Except those times you dropped me."

"In rehearsal, love. Never during a performance."

"That bungled fish dive was the worst. I warned you my leg was cramping."

"Gravity is a powerful force. Next thing I knew, you were lying on the marley in a heap of white tulle. Uninjured," he added emphatically.

She exited the building, moving slowly through the courtyard separating the annex from the Crescent Theatre. She felt dazed and off-balance, as though the red double-decker bus rolling past had careened into her.

How *would* I have answered Rafe, she asked herself, if I hadn't committed to doing Gil's play?

When she'd arrived that morning, she'd been content with her partly in, partly out status. Unlike the dancers in class, she didn't pulse with energy and ambition. She'd liberated herself from the demands of coaches and *répétiteurs* and directors. She was no longer defined by critics, whose expectations of a dancer were rigid and specific. The equally strong biases of ballet fans didn't affect her. She wasn't relentlessly counting down the years towards retirement, aware that a valley of physical disintegration waited beyond the heights of achievement.

She relished London living and her Latimer House apartment. She had Gemma for her barre buddy. At drama school she'd acquired seven friends—eight, counting Maxi. She looked forward to performing her comic role in the one-act. She mentored Lisa, the Archway Cabaret stage kitten. In a few months, she'd appear in a debut drama in the West End.

Far more important, she had Dan. Someone to cherish, to laugh with, to love, whose companionship was essential to her wellbeing. Who provided her with an exhilarating and fulfilling sex life after a lengthy period of celibacy.

Taking advantage of BBT's proximity to Regent's Park, she crossed busy Marylebone Road, and followed the walkway to the Jubilee Gate, marking the Inner Circle that enclosed Queen Mary's Garden. The roses adorning arbors and rope swags, and rising up trellises, were profusely in bloom. Many of them looked similar to the varieties Sir Terence Wheeler grew at Tayer Court. With her phone she took dozens of photographs to show Dan, thinking he could identify them, and posed a few selfies with a background of blossoms.

Aimlessly strolling down a paved path, she paused to listen to raised voices, stopping, starting, singing. Glancing at the nearest signpost, she saw that it pointed towards the Open Air Theatre. The rehearsal in process was a timely reminder of the decision made years ago, when she'd ceased to be a professional ballet dancer. She was an actress now, and learning to be a better one.

Because Dan had to attend a business dinner, she spent

the evening by herself, searching the internet for advice on how best to remove the pervasive old book smell from Dame Alicia's memoir. The next day was bright and dry, so she left it on the balcony. At a supermarket, she purchased a box of baking soda, sealing it and the book in an airtight container for the rest of the week. She repeated the same process with kitty litter. And she inserted dryer sheets among the pages to absorb any lingering odor that an average or a particularly sensitive nose might detect.

Because Ellie's daily routine restricted her to Mayfair and Marylebone, the greater part of London was unknown territory. She was therefore pleased to visit unfamiliar South Kensington, where a variety of major and minor museums were located, to meet the curator preparing an exhibition on burlesque. In a vast space filled with garment rails, she was reunited with the multi-layered gown she'd worn—and removed—when portraying *Swan of the Lake*. She shared information about its inspiration and creation. She also recorded a brief descriptive track for the audio guide.

Afterwards, on the terrace, she claimed an unoccupied bench facing the central pond. Opening the phone app she used for video calls, she clicked Aunt Camille's icon.

"The curatorial staff will send you a shortlist of other items they want," Ellie announced. "Colorful ones. *Fiery Bird,* the red number with the floor length feather tail. *Victorian Vixen.* And *Ondine.*"

Camille's lips moved. After a brief delay, the question came through. "I wish we'd known before shipping them over here."

"I know. The curator will be in touch to work out details. He asked me to be the special guest for the press preview and opening reception, assuming I'd appear as Stella Nue. I told him that was a non-starter, and he agreed to introduce me as Ellie. How are my guys?"

"I saw Zack when he was in Concord picking up fabric to make tablecloths. They're having a blast hosting their B&B guests and managing events. This weekend there's a wedding by the lakeshore and a reception in the barn. A nationally known politician's daughter. Lots of bigwigs to impress."

"They will. I have to tell you about my latest vintage purchase, a real rarity. A 1950s Pierre Balmain cocktail dress, cream satin with sequin embellishment. A perfect fit, though I can't imagine where I'd wear it. And get this—it's called 'Taglioni,' after the famous ballerina. A museum in Paris has one just like it."

"Send me a picture. Maybe our designer can draft a modified pattern to include in our evening wear line. That reminds me, the first batch of Stella Boutique sample dresses will be delivered before you get here. Last week I toured potential retail spaces in Boston—Newbury Street and Boylston."

Pleased by this report, Ellie said, "Back Bay sounds good. Square footage?"

"That will depend on how much we're prepared to pay. I've gathered quotes, and the accountant is working the numbers."

"Thanks for everything."

Camille laughed. "It's a joint business venture, there's a quid pro quo. I'm thinking I might convert Camille's Closet in Concord to a Stella Boutique."

"I approve. Let's discuss it when I'm there."

On Saturday morning, before leaving her bed, she heard the torrent lashing the windowpanes. Opening the curtains in the sitting room, she peered at the gloom obscuring her view of the street below. Pedestrians darted along the pavement, huddled beneath their umbrellas.

From Latimer House she speed-walked to the underground station, eager to escape the chilly air that was a dancer's great enemy. She boarded a carriage filled with damp passengers wearing glum expressions and sidled down the aisle to an empty seat. Hefting her dance bag to her lap, she looked up at the tube map banner. Those intersecting colored lines represented the many routes she hadn't yet taken. Later in the day, she'd experience some of them.

In the women's changing room, everyone groused about the weather. Ellie was glad of her long-sleeved leotard and pink cardigan, and she wore sweatpants and leg warmers over her tights. As she and Gemma joined the others drifting in the direction of the studio, her thoughts returned to her conversation with Rafe.

These people she labored with each morning had the privilege of performing a broad repertoire of ballets, here in London and elsewhere in the world. During hiatus, they accepted invitations to appear with prestigious companies as guest artists. They could access the fully equipped gym in the physio suite and relied on the therapists and massage practitioners. The company dietitian and the mental health officer provided guidance and support as required. Each woman had an assigned cubbyhole in the shoe room, containing her preferred brand and style of pointe shoes, fashioned to her exact foot measurements.

Regret, Ellie reminded herself, was a destructive emotion.

She didn't need the income or the benefits provided by a company contract. She could afford to purchase shoes and pay her masseuse. As a burlesque artist, she'd repeatedly circled the globe, performing for international audiences. Even though her name would never appear on Rafe's cast lists, she was firmly embedded in this community. She'd organized the reading room. She attended strategy sessions with development office personnel. If asked to assist with coaching, she would.

Barry ambled into the room and sat on the padded bench at the grand piano.

If he plays a piece from *Les Sylphides,* she thought, I'm going to cry.

He didn't. During barre exercises, he produced honky-tonk tunes. For the demonic combinations ballet master Marcus had devised, he provided a mash-up of peppy classical themes and numbers from popular stage musicals.

Her lunch date with the Archway Cabaret stage kitten would cheer her up. Nobody could be depressed around bubbly Lisa. And, Dan had pointed out, her journey would take her to a very different part of London than the gentrified one in which they resided.

The Central Line train carried her past unfamiliar stations like Notting Hill and Shepherd's Bush. While traveling above ground, she viewed the urban landscape framed by a dingy, rain-spattered carriage window. At North Acton she hopped off and followed directions to the hamburger joint where Lisa worked the afternoon shift. On entering, the smell of grilled meat carried her back to her waitressing days at The Shamrock.

"Gosh, it's grand seeing you," Lisa greeted her. "But you def don't look like Stella Nue. Different hair. No makeup or fake lashes. What'll you have to eat?"

"Just a coffee. I had a green smoothie for what you'd call elevenses."

Lisa lowered her voice. "They pour a proper brew at the caff. Awful mucky, what's served here."

As they walked down the block, she peppered Ellie with questions.

"How do you manage being in two plays at the same time?"

"I'm not. Our one-act performance will be over before the table read for *Fractures in the Heart.* Those rehearsals won't begin till August, after I get back from the States."

When they were seated at a copper-topped table, she asked about her friends at the Archway.

"We're seeing lots of summer tourists, as well as the business blokes who bring their clients. A fortnight ago, I auditioned my act for the management and our promoter."

"Was it the Queen of Sheba bit you told me about on the phone?"

"That's right. She was brown like me. And I want to work on other regal characters." The crinkles around Lisa's eyes smoothed as her smile faded. "Classy ones, like yours. I noticed how still and quiet people were when they watched you, like they were under a spell. Respectful. Different to how they respond to the bump and grind acts." Cocking her head, she said, "I've been researching about Cleopatra, too. Putting together her costume would be expensive."

"You don't need top of the line crystals to sparkle. But even under the lights, cheap fabric still looks cheap. Always do your shopping in person, it's impossible to judge quality and color online. And find a skilled seamstress."

"One of the girls told me about a woman who works from a simple sketch and can purchase materials at discount. I've been saving up."

"Let me know what you need," Ellie responded. "I'll help."

"Yeah? That's awful kind. At the shoe shops I was spoilt for choice. I bought metallic sandals studded with fake gems."

"Be sure to scuff and scratch the soles. You don't want to slip when you're sashaying."

"Where did you learn so many tricks?"

"From experienced performers, who generously offered advice and encouragement. And warnings."

In that respect, there was no difference between burlesque and ballet. The technique and traditions and history of classical dance had been perpetuated through the centuries, from performer to performer, generation to generation.

Act 3

"There's always the next performance to think of."

—Alicia Markova

Chapter 21

The South Bank bistro was packed with other couples attending performances at Royal Festival Hall and the National Theatre complex, or British Film Institute screenings. Ellie, satisfied that Dame Alicia Markova's memoir was purified, asked Dan where she should send a parcel to his dad, without stating what it would contain.

"He's in Birmingham, monitoring a court case, but he's coming to town soon to spend time with Pamela. If you drop it off at the club, they'll hold it for his arrival."

"Every time I walk past, I wonder what's going on inside. The window shades are always down."

"Nothing shocking or, frankly, terribly interesting. Apart from being entitled to wear the club tie, I don't have a great deal in common with other members. They rehash social events or parliamentary debates. Discuss investments and property prices and the vagaries of the stock market. While drinking and dining." With a nod and smile for the waiter, he tapped his credit card on the payment machine and waited for it to spit out the receipt.

On their way to the cinema, they passed a poster for *Who's Afraid of Virginia Woolf?*

"When the play was revived on Broadway," Ellie said, "I was dancing Helena in *A Midsummer Night's Dream* and couldn't go." Harry went without her. "I've heard it's intense."

While the opening scene unfolded, she twined her fingers with Dan's. She seldom saw couples their age holding hands in public places, but in the dark auditorium nobody would notice. She was simultaneously fascinated and repelled by the raging dysfunction on display, as Martha and George flung insults at each other and drew Nick and Honey into the venomous symbiosis of their relationship. It was possible, she discovered, to sympathetically portray appalling and unlikeable characters.

As the closing credits rolled, Dan asked, "Did you enjoy it?"

"It was emotionally exhausting. But I saw how compelling performances can be, even when they don't depend on the actors being charming or attractive. Isn't the tube station in the opposite direction?"

"After a show, I always take a taxi home, and usually find one closer to the National Theatre." They paused at the crosswalk and waited for the pedestrian signal. "I have a very personal question to ask."

She eyed his profile. "Okay."

"What's your weight?"

"I'm not sure how to answer. At the doctor's office, the scale measured kilograms. Her nurse translated that into stone. I had to request another conversion to find out how many pounds." She recited each of the three numbers. "Why do you want to know?"

"You showed me photos of Rafe and other male dancers hoisting you incredibly high. It occurs to me that if I could pick you up from time to time, I wouldn't need to use the machines at my gym as often."

"Seriously?"

"I want to try it tonight. Your place or mine?"

"Yours. Shorter distance to the bedroom. Not so far to carry me."

"I'm not so sure about the carrying part."

"In my experience, one follows the other. You'll have to follow my instructions so you don't injure yourself."

Latimer Row was dimly lit, and the windows of the shop fronts were barred or obscured by drawn shades. Patrons departed the corner restaurant and staff were clearing and wiping down outdoor tables. Dan pressed the keypad beside the unmarked exterior door, entering the code he'd shared with Ellie. They ascended the two flights of stairs. As soon as they reached the flat, she slipped off her high heels.

Rising onto her toes, she reached up and placed an arm around his shoulder. "Now."

He swept her off her feet. "Lighter than I expected." Dipping her down, he added in a teasing tone, "Somewhat." He crossed the sitting room, angling his body so they would both fit in the narrow hallway.

On their wedding night, Harry had struggled when lugging her from the hotel elevator to their room. Tipsy from the bottle of champagne provided by the bar, they had laughed all the way down the corridor, the hem of her white tulle gown brushing the carpeted floor. Aware that a fall could severely damage an ankle or a foot, she clung to him.

Go away, Harry, she chided. Leave us alone.

Dan eased her to the carpet and stepped away. "Was it good for you?"

"Very." She swept her right foot to the side, swirled it behind and pulled it up against her left kneecap to propel herself into a facsimile of a pirouette. Letting herself lose her balance, she tumbled backwards onto the duvet. "Your much-deserved reward awaits."

Her hands moved to his belt and pulled him closer so she

could unfasten it. Desperate to meld herself to him, she hurriedly removed his shirt and trousers. He proceeded gradually, slowly unbuttoning her blouse, trailing kisses down her bare chest. She pressed her mouth to his, embracing him with her arms and legs. Their *pas de deux* began, sweeping away all thoughts of past or future. In this bed, the only stage that mattered to her, he was the perfect partner. But she wasn't giving a performance. She was entirely, intensely herself.

In the morning, her highly regulated internal clock jerked her awake. On the other side of the bathroom door, the shower was running. Propping her head both pillows, she heaved a sigh of deepest delight.

Dan strode into the bedroom, a towel wrapped around his lower body. "Are you aware that you point your toes when you're sleeping?"

"No." Gazing at him, she commented, "And did you know, for a man who isn't a dancer you have really good shoulders? A nice butt. And great knees."

"Knees?" He came over to kiss her. "Coffee will soon be ready."

She used his shampoo and her toothbrush. Instead of putting on the outfit she'd worn last night, she covered herself with Dan's bathrobe. He'd offered to make space in a dresser drawer or the wardrobe. With Latimer House so near, it wasn't necessary.

When she joined him in the kitchen, she accepted the mug of steaming brew. Her fingers pressed an avocado's dimpled flesh, testing the firmness. "I'll make my favorite breakfast, if you have whole wheat bread and a couple of eggs for frying."

While eating her version of avocado toast, they watched a Sunday morning chat show. The presenters and their guests spouted inanities that alternated between amusing and mildly offensive.

As raindrops struck the windows, Ellie said, "After a thoroughly wet week, I was hoping my one free day would be sunny. I'm starved for grass and trees and romping dogs."

"This weather is the reason wise and wealthy humans created museums," he replied. "And why London's got so many of them. We could visit the National Gallery. There's a room filled with French impressionists where you can see the ballerinas Degas painted. We can hunt for all the famous dancers on display at the National Portrait Gallery. And have lunch in the café."

"I like everything about that plan."

In the downstairs vestibule he picked up the umbrella leaning against the wall. They walked briskly in the direction of Latimer House and darted into the residents' lobby.

The weekend porter transferred his focus from his phone and pointed to the padded envelope on his deck. "For you, Miss Lowery. The gentleman who delivered it said he tried ringing before he came but got no answer."

She'd silenced her phone the night before, somewhere between the bistro and the cinema, and never switched it back on. Powering it up, she found several messages—text and voice—from Gil Cooke. Picking up the parcel, she said, "My script."

"Would you rather stay here and read it?" Dan asked.

"That can wait for some other rainy day. This one belongs to you."

During her Monday morning trek to the tube station, Ellie stopped at the imposing brick edifice that housed Dan's club. She pressed a bell beside the door, summoning a uniformed porter, and handed over the repurposed envelope Gil had sent her, now addressed to Sir Terence Wheeler. In addition to the autographed copy of *Markova Remem-*

bers, it contained a note she'd penned on a sheet of the personalized stationery she'd ordered from Smythson of Bond Street.

Last night she'd read *Fractures in the Heart.* Through the interactions of his conflicted characters, Lyla and Randall, Gil exposed their disillusionment. Dialogue and action revealed the destructive effects of distrust, possessiveness, and envy. Ellie recalled the emotional drain of performing ballet heroines victimized and betrayed by men they loved—Tatiana, Giselle, Odette. She hoped she could leave Lyla's despondency and fury in the rehearsal room and on the stage. She didn't want her character's angst following her home or invading her subconscious

Impromptu, the updated and altered version of Molière's satirical comedy, was a fun and lighthearted contrast to Gil's play. To create her impression of movie star Caroline Bryden, Ellie had studied interviews conducted on television programs and award ceremony red carpets. This afternoon the academy's diction coach would help her perfect the breathy intonation and cut-glass accent that she practiced in the shower and anytime she was alone in her flat. She hadn't tried it out on Dan, or told him her character's identity. She wanted to surprise him.

After a class supervised by hard-driving Marcus, Ellie visited the development office.

"We're putting together the final list of attendees for the end of season reception for the company and our contributors," the administrative assistant told her. "I need the name of your plus-one. Preferably somebody willing to make a substantial donation."

"I'm sure I can persuade the person I'm inviting." The names on the printout were listed in alphabetical order, and near the bottom she found Sir Terence Wheeler and Ms. Pamela Ames.

Before walking over to the drama school for rehearsal,

she phoned Dan to inform him of the time and the venue, one of the many hotels on Piccadilly.

"My dad will be your only Wheeler, I'm afraid. Martin postponed the managers' retreat because he was so busy with the flooding in Somerset, and he rescheduled it for the same weekend as your event. And because he can't get away, I'm in charge. We'll be meeting in Brighton, for three damn days. Lou and I are scrambling to prepare."

"Oh, no." She didn't try to contain her disappointment.

"My penance for leaving you dateless will be a generous financial contribution to the Friends' Fund of British Ballet Theatre. And I'll bring back some Brighton Rock for you."

"What's that?"

"A big, hard . . . stick of candy."

She snickered. "My present location isn't suitable for phone sex."

"Nor mine. Not with Lou hovering. Dinner tonight? I could pick up sushi."

"Perfect."

With more than an hour before she was due at rehearsal, she went shopping. From her experience of events similar to the Friends of British Ballet Theatre annual reception, she knew the female dancers would wear items loaned by top designers who wanted to get their creations into press photos. A flashy Stella Nue style garment wasn't suitable. Her treasured Balmain cocktail dress was gorgeous, but a vintage item was perhaps too eccentric a choice.

She wandered the streets of Marylebone until she spotted an array of sophisticated formal gowns in an atelier's old-fashioned bow window. Going inside, she told the shop assistant which one she wanted to try on. A sleeveless column of off-white silk organza, it had an overskirt of transparent crape embellished with a constellation of pale sequins that drifted from hip to hem. Even though it was too large and loose and made for a much taller person, she purchased it. The assistant escorted her to a back room to meet the creator, who pinned it for alterations.

During their run-through of the one-act, she and her castmates showed off their celebrity impersonations. The director frequently halted the action, waiting for the players to stop laughing at each other.

"Let's form an improv troupe," Declan suggested. "The Muriel Baker Comedy Players."

Valerie held up a hand. "I'm in."

"All right, people," their director said, hands on her hips. "Focus. Dress rehearsal is next week. Start bringing the costumes you've chosen. After we finish, I'll have Maxi unlock the prop room so you can look around for items your characters will need."

Graeme faced Ellie. "We should use our award statuettes like dueling swords. *En garde!*"

Backing away in mock dread, she replied, "If Lucas and Caroline ever find out what we're doing, they'll sue us for defamation."

Chapter 22

Counting the rows of seats in the auditorium of the Muriel Baker School of Dramatic Arts, Dan calculated the occupancy rate at one hundred. The stage, slightly raised above the floor, had a projecting apron. Dad, who was in town, had declined to join him. Ellie's ballet company friends and the Archway Cabaret ladies had their own performances tonight. She'd claimed to be untroubled by the absence of supporters, but he regretted it on her behalf.

The student showcase consisted of three productions. A group of adult players presented the opening scene in *King Lear*, in which the aged monarch distributed his three kingdoms. It was followed by a manic dining room romp borrowed from *Fawlty Towers*, performed by smaller contingent of teenagers.

When the blue cloth curtain parted once more, the stage was set with folding Chinese screens, several chairs, and a cheval mirror. A dark-haired young man marched out of the wings, brandishing a paper in one hand and holding an Oscar in the other.

"Come, ladies and gentlemen, I'm not amused by this delay." He called out a series of names. Facing the audience, he declared, "Oh, what a stubborn race are actors!"

Two male players entered. One sported a trilby on his head and a false goatee was plastered to his chin.

Ellie moved in from the opposite side, also clutching an Academy Award statuette. The green sequins covering her gown sparkled and shimmered as she moved. "Here I am. What do you want us to do? What is your idea?" She spoke with an English accent, and her inflection was soft and whispery.

"We must rehearse before His Majesty arrives."

Pouting, she replied, "But, Luke, we haven't memorized our parts."

"Silence, Caro."

Tossing her head, she replied, "Marriage changes people. You didn't speak to me like that before we said our vows." Her retort drew chuckles from the audience.

Dan perceived that Ellie impersonated film star Caroline Bryden, and the fellow glaring at her portrayed Lucas Daltrey. The chap in the hat was obviously spoofing noted thespian Sir Francis Cooke.

Another male character joined them. An oversized press badge was stuck to his trench coat and he gripped a microphone. "You present a new piece tonight? For our king?" he asked, replicating a well-known newsman's Northern Irish twang.

"We do," Cooke responded.

"When do you begin?"

"None of your damn business." Daltrey swatted at the mic. Turning to his fellow actors, he declared, "I am going mad. This stupid wretch comes cross-examining me when I have other matters to attend to."

An Asian girl said plaintively to the reporter, "Sir, we need to rehearse."

"I'm not preventing you. Go ahead. Do what you have to do."

Daltrey, an impatient edge to his tone, said, "These ladies prefer that no one observe them when practicing. Be off! Such impertinence." Beckoning to the man in the hat, he said, "Now, Frank—"

"*Sir* Frank," the actor retorted, prompting a roar of amusement from the spectators.

"You will enter from stage left, with a distinguished air, hat tilted to one side, humming a tune."

The players traded barbs and criticisms, ridiculing each other for their tics and stage tricks. Embedded in the banter were sharp and accurate observations about audience tastes and the perils of overacting. At the conclusion, they received a spontaneous standing ovation from family members and friends and the academy staff. The curtains came together and opened to reveal the beaming cast, bowing and waving. The director introduced their class instructor and invited everyone to mingle with the performers and sample treats and beverages on the tables in the hallway.

Dan had to wait his turn to speak to Ellie.

"Cheeky," he told her. "Better not tell your *Fractures in the Heart* co-star—or his wife—what you've been up to. Is your playwright aware of how his dad was mocked?"

"We hope none of them ever hear about it. Tomorrow, after the final acting for the camera session, we receive our certificates. All of us. According to Maxi, that's unusual. No dropouts. No incompletes. Our entire gang plans to keep in touch." Placing her hand on his jacket lapel, she added, "It helped a lot, knowing you were here."

"Wouldn't have missed it for anything. I'm proud of you."

She ducked her auburn head as though embarrassed by his praise. "I could kiss you for saying that."

"Please do."

He wanted all the kisses he could get before his talented ballerina-burlesque star-actress left London for her faraway homeland.

A luxury hotel's grand ballroom was an ideal setting for the British Ballet Theatre dancers. In their evening attire, Ellie's studio companions were different creatures than the ones she saw each morning. Most of the girls wore their hair long, as she did, and had adorned themselves with necklaces and bracelets that would be out of place—and potentially hazardous—in class or rehearsals. They admired her diamond drop earrings, a costly souvenir purchased in Brussels to mark her final days as Stella Nue. She was introduced to the spouses or domestic partners or significant others who shared their non-working lives. Barre buddy Gemma came with her boyfriend. Drew Mason was accompanied by his fiancée. Principal dancer Leah Sternberg had a husband.

Ellie watched Rafe, dashing in his tuxedo, circulate through the throng of donors and subscribers and sponsors. He shook hands and exchanged greetings and posed for selfies, valiantly doing his part to keep the company coffers full.

Anya Semerova sat at a round table with Marcus Baldwin, assigned the task of keeping her company. Ellie, having never encountered her outside of the studio or the annex hallways, decided to join them.

"What will you do," she asked the older woman, "during summer break?"

"Teach. I coach young dancers at fine academy near London."

"They're lucky to train with you."

"You have plans also, Eeley?"

"I'm going home, to New Hampshire. My mom and her

sister have a ballet school, and I usually spend a week substituting for whichever one scheduled a vacation. And I'll sign up for a barre class in the town near my lake cottage."

"On day you come to us, I see lyrical moving but loss of technique. Now, very much better. Not to accept soloist place is sad."

"My mother would say the same. If I told her."

"Mireille Charpentier, like Rafe, must regret to lose you. Is excellent company, Ballet Bruxelles." Anya reached for her beaded handbag. "I go for taxicab. Tomorrow morning, I can know which people stay too late here."

Ellie was debating whether to get another glass of wine or to approach Sir Terence Wheeler. His statuesque date solved her dilemma by accosting her and introducing herself.

"Your dress is exquisite," Pamela Ames said. "The ballerinas always look so beautiful at these affairs. And the male dancers are divinely handsome."

Ellie regarded Sir Terence. His eyes were the same blueish gray as his son's, beneath identically shaped brows. "You received the book?"

He nodded. "I did, thank you. A charming addition to my collection."

"I discovered it while setting up the new reading room at BBT. Rafe wanted you to have it. With his compliments, as I said in my note."

Pamela patted his coat sleeve. "Terry, I want to tell Mr. Mason and Ms. Sternberg how impressed we were with their performances in *Onegin.*"

Ellie suspected this separation was pre-arranged, to enable a private conversation. She was prepared for it. "Dan was sorry he couldn't be here tonight."

"Do you often see him?"

His question stung. He'd seen Dan kissing her. He must know more about their relationship than he was letting on. "Daily," she replied. And nightly.

"You must be aware of what happened shortly after he left university."

"The boating accident. On the river."

"It deprived him of the older brother who was his closest friend. Brian survived, but emerged from a coma with life-altering impairment. While we struggled to accept the consequences, my wife—my former wife—decided to leave us."

"Nine years ago, when I was twenty, I experienced a sudden life change. I became a widow."

"Dan told me."

"I sought solace—and sanity—in creative work. I didn't want another relationship. Or care that I had so little time for one to develop. So please don't equate my years in burlesque with promiscuity or drugs or sordid activity of any kind." She shouldn't have to say this. It was demeaning.

"I never have done. Dan says you'll soon be returning to the States. How long will you be there?"

"Six weeks."

"That seems sufficiently long for the two of you to gain some objectivity about your situation. As you probably know, your nationality will hinder your professional prospects in this country. British theatrical producers are only interested in American actresses who possess credits for Broadway performances or have achieved considerable fame from films or on television."

She did know, but optimistically assumed that agent Cait could secure her a role in another play. Or, if the part was worth considering, a movie or a series. In reality, as Sir Terence was pointing out, future employment—if any—would most likely originate on the opposite side of the Atlantic.

"Pamela and I wish you every success in your play. And all other endeavors."

She'd never had much faith in Dan's firm belief that time and familiarity would dissolve Sir Terence's bias against her.

All her doubts were justified. Everything he'd said confirmed it.

She searched the ballroom for Rafe. She needed him. Accepting a champagne glass from a passing waiter, she kept her eyes on her friend's curly head. The moment he stepped away from one of the board members, she waylaid him.

"Enjoying yourself, love?"

"I *was,*" she said, with heavy emphasis on the second word.

"Is Sir Terence unwilling to increase his annual donation?"

"I forgot to ask. I did give you credit for the gift of the Markova book."

He peered down at her. "You can't cry here. Come with me." Placing a hand in the small of her back, he guided her to the seating area in the lobby. "What's wrong?"

Ellie blinked several times in an attempt to force back her tears. "Love trouble."

"Who is he?"

"That's the problem. It's Dan Wheeler, Sir Terence's son. We met the day I arrived in London. He arranged for my apartment rental. We had a few casual meet-ups. He took me on a road trip to the West Country. Now we're a couple. But his father isn't a fan. Of me. Or us."

"Why ever not?"

"Stella Nue. Taking off my clothes in cabarets and arenas. And because I haven't told Dan how I was treated by the Colmans, before and during my marriage to their precious son, he has no idea how wounded I am. *Déjà vu.*"

"*Merde.*"

"I couldn't agree more. Dan's dad doesn't only object to my supposedly lurid past. I'm not just a stripper. I'm an American. And an actress. Thoroughly unsuitable for a scion of the landed gentry."

"Not according to established history. For centuries,

British royals and aristocrats have been involved with ladies of the stage."

"He says I'll never get a job over here, after *Fractures in the Heart.*"

"I've got the perfect solution." He took her hand and squeezed it. "Dance for me. Join my eminently respectable company. There's no better way to clean up your sleazy reputation." When she glared up at him, he released her and leaned back. "That last bit was a joke."

"I shouldn't have laid all this on you. Not tonight."

"I'm glad you did. I'm feeling low myself. End-of-season blues. Let's commiserate over drinks and dinner. If lover boy can spare you, we'll dine out in style before you depart these shores."

"He's out of town till Sunday."

"Tomorrow? You choose the restaurant. I'm paying. And I won't even mention that you're a thousand times richer than I'll ever be."

Chapter 23

During a break between meetings, Dan visited the Jewelry Quarter in the Lanes of Brighton, seeking a present for Ellie. Unsure whether she would be pleased or alarmed if he gave her a ring, he considered the necklaces and bracelets on display in the narrow alleyways. In one shop window, he spied three vertically stacked aquamarines—her birthstone—attached to a thin gold chain. The clerk who presented it for his examination described it as a journey pendant.

"What's the significance?" he asked.

"Anything you want," the man replied. "Milestones in a career or a relationship. Maybe the gemstones symbolize past, present, and future."

"I'll take it."

Signal problems on the Brighton to London railway line delayed his return. He reached the city quite late, hungry, and in a foul mood. Trusting that Ellie could improve it, he rang her. No appetite, she said, blaming an attack of nerves. She wanted to stay in and study her script for tomorrow's read-through. And she needed to finish her packing.

"Should we meet for lunch? After devoting the entire weekend to a work event, I'm taking a personal day."

"I should be free by noontime. We can eat here. I want to use up as much fresh food as I can. You get whatever is left in the fridge and freezer."

Moments after he rang off, his mobile chirped. Dad, still in residence at the club, suggested a visit to the nearby shop that sold country sports equipment and clothing.

"I'm considering replacing my waders. And I need a reel of floating fly line. Join me for breakfast. We'll walk over together."

The next morning, Dan responded to queries about his Brighton activities, waiting to raise the subject that was uppermost in his mind. Eventually he got his chance.

"Tell me about the British Ballet reception."

"Rafe Lawrence and the board president took turns reporting on the successes of the season and provided a preview of the next. They gave an update on fundraising progress and urged generosity from existing contributors. Pamela enjoyed her conversations with the principal dancers."

"And with Ellie, presumably."

Dad laid his cutlery across his plate with precision. "She was instrumental in providing me with a copy of Dame Alicia Markova's memoir. Personally signed. Did you know about it?"

"Only that she had a present for you. She didn't tell me what it was." Before he could continue his interrogation, two waiters arrived to clear their table.

A short time later, as they stood before a wall of fly reels, Dan said, "What else did you and Ellie talk about? Besides the book."

"Nothing of significance."

He moved to the rod and reel cases and pretended to be interested in a black nylon model with reinforced end caps. He didn't want it, didn't need it.

Dad wasn't tempted by the waders. "We're expecting a spell of fine weather to the west," he told Dan after purchasing his fly line. "You should spend the weekend at Tayer Court."

He might as well. Ellie would be thousands of miles away. "If Sandra prepares a picnic lunch, we can take it to Harding Hall."

"Brian does enjoy being outdoors," his father commented.

Returning to his flat, Dan successfully fought the urge to check in with his office staff, opting to do laundry and make space in his refrigerator for the perishables Ellie had offered. That, and a treadmill session, kept him busy. Aware that her script reading would wrap up soon, he decided to stroll to the theatre to meet her.

Many years ago, during a family day in London—ostensibly for holiday shopping—his parents had taken him and his brothers to the Sovereign, surprising them with tickets to the matinee performance of a Christmas pantomime. Oll, the university scholar, practically had to be dragged inside and looked ready to bolt from the auditorium at any moment. The Dame broke through his pretense of boredom with a particularly saucy entendre, and he laughed himself into a choking fit. Brian, who hadn't understood the naughtiest jokes, enjoyed the physical stunts and unfolding chaos.

Banners on either side of the entrance portico were imprinted with Sir Francis Cooke's image in naval uniform, one arm tucked inside his coat. Dan was reading the enthusiastically positive review quotes plastered on the wall beneath the awning when the door opened and a bearded man stalked down the shallow front steps.

After a brief glance at Dan, he inserted a cigarette between his lips and lit it.

"Did you attend the table read?" Dan asked.

"I had to," the fellow answered. "I wrote the blasted

thing. Gil Cooke." He pointed his cigarette at the oversized portrait overhead. "Son of."

"I'm Dan Wheeler."

Gil turned his head. "You drove Ellie to a flooded village. In Somerset, wasn't it?"

"And to my family home in Gloucestershire." Watching Gil exhale a thick plume of smoke, he added, "She's starting her acting career in the best way possible. Creating the Lyla role. Sharing the stage with Lucas Daltrey. Just what her late husband would've wanted for her."

"God knows why," Gil muttered. "He was madly competitive."

"You knew him?"

"Lived with him. We were roommates at the Juilliard School in New York City."

Startled, Dan said, "Ellie didn't mention that you were his friend."

"A grossly inaccurate description. What's she told you about Harry Colman?"

"Not a lot," he admitted.

"Understandable."

To you, perhaps, Dan thought.

"He was utterly self-absorbed and spoiled rotten. Domineering, demanding. Jealous, too. Didn't want me anywhere near her, he made that abundantly clear. And he felt threatened by Rafe Lawrence, the dancer. He even resented the gays. How he persuaded her to elope, I can't say, but that disaster of a marriage wouldn't have lasted. He insisted that she give up ballet, he was that controlling. Her nightmare ended when he smashed his car into an unfortunate motorist."

"Ellie did say he wasn't at fault."

Gil shrugged. "His parents are rich and influential enough to have the accident records sealed. I'm doubtful they'd do it for Ellie's sake, to shield her from the facts. They barely tolerated her." Frowning, he said, "Unless you want to trigger memories of the trauma she endured, don't ever inquire about them. Or him."

Stunned by so many unpleasant revelations, Dan asked if she was inside the theatre.

"She left. Right before everything went to hell. I don't smoke any more, but I bummed this cigarette from the assistant director. I hoped it would calm me. Now I'm tempted to buy a full packet." Gil crushed the stub against the side of the building to snuff it. Without another word, he stalked off.

Dan turned and walked in the opposite direction.

He wished Ellie had been the one to disclose the most profoundly painful aspects of her history. From the outset of their acquaintance, she'd spoken frankly about professional challenges, fostering his assumption that her various career shifts had been in reaction to losing a spouse, a form of grief therapy. Gil's discourse pointed to drastically different motivations. After years of marital horrors, followed by a period as a ballet dancer in Brussels, she'd created an alternate identity as Stella Nue. Did her desire to become an actress rise from her need to prove to herself that she was as talented as her husband had been? Or was it a form of posthumous revenge against an abusive spouse?

His trek from Shaftesbury Avenue to Latimer Row had brought him to Wincott & Sons, where Martin Latimer used to lark about serving cheese to customers—including the one he'd eventually married. There was no point picking out a bouquet for Ellie from the bucket outside the florist's shop. She was leaving London tomorrow.

Walking on, he resolved not to mar their final hours together questioning her about Henry Lionel Matthew Colman. The Fourth.

He revised his plan for the necklace and aquamarine

journey pendant he'd purchased in Brighton. Instead of presenting it as a bon voyage gift, it would be her welcome back present.

Not since childhood had Ellie gone three months without filling a suitcase. Her process of travel preparation, refined over her years on the road and in the skies, was so deeply ingrained that it required very little thought or advance planning. Because she'd return to Latimer House, she was leaving most of her clothes in the wardrobe. Anything and everything she needed could be found in her closets at the lake cottage and in her parents' Birchmont residence. After she inserted her favorite dance slippers and two pairs of pointe shoes among electronic necessities and essential toiletries, enough space remained in her carry-on bag for the small gifts purchased for people back home.

When her phone pinged with a message alert, she was disappointed to find that Gil was the sender. He was in the lobby and needed to speak with her—urgently. She texted Lorcan the porter and asked him to direct Mr. Cooke to the penthouse.

"I didn't think I'd see you again until August," she said when Gil entered the flat.

"I bring bad news." His breath was flavored with tobacco. "An unimaginably terrible thing has happened."

Recognizing this as a moment of crisis, Ellie asked if he'd like a cup of tea.

"You must have something stronger."

She offered him the choice of wine, whisky, gin, or vodka.

"Whisky, please. Neat."

Unwilling to subject him to the disarray in the kitchen, she pointed towards the drawing room. "Second doorway on the left. I'll join you in a minute."

When she did, he was standing at a window. "Impressive digs."

She handed him the glass of amber liquid. "Is there a problem with the play?"

"Got it in one. After you and Lucas left the rehearsal room, the Sovereign Group bosses dropped a bombshell. They're pulling *Fractures in the Heart* from the primary site and transferring us to their Ormond Stage. A fringe venue where they stick new and experimental works. Adjacent to St. James's Square. Not," he added grimly, "in the theatre district."

From her perspective, that was a plus. The alternate space would be less cavernous and intimidating than the Sovereign, therefore more comfortable for a neophyte actress. And the location was a five-minute walk from Latimer House. Aware that he expected sympathy, she said, "I'm sorry about the change. I know how disappointed you must be."

"I'm absolutely furious. My script won top prize at the play festival. It's stage ready. We have a director and dream cast. I'll ask Father to intervene, though I can't say whether it will do us any good."

"Keep me posted." On a brighter note, she added, "Lucas was amazing today. He's a perfect Randall."

"His participation is nothing short of miraculous. Lucky for us that Caroline had a baby a few months ago. He wanted a project close to home."

"He talked about having an intimacy director for the fights and the final scene. Will we?" She hoped so. Shedding clothes on the burlesque stage was no preparation for climbing into bed with a famous sex symbol.

"Talk to Joan Wadsworth. It's her decision."

Hearing a characteristic knock on the door, she said, "Here's Dan. He's taking all the food that would spoil while I'm gone."

Gil handed her the empty glass. With a smile, he added, "I never got the chance to say what a brilliant Lyla you are."

"I wasn't sure. Joan wanted us to read the text without actually acting it," she said on her way to the door.

To her surprise, her invited guest addressed the uninvited one by name. Confused, she glanced from Dan to Gil. "You know each other?"

"We had a brief encounter," Dan said. "At the theatre."

"I'm off to seek Father's advice," Gil told her. "Thanks for the drink."

Ellie walked him to the door. "This change might be for the best."

"I'm not optimistic. Though I suppose if all the Ormond performances sell out, there's a chance of moving to the Sovereign later in the season. I mean to start that conversation. And I'll be counting the days till you're back." When his lips brushed her cheek, the stubble beard grazed her jaw.

She found Dan in the kitchen, surveying the chaos.

"Poor Gil," she said. "The only nepo baby drama student at Juilliard who didn't seem to belong there. He was always so self-conscious, assuming everybody expected him to be as brilliant an actor as Sir Francis. He shared a dorm room with Harry. At some point they lost touch with each other. I can't remember if he was still in New York when—" She swallowed. "I don't think he was at the funeral." On her way to the refrigerator, she said, "I promised to feed you lunch. I'm going to cobble together a couple of sandwiches. How did everything go in Brighton?"

"My main presentation was well received. I moderated a managers' panel. Others were responsible for the onboarding activities for recent hires. Lou is familiar with the town and arranged the evening activities. She must have kept the attendees well entertained. They yawned throughout the Saturday and Sunday morning sessions."

"After the Friday night gala, Saturday morning class was a hard slog." Removing a block of cheese from its compartment, she added, "Rafe took me to dinner at the Wolseley, to cheer us both up. He gets gloomy at the end of the season, even a successful one. And I was feeling low." She yanked a leaf from the head of lettuce. "Guess why."

"Dad." His fingers caught a loose lock of her hair. "Let's not spend these precious hours together talking about him. By this time tomorrow, you'll be at Heathrow."

"Fair enough. We'll do whatever you like."

"Romantic dinner at the bistro. If that's not enough of a mood boost, we can watch a screwball comedy."

She smiled. "I bet you've got other ideas."

"Only one. The best of all."

Chapter 24

Traveling business class on a transatlantic flight was a curiously solitary experience. Partitions closed off Dan's pod, separating him from his traveling companion. If he lowered his side panel he could converse with Hannah, whose seat faced in the opposite direction. But she was sleeping her way across the ocean, cocooned in the complimentary blanket.

Twice a year she combined a trip to her Acorn Films office in Boston with a visit to her parents' Maine farm, and on this one she was in an advanced state of pregnancy. When Martin admitted concerns that he hadn't dared voice to a fiercely independent spouse, Dan had offered to serve as her escort and baggage handler. His relieved boss shifted his annual vacation leave from August to July.

Since Ellie's departure in the limousine that carried her to Heathrow, he'd struggled to conquer the time difference, scheduling the occasional video link-up and regularly messaging her. He'd booked a room at The Maples before informing her of his intention, so she wouldn't feel obliged to invite him to her cottage. She accepted his choice, assuring him that she and the innkeepers would provide what she described as the quintessential *On Golden Pond* experience.

Seeing that film listed on the in-flight entertainment guide, he watched it. The aging couple played by Katharine Hepburn and Henry Fonda owned a seasonal lakeside cottage that did resemble the one in photos Ellie had shown him. He imagined himself sitting beside her on the wooden dock, or on the porch, listening to the cry of loons in the bay.

Movement nearby alerted him to Hannah's wakefulness.

"Did I sleep through meal service?"

"No."

"Good." She patted her bulge. "Little one makes me peckish." Unbuckling her seatbelt, she said, "Better stretch my legs. And I need the loo."

Dan scrolled through the classic film offerings. Inclined to stick with Katharine Hepburn, he pressed the icon for *The Philadelphia Story*. He enjoyed *Holiday* but wasn't keen on its central conflict, fierce parental opposition to a romantic attachment.

When he'd phoned Tayer Court with news of his journey to New England, his dad's response was muted. He stirred a semblance of interest by citing his planned fly-fishing excursion with a local guide recommended by Zack and George.

Hannah returned to her seat with two mini-packets of biscuits and passed one to Dan. Her head fell back against her headrest. "I should get some work done," she said, as if trying to convince herself. "I have to get through two full days of Boston meetings before I can escape to the Maine coast. Why aren't you staying with Ellie? That cottage must be an ideal love nest."

"I wasn't asked to change my reservation." Removing his watch, he re-set it to five hours earlier than London time.

"I had a feeling the two of you would hook up, that day she made Shamrock Burgers. When you brought her to Stanwell, I was certain of it."

"You provided the setting for our first kiss. The terrace."

"The kitchen, for Martin and me," she said reminiscently. "I don't understand Terry's opposition."

While waiting in the upper-class lounge for their call to board the aircraft, Dan had vented to her about his father's prejudice against Ellie. "At Tayer Court, he gave off an uncharacteristic lord of the manor vibe. Whatever transpired at the British Ballet reception upset her even more." He shifted in his seat. "I'm disappointed by Dad's attitude, but it's overshadowed by a greater concern."

"I can't imagine what it could be."

"Her husband. The playwright was at school with Ellie and roomed with Harry Colman. Who, according to Gil Cooke, was appallingly selfish and thoroughly beastly. He described their marriage as a disaster. A nightmare."

"Wow." Hannah pushed her curls off her brow. "I guess that's why she hardly ever talks about it."

"None of my prior relationships lasted very long. Perhaps the failure was mine—or maybe it wasn't. At the start of this year, I deleted the dating app I'd been using. From the moment I encountered Ellie, I was fascinated. Talented. Hardworking. Successful. Determined. I've been afraid I'd scare her off by wanting so much, too soon. Only to find out that her marital history is an even bigger obstacle. Wouldn't you say it's problematic?"

"Not necessarily," she hedged. "I mean, she wouldn't want to get involved with another jerk. After being married to horrible Harry, she needs a decent chap. Exactly like the one flying across an ocean to spend time with her."

The seasonal cottage overlooking a narrow bay provided Ellie with a respite from the demands of her various professions and reconnected her to happy summertime activities.

Her grandad taught her to swim in the shallow water. It was deeper at the far end of the dock, where she and her siblings had jumped in—or pushed each other off. During her moody adolescence, she'd escaped with the family dog for solitary walks on the private dead-end road winding through the woodland. The heirloom dining table had been used for countless card games and puzzles. Like her, the loons calling to one another at dawn and throughout the night were descendants of prior inhabitants.

Each morning began with Pilates, her warm-up before online class. A section of the porch floor was covered with the large square of marley she'd danced on throughout the pandemic, and her portable barre was a permanent fixture. While dipping into *pliés* or stretching a leg in *tendu,* she heard chickadees chirping on the hemlock branches and a constant buzz of boats and jet skis in the bay. On alternate days she drove to a Wolfeboro dance studio for morning barre and center work, followed by a lunch with George and Zack at The Maples, if they weren't otherwise occupied. Or she visited Cousin Phil, who lived at the boarding school in staff housing. Sometimes she booked a massage at an upscale spa at the bridge by the falls.

On July Fourth she'd invited Mom and Daddo to lunch, and Phil brought his stepmother. Her brother Liam hadn't been able to take time off from The Shamrock, and her sister Marie spent the holiday at her partner's house on Martha's Vineyard. Despite these absences, Ellie and her guests had recreated past gatherings. Her dad had grilled salmon and her mom steamed the peas. Her cousin sliced tomatoes and mushrooms for the salad. Seated around the table, they reminisced about family members living or deceased. Just before sunset, when the house was empty and silent, Ellie settled into her favorite porch chair to watch the parade of boats heading down to the fireworks show at the village bandstand. When darkness descended, she could see and hear the smaller pyrotechnic displays along the opposite shoreline.

This afternoon she'd mopped the kitchen floor, dusted every surface, vacuumed carpets, plumped pillows, and wound the mantel clock. The flight app on her phone informed her that Dan and Hannah had landed in Boston on time. He'd boarded the scheduled bus to Concord, which was due in less than two hours. Before meeting him, she wanted to stop in Birchmont to see her mother.

He wouldn't mind if she showed up in shorts and t-shirt. But the dance academy pupils and parents and staff were expected to adhere to the dress code, slightly less rigorous than during Ellie's youth. She changed into a sundress and sandals, adding her gold hoop earrings and a necklace and a cuff bracelet. She didn't bother to pin up her hair, still damp and stringy from a midday swim.

One of her parents' vehicles, a years-old black Mercedes, was reserved for her use when in New Hampshire. Cautiously she reversed, avoiding collision with several broad tree trunks, and followed the one-and-a-half lane private road, prepared to pull aside to make room for any oncoming cars.

She found her mother seated before a computer screen, inspecting a series of promotional poster designs. Ellie neither expected nor received a welcoming hug. Ballet dancers, active or retired, came in two flavors: expressive and emotional or reticent and introverted. Aunt Renée was the former, embracing her pupils when they excelled or needed a comforting gesture. Mom was the latter, sparing with praise.

"Rafe says hello," she told Ellie. "We were on a video call this morning."

"He's supposed to be on vacation."

"For an administrator, there's no escaping work." Mom's hand made a graceful ballerina sweep across a stack of papers. "Feel free to pitch in."

"Next time. I can't stay long—the bus to Concord has already crossed the state line. Did Rafe find someone to coach at your summer intensive?"

"He suggested names for my list of prospects. Renée and I are in discussion with an academy on the seacoast, exploring the possibility of joint sponsorship and shared expenses. With training to take place here." Mom smiled. "Rafe had a lot to say about you."

She knew what was coming.

"Is your friend's play worth giving up your best—probably last—chance of dancing with a major company? As a soloist."

"You two shouldn't conspire against me."

"Not against," Mom insisted.

Ellie's phoned pinged. Taking it out of her purse, she said, "Dan just passed through the tollway."

"When will your Daddo and I meet him?"

"I'm not sure. Trust me, you will. It's payback time. After going a couple of rounds with his father, I get to inflict my parents on him."

"If you think we're so bad," her mother retorted, "I've got a collection of embarrassing baby photos I can show him. Better yet, the video of your first dance recital."

"What's so incriminating? I won the top award."

"Your behavior when the judges presented it to you."

"Five-year-olds jump up and down when they're happy," Ellie pointed out. "Admit it, you were proud of me."

"*Toujours, chérie,*" The phrase was equivalent to a hug. French was her Québécois parent's love language.

"Dan wants to see the pub and sample a genuine Shamrock Burger. I'll let you know when we plan to drop in."

"How will you spend the anniversary?"

A question Ellie should have anticipated. "With Dan. Touring the lake on the motorship Mount Washington. Not thinking about it."

Minutes after she reached the station, the bus eased into a parking bay. Passengers stepped down and waited for the driver to remove their variously colored roller bags and duffels from the luggage compartment. Her pulse raced as she watched for Dan's tall figure. As he waited for his suitcase, the wind ruffled his dark hair. Her heart and head filled with feelings she wasn't yet brave enough to express.

They embraced. And kissed.

Leading him to the Mercedes, she asked, "Was your flight okay?" She pressed the remote to raise the trunk lid.

"Not bad. Occasionally bumpy—headwinds. Awfully long. Hannah says hello." He shrugged. "And other things I can't recall. Half my brain is still in the clouds, despite two hours on the bus. Nice car."

"A loaner from my parents."

Making his way to the driver's side, he stopped, realizing his mistake. They both laughed.

Following the speediest northward route, she pointed out personally relevant landmarks. A place she'd once stopped so a moose could cross the road. The spot where, years ago, a tornado had ripped away the treetops and scattered them on the ground. At the summit of a hill, she pulled off the highway at the sign designating it a scenic viewpoint. From that vantage, they could gaze upon the lake spread out below, shimmering blue, dotted with green islands, surrounded by rounded mountains.

"Considerably larger than I expected," Dan said.

"You'll get a better sense of its size when you're in the middle," she replied. "According to your hosts, the room rate includes a voucher for you and a guest to take a cruise on the motorship that stops at all the lakeside ports."

He looked away from the vista. "You'll be my plus one?"

"Of course. Zack will make the reservation. Tell him we want the Sunday sailing. That's when the ship comes to my bay and passes right by the cottage."

Chapter 25

"America's Oldest Summer Resort," Dan read from the sign positioned at the Wolfeboro town line.

"An honest boast," Ellie affirmed. "Before the Revolution, a British royal governor decided that he preferred spending the warmer months near a lake instead of on the seacoast."

She signaled a left turn and entered a straight driveway lined with parallel rows of old maples, from which the property derived its name. The white clapboard Federal-era farmhouse had rows of sash windows set between dark green shutters. Roses bloomed in shades of pink and red. Perennial beds were full of kaleidoscope colors: indigo blue bellflowers and purple delphiniums and magenta lilies and towering yellow sunflowers. The parking area contained two SUVs, one hybrid and one electric, and a Volvo.

Before Ellie switched off the engine, Zack bounded through the front door. He seized the handle of Dan's wheeled suitcase and ushered him into the house.

"The parlor," he said, indicating a room on one side of the foyer, then pointed in the opposite direction. "Dining room." Trailing his free hand up the stairway handrail, he said reverently, "Maple wood."

Ellie retreated to the kitchen, situated where the main house and the modern extension met. She found George on the other side of the dog gate.

A young Golden Retriever and a tiny tri-color Papillon trotted over. "Hello, Rudi." She patted the caramel head of Zack's pet, named for Rudolf Nureyev. "Hi, Dita." Like burlesque star Dita von Teese, George's small companion had a diva personality.

"Perfect timing," he greeted her. "You can be my taste-tester."

She sniffed and the aroma drew her to the granite-topped island. "Cinnamon buns. Wow, that's a lot."

"We're fully booked for the weekend."

"Zack couldn't wait to give the tour. I didn't rate so much as a hello."

"You know how he is. Don't take it personally."

"I didn't." She bit into the yeasty, spicy, sugary bun. "Sinfully yummy."

They had time to exchange news before Zack swept through the dining room to the kitchen, followed by Dan.

"Welcome to The Maples," George greeted him. "Has jet lag kicked in?"

"Starting to."

"If you have issues with dogs—some guests do—we'll keep ours in here."

Dan leaned over the gate and scratched behind one of Rudi's dangling ears. "I'm mad for them. I tell my Somerset friends that's the main reason I visit."

"You ought to have your own," Ellie told him. "Your flat and office are in the same building. With access to Green Park for exercising."

Zack lifted Dita off the floor for a cuddle. "You'd love living in London, wouldn't you, precious?"

Ellie tore off a portion of cinnamon bun and passed it to Dan. "Preview of tomorrow's breakfast."

Zack placed the dog on the floor, saying, "You can have a cup of tea to go with it. Or locally brewed craft beer."

"Beer sounds wonderfully refreshing."

"On Saturday," George said, "we've got a wedding dinner in the barn. Our caterer lets us add our overnight guests to the order, with a day's notice. Let us know if you're interested."

"He'll be at The Shamrock. An essential cultural experience."

"What can we serve you this evening?" George asked.

Dan shook his head. "Not much. I was eating my way across the Atlantic. In business class."

"French omelet?" Zack suggested. "Our neighbor supplies us with fresh eggs every day."

"I'll gather the herbs," Ellie volunteered. "And show Dan the outbuildings."

When she turned towards the back door, George said, "Barn's open. A florist is coming by soon to decide where to place the arrangements."

After picking chives, thyme, and tarragon, she led Dan to the structure behind the house. The entire space was filled with round tables surrounded by gold-painted faux bamboo chairs.

"For rehearsal dinners or wedding receptions," she explained. "On Sunday afternoons, it's a concert venue for local musicians. During the week there are lectures and author appearances and contra dances. A monthly craft show sets up on the grounds. Not a day goes by without an inquiry." She led him around the granite boulders protruding from the lawn towards a classic white gazebo, encircled with a flowery border. "Couples can exchange their vows here. Or down at the lake, against a background of mountains. That path leads to the water and a dock."

He reached for her hand. "I've missed you."

"What did your father say when he learned about your trip?"

"He warned me that you Americans drive on the wrong side. And he wished me tight lines. Fisherman speak for good luck. The equivalent of *merde* for ballet dancers."

The enormous motorship's engine rumbled as it churned the waters of Wolfeboro Bay. Her horn sounded a farewell blast for the spectators on the docks.

Dan looked up from his phone. "Hannah offers to collect me from The Maples on her way back to Boston." Ellie moved closer, and her shoulder pressed against his upper arm.

"Tell her she'll find you at the cottage. You're spending the night with me. It's your only option. I told Zack and George to release your room, and by now they've probably let somebody else have it."

Their fellow passengers either gathered at the rail to study the scenery or had gone inside the main cabin to queue for the brunch buffet. After gorging on the Shamrock Burger and Fingal's Fries that Liam Lowery had served him last night, he had no appetite.

Ellie jutted a finger towards a bulge of tree-covered land. "Rattlesnake Island."

"How did the snakes ever get over there? Can they swim?" A common question, apparently, because a male voice crackled over the tannoy, recounting various legends connected to the naming of the island. Sensing his mobile's vibration, he assumed it was Hannah. "Email from Dad, planning Brian's birthday."

"No message for me? 'Hands off my son, you vixen!' Harry's parents never said that to my face, but they were thinking it. I could read those thought bubbles hanging over their heads."

This confirmed what Gil had told him. "You didn't get on with them."

"They didn't care for me. I was the wrong girlfriend for their darling only son. They probably thought I pressured Harry into eloping, not realizing his influence over me was stronger than mine over him. I was a teenager, after all. And waiting so long to tell them was his idea. Not mine." Gazing at the white clouds high above them, she added, "The Colmans never understood that what he wanted and what they wanted for him were very different. They assumed he'd outgrow his love of acting."

"How long after marrying him did you regret it?"

Her auburn head swiveled in his direction. "Never. From the moment we met, I sensed that we belonged together. So did he."

"No friction at all?"

"How do you mean?"

"Clashing performers' egos. Professional jealousy. Competitiveness."

"None of that. Sure, we could get cranky with each other, like stubborn people do. But we didn't stay mad for long. We laughed way more than we quarreled. He teased me about being promoted to soloist before I was old enough to vote or be served a bar drink. At his graduation, I threw confetti over him when he marched down the aisle with his diploma." Her tone shifted when she said, "We relied on each other in the tough times. Sometimes—not often—he wasn't cast in the role he wanted most. My job at City International was physically exhausting, but that was nothing compared to the emotional and psychological strain. I'd come home to Harry and vent after being advised—again—to consider breast reduction surgery."

He couldn't believe what he was hearing. "Someone said that to you?"

"Frequently."

"Why?"

"Normal sized tits were problematic. The mean, flat-chested girls in the corps were jealous of my rapid rise through the ranks. They called me Ellie Mae—a busty airhead hick on *The Beverly Hillbillies* television show. Or Jessica Rabbit, from the animated movie. I stuck it out. Until Harry convinced me that doing plays with him would be easier and way more fun. He was right. Cleavage was no longer an issue."

Everything she'd said contradicted the playwright's description of her marriage, and he couldn't doubt that her version was the accurate one. Harry Colman was the love of her life.

She went on, "He liked to say that he could afford to be a poor stage actor. But I know he could've had a career in movies or television if he wanted to. Because he was an only child, we were supposed have two kids. Whenever I felt ready. He really wanted to be a dad." She pointed to a distant vessel on the starboard side. "There's the mail boat. In summertime, it makes deliveries to all the inhabited islands."

Ellie's reminiscences of the late Harry Colman had summoned a ghostly companion for the duration of their journey around the lake.

While collecting his belongings from The Maples, Dan pondered the facts he'd learned about the first man to love the woman he was in love with. Ellie's husband had been a paragon, not a prick. Harry had been her soul mate. Could a person have more than one in a lifetime?

He thanked Zack and George for a pleasant stay, patted each dog, and climbed into her car. For the rest of their time together, he needed to conceal from her how shaken he was by her revelations.

She diverted from the main road to a lesser one and turned onto a private tarmacked lane that wound through forest. Most of the houses, she told him, were seasonal, and few were occupied year-round. Her shingled cottage, among the oldest in the compound, perched on a ridge high above the water. Most of its windows faced the green folds of mountains on the other side of the bay.

They ate their evening meal on the screened porch, talking over the persistent buzz of watercraft speeding back and forth. She wanted to know more of his history with Martin. He gave his side of the tale she'd heard during their stay at Stanwell House and related what he knew about the Latimers' courtship. After tidying the kitchen, they descended a steep wooden stairway to the dock. She pulled two chairs close together and they sat down to watch the sun slip behind the hills. The clouds were tinged pink and gold, and gradually the sky changed from blue to violet to deep purple. With the receding light, a pale silhouette of moon appeared and the stars emerged.

"What made you think there was friction between Harry and me?"

"That's what Gil Cooke said."

She turned a startled face towards him. "He did? When?"

"The day of your table read. I rocked up to theatre to find out how it went. He stepped outside for a smoke, and we introduced ourselves. He mentioned sharing a room with Harry at school. He described your husband as an extremely disagreeable chap."

Her dark eyebrows jutted downward. "That's bizarre. They were friends. He was actually present when Harry, the most popular person in the whole school, invited me to go clubbing with a bunch of drama students. That was the beginning of us as a couple. For weeks, Gil was the only one who knew about our Weehawken elopement. We didn't tell our parents till the start of fall term." She banged her fist on the chair arm. "Why would he talk trash about Harry?"

Envy, Dan deduced, because that's exactly what he was feeling. "He told me you were traumatized."

"By people at City International Ballet. Never by Harry. He was everything to me."

So many years after his untimely demise, her husband still possessed all the pieces of her fractured heart.

Ellie came awake to the cry of loons calling to one another somewhere in the bay. She eased herself from under the covers, careful not to wake Dan. Quietly creeping to the kitchen, she took a glass from the dish drain rack and filled it from the jug of well water she kept in the fridge. A thick, impenetrable fog hovered over the water, obscuring the opposite shore and its layers of green mountains.

The glowing digits of the microwave clock warned her that Hannah would appear in approximately five hours. After lunch, she and Dan would depart for Boston and the airport, well in advance of their early evening flight to London. Returning to the bedroom, she saw that Dan was asleep, his bare torso rising and falling with each deep breath. The mattress shifted as she settled next to him.

"What's the time?" he mumbled.

"Not quite seven."

He rolled onto his side. "You were right about this place resembling the setting in *On Golden Pond*. The lake. The loons. I've never seen a sunset like the one you ordered up for me yesterday. None of the images on my mobile fully convey its splendor."

During his brief time in the bathroom, she shed her sleep shorts and camisole. On his return, his answer to her clear invitation was to comb her hair with his fingers. Warm palms slid to her breasts and along her ribcage, evoking a gurgle of pleasure.

Last night she'd been aware of an urgency to Dan's passion, and this morning it was even more evident. In his determination to ensure her satisfaction, he produced the most exquisite sensations, culminating in a pleasure so intense that it felt surreal.

Lying against him, cheek to chest, feeling his heartbeat, she shared his conviction that they could overcome and withstand any and all difficulties.

She wondered whether he ever thought about marriage. When—or if—he proposed to her, she would joyfully accept. This time she preferred a longer engagement, in the belief that his father needed to know her more fully. She already had the dress, the spangled organza she'd worn to the BBT reception, an unvirginal off-white, exactly right for a second wedding.

They each took a turn in the tiny shower stall in the adjacent bathroom. The porch, where she intended to serve breakfast, was chilly, so she put on her fleece hoodie and gave him Liam's. The loons, trawling for their morning meal, continued to serenade them, and each other.

A bonded pair, she thought. Like us.

After clearing the table and washing up, they walked all the way to the summit of the nearby headland.

"What will you give Brian for his birthday?" Ellie asked on their way to the cottage.

"I haven't decided."

"You could print one of your jackdaw photos and frame it, to hang in his room."

By mutual agreement, they'd left their cellphones behind on the kitchen table. When Ellie picked hers up, she saw the voicemail icon and a number with a New York City area code. After listening to the lengthy message—twice—she fled to the porch to ponder her response to a call she couldn't ignore. She stared across the bay at the mountains range, illuminated by the sun. A hummingbird soared down from a branch to the nectar feeder hanging from the nearest tree.

She heard Dan's suitcase rolling across the living room floor.

When he joined her, she blurted, "I had a weird telephone call. From the Colmans' attorney."

"Oh?"

"They're inviting me to their house on Long Island. They'll take care of my travel. Round-trip flight from Manchester, in premier class. A car and driver from La Guardia to Southampton and back."

"They must need to confer with you about a legal or a financial matter."

"Doubtful. Actually, impossible. I inherited both of Harry's trust funds and was the sole beneficiary of his life insurance policy." She exhaled heavily. "I don't want to see them."

"Can't you devise a plausible excuse?"

"I won't try. Harry would want me to make nice."

He stepped away from her. Lowering his voice, he said, "I can change my plane reservation and go with you."

"That wouldn't be fair to Hannah."

"What about your Aunt Camille?"

"She's having a holiday in Quebec, at a cousin's cottage in the middle of nowhere. It's okay. I'll survive." A movement near the dock caught her eye. "Look—the loons. Let's go down to the water so you can see them up close."

Chapter 26

Years had passed since Ellie had entered the gated compound in Edge of Woods, an area of Long Island between
Southampton Village and North Sea. Towering deciduous
and evergreen trees encircled the lime-washed brick house,
centered within an exquisitely manicured lawn. Over a
century old, it was a rare survivor, an old-money, old-fashioned residence that hadn't been razed and replaced by a
monstrosity of a modern mansion.

Her father-in-law's hair had turned silver and his face
and neck were thinner, though tanned from the summer
sun. Releasing her from a surprisingly tight hug, he said,
"Delighted to see you again."

"Good to see you, Mr. Colman."

"Henry, please. We're glad you were able to come so
soon. Your flight was on time? I hope you didn't encounter
any traffic jams on the expressway."

"No." She might have been talking to Daddo. Travel
details, traffic report. She guessed he was about to mention
the weather.

"Fortunately, the humidity has receded—you've arrived on the best day we've had all week. Up north in New Hampshire you must have been spared the misery."

"We did have a muggy spell."

"Leave your bag right here, and Faye will take it up to the guest quarters." After hesitating, he added, "We didn't know whether you'd wish to stay in Harry's bedroom. Lana's on the terrace. If you want to freshen up before joining us, the powder room is there." He pointed at a door down the hall. What will you have to drink?"

"A glass of white wine would be perfect."

The downstairs bathroom was papered with fern leaves on a cream background. Examining her reflection in the gilt-framed oval mirror hanging above the sink, she decided she looked not bad for someone whose journey had included one hour driving, forty-five minutes in the airport, over an hour in the sky, and ninety minutes in a chauffeured car. She freshened her lipstick and ran a comb through her hair.

Before opening the door, she whispered, "Help me, Harry."

The kitchen layout was unchanged, no walls had been removed to open it up or enlarge it. She stepped through French doors to the brick-paved terrace adjacent to the swimming pool. Henry rose from his chair and presented her wine. Lana, stretched out on a lounger, wore a cotton tunic over her slacks and dark glasses despite the afternoon shade.

"Don't get up," said Ellie, leaning over to give the older woman a semblance of an embrace.

Lana removed her sunglasses. "Splendid to see you again. Your parents are well? And your brother and sister?"

Ellie sat down in a vacant chair, wondering if this was a hallucination. The Colmans' cool politeness was replaced by genuine warmth.

"Everybody's fine. Mom and her sister are busy running their dance academy and teaching. At this time of year, my father spends part of the week on the seacoast. He has a saltwater fishing license and a fancy boat and claims to be retired. Liam's not convinced. He manages The Shamrock, but Daddo is still actively involved. Marie's in Boston, doing her best to keep us all alive as a medical researcher."

"They must be happy you're home. For how long?"

"I return to London in ten days, to start rehearsals for a play. A debut drama written by Gil Cooke, Harry's roommate at Juilliard. You must remember him."

"When did he find you?" Lana asked.

Ellie's arm froze before her wineglass reached her lips. "Find me?"

"Whenever he telephones, he asks us about you. At Christmastime. On Harry's birthday."

Henry added, "When he requested contact information, I sort of fibbed and said we didn't know anything. It didn't feel right to give out your parents' number or address."

During the years of Stella Nue-ing around the world, cocooned by tight security protocols, she'd been shielded from casual contact with faithful fans and obsessed weirdos. But not at the smaller, intimate Archway Cabaret, where Lisa the stage kitten had delivered Gil's unsigned note.

He'd never mentioned his conversations with the Colmans, or any prior efforts to track her down.

"We're serving crab cakes for dinner," Lana announced. "They came from the market, pre-made. Faye bought a fish stew as well. And she'll make a tossed salad. We rely on her for an evening meal if we have company. I take care of the simple ones. Toast and eggs, or cereal in the mornings. Sandwiches for lunch. I don't see very well. Macular degeneration."

"Is there a cure for it?"

"None," Lana replied, "although more effective treatments have been developed. I don't drive. I'm thankful to have ebooks, with type I can enlarge. Audiobooks are a godsend."

"I know what you mean," Ellie told her. "Traveling so much, I appreciate the convenience and portability. But I prefer print books." She glanced at Henry. "You have lots of them, I remember."

"In the evenings I often read to Lana. Our tastes in literature are different. She's expanding my horizons."

"Tomorrow morning," Lana said, "I'd like to show you items that were Harry's. We wondered if you might like to have some of them."

After all this time, she marveled, they're offering keepsakes?

"The hammock is gone," she realized.

"It became an eyesore," Henry told her. "At our advanced age, getting into it was no easier than climbing out."

The conversation shifted in to areas common to wealthy people. The real estate market, the preference for new construction over existing houses, and the poor manners or blatant obnoxiousness of inconsiderate beachgoers and boaters. After the older couple excused themselves to change for dinner, Ellie made a brief excursion through the property, walking from the pool house across the grass, past immaculate perennial beds to the shadowy coolness beneath the fir trees. She remembered Harry pointing out the place where he'd built forts with his friends. Two large tree trunks formed a natural proscenium for staging plays.

Entering the house, she went upstairs. She opened the door to Harry's room. The furniture was the same but personal items had been removed. They had shared his bed for a full week when the ballet company was on summer hiatus and his parents had been on a Danube River cruise. Staying at a house with a large yard and a pool had been a welcome change from his dorm room and the tiny Manhattan apartment she shared with her ballet colleague Melinda. They ate takeout pizza on the terrace and attended a play and visited a beach but didn't swim because of reported shark sightings. One night, Harry grilled steaks but was so preoccupied and jittery that he almost burned them. She discovered the cause of his uncharacteristic nervousness when he proposed to her. During a make-out session. In the hammock.

On the train, returning to the city, they planned a speedy wedding in the nearest accessible New Jersey location. The following weekend they went to Weehawken with a hastily obtained marriage license, overnight bags, and the requisite two witnesses. Melinda, her bridesmaid, had smuggled Ellie's *Swan Lake* Polish princess costume out of the CIB wardrobe room. Harry's best man was a castmate from the spring production at Juilliard.

Looking back, she was astonished by her readiness to become a bride at seventeen. She'd had few life skills after spending most of her years in a ballet studio. Harry, mature for his age, educated in the best schools, supported by trust funds that spewed out money, was better prepared for the responsibilities that came with marriage.

After the seafood dinner, Henry invited Ellie to join him and Lana in the formal living room. The silent audience for their conversation consisted of family members whose portraits decorated the wood-paneled walls.

"Last year we sold our Barbados property. Air travel has become so fraught, and in recent years our enclave there has changed a great deal. We'll continue living in this house as long as we're able. Because we would've signed it over to Harry, Lana and I hope you might want it."

She examined the two expectant faces before formulating a response. "I'm already part owner of a seasonal lake cottage. A house in the Hamptons would require a lot more attention. And maintenance."

"You might find it convenient," Lana said, "if you return to New York to work."

Living there, or here, without Harry was as unappealing a prospect as living in London without Dan would be. Imagining her existence as a Broadway or Off-Broadway performer gave her no pleasure. The professional theatre world was populated with an infinite number of aspirants and very few successful ones. The leading role in a London play would enhance her resume, but it couldn't ensure future success on this side of the Atlantic.

Mustering a smile, she told them, "This conversation seems premature for a healthy couple in their sixties. During dinner you described your activities—the golfing and pickleball and chess nights. You'll be enjoying this lovely home for decades."

Henry cleared his throat. "That's our hope. Losing our son at such a young age is proof that nothing can be taken for granted."

In what Lana referred to as the morning room, two flat cardboard boxes waited for Ellie on the glass-topped coffee table. Light poured from the picture windows behind the sofa where she sat, spilling onto a pale floral rug in the middle of the tiled floor.

"If you want to look at the contents without me here, I don't mind."

"Please stay."

Her mother-in-law's diamond rings glittered as she placed a hand on one box. "Childhood mementoes. His summer camp name badges. Certificates from the tennis tournaments and archery competitions. Newspaper clippings."

Ellie removed the lid and picked up a file folder. The articles about Harry's high school plays and sports achievements were illustrated with photographs she'd never seen. Sorting through loose papers and documents, she recognized a narrow oval emblem hovering above several typed paragraphs of type. It was his acceptance letter from The Juilliard School.

If not for this, she realized, we wouldn't have met. Or married.

Opening the second box, she found a DVD sleeve marked *Much Ado About Nothing*. She held it up. "Have you watched it?"

"A few times. Not recently."

Here were playbills from the Shakespeare comedy and *A Streetcar Named Desire*. Beneath them she saw a cellphone with a coiled charging cable, an older model he'd probably used in high school. At the hospital she'd received the one she knew so well, full of photos and their messages and his saved webpages. She stared down at the printout of *Bare with Me*. "I didn't know he sent you my student thesis."

"He was as proud of your hard work researching and writing it as he was of what you achieved at City International Ballet. He never told us why you left."

"Frustration. Impatience. Unhappiness. As you know, there's no effective antidote for grief. I couldn't go back to CIB, so I accepted the offer from Ballet Bruxelles. Living in a different country was sort of therapeutic. I liked working for Mireille Charpentier, and Rafe Lawrence was there. After he retired from dancing and took an administrative position in London, I stayed on for one season more. Then I came back home."

"And your early interest in burlesque led to the surprising career shift."

"That's right. I developed my Stella Nue act at a New Jersey cabaret, and with help from friends expanded it into a show that we could take on the road. After conforming to all the restrictions of ballet, I was in complete control. Although I eventually discovered a downside to my success."

"You do seem to have a strong aversion to it," Lana observed.

"I haven't stopped dancing," Ellie said. "I take daily class at British Ballet Theatre, where Rafe is artistic director.

He wanted to hire me as a soloist, but I'd already agreed to do Gil's play." Hearing the break in her voice, she paused. "After all these years, I have a chance to prove that Harry was right. He believed I was destined to be an actress."

"Did he ever tell you how I got my name?"

She shook her head.

"My father adored the movie star Lana Turner. According to Henry, my remote connection to a Hollywood glamor queen caused our son's obsession. I hope you're as passionate about acting as Harry was. If not, you might someday feel as trapped as you did in ballet and burlesque."

Ellie reeled from the brutal truth of that statement.

"Henry and I wonder if you're seeing anyone."

"I am."

"Gilbert Cooke?"

"A different Englishman."

"Yesterday, I didn't speak as frankly about him as I wanted to. Henry calls me a worrier and accuses me of creating worst-case scenarios. But I know he shares my concern about Gilbert's determination to contact you. He never explained why. If he wanted you to perform his play, he should've said so."

Ellie wouldn't upset Lana by voicing her own doubts about his motives, or reveal the outrageous untruths he'd told Dan. "Except for Harry and me, he didn't have any other friends at Juilliard. That's probably why he wanted to get in touch." Reverting to a happier subject, she said, "The man I'm seeing is a corporate executive I met shortly after arriving in London. Even though we don't have much in common, we're very compatible. But his father doesn't like me. Dealing with that—again—is difficult."

"Henry and I never disliked you, Ellie. We weren't able to know you very well, because your dancing took up so much of your time. Harry shouldn't have waited so long to tell us about the marriage. We would have preferred that he complete his college degree first. But we saw how happy he was."

"Dan tells me not to fret, that his dad just isn't well enough acquainted with me yet. I hate being the cause of tension between them."

Lana leaned forward. "It sounds like your Dan has made his choice. Harry, who made the same one, wouldn't want you to be alone. Neither do his parents." With a brisk nod, she said, "Now, about shipping these items to you. Where should we send them?"

"The lake house. I'll write the address for Faye."

Lana stood and moved to the window to tweak a fold in the striped curtain. Turning around, she asked, "Is there any chance your play might transfer from London to New York?"

"None at all. It's a four-week run. At a minor theatre."

"I wish we could see it. Perhaps after it closes, you'll reconsider turning down that offer from the ballet company. I can't help thinking that's where you belong."

Until this moment, Ellie had never detected any similarities between Harry's mother and hers.

☆

The constant motion of passing pedestrians, the hum of voices, the beeping from electric carts, the strange overhead lighting and industrial carpeting underfoot, instilled a reflective mood. An open book rested on Ellie's lap, unread, as she pondered recent conversations. Like the chorus in a Greek play Harry had performed, the most important and influential people in her life chanted in unison, all of them urging her to resume her ballet career. Mireille. Rafe. Anya. Mom. Lana.

Accepting Rafe's invitation to join his world-renowned company would allow her to remain in London. She could move from the studio, where she felt so safe, and onto the stage, to perform favorite roles and meet the challenge of new ones. After turning down the soloist position, she'd pushed away her regret and pretended to herself that she was content. Now, caught up in her airport epiphany, she sensed the awakening of a long-dormant desire to display her talents and find out how far into the future they would carry her. Dan—and his father—could watch her dance. Her status within BBT might prove to Sir Terence that she was a respected and respectable artist, worthy of his son's love.

Which, she reminded herself, she already was and had been all along.

She felt no remorse about extricating herself from *Fractures in the Heart*. Gil's untrustworthiness, as revealed over the past few days, was another compelling reason to do so. He'd told Dan falsehoods about her husband and her and their marriage. He had concealed from her his determined efforts to obtain her contact information from the Colmans. After she dropped out of the production, she wouldn't have to see him again.

Rehearsals hadn't started yet. The director could easily re-cast Lyla. Cait Murray represented dozens of experienced, prominent actresses who could better serve as a foil to Lucas Daltrey. His wife Caroline ought to be a prime contender.

Sorry, Harry.

Ellie's fellow passengers in the lounge swarmed in the direction of the uniformed man at the check-in desk, who must have just announced the pre-boarding process. Ignoring the mix of humanity that would share her flight to Manchester, she dug into a pocket for her phone.

Swiping through her list of contacts, she pressed Rafe's photo.

Your favorite sylph, she typed, *has decided to return to her glade.*

Chapter 27

During the pilot's command for the flight attendants to prepare for descent into London airspace, Ellie tucked the script into one of the compartments of her enclosure. For the past two weeks it sat on the dining table at the lake cottage, untouched and unread. After her fleeting trip to Long Island, she'd avoided it altogether.

When Ellie phoned her London theatrical agent to discuss terminating her agreement with the Sovereign Theatre Group, she didn't reveal that animus towards Gil Cooke was a motivating factor. She expressed concern about her ability to rehearse and perform her role in *Fractures in the Heart* while simultaneously fulfilling her responsibilities at BBT. Cait Murray was adamantly opposed. Withdrawing at such a late date, she declared, would upend the production and its promotional campaign and cause severe reputational damage. Ellie, valuing her professional integrity and aware of the importance of preserving it, agreed to continue with the play.

"The Sovereign Theatre Group can't extend the run—

another production is scheduled at the Ormond shortly after yours closes. Your weeks of double duty will pass in a flash," Cait consoled her. "Exhaustion will ensure that you sleep through the night."

The time difference between New Hampshire and London had regulated her final weeks at the lake, as she and her New York manager and Rafe and his staff worked out details of her BBT contract. She'd carried the final document to the Birchmont Dance Academy so her mother and her aunt could witness her signature.

She hadn't admitted to anyone her increasing unease, based on experience, about her work schedule's effect on her relationship with Dan. She kept him apprised of developments as they occurred, and he responded politely but unenthusiastically. He sounded distant, unsure, just when she needed to prepare him for the impact of her dual career. They would both have to adjust to the multiple demands on her time, energy, and attention. After the fateful weekend in the West Country, she'd spent most or all of every evening with him. That wouldn't be possible for as long as she remained a soloist at BBT.

She'd been on the cusp of a fulltime dance career while dating Harry, and after marrying him she received multiple promotions. At City International Ballet, she was contracted for thirty-six weeks per year, leaving several months to lead a relatively normal life—for a dancer—and between seasons she'd gone elsewhere for class. British Ballet Theatre had employed her for a full fifty-two weeks, with salary and benefits and summer vacation leave.

She wouldn't let the past color her expectations. Despite the common culture within ballet companies, there were many differences. At City International, performers at every level of the hierarchy existed in an atmosphere of intense pressure and competition, too often resulting in injured bodies, bruised egos, and bad behavior. The coaches were no happier—Sven Eilert hadn't remained beyond one season, and Mireille Charpentier stayed only two. She ran Ballet Bruxelles like a finishing school, maintaining strict formality in the studios and insisting that her people treat one another with politeness and respect. The contradictory effect of conformity and restraint was an explosion of personality and passion in rehearsals and, more importantly, on the stage.

Rafe had infused BBT with his "ballet is serious fun" outlook. His dancers gave every impression of being happy and healthy, compatible and comradely. They smiled a lot, and they laughed. They socialized after hours. They pranked each other—with affection, not malice. They moaned about Marcus Baldwin's and Anya Semerova's complex combinations but feared neither, or any other coach or staff member.

The plane bumped its way through cloud cover and followed the broad and winding ribbon of the River Thames. When it touched down on the assigned runway at Heathrow, the sun was setting.

The driver Ellie had hired through a door-to-door car service was waiting for her in the arrivals hall, bearing a white placard with her Colman surname plainly written in black marker. She asked him to wait while she made a quick run along aisles of the mini-market, purchasing a sandwich and a bottle of coconut water. In the short-stay car park, he opened the rear car door for her before stowing her suitcase in the boot. As soon as he was behind the wheel, he made a phone call.

"Traffic's buggered up," he told her, "in all directions. Tube workers striking. Again. Till tomorrow."

"It's okay. I'm not in a hurry."

She was already home.

The feeling intensified when she entered the Latimer House flat. She messaged her thanks to Dan for stocking the fridge with milk and eggs and butter. He'd also left a loaf of bread and a selection of fresh fruit on the kitchen counter.

When she'd eaten her airport sandwich and popped a melatonin pill, she climbed into the Biedermeier sleigh bed, made up by the cleaning lady.

In the morning, making no concessions to jet lag, she traveled through the flowing underground system to her new place of employment.

Her barre buddy Gemma, freshly promoted from the corps to soloist, commiserated with a girl complaining about traction alopecia.

"If I lose any more hair, I'll be almost as bald as my grandpa."

"Save the tight bun and hairspray for performances," Ellie advised the young woman, who didn't yet know they were colleagues. "Wear a loose, messy bun in class and rehearsal. Switch to baby shampoo, or something just as mild. Don't use a permanent hair color—chemicals are drying and increase breakage. Regular scalp massage helps, too."

At the barre, Ellie was glad to work her legs after spending the previous day confined to the plane's first-class cabin. She concentrated on the placement of head, shoulders, arms, wrists, hands, fingers. When changing from her slippers to pointe shoes, she considered a session in the physio suite to strengthen her muscles. She wouldn't participate in rehearsals until Rafe figured out where he'd fit her into the repertoire, but she wanted to be ready.

The dancers were battling gravity in the final *grand allegro* combination when he entered the studio. The final group finished, decreasing their velocity to avoid crashing into the mirrored wall. Marcus clapped his hands and invited everyone to gather near the front of the room.

"Attention, everyone. Rafe has an announcement."

Ellie grabbed her towel from her bag and dried her damp forehead and neck.

"Fear not, I won't keep you from your coffee and carbs

for long," Rafe began. "I came to tell you about a new addition to our company roster. Although we preserve the classical tradition at BBT, we also strive to be flexible and innovative. We've therefore created a unique category of performer. Please join me in welcoming Ellie Lowery as our supporting solo artist."

During the eruption of applause, Gemma Banks hugged her. Leah Sternberg headed the line of others eager to do the same. Receiving their congratulations, Ellie could read the thoughts whirling inside their bunheads. *Which of my parts will she take? What men are they pairing her with?* The questions were normal, even in this remarkably cohesive company. She was wondering, too.

Raising his voice above the commotion, Rafe went on, "As you may be aware, I had the great privilege of partnering her at City International and Ballet Bruxelles and on various European stages."

As the dancers dispersed, he took her aside.

"Our personnel director prepared the documents for updating your skilled worker visa. You need to review and sign the paperwork so it can be submitted. She's also got your identification badge, which has the bar code you need for canteen access and food purchases. By tomorrow you'll find your name on a shared dressing room and a compartment in the shoe room. Your preferred brand lasts longer than most, so you won't be as great a drain on our budget as some of your colleagues. Might as well stop by the wardrobe department, so they can take your measurements."

A necessary ordeal, one she'd always hated, and she steeled herself for the usual embarrassment. But the cheerful, chatty woman responsible for recording her height and bust and waist didn't make her feel like a freak.

"Eighty-seven point five centimeters on top. You wear a thirty-four bra?"

"I'm afraid so."

"We accommodate all sizes, dear. Not in ways that restrict the lungs or hamper upper body movement, either. Some of our ladies come back to us after having a baby and rely on us to make them look perfect. Don't tense up, now."

Ellie tried to relax while the tape was stretched between her shoulder blades, along her torso, and around her waist and hips. An assistant wrote down the numbers as they were announced.

Returning to her flat to change clothes and grab a bite before an afternoon meeting at the Sovereign Theatre, she found an exuberant arrangement delivered from the Latimer Row florist. In response to her grateful text to the givers, she received a prompt reply from Martin: *Let's discuss a long-term tenancy, ballerina!*

Stepping onto the narrow, sun-bathed balcony, she considered ways to personalize it. Some evergreen topiaries, like the ones that abounded outside shops, pubs, and townhouses. There was plenty of light. Meyer lemons would surely flower and fruit here.

I could get a dog, she thought.

Her parents used to have one. Liam still did. She'd always wanted one of her own.

She required a compact breed suited to a cosmopolitan lifestyle. A specific dog that lived with her at Latimer House and spent the day in Dan's upstairs flat—or in his office. Before she left for morning class, they could both take it to Green Park. During his lunch hour, he'd be able to provide it with midday and after work exercise. When she had afternoons or evenings off, they could all return to the park. On Sundays, they would go on excursions in the countryside. She intended to consult Gemma Banks. The magnificently massive canine that shared her tiny flat was a very visible presence in her social media accounts.

A celebration was in order, she decided, before Dan traveled to Gloucestershire for his brother's birthday. A restaurant reputed to be one of Mayfair's oldest and most beautiful was within walking distance of their respective abodes. Top-tier establishments held a place or two open for famous diners, and if relying on the Stella Nue name was necessary to secure one, she would.

Dan didn't answer by the second or third ring, as he usually did. She was mentally composing a message for his voicemail when he picked up.

"Good news," she chirped. "Rafe came to the studio and made the official announcement to the entire company."

"You danced this morning? After that long flight—and the time zone shift?"

"The best way to bounce back from jet lag. I'm calling to invite you to that old world place on Jermyn Street. I'm hungry enough do justice to a gourmet meal."

Silence.

"Doesn't have to be tonight. Anytime this week is fine."

"We should talk," he told her, his tone heavy. "Soon. I've got something important to tell you."

"I'm listening."

"In person."

That sounded bad. Terrible, in fact. She had a premonition—no, a conviction. Dan was about to dump her. Pushing past the fog of dread that enveloped her, she said, "Go ahead. Do it now, if that's easier."

"It's not."

Her dancer's superstition kicked in, warning her not to let negative vibes invade her domestic space. Might as well end the relationship where it began. "Meet me at the Ritz. Rivoli Bar. Six o'clock," she added, hoping he hadn't detected the quiver in her voice. With a shaking hand she put her phone on the table beside the sofa.

He owed her an explanation. And he was man enough to face her while giving it. She'd heard of guys who sent their partner a final farewell text. Would that be way better or more harrowing than what was about to transpire?

She had no history of breakups. She'd married her only other boyfriend.

A month ago, she'd anticipated a proposal and had planned what to wear at their wedding. What a colossal jinx that turned out to be.

To lose Dan on this of all days, her first as a BBT employee, seemed monumentally unfair. While reentering a profession beset by insecurities, she would be deprived of emotional support. Her family members were thousands of miles away. Harry, who'd been at her side at Juilliard and during her tenure at City International Ballet, was dead. Rafe, her longtime confidant and now her boss, had myriad responsibilities.

I definitely need a dog, she concluded.

He felt his resolve ebbing with every footstep. But doubt and regret were overpowered by his desire—no, his need—to curtail the agony he'd endured since he'd last seen Ellie. He loved a woman whose heart was severely and permanently shattered. He couldn't heal it and had no hope of ever possessing the whole of it.

He walked past the round table of their initial encounter many months ago. She occupied a sofa, her vibrant beauty exceeding that of the naked goddess in the decorative mythological panel over her head. On the table before her was a blueish cocktail in a martini glass, not the one she'd ordered the night they met.

After he sat down across from her, the waiter brought him a bar menu. He handed it back and requested his favorite single malt, a short pour for an outrageously high price.

Ellie's eyelashes fluttered. "Brian will be happy to see you again so soon after his Games Day. Did he enjoy it?"

"He was awarded a prize for effort. It meant a lot to Dad and Sandra and me."

She responded with a fleeting half-smile before saying coolly, "We might as well dispense with the small talk. I've watched this scene in plenty of television shows and more movies than I can name. That night at the cottage, when we were in bed, I sensed a change in you. It was even more obvious the next morning."

"While I was with you that day, I wondered if we were—" He looked up at the glassy figure on the wall. "Since coming back to London, it became clearer to me that I'm not ready for a—that I couldn't let our—" God, this was worse than he thought it would be.

"That sounds like the preamble to, 'It's not you, it's me.'"

"My feelings for you are unprecedented. Please understand that."

"Are? Or were?"

"It's because I care about you that I have to be completely candid. We both have demanding careers. You've got two of them. Martin has a habit of turning special projects over to me, either to manage or to delegate, but either way, my role is supervisory. I spend so much of my free time—weekends, I mean—in Gloucestershire. A committed relationship is . . . " He ran out of words again.

"Is what?"

"The timing's not ideal. For either of us." Unable to expand on this feeble explanation, he added, "If you ever need anything, you can ring me. I mean that."

"Good to know." Her voice was so devoid of inflection, he couldn't tell if she was being sarcastic. She picked up her glass to empty it, then placed it on the scalloped paper mat. Taking the keys to his flat from her jacket pocket, she dropped them in the middle of the table. She rose and picked up her handbag from an empty chair. "Tell your father I said hello. And goodbye."

Dan had spent days summoning the fortitude for this conversation. Ellie, intuiting what he would say, dispassionately hearing him out, suppressing her emotions, was the strong one.

He heard her murmur something to the man behind the bar before she exited.

As he swallowed the last of his whisky, the waiter appeared with a second glass on his tray.

"The lady said you wanted another."

She was right.

After pressing the ignition switch to shut down the Jaguar's engine, Dan reached for the birthday gift on the passenger seat. The wrapping on the framed jackdaw photo was printed with colored balloons. He never could guess how Brian would react to unfamiliar items, but removing the paper would employ motor skills his physical therapists had spent years restoring.

When he signed in at reception, the woman on duty said, "If we gave a prize for popularity, your brother would be today's winner."

Dad had stopped in on the way to his Bristol office. At lunchtime, Sandra brought over the birthday cake she'd baked.

"Can you find out whether Dr. Daventry is able to see me? My dad was in a hurry this morning and couldn't ask if there's a decision about arranging Brian's visit to Tayer Court."

"Wouldn't that be grand? No need to page him, you'll find him in his office."

At the far end of a broad corridor, the chief administrator conversed with a tall and slender female. Whatever he said made her turn.

His chest ached as though he'd received a blow.

"Lady Lucinda was with Brian for a quarter of an hour," Dr. Daventry said. "In the day room."

Her iron gray hair was bluntly chopped in a pageboy style. It used to be glossy brown-black and coiled in a bun behind her head. He couldn't help asking, "Does Dad know you planned to come today?"

"I'm on the list of permitted visitors," she declared. "I always have been." Her voice was different, too, pitched lower than he remembered.

Every parting line he could think of sounded like an insult. *How considerate of you, traveling all the way from Scotland to spend fifteen minutes with your brain-damaged son. Thanks for remembering Brian's birthday, it almost makes up for ignoring mine.* Choosing not to be blatantly rude to the person who had taught him manners, he said nothing at all.

I've got problems enough, he thought, hurrying towards the day room. I don't need this one.

Brian was wearing a baggy sweatshirt embroidered with a bright red Scottish lion. He grinned up at Dan before dipping a spoon into his bowl of chocolate ice cream and the remnants of Sandra's sponge cake.

"Happy birthday, Brian. Hello, Norman."

"I've been telling him he'd have a fourth visitor," the attendant said. "That's a record for one day. You. Sir Terry. Sandra. And your mum."

"Has she visited before?"

Norman shrugged. "Can't say. If so, it was before my time."

"Or when you were off-duty."

"Nah. I'd have been informed. What we got here?" Norman asked, pointing at the parcel.

"A picture to hang in his room." Dan sat with his brother at the table. "How's that ice cream?"

Brian nodded vigorously.

"Here's a birthday present. You can open it." He watched the unsteady hands pull away the paper, revealing the image. "This is Jack. Our bird friend in the garden at Tayer Court." It wouldn't be fair—or productive—to ask if Brian remembered. Would he retain the memory of this one-sided conversation? Regarding Norman, he said, "Tell me about his interaction with his prior visitor. What did she say to him?"

"She described where she lives and what she does there. She told him about watching seals and sea eagles from a jetty. Walking in the hills when the heather blooms. Sounded just like you, talking about that bird in your dad's garden."

Dan disliked being compared to his mother as much as he did the description of her idyllic Highland existence.

Brian's forefinger tapped the picture.

"Norman will hang it in your room." Dan asked if he looked forward to the next movie night, nodding at the replies Norman gave. He wanted to outstay their estranged parent but suspected Brian needed quiet time after the unprecedented parade of people.

Before going, he ruffled the thatch of dark hair so similar to his. The same shade their mother's used to be.

His hope that she'd left the premises was dashed when he saw her seated on a bench that was directly and unavoidably in his path. Sunglasses shielded her eyes, and she'd tied a scarf over her hair.

As soon as he was within earshot she said, "I've identified your motorcar. You used to dream of owning a Jaguar."

He was in no mood to entertain her reminiscences.

"Coming to Harding Hall was difficult for me," she went on, "in this anxious time. My father is declining rapidly, and he's putting his affairs in order while he's able. Your uncle and I are co-executors. You bear the Wheeler surname, but you're equally a Neast of Tredington. Under the terms of the will, you'll receive a legacy."

"I neither want nor need it. Tell my grandfather to assign it to Brian."

"His share will be placed in a trust, to be jointly administered by you and your father." Her fingers plucked the ends of her scarf. "I met the members of his care team, who gave me all the details of his therapy regimen. They told me how often you and Terry visit him. Dr. Daventry sends reports, but I'm glad to see for myself that he's healthy and comfortable."

"I was unaware it mattered to you."

"My love for my sons is constant, unaffected by time and distance." She placed her fidgety hands in her lap and clasped them. "Depression is as unpredictable as it is cruel. Although mine began as situational, it was later diagnosed as clinical. When I lost all desire to continue my existence, I dreaded inflicting another tragedy on those I never stopped loving."

"You think you didn't?"

"My condition forced me into a terrible choice. I don't expect understanding or compassion from you. What I did was absolutely necessary for my self-preservation. And it was kinder and better to go. By staying, I would've caused all of us a great deal more anguish."

He'd told himself the same thing, to salve his conscience, before and after informing Ellie of his decision to part from her.

"My husband is coming to collect me. I daresay you prefer to get away before he arrives." She removed her sunglasses and peered up at him. "You're resilient, like your father, I've always known that. And you've done well professionally. Your personal life is a mystery to me. I do hope it brings you happiness."

"It did. Until a fortnight ago."

"What happened?"

"She was put off by Dad's refusal to condone our relationship. A repeat of past trauma—her late husband's parents never accepted her. That, combined with demand-ing and conflicting work schedules, made our situation even more untenable."

He wouldn't admit that his qualms about Ellie's attach-ment to a dead husband had led to the break-up. Or that since being abandoned in the Rivoli Bar, his love for her had intensified. Along with his regret.

"It's been ages since I've dished out motherly advice, and I may never have another chance. Follow your heart, Dan. Wherever, to whomever, it leads."

Depression wasn't supposed to be contagious, but during his brief exposure to a sufferer, he'd contracted something that closely resembled it. Driving back to Tayer Court, he won-dered if his mother's next destination was the churchyard. He imagined her walking past graves of dead Wheelers and Dimerys and Tayers on the way to Oll's burial place, shaded by the spreading branches of an ancient yew tree.

The only time she visited the unconscious Brian's hospital room, he'd been attached to monitors and the machine that regulated his breathing. Her reaction was so frenzied that a medic put her under sedation, and she remained bedridden at home until the day of her eldest son's funeral and inter-ment. Dan's grandparents, the Earl and Countess of Treding-ton, wanted to send her to a sanitarium for treatment. Dad, rejecting this drastic measure, arranged her sessions with Dr. Blair and chauffeured her to Bristol every week.

The therapist introduced the Wheelers to his brother, who was spending his annual holiday in the city. Soon afterwards, Dan's mother decided to drive her herself to the appointments. The following week she was late returning to Tayer Court—Mr. Blair from Scotland had invited her to tea. One rainy evening she rang the house to say she'd met her new friend for drinks at the Grand Hotel on Broad Street and would stay the night, since she was too tipsy to be behind the wheel. She spent the following weekend in Weston-Super-Mare, ostensibly by herself. On her return, she tearfully confessed that the Scotsman had been with her, but swore she hadn't violated her marriage vows. She also stated her intention of seeking an immediate divorce, on the grounds of incompatibility, and would move to her parents' Georgian mansion just outside Gloucester. At some point she left them to join her Mr. Blair in the Highlands. Six months after she received the final decree, she married him.

Dan tried not to dwell on that fraught period, preferring to recall years when his family had been intact. He and his brothers had played cricket on their pitch behind Kington Cottage, where they grew up. On rainy days, they sat at the dining room table with their miniature cars, rolling them across the flat surface. They raced along the public footpath through the woods and at the edge of the fields. They rode their bicycles to nearby Tayer Court, always receiving a warm welcome from the Wheeler grandparents.

They spent Christmas and Boxing Day at Tredington Hall, chafing at the formality and ritual, and picking quarrels with their Neast cousins. Muddy shoes and antique Aubusson rugs didn't mix well. The elders scolded whenever drawing room conversations were punctuated by repeated pings and buzzing from handheld video games.

Just beyond Sandra's house, Dan approached a tractor with an extended hedge-cutting arm and had to reduce speed. The lane was narrow with many bends, and he couldn't risk overtaking. Impatient to reach the one place where Lady Lucinda Blair would never turn up, he watched the blade's teeth slice through tangled branches, leaving behind a green trail of chopped stems and shredded leaves. Broken and wasted, like his hopes of a future with Ellie.

In the kitchen his father greeted him gleefully, saying, "When I popped in to that fishmonger's on the city's east side for scallops, he tempted me with this beauty." He peeled away butcher paper to reveal a large salmon fillet.

Dan set his key fob on the worktop. "Mother was at Harding Hall." He had never called her that in his life, but to him she could no longer be Mum.

Apparently unperturbed, Dad prodded the pink flesh of his purchase. "I know. Daventry rang after their conference. No adverse effect on Brian, he said."

"It was otherwise for me. A strange and exceedingly awkward reunion."

"Poor Lucy. One of our firm's Gloucester clients told me Old Tredington is fading and isn't likely to cling on more than a week at the most. I'll let you know about his funeral or memorial service, whatever the Neasts arrange. Both of us have to attend, you understand."

Dan moved to the window. The canvas cover of the barbecue was draped over a patio chair, billowing in the wind like a sail on a boat. "Oll was his favorite. He never seemed terribly interested in me or Brian."

"Titled chaps of his generation invest the firstborn male with primacy. Oliver would've inherited my baronetcy, if he'd outlived me, as you will when I pop my clogs. Your uncle will soon become master of Tredington Hall. Eventually the title and estate will pass to his eldest son—the one you used to kick under the table at Christmas dinner. Lucy was fortunate in being the only daughter. It conferred special status and infinite privileges."

A sudden and staggering bolt of insight struck Dan. The two of them had each loved and lost a woman who was unable to fully reciprocate their love. This realization emboldened him to pose a question he'd suppressed for many years.

"Do you still feel a connection to her? Despite everything?"

"After more than two decades as husband and wife and raising three boys together, a legal judgment didn't entirely dissolve our bond. Your brothers' accident changed her from the person who loved us and lived with us. The passage of time does foster acceptance of what used to be painful and incomprehensible. I sincerely hope Lucy found the serenity she desperately desired."

Dan wondered if Ellie was feeling serene. He wasn't.

Shortly before coming to Gloucestershire, he'd stopped at the Ormond Stage. Her name and photo appeared with Lucas Daltrey's on the eye-catching promotional banner draped over the entrance. It had lured him into the box office to purchase a ticket for the opening performance.

He delayed his departure until Sandra returned from a shopping expedition to Thornbury. She presented him with a thick wedge of Double Gloucester and a paper sack of chocolate chip cookies.

"These can't be as good as yours," he told her, tucking them in his overnight bag.

"I don't bake them nowadays. Wouldn't be fair to Terry to tempt him when he's so disciplined about his diet. I tell him when a man reaches a certain age, he should eat anything he wants. I reckon he keeps himself slim for Pamela."

Dan discovered that despite his low spirits, he was capable of laughter.

Dad came through the garden door. "What's so amusing?" He removed his hat and kicked off his garden shoes.

"You are."

He drew half a dozen shiny red tomatoes from his garden trug before handing it and the secateurs to Dan. "Cut some roses to take with you. You'll be spoilt for choice. We had rain enough a few weeks back to produce a lavish late summer flush."

Chapter 28

Ellie, mulling over her woes, failed to follow developments in the murder mystery episode she thought she was watching. The suspenseful soundtrack drew her attention back to the television, and she discovered the suspected killer had just been killed. After that, there was no point paying attention.

When Gil, a constant presence at rehearsals, invited her to his dad's closing night party, she turned him down. In a meeting with a Sovereign Theatre Group publicist, she and Lucas had learned about their scheduled promotional activities for *Fractures in the Heart*. She'd arrived at the supermarket without a list and forgot to pick up lemons and hummus and steel cut oats. A disappointing voicemail from the animal shelter informed her that the young mongrel in an enchanting website photo required a suburban or rural home with outdoor space.

Her days were busy. Her solitary evenings were excruciating. Without Dan, the hours dragged by. She missed their shared meals. The cute way he furrowed his forehead when they watched television. His kisses. The gloriously fulfilling sex.

Her cellphone buzzed a text notification. Ever hopeful, she pressed the icon. Rafe's face popped up.

Lurking in your territory @ The Wolseley. Dinner companions departing. Care to join me for a nightcap?

Easy decision.

Recovering from a rough day. You come here.

She contacted Lorcan's evening replacement at the lobby desk, letting him know she expected a visitor.

She saw no reason to change out of comfy loungewear for a man who knew her body almost as well as he did his own and wouldn't care about her messy hair. She did straighten the sofa cushions and stowed her rolled-up Pilates mat in the corner. She swept up the pink petals that had dropped from the bouquet that had arrived early in the week. She'd compared the roses to photos she'd taken of the nameless plant at Tayer Court, the one Sir Terence referred to as TC37. Dan, identified as the giver by her doorman, hadn't included a note.

Peace offering? Condolence gift?

Before showing Rafe around the flat—this was his first visit—she offered him a drink.

"Make it non-alcoholic. I'm well beyond my limit."

"Orange squash?"

"That'll do."

She concluded the tour in the study. Pulling aside a curtain, she took him onto the balcony to gaze upon nighttime Mayfair.

"What luck, living in such splendor. And close to the Ormond Stage."

"I'm considering a move," she told him when they went inside.

"Where to?"

"Near Regent's Park. And BBT. I can't continue living

a street away from my ex." Eventually Dan would find her replacement, and there was a strong likelihood of uncomfortable encounters in Latimer Row, and in the bookstore, or at the cheese shop. She'd see them at the wine bar, seated at his favorite table.

"To rent or buy?"

She shrugged. "Either. My financial advisor is always saying I need to diversify my investments—though I doubt he was thinking about London property. After class tomorrow, I'm meeting an estate agent to check out two flats. A one-bedroom penthouse on Fitzroy Street, with roof terrace and garden views. The other, on Cleveland Street, has two bedrooms for the same price. Both have high ceilings and lots of light." She liked the canine-friendly wooden flooring and their proximity to a dog daycare facility with a five-star rating.

"You know I'm in Grafton Mews. We'd be neighbors. That's the appeal, right?"

"Naturally."

"I'm here to tell my favorite sylph when she'll take flight. It's time we discussed the Autumn Gala."

That sounded promising. "Okay."

"Late November. Royal Albert Hall. Double bill. *Les Sylphides*—although I'll use the original title, *Chopiniana*. Paired with my ballet about Chopin and Liszt and their mistresses." He leaned forward, palms pressed against his knees. "A program of contrasts. The dreamy poet and two dozen sylphs fluttering about in the moonlight in Romantic style tutus. Followed by the drama and tortured passion of two musician friends and their human muses. You stated unequivocally that you're ready to return to the forest glade. How do you feel about lifts?"

"Who's doing the lifting?"

"Drew Mason. I'm putting you in the opening *pas de trois* and the C minor waltz. You'll have the D flat mazurka as well. Supported arabesques. *Jetés* and *pas de chats* and *port de bras.*"

"I remember. When do rehearsals start?"

"Not till the middle of October. After your play closes."

His duties as artistic director didn't leave spare time for creating choreography, and the debut of his new work was a major event. The gala was destined to attract an international audience and would be a magnet for dance critics from major publications. They would see her reprise a favorite part in her most beloved ballet.

"I've got plans for my solo supporting artist." He slurred his words. "Supporting solo artist, I mean. I'm thinking White Cat in *Swan Lake*, first cast. Lilac Fairy, third or fourth cast. A stepsister in *Cinderella*. Maybe Sugar Plum in *The Nutcracker.*" He placed his empty glass on the table at his elbow. "A *prima,* you can probably guess who, retires at the end of season—there's an announcement coming. It has a huge impact on our two-week European summer tour of *Giselle.* I've long imagined you as a fierce and fearsome little Myrthe."

"With this hair?" She pulled at a strand. "Every Queen of the Wilis I've ever seen was brunette."

"Doesn't have to be."

"Me, as Myrthe." She shook her head. "How much drinking did you do at the Wolseley?"

"Not so much that I'll forget to put you on the *Sylphides* cast list."

"Move farther downstage," Joan Wadsworth instructed Ellie. "About five paces. Don't turn back when Lucas speaks his line. That will heighten the tension."

Ellie marked the movement with her hands, like a dancer—awkwardly, because of the script she held. She stepped past the faded sofa that represented a bed, and remembered to avoid the pieces of tape indicating where the other furniture would be positioned.

She wasn't sure whether she should be glad or sorry Gil hadn't joined them in this rented rehearsal studio. The longer she delayed telling him about her contract with BBT, the worse his reaction would be. On the other hand, concealment felt like payback for all the whoppers he'd told Dan.

During their break, Lucas warned her of probable changes to their dialogue and adjustments to the blocking. "That's common with new plays. Because nobody is familiar with the text or staging, the audience won't know when we muck something up," he said reassuringly.

Having learned her speeches and cues as currently written, she hoped she'd pick up alterations as easily as she did shifts in choreography.

"It's an adjustment, expressing character conflict through words instead of ballet mime."

"You've done it before."

"With Beatrice and Benedick, verbal sparring was a game, a competition. They were witty and funny. Lyla and Randall are intentionally cruel and insulting."

"When Caroline and I worked together on *Forsaken Fortune,* our director tried to put us at odds off the set and on, to build up the conflict between us. He didn't know that we'd been secretly married for months. When you come to Hampstead for dinner, you'll hear all about it from my wife."

"I'm eager to see those matching Oscar statues. And the baby."

"That you will. We'll let you hold our awards and our boy. Not at the same time."

On Sunday, her day off, Ellie attended a reunion of her drama class. They met at a Chinatown noodle bar, claiming the largest available table and requisitioning extra chairs. Everyone was bursting with news. Simrat would voice a popular children's book character for a renowned animation studio. The improv troupe formed by four members of the group—Graeme, Rose, Val, and Declan—had secured a weekly pub gig. Tony the Canadian was cast as a constable in an amateur Agatha Christie play in Hampstead. Archie, employed by the academy part-time, received an hourly wage and free tuition to an advanced class.

Before going their separate ways, everyone promised to come to Ellie's play. She accepted the chorus of "break a leg!" in the spirit it was given and refrained from cringing. As a dancer, she found it impossible to appreciate that phrase.

Chapter 29

The week before *Fractures in the Heart* transferred to the Ormond Stage, Ellie detected a faint glimmer of light at the end of the depressingly long tunnel of preparation. Gil accompanied the production team on a tour of the green room and dressing rooms and props storage area. One side of the stage was arranged as a sitting room, separated from the bedroom by a divider with a doorway opening.

While Joan and the stage manager conferred in the wings, Gil sidled up to Ellie. Over the summer he'd shortened his sandy hair and let his stubble beard grow out, and kept both neatly trimmed. "There's an exciting development to report. I can't tell the others yet, only you. Media interest and the surge in advance bookings did what Father and I couldn't. The Sovereign board is strongly in favor moving *Fractures* to the big theatre next spring. Don't worry, we're not recasting."

"In my case, you'll have to. I can't continue as Lyla."

"No false modesty. You're giving a great performance."

"I've signed a contract with British Ballet Theatre. Tomorrow I start rehearsing *Les Sylphides.*"

"I don't believe it."

She reached into her shoulder bag, pushing aside packets of gel blister pads and a roll of toe wrap tape and a paperback until she felt the slick plastic of her employee identification badge. "For real," she said, holding it up.

"But why?"

"Lots of reasons. I've known Rafe Lawrence since I was in the *corps de ballet*. He used to partner me."

"I know. Are you sleeping with him?"

"No!" She was so shocked by the question that she didn't immediately realize how offensive it was.

"You used to."

"Never." She'd only considered it when clawing her way up from her pit of grief, after he'd extricated himself from his second mistake of a marriage.

"That's the impression I got in Bruges, when I saw the two you together onstage."

She choked on her indrawn breath. "Saw us? In what?"

"An unsubtle and overblown version of the *Eugene Onegin* opera."

His scathing description of a beloved ballet nettled her. "It's regarded as a masterpiece."

"I can't tell you the title of the one I saw in Amsterdam. Its score was unmistakably a Bach composition."

"Tribute." Had he stalked her all over Europe, or just through the Low Countries? She didn't want to know. She wondered if he'd also witnessed any of her Stella Nue shows before her arrival at the Archway Cabaret. The possibility that he'd repeatedly watched her disrobe was revolting. "You could've told me that you attended Ballet Bruxelles performances."

"Didn't seem important."

Another misleading statement. He hadn't wanted her to know. Because he knew perfectly well that she'd think it was creepy.

After closing night, she consoled herself, I won't have to see him again. Ever.

To her relief, his name never came up during her evening with Lucas and his wife Caroline at their Hampstead townhouse. She felt comfortable enough to confess how they had been caricatured in her drama class play. Unfazed by her admission, they declared that their visibility since the release of *Forsaken Fortune* and its sequel had desensitized them to ridicule. They'd been targeted by every comedian on each side of the Atlantic, and most scathingly, in a Saturday evening sketch show on American television.

The next morning Ellie went straight from class to her *Les Sylphides* soloists' rehearsal. She and Gemma Banks and two other young women joined Drew Mason in the studio, with Anya and Rafe coaching them and a beaming Barry at the piano. The process was as exhilarating as it was arduous, and the familiar strains of Chopin's nocturne fed her soul and infused her body. Every note was embedded in her brain, and though five years had passed since she'd last performed Michel Fokine's delicate choreography, she discovered the durability of muscle memory. Drew's hands on her waist, raising her off the ground, felt novel but also natural.

Rafe, characteristically upbeat, declared it to be a promising start.

Anya approached Ellie to give helpful guidance about the timing of her *bourrées*. "Tomorrow, we repeat section."

The women of the corps drifted in to observe while waiting for their session with Marcus. The staging required them to be omnipresent, alternating between movement and still poses to form picturesque tableaux.

When Ellie removed the pointe shoes and protective padding from her hardworking feet, she stuffed them into her GaitGuard sneakers and trotted over to the Regent's

Park station. Her own image stared back at her from the *Fractures* posters, wearing the same lost expression she sometimes faced in her bathroom mirror. Glamorous, sexy Stella Nue was replaced by pensive Lyla.

Returning to her temporary residence, she showered and ate a late lunch. She had time to nap or read until time to walk over to the Ormond Stage. Instead, she powered on her laptop to review photographs of the two prospective properties she'd visited. She then read everything her internet search produced about the character and care of a moyen-klein poodle.

Going to the theatre, she avoided Latimer Row, the most direct route. If she passed Dan's building, he might see her from his office window and assume that she wanted him to.

The eve of the press preview was fraught. After a problematic run-through, everyone assembled for production notes, tossing off the overused adage that a glitchy tech week ensured an error-free first night. Ellie and Lucas collapsed onto the sofa of the living room set, and their understudies settled in the armchairs. The tension was as palpable as the exhaustion.

When Joan, admirably calm, completed her commentary, she asked the playwright if he had anything to add.

"I know it's awfully late for a blocking change," Gil said. "The one I have in mind for Ellie is simple." He turned to her. "Come over here, and I'll demonstrate."

She got up.

"Watch us, Lucas. You're facing each other, like this, when you say, 'I won't apologize.' Pause. Turn. 'Unless *you* do.' Ellie, when I walk towards the bedroom, you follow. Try to stop me. Get physical."

When she was close enough to grab his arm, he backed up. The hard heel of his shoe pounded the bridge of her foot, crunching the toes.

From Ballet to Burlesque
to the Boards and Back

In the spring, when I interviewed the diminutive auburn-haired beauty in her luxurious suite at the Ritz, she was the glamorous international burlesque star Stella Nue. Today, gracing a table in a Mayfair restaurant, she's Ellie Lowery, professional ballerina—and debut London actress. She appears as Lyla Carrigan in the new drama *Fractures in the Heart,* which opened this week at the Ormond Stage. Recently recruited by British Ballet as a soloist, she's currently rehearsing *Les Sylphides* for the company's highly anticipated Autumn Gala.

She thrives on variety.

"I received my initial dance training from my mother and her sister," she explains. "When I was married to an actor [the late Harry Colman, her Juilliard schoolmate], we performed together. I wrote a student thesis about burlesque and years later developed my own act."

Throughout the twists and turns and career shifts, the twenty-nine-year-old Lowery has consistently excelled in her endeavors.

The swan costume she wore at the Archway Cabaret is on permanent display at the fashion museum, and several others can be viewed as part of a new exhibition. Lola LaFlamme, one of Lowery's many former burlesque colleagues at the opening reception, credited her as an inspiration and a mentor.

According to playwright Gilbert Cooke, son of Oscar-winner Sir Francis, she was his only choice to portray the conflicted wife in his tale of a splintering marriage.

"Lyla is complex," Lowery says, "and Ellie's portrayal of her character's weaknesses and strengths is brilliant. As the possessive and self-absorbed Randall, Lucas [Daltrey, her co-star in the two-hander] goes well beyond the cliché version of a jealous husband."

What is it like, co-starring with a heartthrob who also possesses an Academy Award and major acting honors? Lowery concedes that in the run up to rehearsals, it was a daunting prospect.

"I can honestly say that working together has been a privilege and a pleasure, and I've learned a great deal from our onstage collaboration. Becoming acquainted with Caroline [Bryden, Daltrey's wife, mother of their infant son] was a bonus. When reading press accounts of their whirlwind romance and secret marriage, I never imagined I'd someday regard them as friends."

What of her own love life? When asked if a special someone waits for her to exit the stage each evening, she laughs softly.

"If I described my schedule in detail, you'd understand why not. I spend all day dancing. Every night I'm at the Ormond Stage, being Lyla."

Dan read through the final paragraphs a second time before turning the page of his newspaper. There she was again, in an advert, curled on bed in a fetal position with a frowning Lucas Daltrey stretched out beside her. They were surrounded by glowing and exclamatory review quotes printed in bold type.

She was inescapable. He encountered her image in social media promotions, on the posters lining the walls of tube station escalators, and in larger versions hanging in the tunnels. At Green Park, someone had placed a red heart sticker on the face he used to kiss.

Tonight, for the first time since her abrupt departure from the Rivoli Bar, he would see the real Ellie. She didn't know he had a ticket for opening night, because an envelope containing five of them for various dates had been dropped off at the office. He gave a pair to her fangirls Lou and Kelly, one to his secretary, and left another two at the club for his father and Pamela.

Ellie and Lucas Daltrey proved their unmistakable chemistry from the first minutes of their opening scene. The hours she'd spent in morning class and rehearsal hadn't dimmed her energy, but he detected a hitch in her stride. He supposed it was a late addition to the script, which she'd let him read when he was in New Hampshire, although it wasn't explained.

At the interval he went to the lobby bar, so packed with patrons that he didn't bother ordering a drink. The playwright stood against a wall. When he noticed Dan, he began weaving through the crowd with intent.

"Hello again. Enjoying the performance?"

"It deserves every accolade."

Gil's sandy head bobbed. "We hope for similar success in six months, when we transfer to the Sovereign Theatre. I've recently completed my next play, a satirical comedy, to prove my versatility. And Ellie's. She doesn't know about it yet, so don't tell her."

"I won't." He'd never been so glad to hear the chime that would send the audience members rushing to their seats. It prevented him from calling out the other man as a liar, which he was sorely tempted to do.

The rising curtain revealed a shirtless Lucas, wearing

trousers without a belt, picking up pieces of broken crockery. Ellie sat slumped on the edge of the bed. Her hair was mussed, and her untucked blouse was partly unbuttoned, revealing her bra and exposed cleavage. One bare foot was wrapped in a flesh-colored bandage.

When he'd made love to Ellie that last time, Dan had been the mournful one. She'd twined her legs around him and rested her cheek on his chest, unaware of his inner turmoil. He hadn't spoiled the moment for her by sharing his distress. He told himself it would ease, eventually. But after he returned to London, she telephoned him to describe her rapprochement with Colmans. She'd accompanied them on a gravesite visit and accepted a box of memorabilia they offered her. They wanted her to occupy their house when they no longer wished to live there. Though she didn't say so, it all added up to a symbolic reunion with her late husband.

The second act depicted the complete disintegration of the couple's marriage. In Randall, the playwright presented his version of Harry Colman—an egotistical bully, belittling his wife while demanding her devotion and fidelity. In the final moments, Lyla stood alone on the stage, free of the emotional and physical abuse she'd suffered. The lights went dark, and the curtain fell.

Deafening applause shattered the hush that had descended over the auditorium.

Up went the curtain, revealing Ellie and Lucas. With hands clasped, they bowed in acknowledgment of the enthusiastic acclaim.

The stranger seated next to Dan looked over at him and commented, "A star is born."

Star. Stella. Ellie.

He wondered whether she saw him in the middle row, clapping so hard that his palms stung. His chest ached with pride—and pent-up, undeclared love for the woman he had relinquished, without telling her the real reason.

Arriving in the physio suite, Ellie felt sure that today she'd be allowed to put on her pointe shoes again.

Because everyone understood the potential danger of stage work, her nonspecific explanation for the severely bruised toes was accepted without question. In class she performed her barre and center routines in dance slippers and refrained from bouncing and leaping. During rehearsals, she was permitted to mark any sections that might hamper recovery. Drew made every effort to be accommodating. After each lift, he set her down gently, reducing but never eliminating the pain of landing.

"Before I saw those x-rays," her myotherapist said, "I was afraid they'd have to change the title of your play to *Fractures in the Foot*."

"Not funny."

"Are you using stretch bands and your foot roller?"

"Yes. And I'm trying not to limp."

"Good girl. Shifting your weight to the other leg would impact your hip, and we can't have that. The skin over the metatarsal has turned a lovely greenish yellow, an improvement over that ghastly purple. By gala night, you'll hardly remember you were injured."

Oh, but I will, she silently contradicted, as he manipulated each toe joint.

"How much does that hurt?"

"A minor twinge. Can I practice in my Mindens today?"

"With ample cushioning in the toe box and tape over the bruise. Come back after rehearsal so I can check you over. We'll have an ice bath ready."

She danced on pointe for the nocturne and her solo but removed her shoes for the second *pas de deux* with Drew, and the final *grande valse*. The next day she wore them longer, with no adverse effects.

Incremental progress. Constant striving for perfection. The essence and the infinite challenge of ballet.

After another evaluation by her new best friend in the physio suite, she sank her feet into the vat of icy water he'd prepared for her. She read the latest email from her agent Cait, who was fielding inquiries from movie casting directors and theatrical producers. Ellie tapped out instructions to decline all audition requests but added that she'd might consider endorsements for dancewear.

No more acting jobs, she typed. *Until I retire from this one.*

Sorry, Harry.

Hours later when she passed through the Ormond's stage door, her mood was chipper. In preparation for her penultimate performance as Lyla, she put on the costume that didn't look like one—a blouse and jacket and pencil skirt—and sat down at the mirror to apply her makeup. She joined Lucas in the green room for their ritual cup of lemon-infused tea.

"You really are amazing," he told her. "Hopping about and twirling on a mashed foot before emoting all evening on the stage."

"I also squeezed in a phone chat with my Aunt Camille about Stella Nue merchandising. What about you?"

"I watched Caroline feed the sprog. Babysat him while she was at the gym. Rinsed sick off his onesie and my shirt. Fell asleep reading a screenplay."

"Must not have been any good," she surmised.

"This late in the year, the most intriguing productions have already been cast. Not sure I can fit in something before resuming *Fractures.* I'm gutted that you can't face working with me again."

"You know that's not the reason. Caroline will be a fantastic Lyla. She'll probably receive an Olivier nomination. You're sure to get another one yourself. I predict two more matching awards."

"I told her ripping up at me every night for a paying audience means we'll never need to quarrel at home."

At the conclusion of the second act, they met in the middle of the stage. While waiting for the curtain to rise, Lucas whispered, "You're going to miss this. Admit it."

"I'll miss *you*," she replied, squeezing his hand.

"You won't get the chance. We'll keep in touch."

After the usual number of bows, they returned to their dressing rooms. Ellie unfastened the lower buttons of her top and slipped it off. She hung it with her skirt and jacket on the clothes rail and changed into the long-sleeved jersey and track suit bottoms she wore for her five-minute walk back and forth from Latimer House. She never bothered removing her makeup for the quick trip through the darkness.

Before she could grab her fleece hoodie, somebody tapped on the door.

Gil stepped past her, satchel in hand. He placed it on her makeup table and pulled out a stack of papers tied together with a crimson ribbon. "The first draft of my next play. A modern version of *Much Ado*. Romantic comedy with bite."

Unclenching her jaw, she replied, "I don't want it."

"You told me how much you enjoyed playing Beatrice."

"Because I had Harry for my Benedick."

"There's no conflict with the ballet contract. This play won't go into production before next autumn."

Fortified by the knowledge that their association was nearing its end, she said, "Gil, we're finished. I mean forever. I shouldn't have to tell you why, but I will. You repeatedly asked my in-laws for information about me. You never told me you attended Ballet Bruxelles performances. You deliberately crushed my foot, to stop me from dancing. Most unforgivable of all, you told Dan Wheeler those awful, vicious lies about Harry."

"I lived with him before you did," he shot back. "He had a dark side."

"We all do. Nobody's perfect, everyone has flaws. He was a normal human being. I can't say the same about you."

"You've got no idea what your precious Harry was like when you weren't around. He talked about you. A lot. When he was with me." He took a step towards her and shoved his mobile at her.

"Go away, Gil. I'm tired. And fed up with your nasty tricks." She snatched her hoodie from the chair.

"Wait. I want you to hear this." His forefinger slid across the surface of his phone. "I'll raise the volume."

Before she reached the door, the unforgettable mellow voice, forever silenced so many years ago, made her stop. And listen.

Chapter 30

Harry: I'm her first. She was never intimate with anybody else.

Gil: How can you be sure? Not all those ballet boys are gay.

Harry: I'm one hundred percent positive. Do I have to spell it out for you?

Gil: You've seen how those chaps pick her up. Their hands on her tits. Grabbing her crotch. I reckon she gets aroused, being touched like that. Everywhere.

Harry: It's a performance. Not an orgy.

Gil: All those bodies rubbing up against her, and practically no clothes on. None of the girls in her group have a figure like hers. They starve themselves until they stop having periods. And they look like they'd break into pieces if you shagged them.

Harry: Ellie's sensible about food.

Gil: Can you make her come every time you two have sex?

Harry: Get your mind out of the gutter, man.

Gil: Better enjoy it while it lasts.

Harry: What makes you think it won't?

Ellie's fist knocked the phone out of his hand. "Did he know you recorded that conversation? When was it?"

"I visited him in Williamstown, when he apprenticed with the theatre there. You were in Montreal."

She'd accompanied her mother, hired to lead an intensive at her former ballet company, with the added benefit of a tuition waiver for Ellie. Mom had been a broken record, carping at her about sleeping with her boyfriend, warning her not to get pregnant. Right after she returned to New York, Harry took her to his parents' empty house out on Long Island, where he proposed.

Gil was anxiously checking his phone for damage. Looking up, he said, "Harry married you so he could keep you to himself. He was jealous of other guys, all the time. He told me so. Often."

"That's not true. He wasn't insecure about me, or us. He knew perfectly well he had no reason to be." Her glare dared him to contradict her. "You loaded your characters with your twisted feelings about him and me. You exploited us. And tarnished our marriage. I'm only Lyla when I'm on the stage. Randall isn't Harry. He's *you*. Keep away from me, or I swear to God, I'll tell your father how you've treated me."

"He won't believe you."

"Don't be so sure." His expression proved that she'd landed a blow where he was weakest. "I'm a gifted actress, all the reviewers say so. I intend to be very convincing when I tell Sir Francis Cooke that his son is a duplicitous rat. And if you don't leave me alone, I'll report you to the Sovereign Theatre Group personnel department."

"For what?"

"Harassment. Physical injury. And invasion of privacy. Mine and my late husband's."

She picked up her bag and burst thorough the dressing room door, slamming it behind her. She wished she could lock him inside.

Walking through the murky darkness, she became aware of an exhaustion that was equally emotional and physical. Halting beside an iron railing beaded with raindrops, she thrust her arms into the sleeves of her hoodie and fumbled with the zipper. The nearest streetlamp cast a beam onto a brass plaque beside the door.

She was standing in front of Dan's club.

He'd told her to contact him if she needed anything. She was desperate for an unthreatening, comforting presence.

She fumbled with her phone. Hearing Dan's voice giving instructions about leaving a voicemail, she canceled the call. She could think of several reasons he hadn't answered. He didn't want to talk to her. He'd gone to a movie. Or he could be inside this very building. Club members were prohibited from using mobiles in the common areas and were advised to keep them switched off.

She found the club's number on the website and dialed. "Is Mr. Wheeler there?" she asked the person on the other side of the brick wall. "Maybe in the bar?" At this late hour, the dining room would be closed.

"We're unable to relay that information, Madam."

"If you can find him, I'd appreciate your letting him know that a friend of his is standing outside. In the rain. Thank you."

While waiting, she examined her messages and found a fresh text from Gil. She deleted it without reading. And blocked him.

The glossy black door opened. Heedless of the raindrops, she pushed back her hood to expose her face.

"Ellie?"

The father. She wanted the son.

"I specifically asked for *Mister* Wheeler," she blurted. "You're the Sir."

"Dan's not here. He's seeing whatever is on at the cinema in Curzon Street."

"Oh." One of her guesses had been correct.

"I've been at an orchestral concert, my way of relaxing after a most trying day. We attended his grandfather's memorial service at St. Mary Abbott's Church in Kensington, and a family gathering afterwards. My former wife was there with her husband." He cleared his throat before saying, "Forgive my inability to invite you inside. I'm prevented by our extremely strict rules about correct attire for members and guests."

Her composure crumbled. She bent her wrist and pressed it against each eye in a futile attempt to push back the tears.

Moving closer, he said calmly, "I doubt there's a safer street in London, but a female in distress shouldn't wander about alone at this advanced hour. I'll walk with you to Latimer House."

"You'll get wet," she said shakily.

"You think I've never been rained on? I'm British. And a gardener. Come along." He was silent until they reached the corner. "Pamela and I were impressed by *Fractures in the Heart*. It forced me to reconsider my prejudice against modern dramas. Dan said you provided our tickets."

"Yes." Almost home—she could see Latimer House at the corner.

He opened the residents' door and followed her inside. "Good evening, Angelo," he greeted the night porter.

"Hello, Sir Terence."

Ellie, eyeing her escort's damp blazer, told him, "I'll go upstairs for my umbrella. You can borrow it."

"If it's not an imposition, I'd prefer the drink I didn't have a chance to order in the bar."

"Oh. Okay. Sure."

During their elevator journey to the top floor, she lowered her hood. "How do you know Angelo?"

"He was our club doorman. Dan and I recommended him to Martin Latimer for the night porter job when Lorcan took the day shift."

When they entered the flat, she went directly to the kitchen and pointed to a cupboard. "That's where you'll find Dan's favorite single malt. Glassware is in the next one over. I want to clean up."

"What shall I pour for you?"

"White wine, please."

The reflection in her bathroom mirror should have appalled her, but she was past caring. Her guest's opinion of her was so low, her bedraggled appearance couldn't diminish it. While soaping and rinsing her face, she wondered whether he'd come here with an agenda. She hoped he'd speak his piece without delay and leave. She'd experienced more than enough angst, on stage and off, for one night.

He'd taken their drinks to the informal sitting room, and was studying the framed travel poster of a gondolier passing beneath an arched bridge over a Venetian canal.

"You must have been here before," she surmised.

"Occasionally." He handed her a very full wineglass.

"After the Autumn Gala, I'm moving out. I'd rather not live this close to Dan. I wouldn't have tried to reach him if I hadn't been upset by—by something that happened at the theatre. It was a reflex."

"I'm a willing surrogate. Perhaps I can help."

"Nobody can," she said bleakly, gravitating to her favorite spot on the sofa. "Gil Cooke, the playwright, barged into my dressing room. I threatened to inform the management if he bothers me again. But I won't have to. The show closes tomorrow."

"Be specific. Did he get physical? Were you attacked?"

"He's not daring enough to go that far. He plays mind games. His methods are stealth and manipulation. Not many minutes ago, I discovered that when he was my future husband's roommate at Juilliard, he tried—and failed—to undermine our relationship. He used that same trick on Dan, telling him I was married to a possessive jerk and my marriage was a nightmare. It was the worst kind of gaslighting. I didn't know about it till Dan came to New Hampshire. I told him about the real Harry, how much we loved and supported each other. Always."

"How did he react?"

"He was surprised. He'd believed everything Gil said."

"You hadn't previously spoken to him about your husband?"

"Only in general terms. We met at school. He was a really good actor. That's about it."

"You've just solved the mystery of my son's abrupt—and most unexpected—decision to detach himself from you."

"It should've been perfectly obvious. You won, Sir Terence."

"Please call me Terry. I can understand why you think so. My part in the rupture, if any, was negligible. Outwardly, Dan gives the impression of being the quintessential middle child. But that easygoing temperament conceals a longing to measure up to others. He spent years in the shadow of an impressive and accomplished older brother. He had a lively younger sibling who was quite the charmer. His sense of self changed drastically when we lost Oliver and, in a different way, Brian. While he was adjusting to an altered identity, his mother left us."

"I know." She looked straight at him when she said,

"All the years after losing Harry, I wasn't seriously—or casually—involved with anybody. When I met Dan, I was instantly attracted, but I wasn't looking to fall in love. Certainly not so fast, in the all-consuming way I doubted I'd ever experience again. I believed he felt the same about me. Until he told me he wanted to end our relationship. That was crushing. But I had to accept his choice."

"In doing so, you apparently confirmed his belief that you couldn't love him as much as you did your husband."

"I do." Ellie got up and crossed the room to close the curtains, blocking out distant star-like lights that glowed in other windows. "And it makes no difference."

"Shouldn't it?"

"Living after loss, coping with hardship in my work life, taught me to accept situations that I can't change or control. Like Dan, I responded based on my history. Neither you nor I can be sure about his motivation. Whatever it was, I'm certain he wouldn't want me clinging on, or guilting him into staying with me. Which would only prolong and increase his misery. Missing somebody who is still alive, living and working in the next street, is agony. Every day since the breakup has been a challenge. But I've experienced a loss that's far, far worse. Like you and Dan did. It doesn't, it mustn't define us. Not entirely."

"Agreed."

"Years ago, my grief counselor told me that when the most terrible, unimaginable thing happens, there's an urge to look for meaning in it. That impulse, she said, can be redirected towards a purpose, and action. So that's what I did. I created a charitable foundation. I followed Rafe to Ballet Bruxelles. I became a burlesque performer and built a name brand and a business. I accepted the role in Gil's play." She pointed to the dance publication on the coffee table. "I'm back where I started. When I signed my BBT contract, I didn't know Dan was about to cut me loose. Work can't cure heartbreak, but I'm thankful to have a job that takes up a lot of my time. And concentration."

Terry picked up the magazine and studied the table of contents. Looking up, he told her, "After reading Dame Alicia's memoir, I was inspired to seek out a substantial and heavily-researched biography. I was unaware that one of her sisters was a Windmill Girl and performed at a theatre not far from here. For thirty years it was famous for its nude revues and other forms of entertainment. Daily shows at the Windmill continued throughout the war. And during Blitz, when the bombs were falling all around the building."

"There was a movie about it," she recalled, wondering why he'd raised a thorny subject.

"Doris Marks never appeared without clothes, but her costumes were quite revealing. She was a soubrette, singing comic songs and dancing. Her employer, the rich old lady who created the nudie show, financed Alicia Markova's touring company. I admit, I'd never known of the strong historical connection between classical ballet and burlesque in Britain. If you're interested, I'll lend you the book."

"I'd like to read it."

Setting down his empty glass, he said, "I'm a solicitor. If you require an attorney to act on your behalf, I can provide recommendations. Mr. Cooke has demonstrated that he's unstable. You not only need to be wary of him, you should protect yourself."

"I've spent enough years as public figure to know the risks of bad publicity. Taking action against Gil would backfire on me and cause a hell of a lot of trouble at a sensitive moment in my career. Liar that he is, he would accuse me of enticement and drag in my Stella Nue exploits to justify his behavior. He isn't stupid. He's very ambitious. And he can't bear disappointing his father. My threat of exposure should be sufficiently daunting."

He stood up. "Nevertheless, I advise caution." Removing a business card from his inner jacket pocket, he said, "Take this. If you require legal advice or assistance of any kind, you should get in touch."

She followed him to the foyer. "All I want is your promise not to tell Dan. He already knows Gil deceived him. What happened at the theatre tonight doesn't concern him."

"He'd be extremely concerned, I assure you."

"He doesn't need to know," she said firmly, and pulled an umbrella from the stand near the door. "Good night— Terry."

Chapter 31

"Ready for your close up?" Ellie asked Gemma as they sat on the studio floor, unpacking their dance bags. "On World Ballet Day, everybody gets their fleeting moment of fame."

"Last year, my mum complained that she didn't see me often enough."

"The producer will have studied our website to pick out principals and soloists. If there's a camera pointed in your direction and its red light is on, don't wobble."

This wasn't her first time participating in the annual televised celebration of their art. For twenty-four hours, dance companies around the globe were appearing in real-time broadcasts of their morning class and rehearsals. Live and pre-recorded backstage tours rounded out the content. Interviewers would speak with selected personnel—artistic directors and their dancers, choreographers and costumers, set designers and builders, rehearsal pianists and conductors, sound and light technicians.

"What do you think about my leo?" Gemma asked anxiously. "Too much?"

"Not if you're trying to be noticed." Ellie stood up to pull the black warm-up trousers over her tights, positioning the elasticized waistband just below her midriff.

"You could've made an effort," her colleague complained.

"It's not a fashion show. Viewers want to see what we look like on a normal working day."

"Which this definitely is not."

According to the document all British Ballet Theatre employees received via email, class would be delayed by fifteen minutes. The technicians and camera and microphone operators were in position. Anya stood at the piano while a woman pinned a wireless lavaliere mic to her blouse and searched for a place to stow the power pack.

"Take it off," the producer called. "She'll create static when moving around. The boom can pick up whatever she says. Mr. Piano Man, give us a tune so we can check Ms. Semerova's levels when she's talking."

Barry pounded his keyboard, producing a crescendo of chords. Anya counted to twenty. The woman, crouched in a corner, removed her headphones and held up her thumbs.

"Will your mother be watching?" Gemma asked Ellie.

"If she gets up before dawn. The replay will be online till the end of time. She and my aunt will make their students study it."

"In a fortnight your whole family will be here for the gala. You must be excited."

Mom and Daddo, her sister and brother, and both aunts were arriving two days before Thanksgiving and would be eating their turkey dinner at her flat. She'd ordered a large bird from the Latimer Row butcher and would rely on Daddo and Liam to roast it and delegate preparation of the side dishes and desserts. The following night, they would witness her performance in *Les Sylphides*.

Marie the scientist would want to visit the Science

Museum and the adjacent Natural History Museum. Mom and Aunt Renée had made an appointment with Drew to discuss his possible participation in their academy's summer intensive. Camille, familiar with London, was capable of entertaining herself. Liam and Daddo intended to check out authentic Irish pubs, after stopping by that Blarney Burger outpost near Shaftesbury Avenue. They had also expressed interest in a sightseeing cruise on the Thames, from Westminster to Greenwich.

Ellie dipped into a *grand plié,* carefully aligning her hips to prevent overworking the flexors.

Rafe and the director of publicity stood just outside the studio. They were armed with handheld microphones and would offer a brief on-camera intro before the switchover to the studio feed.

"Remember, people," the producer called, "don't be distracted by our monitors or the camera. Pretend we're not here."

"Easy for him to say," Gemma muttered.

"Quiet on the set. Places, everyone."

As soon as class ended, viewers of the BBT livestream were treated to an interview with ballet master Marcus, who offered a preview of the season and the Continental summer tour and all the preparations it entailed. This was followed by a recorded segment in the wardrobe department and a demonstration of how a sylph's Romantic era tutu was constructed.

After watching the monitor for a few minutes, Ellie zipped up her bag and left the studio. She took the elevator to the ground floor to meet with the company's mental health practitioner.

Without naming Gil or his profession, she described his years-long stalking campaign, his dishonesty, and his attempt to hobble her. She recounted many of the details but not the location of their final encounter.

"This person exhibits the classic traits of pathological narcissism," the woman told her. "Lack of empathy. A sense of entitlement. Absence of remorse. Egocentric. Manipulative. Dominating. Your independent nature undermined his need to control. He acted out whenever you exerted your autonomy—starting a relationship with another man, signing with an agent someone else recommended, accepting the BBT contract. And there's an overt, longstanding sexual component to his fixation."

Like Sir Terry, the therapist recommended seeking legal remedies if Gil contacted her or doorstepped her. She provided a print-out with information on narcissistic personality disorder and encouraged her to return whenever she needed to talk.

"Emotions from a traumatic incident can resurface. You've probably had recurrences of the feelings you experienced at the time of your husband's death."

Ellie nodded. "And the physical sensations."

Her pulse raced when she let herself remember the heart-stopping phone call from the hospital. She felt dizzy reliving the longest car ride of her life, when Cousin Phil had driven her to the medical center. Her memory of the doctor solemnly informing her that nothing could've been done for Harry produced tremors.

She climbed a stairway to the dressing room section for soloists and principals. Her practice tutu, a facsimile of the one she would wear in the performance, was formed by layers of calf-length white tulle. Carrying her dance bag, she crossed the bridge connecting the annex to the theatre for a *Les Sylphides* stage rehearsal. While waiting for the film crew to complete their preparations, she chatted to Drew and sipped from her water bottle.

"It's almost time to go live," the director informed them. "Rafe, you and Ms. Semerova will face the camera. After a quick explanation of what's about to happen, introduce the dancers."

Ellie's damaged foot was fully functional, and ibuprofen

blotted the residual ache. Because this *pas de deux* had many hops and jumps and arabesques, she was thankful when Drew released her hand so she could begin the final *bourée en courir* into the wings.

When Barry, down in the pit, stopped playing, she returned to the stage to hear Anya's comments.

"Eeley, is good how you keep hands light and curved arms. Make shoulders stay down more for arabesques. In lifts, tilt face away from partner so audience will see. In this, smiling much is okay. And remember, audience will be on three sides, not just in front of you."

The cameraman moved in closer for Rafe's brief remarks about choreographer Michael Fokine and why *Les Sylphides* was referred to as a *ballet blanc*. When he handed the microphone to Ellie, she described the ballet as a favorite and said she looked forward to performing it for the gala. She passed the mic to Drew, who told her he'd be careful where he placed his hands so he wouldn't crush the delicate little fairy wings that would be attached to her back.

"You survived," said Gemma, when Ellie joined her in the crowded staff canteen.

"Apparently." She pried the lid off a yogurt cup. "What's next for you?"

"Walking the dog. Leah has vouchers from the new Pilates studio on Marylebone High Street, so we'll go there to schedule a trial class. We're both on tonight, in *Sylvia*. Have you checked the casting board? They've posted *Nutcracker*."

"I saw it."

"What parts did you get?"

"First cast, Columbine doll. Sugar Plum, third cast. You?"

"Second cast, mirliton *pas de deux*. Columbine, fourth cast. Clara's friend, first cast. They bring in pupils from a

Camden Town dance school for the party scene. I used to be one of them. We were in awe of the professionals and terrified of making mistakes. As you'll see, the current crop of kids is fearless. And rambunctious."

"Thanks for the warning."

When Ellie finished her snack, she tossed the empty container into the recycling bin. This corridor, which led to the staff and artists' entrance, was off-limits to the television people. The desk attendant offered a cheery farewell as Ellie pressed the door's metal bar. On the other side, she sucked in deep breaths of fresh October air and squinted from exposure to the afternoon glare. As usual, her sunglasses case had sunk to the bottom of her bag. She placed it on the brick retaining wall and scrounged around, teeth gritted in frustration.

"Ellie."

Dan sat on the bench directly across from her.

Her heart, which had settled in to a normal rhythm after her exertions, pounded against her ribcage. "This must be what the staff therapist meant by the term doorstepping. Why are you here?"

"Last night Dad messaged me with information about World Ballet Day. I skived off work so I could watch, only nobody would let me inside this building, or the theatre. I sat here and watched your rehearsal on my phone. And stayed, hoping I'd get a chance to tell you how magnificent you were."

She managed to produce a faint smile. "Thanks. Nothing like what you saw at the Archway, right?"

He maintained his sober expression. "And I need to apologize. For my colossal mistake."

Borrowing the phrase her therapist repeatedly used, she said, "Tell me more about that."

"From the moment you left me in the Rivoli Bar, I've been utterly wretched. And damned lonely."

"Me, too. Apology accepted." She sat beside him and released her bag's strap. "You wanted me to believe our work schedules were the reason you gave up on us. But you started having doubts and second thoughts after the boat trip, didn't you? Because I told you about Harry, and how happy we were."

"Yes."

"Here's something I didn't tell you. That day was the ninth anniversary of his death. I chose to spend it with you. I was thinking about our future, not my past. I never would've mentioned Harry if I hadn't been so enraged by Gil's lies about him. I owed it to my husband, to all of us, to refute them. I wish you'd told me then how it made you feel."

"Many months ago, trying to define Englishness for you, I mentioned cricket and kings. But I left out another characteristic—our chronic tendency to repress or withhold emotion. I was relieved that you hadn't been tyrannized, like your character in the play. I was also very much afraid you could never care about me in the way you did for the special person you lost."

"I can't. I don't. You're totally different. Harry liked gin. You prefer whisky. He was a New Yorker. You're British. He eloped with the teenaged ballet girl. You met a burlesque performer who wanted to be an actress."

"Unlike him, I didn't immediately realize you were my dream girl. Probably because you were a world-famous performer, swanning around the stage and taking off your clothes. I didn't dare hope I'd ever become acquainted with the alluring Stella Nue. Or imagine I'd meet her within an hour of leaving the show."

"When you joined me in the bar that night, I felt a spark. Camille knows. She said you offered to assist my apartment search because you had an ulterior motive. I told her I wouldn't mind if you did. By closing night, I was hoping you'd ask me out."

He ran his fingers along her neck and traced her shoulder. "I messed things up so badly. Dad said I should've admitted my concerns instead of making assumptions."

She stared at him. "He did?"

"More than once. He regrets his behavior, too. I assured him I'd put things right. In fact, I was planning a dramatic, ostentatious gesture. I meant to turn up on the night of your gala performance, with an armful of roses, and ask you to forgive me for being a such an idiot."

"Like a reconciliation scene from one of your black and white movies." Covering his hand with hers, she said, "No need to go to all that trouble. You're here, that's what's important. And you'll be at the Royal Albert Hall. I had lots of reasons for joining BBT, but the one nobody knows about is my secret longing for you to see me dance in ballets."

"I just did." He held up his phone.

"That was a rehearsal, it doesn't count. I've already assigned all my comps to my family—my parents and brother and sister and two aunts are coming over. I'll ask Rafe if I can have some of his seats, if you agree to an exchange. Tickets to the gala, in return for a favor. A really big one."

"Go on."

"My flat has enough bedrooms for Mom and Daddo and Liam and Marie, but not for Camille and Renée. Could the aunts use yours? Having all the family close would be so convenient."

"Certainly. I'll stay at the club."

"Oh, no." Hooking her arm through his, she said, "You'll be rooming with me."

Chapter 32

Many months ago, Ellie arrived in London to strut her stuff at the Archway for a few weeks and embark on her professional acting career. She hadn't imagined that she'd be cast in a ballet she loved and had never expected to dance again, or that she'd perform it in one of the world's most famous theatres. Standing backstage, adrenalin flowing, she was conscious of her usual contradictory impulses. She wanted to run to her dressing room and hide. She was impatient for the overture to begin and the lights to come up.

Members of the *corps de ballet* were busy with their warm ups, stretching their limbs, practicing steps. Their variously colored woolen shawls, knitted leg warmers, and bulky padded gilets contrasted with white shiny bodices and foamy skirts. Rafe was making the rounds, offering words of encouragement to neophytes before addressing similar words to each of his soloists.

Her affection and gratitude surged as she watched him move from sylph to sylph, his regal movements calling to mind his portrayals of Siegfried, Albrecht, Desiré, and

Oberon. Later, he would demonstrate how well he could rock a tuxedo.

After a brief dialogue with Drew, Rafe approached her.

Reaching out to adjust her floral coronet, he said fondly, "This gladdens my heart. Seeing you here, where you belong, for all the best reasons. Not to escape the meanness you experienced at City International. Or for the comfort you hoped for when joining me at Ballet Bruxelles. You'll never again be Rafe's Waif. You're perfectly balanced. And I don't mean on your feet."

"I'm a dancer who found out how to live her best life when not in the studio or onstage. With Dan. And our dog. And my friends."

"I look forward to creating a ballet on you. You're so loved up, it should be something romantic, don't you think? With a very happy ending."

"Cut the sentimentality, or I'll cry and mess up my face." She fluttered her false eyelashes. "When I quit burlesque, I swore I'd never wear these again. Now I am. For you."

He kissed each of her cheeks. "*Merde,* my darling sylph."

"Back at you, my forever partner."

The people she loved best were scattered throughout the horseshoe-shaped auditorium. Many of her relatives. Dan and Terry and Pamela. Lou and Kelly.

She fluffed up her tulle skirts and filled her lungs, conscious of the satin encasing her torso. Disjointed notes emerged from the orchestra as the musicians tuned up. Dancers removed their fleeces and leg warmers and made final adjustments to their shoe elastics and ribbons. When the instruments quieted, the crowd fell silent. They applauded the conductor as he took his place.

Ellie drifted into her spot on Drew's left side. Leaning across him, she pursed her lips at Gemma, miming a kiss. The third female soloist stretched out on the floor at their feet.

Drew prodded her with the toes of his slipper. "Don't fall asleep down there."

Their central grouping was surrounded by twenty sylphides, ten on either side of the stage, some standing and some kneeling. Their hair was identically styled and topped with a circlet of pale flowers.

Hearing an increase in the overture's tempo and volume, Ellie angled her head towards Drew's shoulder blade, careful not to let her rouged cheek brush his white sleeve. She raised her hands to her chest, fingers cupped. After sliding her right leg back in *tendu,* she adjusted her balance to ensure that her left leg wasn't supporting her entire body. She would maintain this pose until her cue to soar and to shine.

British Ballet Theatre board members, donors, and special guests descended to the colorful and, in Dan's opinion, excessively decorated bar in the theatre basement for a private reception. The walls were peacock blue, with ornamental tiles, and he was walking on a Moroccan-style carpet. Ellie's mother and aunts held court on a tufted sofa upholstered in gold velvet. Patrick Lowery and his son Liam were chatting with a bartender.

The one Lowery Dan hadn't met during his brief time in New Hampshire, more subdued than her charismatic relatives, stood beside him, observing the crowd. Turning to her, he commented, "Assembling a Thanksgiving feast for eight people in a foreign city didn't faze them at all."

"They loved doing it. Too bad Ellie spent our national holiday in the studio. At least she worked up a good appetite."

"Why didn't you have ballet training?"

"I was a girl jock. Track. Softball. I still play, with colleagues at my research institution. My partner's specialty is sports medicine—if I bust something, she can patch me up. Tomorrow she'll wake up to my pics of the creepiest exhibits at the Hunterian Museum. Bones and skulls. Surgical instruments. She'll probably insist on coming to London for our honeymoon, so she can see them herself."

"When is the wedding?"

"Within the year," Marie replied. "Most likely on our island—Martha's Vineyard. My sister wanted us to exchange vows at the lake cottage. On the dock, with the mountains as a backdrop."

Was that Ellie's dream location? Before asking her, he needed to get through the preliminaries.

The conversational buzz subsided when the artistic director called for attention. After thanking the assembled donors for their support and praising his staff, he acknowledged the performers' diligence when preparing two ballets within a relatively short time, while rehearsing other works in the repertory. His voice cracked with emotion as he expressed his extreme pride in the entire company.

Ellie, no longer the fairylike creature who had danced across the stage, had resumed her human form. At Dan's suggestion, she wore the full-skirted, blue-green dress he remembered from the after-party the night of her final appearance as Stella Nue. Her auburn hair, freed from the ballet bun, was held away from her face by a diamanté band.

"Who's the guy talking to your main squeeze?" Marie asked him.

"My dad, who recently joined the BBT Board of Directors." The two of them looked very much at ease, sitting side by side on a sofa.

He passed through the crowd to join them, positioning himself on an adjacent armchair boldly patterned in kaleidoscope colors.

Dad said, "We're discussing my TC37 cultivar. I was telling Ellie I'd like to call it *Chopiniana.*"

"That would suit a white rose," she said. "I have a better suggestion for your pink one. Stella Nue." When he didn't say anything, she asked, "Too risqué?"

"Just enough to attract buyers' attention. But that name is a registered trademark, isn't it?"

"I'll grant you a license for commercial use, royalty-free, for one pound." She added, "With conditions. I've provided start-up funding for Harding Hall's new dance therapy program. I want you to contribute a portion of your profits to it. In Brian's name."

"That's extraordinarily generous. Isn't it, Dan?"

"Indeed," he replied.

Ellie flagged down a server and asked to borrow his biro. "What price does your grower charge per plant?"

"Twenty-five pounds."

"You receive a percentage of the sales. Net or gross?"

"Net. The shipping fee is an add-on. My share out is in the region of fifty per cent."

"At Tayer Court, you said you expect to sell five hundred plants from your catalog."

"You've got an exceptional memory."

"Occupational necessity." Ellie jotted numbers on a napkin. Looking up, she announced, "Just over six thousand pounds. From the United Kingdom. For years, Aunt Camille has dealt with international suppliers and knows all about customs regulations. She can research our Department of Agriculture certification process and requirements for importation of plants. Canada, a Commonwealth nation, has a parallel entity. I can't predict when we'll find overseas growers to handle grafting and distribution, but we can start looking. For North American regions, you'll need to test for hardiness. New Hampshire would be ideal, with a span of USDA Zones 3 to 6." She studied their faces. "Am I going too fast?"

"When Dan described you as an astute businesswoman, he didn't exaggerate."

"There's a close alignment between creativity and commercialism, Terry. You know that."

His father got up. "Pamela's giving me a meaningful look. We've got an early morning flight to Milan. When we're back, we'll bore you both senseless with our descriptions of culture cramming at La Scala."

Dan moved to the place beside Ellie. "I've tried to get you alone for days. This isn't the most private of settings, but I'm not waiting any longer to say what's on my mind."

She scrawled another number on the napkin and drew a line under it. "I'm listening."

To make sure, he took away the pen. "It's important."

That got her attention. "I'm having Rivoli Bar flashbacks."

"This is the opposite of a brush off. Harry's favorite tipple was different to mine," he began. "In choosing a wife, our preferences are exactly the same. When you feel ready to marry again, if you ever do, I'd very much like to be your next husband."

"Oh, you will."

"You're sure?"

"I've already decided what I'll wear for our wedding. Terry has seen it."

"How? Where?"

"At the BBT Friends reception, when you were out of town. It's a designer gown. Ivory silk with sequins scattered on the overskirt. It'll be my something old."

"Here's something blue." He reached into his jacket's inner pocket. Taking her hand, he turned it over and placed the necklace in her palm. "A souvenir from Brighton. It's called a journey pendant. Ours is just beginning."

"These are aquamarines. Our birthstone. That's why you wanted me to wear this dress—it matches." She turned and held her hair away from her neck. "Put it on."

Securing the tiny clasp, he whispered in her ear, "I love you, Ellie Lowery. Mrs. Colman. Stella Nue."

She swiveled around. "I'm absolutely certain I fell in love before you did."

"I suspect we'll be debating that point for the rest of our lives," he said, before kissing her on the lips.

On moving day at Latimer House, Ellie's assigned task was watching over Hannah, whose due date was fast approaching. Much easier than keeping her curly-coated moyen poodle pup distracted and entertained, and away from all commotion.

"Let me know if I can bring you something," she said to her human charge when she had successfully depleted Jasper's not entirely endless capacity for activity. "Cup of tea? Glass of water? A biscuit?"

"There's no room in me for anything besides my not so little girl. If you don't need the mahogany chest in the main bedroom, you could let Martin know it can go to Stanwell."

Ellie found the noble marquess in his former study, dismantling desktop computer components and cursing under his breath.

"Having second thoughts?" she teased.

"Not yet," he panted. "You?"

"Too late for that. Dan's treadmill just came up the service lift and is being reassembled in the room where I keep my portable barre."

Ellie and Dan had accepted Martin's offer to become permanent tenants. A multitude of responsibilities in the Milver Vale had reduced his visits to London. Hannah planned to keep busy with their expanded family and after maternity leave would resume work on the Thomas Hardy biographical film. They were removing personal possessions—photos, mementos, any pieces of furniture with sentimental or practical value. In future, Latimer Estates would receive a substantially higher rent for Dan's flat than he had paid.

Eyeing the framed travel pictures of Italian cities and Bangkok and a river in Thailand, she asked what Martin meant to do with them.

"They're destined for a charity shop. At Stanwell, we've got an entire series of Venetian views by the master painter Canaletto. Dan needs the space for his cinema posters. Arrange things as you please. Make this your home. Because it is."

Dan carried a stack of books into the room. Stepping around the computer screen, he went to the built-ins and began filling the empty shelves.

"When will you get round to putting a ring on this lady's finger?" Martin asked him.

"I'm waiting for Ellie to tell me what she wants. Unfortunately, I haven't got a stonking heirloom diamond like the one that sealed your engagement to Hannah."

"You gave me this." Ellie touched the gemstone pendant dangling from its gold chain. "It stays on in class and during rehearsals. If I had a ring, I'd constantly be taking it off. Anyway, we haven't set a date yet. Or decided on a location."

"Getting the dog was a higher priority," Dan added. "Where *is* Jasper?"

"Fast asleep in the parlor on his cushion, curled around his favorite fish toy. Looking adorable." Ellie presented her phone so he could see the most recent photo.

Martin coiled the cables he had detached and placed them in a carton with the keyboard. "I could use an extra set of hands carrying this lot to the van."

Ellie opened the glass door and stepped onto the balcony. The leaves of her potted Stella Nue rose, a housewarming gift from Terry, were changing from green to yellow, but it continued to bear flowers. Their petals were as pale and pink as a satin pointe shoe.

Epilogue

A Christmas Eve snowfall wasn't unprecedented in New Hampshire. For residents of South Somerset, it was a thrilling phenomenon. At mid-morning, flakes dotted the gray slate roof of All Saints church in Milverston Magna, where Lady Nina Gwendolyn Latimer was christened. By early afternoon, a layer of white blanketed the Stanwell House lawn and gardens.

British Ballet Theatre had issued a survey to collect information about company member's religious affiliations, to determine who and how many wished to be released on Bodhi Day, any night during Hanukkah, in the run-up to Christmas or the aftermath. Ellie asked for and received a three-day break from duties in *The Nutcracker.* She wouldn't perform Columbine again until Boxing Day, and her next appearance as the Sugar Plum Fairy would come later in the week.

Dan removed his Jaguar from the storage facility, and they drove to Tayer Court to collect Terry, who was also invited to join the festive activities in the Milver Vale.

After lunch, Hannah put her infant daughter and boisterous son down for their afternoon naps and caught up on her own sleep after a wakeful night of feeding. Martin, Dan, and Terry bundled themselves into winter jackets and took the household dogs and young Jasper for a ramble.

Ellie went to the guest room bath to fill its soaking tub with hot water and luxuriated there until the temperature cooled. Thoroughly relaxed, she stretched out on the four-poster bed and reviewed this year of transformations.

In springtime, she'd arrived in London for the final weeks as a burlesque artist. She fell in love with a corporate executive. She completed a drama course and earned a certificate. Her visit with Lana and Henry Colman had resulted in a warming of their relationship, and disturbing insights into Gil Cooke's character. Her portrayal of Lyla Carrigan was favorably received by theatrical critics and audiences. Rafe's firm friendship comforted her during the separation from Dan, and his confidence had sustained her while rehearsing *Les Sylphides* and other ballets. Terry had named his pink rose Stella Nue.

Awareness of Dan's presence pulled her out of a dreamless doze.

"I let you sleep through teatime," he told her. "Would you like me to bring a tray from the kitchen."

"Stay," she said, patting the duvet.

After making love to her with exquisite tenderness, Dan propped himself on one elbow.

"We walked all the way to the River Milver, where the topic turned to angling. Hearing Dad expound on certain types of lures, I decided he ought to fish the streams of New Hampshire. Shouldn't we have the wedding there, during our August vacation time? At the lake cottage."

"Yes, and yes, and yes. Zack and George's party barn at The Maples is the perfect place for a reception. Decision made. We can tell everyone tonight."

Dinner for six was served on the mahogany dining table. Terry traded gardening tips with Martin's mother Isobel. Hannah asked if Ellie would consider a cameo appearance in a movie in the earliest stage of development.

Before she could answer, Dan tapped his knife against his water glass. He rose to make their announcement, extending an invitation to everyone present.

Martin bounded out of his chair and kissed Ellie's cheek. He slapped Dan on the back and hurried to his wine fridge for several bottles of champagne. After it was consumed, no one but the nursing mother could claim sobriety. Her tipsy husband escorted her up the staircase, followed by a wobbly Terry and an amused Isobel.

"We needn't go up just yet," Dan told Ellie. Taking her by the hand, he led her to the terrace.

The clouds that had delivered the snow were dissipating. Ellie gazed up at the black sky, speckled with bright and twinkling light. "This is where we kissed the first time."

"Let's do it again."

Leaning against him, she said, "Yes, please. I want as many kisses as stars in the sky."

"I'd better get busy."

And he did.

Author's Note

Although *Sequins and Starlight* is not my first novel with a dancer protagonist, it's the only one set within the contemporary ballet world. My own training and experience feel quite distant now, apart from an almost-daily ballet workout routine. I therefore immersed myself in memoirs and autobiographies by professional dancers, choreographers, and artistic directors, too numerous to list.

I also delved into the critiques and analyses of the art by its practitioners—past and present—and explored current developments and trends and challenges within the dance industry. Among the most helpful titles: *Turning Pointe: How a New Generation of Dancers is Saving Ballet from Itself* by Chloe Angyal, *Passionate Work: Choreographing a Dance Career* by Ruth Horowitz, and *Ballerina: Sex, Scandal, and Suffering Behind the Symbol of Perfection* by Deirdre Kelly.

Backstage tours at the Royal Ballet and Opera in London were also immensely helpful. Not only did I have access to the many departments so crucial to a production—wardrobe storage, practice studios, scenery shop, and more, I encountered several of my favorite dancers in the corridors or the lift. I'm similarly indebted to the London Ballet Circle. My membership proved valuable in so many ways during the writing process, as I took advantage of an extensive program of interviews with performers and ballet company personnel in Great Britain and beyond.

I extend heartfelt thanks to all ballet dancers—female and male—who have inspired and entertained and amazed me through the years. Many, whose talent carried them to the heights of fame, were fortunate in realizing their cherished dreams of success. Others, for various reasons, were unable to pursue their preferred path, stymied by injury, physical changes, dismissal, and other difficulties. I honor all of them, known and unknown, struggling or successful.

Research was necessary to accurately represent the equally fascinating world of neo-burlesque. I attended a seminar presented by performers in my area. I studied performance videos and films and interviews with contemporary stars—Dita von Teese and others. I'm hugely indebted to the extensive work by Leslie Zemeckis, producer of the historical documentary *Behind the Burly Q: The Story of Burlesque in America* and author of the nonfiction book with the same title.

As someone who went on the stage at age ten and remained there through graduate school, I could rely on personal experience of acting classes and rehearsals and theatrical productions. Back then I didn't dream I'd eventually trade performing with casts of dozens for this solitary but equally fulfilling career as an author.

I always intended to write a follow up to *A Change of Location*, which preceded this novel, pairing minor character Dan Wheeler with a ballet dancer who had previously performed in burlesque. The resulting novel let me and my readers spend more time with Hannah and Martin and revisit the fictional Milver Vale, based on an area I know well and dearly love. If it appears that I inserted a natural disaster for story purposes, I must clarify that not so long ago, the river in that region did unfortunately flood and overflow its banks. The effects were disastrous for close personal friends and multiple villages. Rainfall frequency and storm severity has increased in many parts of Great Britain, requiring strong local response and reinforcing community spirit and initiative.

I made use of my familial connection to Gloucestershire, particularly Thornbury and its environs. My forbears, like Dan's, were Wheelers and Dimerys and Tayers, interred beneath the yews of St. Mary's churchyard or named in memorials inside the building.

To a great extent, *Sequins and Starlight* is a love letter to London, in particular the places where I spend so much of my time when there. My main characters are following my footsteps through Mayfair and Marylebone, shopping, strolling, drinking and dining, and copying my many journeys in the underground system.

Sir Terence Wheeler's activities as rosarian are very much inspired by reality. My late paternal grandfather was an avid rose grower, as is my mother. I tend over two hundred rose bushes of all varieties in my gardens. And I relish time spent in the greatest and most notable English gardens during peak rose flowering season.

For several decades I've been fortunate to occupy a second home beside the waters of Lake Winnipesaukee in New Hampshire. Any resemblance between Ellie's shingled cottage and mine—its setting, mountain views, proximity to Wolfeboro—and her attachment to it, are not at all coincidental.

I extend much gratitude to the Gallica Press crew. I'm also very fortunate to have other talented and expert collaborators. Erin Al-Mehairi of Hook of a Book, whose editorial expertise I value. Deborah Bradseth, for turning my cover concepts into gorgeous designs. Michelle Argyle at Melissa Williams Design, who yet again produced an interior that matches the story elements.

As ever, I'm endlessly grateful to my husband, the best and more supportive spouse any author could hope for, my favorite companion on visits to the Rivoli Bar at London's Ritz Hotel. This book, like the sixteen that preceded it, is dedicated to him.

Ballet Glossary

Arabesque
Position on one stationary leg with the other held straight behind.

Ballet blanc
"White ballet"—an entire classical ballet or a scene in which the principal female dancer and *corps de ballet* members wear white costumes. Their characters are often ghosts, fairies, sylphs, enchanted maidens, or apparitions. (*Swan Lake, Giselle, La Sylphides, Les Sylphides*)

Battement frappé
The ball of the foot glides over the floor and is swiftly extended from a flexed position against the lower calf of the supporting leg.

Bourrée
A series of very small, rapid, even steps with the feet close together crossed in fifth position and the legs held straight; the dancer skims across the floor.

Bourée en courir
A "running" *bourrée,* in which the dancer glides swiftly over the floor.

Corps de ballet
The ensemble of ballet dancers, performing as a group.

Coryphée
High-ranking member of the *corps de ballet.*

Danseur
A male dancer.

Echappé
The feet move from a closed position to an open position.

En arrière
Moving backwards.

Entrechat huit
From the fifth position, the dancer leaps into the air, rapidly and repeatedly crossing the legs before and behind, beating them multiple times. In this type, four changes back and forth are made.

Glissade
Gliding movement from *plié*, with feet in fifth position to fifth position.

Grand allegro
Typically done as the last part of center work in ballet class, big jumps performed to a fast tempo.

Grand plié
A full, deep bend with knees parallel to the floor and the heels rising from the floor.

Grande jété
A long, forward moving horizontal jump, starting from one leg and landing on the other. Because both legs are parallel to the floor, it looks like a split performed in the air.

Jété
A jump from one leg, landing on the other.

Merde
The French term for "shit," traditional "good luck" for ballet dancers.

Pas de basque
A step in three parts, transferring and alternating weight from one foot to the other on the spot.

Pas de chat
A sideways jump, with legs and feet forming a diamond shape when in mid-air.

Pas de deux

A dance duet, usually performed by a female and a male dancer.

Pas de trois

Performed by three dancers.

Pas de six

Performed by six dancers.

Petit allegro

Performed during ballet class center work, a series of small, fast jumps.

Piqué

The raised and pointed foot of the working leg moves down to touch the floor and moves up again or is lowered to become the supported leg. Usually part of a turn.

Pirouette

A turn done in place (not traveling), with one or more rotations, in which the supporting leg is held straight and stationary.

Port de bras

Exercise of arm movements based on the five standard positions, sometimes involving the upper body, with bends from the waist in a forward, backward, or circular direction.

Prima (ballerina)

A principal female dancer in a ballet company.

Répétiteur

A staff member of a ballet company responsible for leading daily class, and staging and rehearsing ballets, who reports to ballet master or artistic director.

Rond de jambe à terre

Half-circle made on the floor by the pointed working foot.

<u>Tendu à la arrière</u>
Stretching the leg backwards with the foot remaining in contact with the floor.

<u>Tombé</u>
A falling motion, with the working leg raised up, then falling forward, backwards, or sideways. A means of transferring weight from one leg to another, often a preliminary to a traveling step.

<u>Tour</u>
A turning of the body, usually combined with another movement such as a *jété*.

<u>Tour en l'air</u>
A turn performed when airborne, usually by a male dancer.

About the Author

Margaret Porter is the award-winning and best-selling author of seventeen novels in multiple genres. A former stage actress, she also worked professionally in film, television, and radio. Additional writing credits include nonfiction, newspaper and magazine articles, and poetry. She and  her husband live in New England. Information about her books and aspects of her life and career can be found at www.margaretporter.com.

* 9 7 9 8 9 8 5 6 7 3 4 6 3 *